THE OUTSIDER

Dulan's curiosity was almost out of control. There was so much he didn't know. He hardly knew where to begin.

"What's it . . . like on the Outside?" he said at last. "Why would anyone choose such a primitive existence when there are other options open?"

"I suppose that freedom has something to do with it," said Bea, her eyes flashing. "I don't know that I accept the term 'primitive' either." She curled honey strands of her shoulder-length hair around long, slender fingers. "Com life certainly has its advantages. Life is always predictable and unchanging. The feeling that God's in his heaven . . . it can lull you right along."

"But . . . ?" asked Dulan.

"But? The obvious. The price is great—your soul. There's no place for individuality or independent creative thought or emotion. Individuals end up on the frontier."

"Why?"

"I suppose that freedom has something to do with it," said Bea. She sat for a moment, lost in some private dream, then continued. "You don't see it in the com because the social order doesn't allow it, but there are people in this world who glory in freedom, who scream their independence to the world. . . ."

Bantam Books by Mike McQuay
Ask your bookseller for the titles you have missed

JITTERBUG
LIFEKEEPER
PURE BLOOD

LIFEKEEPER

MIKE McQUAY

BANTAM BOOKS
TORONTO • NEW YORK • LONDON • SYDNEY • AUCKLAND

To the lawyers at Fagin, Hewett, Mathews and Fagin; especially to Charles, Betsy and Bill, with thanks.

LIFEKEEPER

A Bantam Book / published by arrangement with the Author

Bantam edition / May 1985

ISBN 0-553-25075-2

Published simultaneously in the United States and Canada

Bantam Books are published by Bantam Books, Inc. Its trademark, consisting of the words "Bantam Books" and the portrayal of a rooster, is Registered in U.S. Patent and Trademark Office and in other countries. Marca Registrada. Bantam Books, Inc., 666 Fifth Avenue, New York, New York 10103.

PRINTED IN THE UNITED STATES OF AMERICA

O 0 9 8 7 6 5 4 3 2 1

For my wife, Margaret, whose love makes all things possible.

"... for the world, which seems
To lie before us like a land of dreams,
So various, so beautiful, so new,
Hath really neither joy, nor love, nor light,
Nor certitude, nor peace, nor help for pain;
And we are here as on a darkling plain
Swept with confused alarms of struggle and flight,
Where ignorant armies clash by night."

—Matthew Arnold
Oldworlder (expunged)

So it was that Isaac Complan went to the mountain top to dwell for a time with the Lord. And he found him robed and hooded, strolling along a twisted path that wound through a dark thicket of bramble.

Upon his approach, the Lord said, "You seem troubled my son."

Whereupon Complan fell to his knees on the pathway and covered his face from the majesty of God. "My Lord," he spake. "I cower from the awesome responsibility that you have placed upon my unworthy shoulders."

And the Lord answered him, saying, "It is really not such a difficult task to remake a world. Many before you have gladly shouldered the same yoke."

"But, Lord, where do I begin?"

"Begin at the beginning," the Lord said gravely, "and go till you come to the end; then stop."

—*Book of Complan* (5-3, 4)

The worst thing in the world, next to anarchy, is government.

—Caravan fable

1

July

Rain.

For the third straight night, rain fell upon the remains of the ancient city, filling the follies of men with the stability of Nature. The broken buildings stood silent. Dark, thrusting sentinals they were, tombstones fifty stories high—a mammoth graveyard for a dead culture. Once a symbol of pride and accomplishment, the city was now no more than stone canyons reaching for the heavens. Reaching too high. Stone tower windows, the glass centuries gone, freely admitted that which they had been designed to keep out. The rain purged the steel and concrete, inside and out, mocking the creators of such blasphemy. Through the cracked and broken streets and sidewalks, the Earth took slowly back what was once hers, what would be hers once again.

And the wheel turns.

The black sedan slowly coughed and grumbled its way through the slick, wet cityscape, trying to make the streets remember, just for a while, what they had once been. The ancient towers loomed around them, twisted edifices, wind-howling mountains, black silhouettes against a starless night. And the sedan pushed forward, easing its way around the hulking barricades of its rust-ridden brothers. For the streets were tangled with sedans, and coupes, and convertibles that had been abandoned when the rain rained red, and the sun never peered from behind a curtain of noxious gases.

It was summer, but the long bout of wet weather had brought a chill dampness that seemed to seep through the bodies and settle directly in the bones of the four men in the creeping car. They sat huddled in the moving chamber, their muscles tightening involuntarily in a futile attempt to ward off the unseasonable cold.

"This your first time outside the com, Doctor Dulan?" Sergeant Jarsen asked his companion in the backseat.

"Am I that obvious?" the man answered.

The Sergeant shook his head in a very curt, very military manner. "They all look at it like you do, first time out." Hoagy Jarsen had spent a good part of his forty-three years in the military service of his country. It was a good thing to do, and he knew it, and every night when he went to bed he slept deeply and peacefully because he was doing a job that needed to be done. He was small like a bobcat is small, and wiry because he took pride in keeping his body in shape. He wore a moustache cut to regulation, a uniform that was pressed to tight creases, and eyes that never connected up to his brain in any sort of intelligent manner. He was a soldier.

Dulan looked at the man for a moment before answering. "I knew that the cities were out here," he said finally, "but I had no idea they were so . . . massive." Doral Dulan was twenty-five, but he looked older simply because of the smoldering intensity of his eyes. They called him Exceptional, and he didn't even look like they did. His skin was burnished copper, his close-cropped hair raw cotton painted black. His face was long and aristocratic, and people who worried about such things said that he was a genetic throwback. Dulan didn't worry about such things.

"What city is this?" he asked Jarsen.

The soldier looked at him, perplexed. "Why?" he asked.

"Ancient history is a kind of hobby of mine."

Jarsen lowered his brows to narrow his dull-eyed stare, but it didn't make him look any smarter. "Oh," he said, and shrugged. It looked to Dulan like the man really tried to think for a minute, but then he gave it up and leaned toward the passenger in the front seat. "Hey, Jimbo. What was this place called back in the old times?"

"Why?" asked Jimbo.

"Because there's a man back here would like to know, that's why," Jarsen said self-righteously, then winked at Dulan.

Jimbo tried to think about it too; he really did. "I think it was a man's name," he said. "But I can't recall it right off."

"Never mind," Dulan said, sorry that he had brought it up. "It's not important. Was the city destroyed by the war?"

"Naw," replied Jarsen, settling back against the worn upholstery. "There'd be craters and lots of burned out places. This decay is mostly natural. I guess all the people left when the southern territories began to fall. Can't say as I blame them. I'd hate to get caught in one of these places with my pants down."

The two MPs in the front began chuckling.

"I don't know that the fighting ever did get up this far," the man continued. "You'd know what I mean if you'd seen some of them other places down south. What a mess."

Dulan couldn't keep from staring out of his window, transfixed by the spectacle of the dead city. "Everything went up . . ."

". . . Instead of down," the Sergeant finished. "Damndest thing I ever saw. How would you defend something like this?" Jarsen shivered, and Dulan wasn't sure if it was from the cold or the Old World reflection. "I'll tell you, Doc, it gives me the creeps. Them people back in the old days must have really been strange."

"Possessed," Jimbo said mechanically.

Steeped in evil. Nobody said it, but they all thought it, for it was the traditional description, the words of Isaac Complan. Steeped in evil. It hung in the car like the dampness hung in the air.

A woman's voice crackled through the small radio attached to the dashboard. "Mobile Fifteen . . . Mobile Fifteen . . . this is Comcen . . . please respond."

Jimbo Wollams reached down and picked up the attached microphone, scooting sideways in the front seat so that he could look back at Jarsen for instructions. "This is Wollams in Fifteen. Go ahead Comcen, talk to me."

The voice, lisping static, began again. "Subject of Priority One search...Daniel T. Jones...has been located...Destructor's tavern in inhabited sector, over."

"Acknowledged, Comcen." Jimbo raised his eyebrows in Jarsen's direction. The Sergeant nodded vigorously.

"And have them tell those ignorant jackasses to stay put until we get there," Jarsen said. "I don't want that old boy slipping away from us like he did last time."

Jimbo brought the crimp-corded mike to his lips. "We are proceeding to the inhabited sector. Please have the search team continue surveillance until our arrival. That's all."

Jarsen reached out and clapped the driver on the shoulder. "Come on, Wynna. Let's see if you can get us over there without getting lost."

Wynna growled and turned the wheel full. They bounced up over the remnants of a crumbling curb onto a sidewalk. They swung around, nearly bouncing off the side of a high-stooped brownstone, and were pointing back the way they had come. He drove there, on the sidewalk, for another block, then turned down a narrow, water-filled alley. The alleyway was overgrown with tall weeds and tall buildings, and Wynna gassed the machine full and charged along the clogged roadway, green drippy leaves and stalks batting them from all sides as they invaded virgin territory. Dulan sat up straight, tensing. The dying screams of small animals assailed them; the towering buildings seemed to close in all around them.

"Where are we going?" Dulan asked, craning his neck around, trying to keep an eye on everything at once, diligently trying to look them out of any trouble that might arise.

"There's this Outsider we've been hunting," Jarsen said casually, and he bunched up his face as if he had just taken castor oil. "Beats the holy crap outta me what they'd want him for, but you don't call a Priority One to see what time of day it is, if you know what I mean." He poked Dulan in the ribs to emphasize the point. The black man smiled automatically. "Anyway, I've got orders to take him to Forty-Three same as you. It's just a few K's out of the way now, and it will save me another trip later on—you don't mind, do you?"

The question was obviously not designed to give Dulan a real choice, so he simply continued looking around. After a few minutes, they finally cleared the alley and broke into partially open street again. Dulan felt himself relax as he turned to Jarsen. "Are you stationed at Milcom Forty-Three?"

The man looked surprised at the question. "Me?" he laughed. "Inside a milcom? No way. That's top secret hush-hush stuff going on in there. I'm just regular army. We're stationed at a Class Three near the airstrip where I picked you up. Our official title is Special Material Receiving and Disbursing, but mostly we're just a glorified delivery service for people like you going to Forty-Three. We also keep an eye on the Outsiders here in the city. You know, make sure the dumb fuckers don't get all boozed up and hurt themselves. There's a sorry lot for you."

"The base is also a female recruitment center," Jimbo said, dancing his eyebrows in the front seat.

"Recruitment?" Dulan asked.

"Yeah," Jarsen responded. "When they're brought in, we run medical tests and set up pre psyche-pro files on them."

"There's one of our jeeps," Wynna said, pointing. The vehicle was sitting in the middle of the street, rain puddling up on its canvas top. It was near a building every bit as diseased as the rest of the city. The large windows in the front were boarded up, but there were small, flat shafts of light slicing through the cracks between the boards.

"Okay, pull it over," Jarsen said, and he sounded tired.

Wynna pulled up next to the jeep, and he and Jimbo piled out of the car. "Take it easy, you guys," Jarsen called to them, as he searched around by his feet, fishing for his gun belt. He opened his door so they could hear him better. "Don't mix it up with these people unless you have to. We're supposed to take this Jones character in one piece."

Jarsen found his belt; resting it over his shoulder. "Sit tight, Doc," he said. "We'll be right back."

"Mind if I come along?" Dulan asked.

Jarsen climbed out of his open door and began hooking on the belt. "Out of the question," he said flatly. "I'm responsible for your safety, and these people"—he gestured toward the building—"they're not civilized like you and me. Anything could happen."

The corners of Dulan's mouth turned up in a slight smile. "Do you smoke, Sergeant?"

The man pursed his lips. "Smoke? Why, sure."

Dulan reached into his pocket and pulled out a small metal box. "Have you ever seen one of these?" He handed it to Jarsen.

The Sergeant looked around suspiciously, then climbed back into the car, shutting the door. "Can't say that I have," he answered, turning the object every which way in his hand. "What does it do?"

"I'll show you," Dulan replied, taking it back. There was a small lid that turned on a hinge. He flipped it open. "When you turn this little wheel, it rubs against this piece of flint. The friction causes a spark—there you see—to jump, igniting the wick, which is soaked in fuel. Voilà! Instant fire."

Jarsen's eyes grew wide as he watched the tiny flame dance before him. "That's right remarkable," he said.

"It's yours," Dulan said, snapping the lid closed, suffocating the fire.

Jarsen looked around again to make sure no one was watching, then took the machine and slipped it into his breast pocket. "Look," he told Dulan. "It's my ass if anybody finds out about this, so, if anybody asks, you stayed in the car, right?"

"Fair enough," Dulan answered.

"Now watch yourself in there," Jarsen ordered, as he opened the door and climbed back out. "Stick close to me. Outsiders, especially Destructors, can be unpredictable."

Nodding, Dulan got out of the car. Jarsen moved around to where he stood and wrapped a beefy hand around his forearm.

"No kidding, Doc. First sign of trouble, I want you to get the hell back out that door."

Jarsen walked over to the jeep and spoke quietly for a short time with its three occupants. Then he walked directly to the battered wooden door of the tavern and disappeared inside. A moment later he poked his head back out, giving Dulan and the MPs the high sign.

The man seemed stern, businesslike. Dulan had the feeling that he had done this before—and that he liked it. He moved to the door.

"Jimbo, you and Wynna post yourselves by the door. Nobody goes in or out." Jarsen looked at Dulan and smiled with crooked teeth. "C'mon, Doc, let's go get us a beer."

He swung the door open to hazy light, a smoke-filled dream. The room was much longer than it was wide, and it billowed so with smoke that Dulan felt that he had walked into a cloud bank. A long makeshift bar covered the entire wall to their left, and on a shelf behind it were rows and rows of unmarked brown and amber bottles. A grave-looking man wearing an apron was busy lining all those bottles in neat military rows. The rest of the room was filled with tables made from boxes with planks attached, and the tables were filled with people. They were tattered and dirty and, without exception, their faces strained with the bitter lines of total defeat. Men mostly, they drank from brown bottles and smoked big-bowled pipes, which continually fed the stifling atmosphere with thicker and thicker layers of haze. And as they smoked and drank and laughed and talked, Dulan could feel that it was just a charade. They were putting in their time until they died.

Dulan's eyes began to sting from the smoke as he and Jarsen walked slowly toward the bar. The light came from kerosine lamps placed strategically around the chamber. They turned the place jumping yellow, and left long slabs of black shadow where the jumping yellow couldn't reach. Dust hung everywhere. It danced in and out of the smoke stream and settled in thick, crusty layers on everything that wasn't engaged in constant motion. It strangled the air, making Dulan breathe in shallow gasps, leaving a gritty taste on his tongue.

They reached the bar, the sound in the room low and rumbling, like a distant thunderstorm. The bartender approached them warily.

"Looking for Dan Jones," Jarsen said congenially, smiling broadly at the man.

The bartender's eyes narrowed as he stared directly into Jarsen's face. "Sorry, Sarge. I just juice them up, I don't ask for dossiers." The man turned his back and continued his bottle straightening. He'd take each one down individually, wipe off the dust layer on his apron, then put it back in line. Dulan got the feeling that it was a never-ending occupation.

Jarsen didn't move. It was as if he were a snake, coiling, ready to strike. He leaned his weight against the bar and made himself comfortable. Dulan watched him carefully, watched the obvious pleasure that the man was taking out of the mounting tension.

"So you say that Dan Jones isn't here, is that right?" he said to the bartender's back.

"I don't know the guy," the man said without turning around. "It's a wide world; he could be anywhere."

"Even here."

"Anything's possible. Can I get you a drink? That *is* what the place is for."

"Why sure," Jarsen answered. "How about a beer for me and my buddy? A nice cold beer."

The man turned, two dusted bottles in his hands. He set them on the bar and opened the tops with a church key that hung from a string on his apron. "You want cold beer," he said, "you'd better move farther north."

Jarsen smiled theatrically and took a sip from the bottle. He immediately made a face, spitting out his mouthful and dropping his bottle with a crash to the floor. The rumbling in the room stopped for a long second, then began again. Dulan looked at the floor. The spilled beer had turned the dust layer to fine mud, and he could see that beneath the dirt was a linoleum floor.

"Hey!" the barman yelled. "Those things are hard to come by."

"It tasted like horse dung," Jarsen explained in a condescending voice. He wiped his mouth with the back of his hand. "I think I'd better try another." With that, he grabbed Dulan's bottle up off the bar and turned it to his lips. This time, he didn't even swallow before pulling the thing away from his mouth and hurling it at the shelf behind the bar. Several bottles exploded with a loud pop when Jarsen's missile struck home, wetting the shelf and the floor with their precious contents.

The bartender turned slowly to Jarsen, his mouth slack, his face pale. This time, the conversation in the room didn't abate, but Dulan could feel the pressure of hundreds of eyes on his back. He didn't like the sensation.

Jarsen, still casual, said, "Now, let's get this out in the open, all right? I know that he's in here, and you know that he's in here, and one way or the other we're going to find him. It can either be the hard way," he gestured with his head toward the broken bottles, "or the easy way, the simple way." He shrugged. "It doesn't make any difference to me. How about you?"

The bartender hauled out a thick tongue to lick dry lips. Slowly, ever so slowly, he let his eyes wander to a corner of the room where a man sat alone, couched in the shadows. He was half-slumped over a bottle, and seemed completely oblivious to everything around him.

"Thanks for the beer," Jarsen said, and turning, strode resolutely toward the table, Dulan quickly on his heels. He moved right up on top of the man, looking down at him. "Daniel T. Jones?" he asked.

The man leaned his head way back to make fleeting eye contact with the Sergeant. ''No,'' he said quietly.

''Mind if we sit?'' Jarsen asked as he pulled over a packing crate. Dulan, embarrassed and not knowing why, followed suit. He scooted his box directly across from the man.

Daniel T. Jones was tiny, a rodent of a man. He could have been any age between thirty and fifty and was so nondescript that he was probably forgotten immediately by anyone unfortunate enough to meet him. His hair was black and thin, baby fine, and his slit eyes darted continuously, like a cornered animal's. His hands were always in motion, as he doodled idly in the dust that covered his tabletop.

''You're a regular artist, ain't you?'' Jarsen sneered.

''I haven't done anything,'' the man said, but his voice bore no conviction.

''How long have you been away from the com?'' Jarsen asked, making small talk, dragging out the man's agony.

Jones looked up from his doodles and stared at Jarsen. ''Fourteen years, give or take.'' Even when he wasn't drawing, his hands were moving, clasping and unclasping.

Jarsen slid his box around to where he was right next to the little man. He made his voice go real low, saying, ''How would you like to go back?''

''I'd rather walk through fire,'' the Outsider replied without hesitation. He half-turned his back to the Sergeant and began once again nursing his beer. Jarsen looked at Dulan in mock astonishment.

''These people have absolutely no manners,'' he said, showing empty palms.

Dulan could only stare. Something was going to happen, and it was going to happen very soon. The pressure was mounting, physically mounting like an unvented boiler. The front door began to look very far away—the distance of a human ocean.

''You're a very rude man,'' Jarsen was saying in a voice loud enough for everyone to hear. His voice had increased in pitch and he was talking very quickly. Suddenly, his hand snaked out and jerked the beer bottle away from Jones's mouth. He slammed it loudly on the table, raising a small cloud of dust. ''Dammit! Look at me when I'm talking to you!''

The noise in the room had quieted to nothing. Jarsen had the floor. It was his show. Jones looked at him once, then turned his back on him again.

A guttural sound escaped from Jarsen's throat, and then something snapped within him. Lunging at the little man, he grabbed him by the lapels of his worn leather jacket, dragged him to his feet, and slammed him viciously into the wall, back first.

Jones groaned loudly.

The sound of scraping chairs behind Dulan. His mind's eye pictured a room full of people getting angrily to their feet, but he didn't have the nerve to turn around and visualize his mental picture.

"Now we do it my way!" Jarsen growled through clenched teeth. Pinning Jones to the wall with one hand, he used the other to extract, with some difficulty, a piece of paper from his pants pocket. He cleared his throat and read to the whole room: "The Central Council of the Community Complex States of North America has herewith determined that the services of Daniel T. Jones are indispensable and immediately required for the continued defense and protection of the Com States.

"By the power vested in me by the Central Council, you are, as of this day, commissioned Private First Class in the Armed Forces of North Am Com States and ordered to report immediately to Military Community Complex number Forty-Three, quadrant four." Jarsen chuckled as he shoved the paper back into his pocket.

"Welcome to the army, friend. You've just been drafted."

Jones's eyes flashed wildly back and forth between Dulan and the hefty soldier. "You can't, you can't," he muttered in confusion. "Dear God . . . please." The man began sobbing loudly.

"Complan, what a baby," Jarsen said, disgusted. He released his hold on the man, and Jones slumped back to his chair, sitting down heavily, crying into his arm.

Dulan could only gaze in astonishment. He had never seen anyone cry before. In the com, it just wasn't done.

"There has to be a mistake . . . something," Jones was saying into his arm. He raised his moist eyes. "Don't you understand?"

Suddenly he zeroed in on Dulan. "You look like an important man," he pleaded. "Tell him, please! They threw me out of the com. Court martial. They can't want me back . . . they can't!" His breath was coming in short, shallow gulps. "I won't go. I can't. There must be a mistake."

Dulan, face flushed, could only cast his eyes downward to avoid the man's gaze.

"Come on, you whining scumbag—come on!" Jarsen grabbed the Outsider's arm, pulling him out of his seat. Pushing and prodding, he began to bully Jones across the room toward the door.

Dulan made to follow. Everyone in the room was on his feet, pressing in close. The Exceptional hurried on weak legs to catch up with his escort. The crowd filled in the empty space; they meant to keep them from leaving with the pitiful little man.

Jarsen unholstered his service revolver and turned to meet them, his eyes glazed, totally involved in the excitement. "This thing's loaded with Funnies!" he yelled. "Is he worth it? Is he worth it?"

Still they came. Dulan's stomach had turned to mush. He could smell them now, all sweat and cheap booze—hear their whispered curses. He felt he would throw up.

Jarsen screamed for the crowd to get back. They didn't. Releasing the safety on his gun, he leveled it. "I mean to use this," he said. "I'd love to use it."

Dulan inched so close to Jarsen that he was touching him. The crowd was on them; he could feel their hot, stale breath.

Wham!

Jarsen fired one shot, point-blank, into the straggly mob. Dulan had never heard a gunshot before. The deafening roar was like nothing he had ever imagined.

Like an ill-constructed house of cards, the mob collapsed immediately, backing away, losers who had lost again. In their wake, a woman lay twitching on the filthy floor. She was dressed in an old sack. A huge, bloody hole gaped squarely in the middle of her chest, and as her hands opened and closed in agony, a huge grin began spreading across her face. Then she began laughing—shrieking.

All at once, Jones snatched his arm free and broke for the exit. He scuffled momentarily with the two men at the door, but it was a futile effort. He was felled very quickly and unceremoniously from behind with a billy club. The soldiers took the opportunity to fall upon the man and pound him mercilessly as he sank to the floor.

"That's enough," Jarsen said. "The orders said intern, not infirm." He walked over to them, and Dulan was never more than a step behind. "You guys are going to get me in trouble yet." He sighed deeply. "Okay, get him out to the car, and put some cuffs on him." He holstered his revolver and looked at Dulan. "You all right?"

"Yeah," Dulan replied, but his voice gave away his nervousness. He pointed to the woman still laughing on the floor. "What about . . ."

"Good as dead," drawled the Sergeant. "Let's get out of here."

The Exceptional, in a daze, followed Jarsen out the door into the wet, wet night.

"I warned you about those fuckers, didn't I?" Jarsen asked. "They got no respect for authority. No respect at all."

The rain was still coming down, but somehow it was a welcome friend to Dulan—a very pleasant alternative to the inside of the tavern.

"Say," said Jarsen, stopping dead in his tracks as if he couldn't walk and talk at the same time. "Think you could see your way clear to have a look at that devil's head before we . . ."

"I'm not that kind of a doctor," Dulan replied.

"Oh," Jarsen shrugged, and continued walking. Jones was lying on the sidewalk, moaning softly. His hair was matted with blood, and the rain poured down on him, puddling in his eye sockets, turning his dark clothes darker. Even unconscious, his fingers fidgeted. The Sergeant walked over to where the Outsider lay and spat loudly on his prostrate form.

Wynna and Jimbo were leaning against the sedan, cupping their hands around cigarettes, trying to light them in the damp air. Jarsen called to them. "Load this filth into the jeep, and tell them to follow us out to Forty-Three. And try to clean him up a little, will you?"

Jimbo wagged his head and threw down the smoker. "Don't ask us to mess with this," he said with distaste.

Jarsen pointed an accusing finger. "Dammit! You messed him up; you clean him up. I can't be delivering damaged goods."

The Sergeant turned his back on them to terminate the discussion and sauntered over to where Dulan was standing. Hands in his pockets, the Exceptional was staring up at the sky, trying very hard to ride out the nausea that rifled through his body.

"Might clear up before morning," Jarsen said. Then, "Remember, not a word about me bringing you in there. It'd be my ass."

Dulan looked him full in the face, then took one last glance at the sky before climbing into the car. So far, this was not at all what he had expected.

. . . And it came to pass in the third year of the Great Famine that a once mighty seaport in a province called Texas was engulfed by a pillar of fire as a sign from the Lord that the people had strayed from the path of righteousness. A time later, a large center of much commerce and population on the Western shore was also smote to ruins in the same manner by God through His human agents. Many lives were sacrificed. The people saw these things and were sorely afraid, and said one to the other that His Will must be done.

—*Book of Complan* (1-13)

The entire fabric of life is destructive. Survival is the only rule in Nature's game. The human body itself is constantly at war as microorganisms vie for control continuously. Intelligence does battle with Ignorance, Reason engages blind passion for possession of the soul. Therefore, war is, must be, the highest of human aspirations for it fulfills the Divine cycle. Times without war are times of stagnation and are inherently evil.

—*The Seminarian's Companion to the Philosophy of Isaac Complan*

The hungry wolf fears naught but the pain in its belly.

—Caravan fable

2

Dulan awoke to the punctuated jab of Sergeant Jarsen's right index finger as it poked him in the side.

"Hey, wake up. We're here."

Laboriously opening his eyes, the black man forced his mind into gear. He didn't remember falling asleep, but he felt more tired than before he had dozed. It was a toss-up whether the motions of the auto during the long ride to the milcom or Jarsen's incessant, monotonous banter had done the trick, but there he was, bleary-eyed and disheveled, ready to meet his superiors.

The sun had already begun to rise, and the rain lingered only in the still-damp earth. Getting stiffly out of the car, Dulan walked around a bit to stretch his legs. The morning air was crisp and refreshing, and immediately put him in a better frame of mind.

He took a quick survey of his surroundings. Was this to be his new home? Gently rolling countryside dotted with occasional scrub oak and considerable underbrush ranged from Dulan's vantage point to the horizon. On a good-sized hillock about one hundred meters away was an operational radar scan station. Behind him, no more than ten meters distant, was what appeared to be a bunker built into a hillside. It was sealed by a huge, ponderous iron door. The facility was unmarked, so Dulan could only surmise that this was Milcom Forty-Three. He had been conscripted at twenty-five from the com of his birth and made to travel halfway across the continent to stand in this spot. He wasn't very impressed.

The jeep was parked beside them. The Outsider named Jones was being roughly ushered from the vehicle by the two MPs who had beaten him the night before. The man was led, still dazed, shackled, and in obvious pain toward the great door. Dulan didn't understand about the Outsider, but then it wasn't his place to understand such things.

"Yeah, that's it all right," announced Jarsen when he saw Dulan staring at the bunker. "Real impressive, ain't it?" The Sergeant moved like an old man to the rear of the car—he was stiff too. Opening the trunk, he produced Dulan's brand-new luggage. "Guess we all got to do our bit, right Doc?"

The black man smiled.

Jones was delivered to the door just as it slid open. As he was taken in, a middle-aged man in a light blue jump suit stepped out into the misty sunlight and trotted toward the cars with his arm outstretched.

Dulan was taken aback at the sight of the man. He was grossly overweight and was fairly bulging out of his jumper. His monster jowls flounced obscenely with every step he took. Such excess was unheard of in the com, and Dulan couldn't help but wonder exactly what he had gotten himself into.

"Doctor Dulan, this is a genuine pleasure," the man said through thick purple lips. "I'm Marv Mensik, Doctor Stuart's personal secretary. The doctor is a very busy man and regrets that he can't come up and greet you himself, but...duty calls. You understand."

Mensik began energetically pumping Dulan's hand as if he were drawing water from a well.

"Glad to know you," Dulan said while trying unsuccessfully for eye contact. Dulan released his handshake pressure, and Mensik took the hint, bringing the protracted greeting to a stop. Mensik stooped to pick up Dulan's bags, but the black man stopped him.

"That's all right, I can get them," he said. "Thanks for the ride Sergeant."

Jarsen cracked his rawhide face for a toothless grin. "Sure, Doc. Anytime." The man climbed back into the sedan and motioned to Wynna. As the car backed up, tracking a parabola in the soft soil, Jarsen rolled down his window, sticking a thumbs up salute through the opening. "Keep 'em flying," he called to Dulan.

"Loose lips sink ships," Dulan returned with as much heart as he could muster, then turned and headed toward the door.

They entered the bunker, a room about ten meters square, practically devoid of furnishings. By the wall to his left was a small guard station, manned by three enlisted men, who at the time were pushing closed the heavy door that separated Forty-Three from the outside world. The guards' only duty was apparently opening and closing that immense slab of metal.

The station comprised three chairs, a small console equipped with a video screen, and a wooden table containing telephone, coffee pot, and the usual array of propaganda magazines. The video screen was presenting a picture of the countryside directly in line with the front of the bunker, and Dulan watched for a moment as the car that brought him drove slowly away and finally off the screen.

"This way, Doctor," smiled Mensik, motioning toward a sliding door on the wall opposite the guard station. "The lift will be back up in a minute."

Dulan carried his bags over to the elevator, set them on the rock floor, and looked around for Jones. They must have sent him ahead, for he was not in the room.

"How was the trip up?" the man asked, still attempting congeniality.

"Quite an experience," Dulan replied, trying to remain civil to the man. He didn't like Mensik at all, but couldn't decide whether his reasons were valid. He realized that he was still really worn out, and sat himself down on his big suitcase. "I've never been on one of these before," he said, motioning toward the lift. "In fact, up until yesterday I'd never ridden in an airplane, or an auto, or seen one of the old cities."

Mensik raised his eyebrows, deep furrows etching his forehead. "You'll find a milcom entirely outside of your experience, Doctor. Unfortunately, after enough exposure, even the extraordinary becomes mundane."

Dulan thought that he discerned a slight twinge of remorse, mixed with more than a little bitterness in Mensik's tone, but being completely disinterested in the man personally, he said nothing.

A barely noticeable rumble could be detected behind the sliding panels, heralding the arrival of the elevator. Dulan picked up his bags and stepped close to the door. In a few seconds the doors slowly squeaked open and the two men entered the small cubicle.

"Why don't you leave your luggage here?" Mensik asked, picking up the two bags and replacing them on the bunker floor. "One of these gentlemen will take them directly to your apartment. You still have a few security procedures to go through, and that will save you from dragging them around. What kind of rocks do you keep in these things anyway?"

"Not rocks," Dulan replied, "books."

Mensik smiled with his gelatin face. "I don't think that you'll find any market for things like that here."

"I don't intend to sell them," Dulan frowned. "Where to now?"

Perpetually grinning, Mensik merely pointed toward the floor. The control box on the elevator wall was numbered in descending order from one to eight, with a G above the one. The fat man mashed the button marked two, and with a jerk, they were on their way.

Dulan's stomach took note of a new sensation as the lift rushed downward. It was an uneasy feeling, but not without its pleasure. There were a million questions running around in his mind, but he kept them to himself, preferring to let every aspect of this new experience burst fresh and unannounced upon his consciousness. They traveled downward for several minutes, and when the lift finally came to a stop, Dulan wondered just how far underground they were.

"About half a kilometer," Mensik said in response to the unasked question. "Everyone wonders the same thing."

As the elevator doors slid open, Dulan was in no way prepared for the sight that greeted his eyes. The lift stood at the center of an enormous circular room. It was by far the largest enclosed space that he had ever seen. The diameter of the big circle, from wall to wall, was every bit of five hundred meters, with a floor-to-ceiling height of perhaps six meters. Inside the outer perimeter were several concentric inner circles composed of blocks of what appeared to be offices and labs. Separating the office blocks were aisles radiating out diagonally from the center point elevators (which instead of one were now ten, stacked back to back and side by side) and extending to the far walls. If the chamber were a huge wheel, the elevators would be the hub and the aisles the spokes.

The inner circles of office blocks were divided back and front by corridors, indicating easy access from the lifts to any point in the voluminous room. The walls of the inner circles went all the way from floor to ceiling enabling two stories of offices to be put in one room. Dulan theorized that the walls probably ran through the whole structure for strength and support, and that the extremely high ceilings helped to alleviate the claustrophobic feelings that sometimes develop with long periods of confinement. The effect worked fairly well—the overall impression given was one of spaciousness.

The walls all seemed made of concrete, while the floor was some kind of aluminum alloy braced by steel girders. The lighting was indirect, inserted into diffusing panels in the walls and ceiling. It was bright but not harsh, and helped create an atmosphere of antisepticness and sterility. The walls were painted warmly, though, and many people were droning around, proceeding with their day's activities, making the whole picture seem harmonious, if slightly impersonal.

It was difficult for Dulan to ascertain the age of the structure. Com architecture and systems hadn't changed appreciatively in over four hundred years. Everything was extremely well-kept and looked, in fact, almost new. But orderliness was intrinsic to com life. He conservatively estimated the age of the milcom at two hundred fifty years.

He tried to take it all in. So this is where they ran the war. He had somehow expected troops and barracks, but so far the three noncoms in the guard station were the only noncivilians encountered.

"First stop, personnel," said Mensik, leading Dulan down one of the main aisles. The black man noticed that each of the spokes was marked with a letter of the alphabet, and each interior ring of office blocks was color coded. They turned down the corridor marked "Green" and proceeded in a clockwise direction. The doors to the offices were consecutively numbered, and these numbers also proceeded clockwise.

The two men came to a stop in front of a door marked 101. Mensik opened the door and motioned Dulan in behind him. The small office was occupied by three women and two men who appeared busily unproductive behind their wooden desks. Dulan was led to a slight, balding man with a nervous twitch, who asked him a lot of questions, the answers to which were banged out directly on a typer. There was no extraneous furniture in the room, so Dulan was forced to stand while being interrogated. After a few minutes of that, pictures were taken and fingerprints made, then Dulan was released.

Mensik held the door open, nodding Dulan into the corridor. Once out of the office, they stayed in the green corridor, still traveling clockwise. They passed several of the main spokes before reaching Operations. The lettering on the door read:

CARL STUART
CIVILIAN COORDINATOR
MILCOM OPERATIONS

"The boss," Mensik said, and gazed at the door as if to deify the writing it contained. He turned the knob and they entered a vacant office filled with filing cabinets.

"Nobody home?" Dulan wondered aloud.

"This is my cubbyhole," grinned Mensik. "Doctor Stuart's office adjoins through that door." He pointed to a door marked "Private."

Dulan glanced around at the bulky records files. "What's all this?" he asked.

"One of the things you'll have to get used to," answered Mensik. "Carl Stuart is very self-dependent. Of course, all personnel records are stored in the computer, but Doctor Stuart prefers his own files. So what can you do?"

"File," Dulan responded.

"Right." Mensik tapped lightly on the door.

"Come," said a muffled voice from inside the office. Mensik led Dulan through the doorway.

"Doral Dulan, boy wonder," the fat man chimed.

The room was marginally furnished, and very proper. There were several more filing cabinets lined like soldiers against the wall, and eight or ten hard-backed chairs positioned just so against the remaining wall space. In the center of the medium-sized room, toward the back wall, sat an aging man at an oversized desk filled with neatly stacked piles of papers and several telephones. He was busily scribbling on a piece of paper and seemed completely oblivious to their entrance.

They stood unrecognized in the middle of the office for perhaps a minute. Mensik became increasingly nervous and agitated. Dulan spent the time surveying the office interior more carefully.

He was struck by the complete absence of personal items: photos on the desk, perhaps a diploma or psyche-pro on the wall, a favorite vase or bust of Isaac Complan—any of the things that lend the distinct human touch to the surroundings in which people spend a good deal of time.

Finally, Carl Stuart put down his pen and looked up.

"Thank you, Marvin. You may go now." Mensik nodded dully and left the room without a word, closing the door behind him.

"So, you're the Exceptional," said Doctor Stuart, reaching across the desk to shake the black man's hand. "I'm Stuart, and all the terrible things you've heard about me don't nearly measure up to the genuine article." He was lean and hard and stern, and his grip was predictably viselike. He appeared to be in his mid-fifties, although his vitality and internal drive bespoke someone younger. His countenance was all straight lines and severe angles, as a face chiseled out of oak, and he was touched very little by the wrinkles that accompany advancing age. Only his burr-cropped hair, white as maggots, gave a hint of his true years. His face was ashen, probably due to the large number of years spent in the underground complex. His eyes were steel: cold, hard, and without compassion. His gaze was unfaltering, and he looked at Dulan as if he were giving him an X ray.

"Sit down, Doctor," he said, indicating a chair near the desk.

Dulan nodded silently and parked himself on the uncompromising wood. Stuart shuffled through a stack of papers until he came up with a file folder. The folder was full of handwritten information; there wasn't a printout in the lot. Stuart flipped through it quickly, then laid it aside.

"You come . . . well recommended, Doctor Dulan," he said, almost sarcastically.

"My record speaks for itself," Dulan answered, wondering why he felt as if he had to defend himself.

Stuart wiped his lips with a handkerchief that lay on the desk top. The odor of witch hazel drifted across the room to Dulan's nostrils. "Indeed," the Doctor said. "According to your file, this is your first experience in a milcom. In fact, it's the first time that you've ever been away from the com in which you were raised."

"That's correct."

Stuart rolled his eyes. "You may find life here a little harder, a little more disciplined than you're used to. This is a military installation and, as such, must be run in a military manner. How do you feel about discipline, Doctor?"

"It's a necessary prerequisite for an orderly society," Dulan answered.

"Yes, yes, but how do you feel about discipline . . . personally?"

"Appreciating the concept, I tolerate the reality."

Doctor Stuart wiped his lips. "When you arrive at your room, you will find an S.O.P. lying on your bed. I want you to read it carefully, frequently, and completely until you fully understand our procedures here. Then I want you to heed it, Doctor. Conformity is the basis of all military life. Conformity and order. I've been project coordinator here for over twenty-five years, and I worked here for many years before that. The milcom is my life, and I love it. As your superior, it is my responsibility to see that you maintain the proper . . . shall we say . . . respect, for our rules and precepts. It is your responsibility to acquiesce to my wishes. Exceptionals don't get special treatment here, Doctor. We all drink from the same philosophical cup. Do you understand?"

"I understand," Dulan said, wishing he could lie down on something that wasn't moving.

"Good." The hint of a grimace (or was it a smile?) flashed across Stuart's lips and he seemed to relax a bit. "You work with computers," he stated, clumsily changing the subject.

"Mostly on a theoretical level," Dulan answered. "I explore the possibilities of the system."

Stuart nodded and laid his hand on the file folder. "Your dossier details your career most adequately. The computer has a very important place in the Divine Plan. Your work here will be of a highly critical nature, and, I should think, most stimulating."

Dulan perked up a bit. "Just what exactly is the nature of my work? No one has ever told me."

"All in good time, my friend. Your research is top secret. It isn't wise to reveal too many secrets too quickly."

Dulan had been exposed to bureaucratic crypticism all of his life, and found it intolerable on every level. He was just about to press his point when a sharp knock resounded on the door, followed immediately by a young woman charging in like an angry bull, Mensik right on her heels. She barged past Dulan, bumping him rudely. Ignoring Dulan, she strode right up to the project director, looking for all the world as if she were going to box his ears.

"My patient was just brought in beaten and chained like some animal." She was livid with rage. Dulan was captivated.

Mensik was huffing and puffing. "I-I'm sorry, Doctor. I told her that you were . . ."

"Never mind, Marvin," Doctor Stuart said, waving the fat man away. "I'll speak to Miss Delacorte." Once again, Mensik silently left the room.

"About Mr. Jones . . ." she persisted, eyes flashing.

"A truly regrettable incident, Doctor. What's his condition?"

"Slight concussion, two broken fingers, some missing teeth—Doctor Stuart, that man was handcuffed and forced here against his will. He . . ."

"Yes, I know. Will he be ready for work tomorrow?"

The woman looked horrified. "Tomorrow! I should say not. That poor man will need at least . . ."

"Day after tomorrow, no later."

"But Doctor Stuart, I . . ."

"No more, Miss Delacorte." Doctor Stuart was outwardly calm, but Dulan could see that he was barely able to tolerate this assault on his authority. The woman pushed on.

"About this method of recruitment. . ."

Stuart raised his arms in surrender. "Please spare us, would you? I'm merely an administrator. I've already conceded the regrettability of the occurrence. What more do you want from me?"

"A little less inaction would be nice."

"You have a lot to learn, young lady. The recruitment of Outsiders has nothing to do with this office. I neither condone it, nor do I have any control over it. But since you ask my opinion, I'll tell you exactly how I feel. I think that Outsiders are not just a nuisance, but a hazard to the well-being of all pure-blooded comites, and that they should be left to wallow on the frontier with others of their ilk. Their continued exposure to com life will only stand to tarnish us by our association with them. In other words, Doctor Delacorte, I find the mere existence of those godless heathens to be an almost intolerable situation, one that I would rectify were it within my power. Now that we understand each other, was there anything else that you wanted?''

The woman stood firm. ''Yes,'' she said, ''the nurse in the clinic, against my orders, put Mr. Jones under heavy sedation. It was not warranted given the patient's condition.''

Stuart grimaced and slowly wiped his lips. ''Need I remind you that you have no authority over the medical department here. The nurse was following my orders in sedating the Outsider.''

''Your orders?''

''That's correct. Now, I'd like for you to meet the man you tried to knock down when you came barging in here.'' Dulan rose from his seat. ''Beatrice Delacorte, Doral Dulan. Doctor Dulan arrived just this morning, along with your Mr. Jones.''

''In slightly better condition, too,'' she remarked coldly. Then a change. ''I'm sorry for being so impolite, really. I've no reason to take my frustrations out on you.''

''Anytime,'' Dulan answered, putting on his most come-hither look. When he shook her hand, it was more intimate than a mere greeting.

''Doctor Stuart tells me that I'm just not used to the system yet,'' she said, brushing some stray hair from her eyes. ''I've only been here a few weeks myself.''

Dulan studied the woman. She was beautiful. Almost as large as him, with honey-blond tresses that hung loosely on her shoulders, quite contary to the short, boyish cut which was the style among most com females. Her eyes were of the palest blue, and seemed to glow, hauntingly, from within—twin beacons of fiery intensity. Her features were soft, and her skin, though slightly pale in color, was clear and, except for a small birthmark on her left cheekbone, unblemished. If anything, that small imperfection made her appear that much more perfect. Her whole manner stirred the Exceptional sexually, and he would have claimed her immediately had they been in the com. But, customs seemed so different in the milcom, he decided to extend his overtures and then play it by ear. One thing he knew for certain: this was a woman accustomed to the freedom of the frontier. No comite would even think about attacking Stuart's authority the way she had done, especially in defense of an Outsider. Another thing he knew: Carl Stuart hated this woman of the outside with a passionless loathing born of righteous indignation. Dulan had no particular prejudices. He treated everyone with equal contempt.

She wore the informal, loose-fitting jump suit that seemed to be the unofficial uniform at Forty-Three. But even under such uncomplimentary attire, the woman exhibited a marvelous fullness of figure, and Dulan found that it required a real effort on his part to keep from staring at her shamelessly. Perhaps things were beginning to look up.

"I'm glad that you came in, Doctor," Stuart was saying. "I have to meet with General Lynch in a few minutes. Do you think that you could help Doctor Dulan find his room?" He picked up a pen and scribbled something on a note pad. When finished, he ripped the paper off of the pad and handed it to her.

"What about my luggage?" Dulan asked, thinking about a change of clothes.

"I think that you'll find your suitcases already in your room when you arrive. By the way, I'd appreciate it if you both would meet me here at 1300 hours for a short tour and orientation. I'm sure that you'll find it interesting and . . . informative."

Beatrice Delacorte spoke up. "Does this mean that I'm finally going to be put to work?"

"The impetuousness of youth," sighed Doctor Stuart. "The wheels of government grind very slowly, Miss Delacorte. You may as well get used to it. Now if there's nothing further. . . ." Suddenly, the old man's eyes narrowed and he glared at the woman. Then he was around the desk and in front of them in a flash. Dulan jumped with surprise. Doctor Stuart was seated in a wheelchair. He had no legs. His empty pants dangled over the edge of the chair as if waiting for something to grow into them.

"Miss Delacorte," Stuart growled. "I've forgiven your little indiscretions in the past, and shall do so this one last time, but my patience with you is rapidly drawing to a close. I'm the authority in this institution, and as such I demand respect. I demand it!" The Director's face was straining and his powerful hands clawed a deathgrip on the chair arms. "If I had wanted you people running in and out of here like lunatics, I would have installed a revolving door."

"I apologize," she said, a barely noticeable quaver in her voice. "It won't happen again."

"I'm sure it won't, by Complan," the old man fumed. "On your way out, would you send Mr. Mensik in to me?"

"I think that's our cue," Dulan whispered. They turned and headed out the door. Mensik scurried by as they passed his desk. Dulan started to say something, but the fat man just nodded his head and disappeared into Doctor Stuart's office, closing the door behind him.

Dulan and the woman left the outer office and walked down the hall. Even through double closed doors, they could hear Stuart's voice as he screamed at Mensik.

They walked in silence for a moment, and Dulan heard a sound he hadn't noticed earlier. It was a voice, gentle and pristine, coming from nowhere and everywhere. It was a woman's voice, talking—no, reading. He recognized the text as a passage from Complan.

"What's that?" he asked.

"Get used to it," she said. "Isaac Complan keeps us company twenty-four hours a day."

Her tone was sardonic, almost frighteningly so. Out of habit, Dulan glanced around to see if they had been overheard. "You're a beautiful woman," he said.

"And you're very disarming, Doctor. I noticed the way you undressed me with your eyes back in Doctor Stuart's office."

"Was I that obvious? I never have been accused of having a great deal of style."

"I'll accept it as a compliment."

"Good," he beamed. "Will we be friends then?"

"It's possible," she answered. "Yes. It's very possible."

Did she want him or not? Dulan was befuddled. He had made all the proper advances, expressed his interest. Why hadn't she responded yet? All the other women he had known had made their sexual objectives clear within the first few minutes of a conversation. What in the round world was she waiting for? Things certainly were different in a milcom.

"Let's begin the road to friendship by getting on a first name basis," she said. "My friends, who are admittedly few and far between, call me Bea."

"Bea," he repeated. "My first name's Doral, but everyone calls me Dulan."

"Then I'll call you Doral," she replied. "You're very self-assured, aren't you?"

"Not really. I simply know the extent of my capabilities . . . and my limitations. In many ways I'm quite backward." He watched her closely. "I hear the war is going well," he said.

She returned his gaze long and hard before answering. "They tell me that victory is at hand," she replied, and the slightest smile pinched the corners of her lips, a smile that he returned.

They understood each other.

They made a turn and headed down spoke D toward the elevator complex. Bea suddenly stopped dead in her tracks and pointed a finger at Dulan. "Why, you're the Exceptional!" she exclaimed, and slapped her forehead. "Of course."

Dulan raised his eyebrows. "How did you know?"

"Are you kidding? They've been talking about your arrival for weeks now. Most people never meet one of your kind in their entire lives, and for an Exceptional to be sent to a milcom is almost unthinkable. I don't know if it's ever occurred before."

"If that's so," he said, "then why am I here?"

Now it was Bea's turn to raise her eyebrows. "You don't know?"

"Nope."

She shrugged, burying her hands deeply into her jumper pockets. "Welcome to the club," she said.

They arrived at the elevators and Bea pushed the big illuminated "Down" arrow. One of the doors opened immediately and they stepped inside. She pressed the button for the fifth floor, and the car began moving.

"Are these lifts the only connection between floors?" he asked.

"As far as I know. I've wondered about that myself."

"What's on the fifth floor?"

"Housing. All civilian personnel live there, if 'live' is the right word for it."

Dulan shook his head. "What about the rest of the floors?"

"It's hard to say exactly. I'm not authorized any lower than level six yet. Seven and eight are security levels. When we have the opportunity, we'll sit down and plumb the shallows of my knowledge. Ah, here we are."

The door slid open and they stepped out. This floor looked essentially like the one they had just left. Bea removed from her jumper pocket the paper that Doctor Stuart had given her, and handed it to Dulan. On the paper was written: 5 D (red) 83.

"This is your address," she said. "It means . . ."

"It means—fifth floor, spoke D," he began moving in that direction, "red aisle, number eighty-three. Right?"

The woman beamed at him. "So what did you need me for?"

"I hate to be alone?"

"Baloney. You're a devious man."

"Guilty," he laughed. "By the way. Why did I have to leave my bags upstairs?"

"They wanted to search them," she answered.

"Oh."

As the battle roared about him, Isaac Complan was possessed withal by a glorious frenzy of the spirit, and with gun, and pinard, and bare hands he did account for the lives of twenty-three men on that holiest of days. It was upon slitting the throat of the last man, that the Lord God appeared to him in a vision. The voice of God spoke through the lips of the dead soldier who Complan still cradled in gore-covered arms. And as He spoke, the corpses of half a hundred men—friend and foe alike—rose from their death places and, joining hands, danced they the gavotte of war. When Isaac saw these things he prostrated himself on the ground, and trembled before the sight of such a miracle.

"Why do you fear?" asked the Lord, and His voice was like the breath of morning and the snort of black night thunder at one and the same time. "You crushed the grapes, now drink the wine."

With firm resolve, Isaac looked up at the spectacle that surrounded him. The carrion bait had been transformed into wondrous angels with pulsing Aspects—the final victory of the just death. And around them, the crater-filled smokescape had become a beautiful, white-sanded beach set against a gently roiling blue green ocean of limitless horizon and erotic, licking breezes. Complan was filled with wonder.

"Isaac," the Lord whispered on the breeze, "there are words that must be said to my people. You will say them for Me."

"But Lord," Isaac answered, and he was on his knees for his legs were like the daffodil in the midsummer wind, "I am but a simple soldier."

And the Lord laughed loud and long, like the cement truck with the strip-geared gondola. "You are an expert practitioner of the greatest human art form. You suit My purposes splendidly."

—*Book of Complan* (6-35 to 40)

Anyone who is found to have in his possession Old World artifacts, literature, films, or tapes which have been enumerated on the expunged list, is subject to expulsion to the frontier without trial.

—from the original *Com State Charter*

3

Level seven was darker than the other levels. Only slightly, but darker nevertheless. That physical reality produced a mental fantasy extension. A murkiness seemed to ooze from the now damp looking walls and hang, mistlike, in the air. Dulan shuddered involuntarily as if chilled, although he knew that the feeling was produced in his own mind. As he drank in his surroundings, the Exceptional dropped slightly behind his companions.

A group of people passed him going the opposite direction. There were perhaps twenty of them moving in double file. They shuffled listlessly, almost directionlessly, along the gently curling hallway, all of them in some manner of physical contact with others in the group. He watched their faces but saw nothing there—only faces, many open-mouthed. Around their necks they wore amulets made of clear acrylic. Within each amulet was imprisoned seemingly insignificant bits of ordinary material—a button, a piece of cloth, part of a zipper. Several of the people maintained a death grip on their pendants.

Dulan stopped and stared as the group staggered past and wondered again what he was doing in a place like this. The war had managed to roll along for over five hundred years without his interference. Why could they want him now? Soldiers were chosen early in life from the results of psyche-pros, and were trained accordingly. Every month or so a new crop would parade out of the walled city in their fresh, clean uniforms to the sound of a marching band and the cheers of flag-waving citizens who lined the streets en masse. None of the recruits ever came back again.

"We haven't got all day, Doctor," Carl Stuart called to him from his wheelchair. "You can go sightseeing some other time."

Dulan frowned and nodded, quickening his pace to catch up. He had already made an enemy of the program coordinator. Stuart was a by-the-book old schooler and was put off by the black man's casualness and easy intelligence. Dulan had circumvented plenty like Stuart in the com and, boss or no boss, was not about to change his attitudes to satisfy an old man's concepts of internal harmony.

Bea crinkled her nose in his direction as Dulan rejoined her. Stuart was using incredibly powerful arms to propel his chair forward at breakneck speed, and keeping up with him was no easy task.

"Very few human beings ever get to see the security levels of a milcom," the old man was saying. "You two should consider yourselves most fortunate."

Dulan smiled. It pleased him to think that it must have been more than difficult for an old heathen hater like Stuart to show Bea his little secrets.

They moved along in silence for a time, the only sound being the never-ending Complanian monologue. Finally, Stuart jerked his motivator to a halt before a door that looked remarkably like any other door. "Here we are," he announced. The door was numbered 131 and had the name Colonel Kwi handwritten on a card that could slide in and out a slot, as if the name changed from time to time. The old man stretched to push open the door, then stopped. He looked with distaste at both Dulan and Bea. "I'm too loyal a citizen to question the wisdom behind the decision to send you here, but I can tell you that I've made it my duty to see that you both conduct yourselves with the proper sense of responsibility as regards the knowledge you are about to acquire." He looked piercingly, almost theatrically, at each of them in turn for signs of reluctance, then threw open the door and ushered them inside the room that lay beyond.

The chamber was almost totally dark, except for tiny wink lights that dotted the walls at regular intervals and threw off a weak luminescence around the bulb. They were forced to stay put for a while until their eyes became accustomed to the subdued light.

Gradually things assumed bumps and contours, and paraded into fuzzy focus. The room was lecture-hall sized, and filled with desks. A group of people occupied the center section of desks. Both male and female, they seemed to be limp in their chairs; in fact, they were strapped in. Around their heads was some manner of metal ring, dangling wires like turnip roots. Their skulls lolled back on heaving shoulders, and they were moaning softly, eerily, as if in a trance.

Dulan heard Bea gasp softly.

"Please," Stuart said, indicating a short flight of stairs just off to their left. "This way." The old man wheeled himself to the stairway and somehow managed to connect his wheelchair to a runningboard next to the bannister. Then, using only the strength of his arms and a will of iron, he hauled himself and his metal mover up the steps by grasping the rail and pulling for all he was worth. Bea and Dulan dutifully followed behind.

At the top of the stairs was a small control booth that looked out over the rest of the room. The blockhouse was also unlit, but it glowed ominously from the dull light emitted from hundreds of dials on dozens of instrument panels. There were two white-robed technicians in the booth, their function apparently to watchdog the controls and the catatonic group of zombies who sat below them. But Dulan barely noticed these things. His gaze was riveted to a large view screen which completely dominated the far blockhouse wall. On the screen was what appeared to be a video tape recording of a bathtub occupied by a very diminutive, very naked Oriental-looking man who was fondling the heavy breasts of a young, red-haired, also very naked woman.

Sex-pix were everyday fare, required viewing, in the com, but this one was like nothing he had ever seen. Com sex-pix were done in a rigid, unchanging style, designed to achieve a certain effect in a given amount of time. This one was not like that. There was no continuity or internal logic to the tableau that was unfolding on the screen. Images changed rapidly, fading in and out, sometimes with no relation to each other—sometimes with no relation to anything; scenes floating fluidly through time and space. Death, dinner, dancing and demagoguery all moved together in beautiful confusion. Many of the quick scenes were comprehensible, even understandable, and Dulan found himself able to follow a small strain of intelligible connections and piece together exactly what was happening up on the screen. Strangely enough, despite all the mass chaos and image shifting, the overall effect was very personal and highly erotic. Dulan felt himself relating to the man in the movie.

"We came in at a bad time," Stuart remarked. "Sexual activity, along with all of its inherent fantasy elements, is terribly difficult to scan with any degree of expediency. Unfortunately, Colonel Kwi seems to be highly prolific sexually and very unproductive otherwise."

"What do you mean?" asked Bea, mirroring the question that skidded into Dulan's thoughts.

Doctor Stuart's eyes narrowed. It was obvious that he was searching for the most concise way of explaining the view screen non sequiturs. "What I mean, Miss Delacorte, is that what you are watching right now is not some strange motion picture, but a live transmission . . . without cameras. It's all happening, at this moment, a thousand kilometers from here and is being brought to us courtesy of those people down there." He reached out and rapped his knuckles on the blockhouse window, a window that was set just low enough for him to see through.

"Telps," she said in a whisper that was almost a question.

"Your parapsychological training stands you in good stead," replied Stuart. "Yes, they're telepaths, but this system is infinitely more advanced than anything that you've worked with in the com." He turned his chair so that it faced the screen squarely, then pointed. "That man is Colonel Kwi, military attaché and third in command of the so-called 'People's Army' on the Northern Front. I have no idea who the young lady is."

She's not your type anyway, thought Dulan. The Exceptional had absolutely no idea what was going on, but there would be time for questions later.

"The Colonel is now, involuntarily of course, sharing his thoughts with us telepathically, through the combined abilities of the twenty people below us. They are individually and collectively attuned to the Colonel's brain waves, and are relaying to us via the electrodes implanted in the alpha bands around their craniums."

Dulan thought of the people in the hall. They were obviously telepaths, but why the bizarre behavior? This talk of telepathy was intriguing. He had heard the term, but never in relation to anything military. But then, civilians never heard about the military at all except on parade day. He could contain his curiosity no longer. "How do . . ." he began, but Stuart silenced him.

"The electrical impulses discharged from the brains of the Telps are being fed into the computer which, hopefully, translates and separates these impulses into simple electric signals which it then identifies and turns back into a visual composite as you see it on the screen."

"Television," Dulan said, remembering something he had seen in one of the ancient books.

The woman raised her eyebrows. "Television?"

"Cathode ray scanners," the Exceptional corrected quickly, realizing the unfamiliarity of the term.

"Yes," said Stuart, "not unlike our cathode scanners. Obviously that's an oversimplification. The human brain is itself a computer of unequalled sophistication, sending and receiving messages at an astounding rate. Thoughts come and go with rapidity and disjointedness. Many are connected to a basic logical progression of events only in the most Freudian of manners."

It was Dulan's turn to start with amazement. Perhaps he was not the only student of ancient history at Forty-Three. How did Stuart know about Freud?

"What the computer does," Stuart continued, "is scan the impulses, rejecting those thoughts that seem too obscure or unintelligible to be of any importance to the main line of reasoning. It then takes whatever patterns are left and translates them back into a composite visual. We think in words as well as pictures, so the speech patterns are scanned in the same way and appear as blurbs at the bottom of the screen. Actual verbalizations run as an auditory track."

Dulan was appalled. He was revered in the com as one of the world's foremost computer experts, and here he was being offhandedly presented with complexities of the system that he had never even dreamed existed. "It must have been quite a task, trying to interpret abstract brain discharges into simple electrical patterns."

"Perhaps not as difficult as you might think," answered Doctor Stuart. "You start with a known, take a group of people, and have them think about the same thing. Check similarities, eliminate nonessentials, find the common denominator. Once you've made one connection—wave impulse to known electrical pattern, the rest is just trial and error. It's like breaking a code. As soon as the first letter is discovered, it's a matter of chipping away until it all comes together."

"It's a new language," Dulan said.

"If you will," Stuart answered. "But one that only the computer understands. Anyway, all this," he again drew their attention to the screen, "is a very elementary interpretation of what's actually happening in that man's mind—the computer's extrapolation of events. It's like trying to watch two things at the same time; you never can get a full grasp of what you're looking at. The brain is too personal and complex an instrument to be even remotely understood in its raw state. The best we can do is skim the surface trying to pick up that basic conscious thread that runs through our thinking and ties everything else together. Then we cut it down some more and interpret it as best we can, in the hopes of understanding in an essential way just what it is that man is thinking."

Dulan was beginning to understand the concepts, and was being physically jolted by the implications. He had questions. "What we're seeing right now may not actually be happening," he said, noticing that Colonel Kwi seemed to be reaching a plateau of excitement, heaving and rolling in the tub, the red-haired girl squealing like a puppy. Husky groans issued through the screen's speaker. He realized that it was far easier to follow the action if he allowed himself to flow with the images on a purely emotional level, rather than trying to break it down into logical patterns. In the chamber proper, the Telps were moaning at ever-increasing intensity, echoing Kwi's agitation.

"You catch on quickly," said Stuart.

"I'm an Exceptional," Dulan answered dryly.

"Well, I'm not," Bea blurted out. "And I'm so mixed up you could make an omelet out of me."

Stuart grunted contemptuously. "A human being's ability to achieve sexual gratification is solely dependent upon his ability to appreciate the sex act as an erotic experience. There's nothing in the book that says we should enjoy sex. That's an invention of our minds. Hence, the mental fantasy elements comprise ninety percent of the actual experience. So, undoubtedly, a very small portion of what you're watching is actually real, at least in the sense that we define reality. That's why I said that we came in at a bad time. This is awfully unrepresentative of what the Telp system can achieve. Other human activities translate through the computer much better."

Bea still seemed confused. Everything was coming too fast for her. "But, what's the point?" she asked, trying to synthesize an overall picture in her mind. "What's it all for?" It was necessary for her to speak in a loud voice in order to be heard over the racket from below which had reached clamorous proportions. Doctor Stuart attempted to answer, but the din from without made it impossible for him to be heard. He shrugged his shoulders and stopped talking.

While they waited for the Oriental to bring his bathtub sex to a conclusion, Dulan looked for a place to sit down, but the only two chairs in the room were occupied by the technicians watching the controls. So he walked to the blockhouse window and watched the Telps. They were weaving obscenely, dancing to someone else's tune. He wondered where their minds were while they shared Kwi's.

The action on the screen and below increased in cadence, then reached a blistering crescendo. All at once there was a loud scream in unison from the Telps, then—silence.

"Look," gasped Bea, pointing to the screen.

The erotic scene had been replaced by something much different. The Colonel had his arms oustretched and appeared to be actually, physically flying. He soared through gelatinous clouds that seemed to have mass and substance, and Kwi was scooping up great handfuls of the stuff and cramming it into his mouth.

"Looks like the stud has flaked out on us again," laughed one of the white-robed men. "That young fluff is just too much for him."

"He's asleep," explained Doctor Stuart.

"In the bathtub?" Bea asked.

Stuart tightened his lips, wiped them with his handkerchief, then turned away from the screen. "Let's hope that his young friend has drained out the water. I'm afraid that there will be nothing but nonsense on the viewer for a time."

"Nonsense!" exclaimed Bea. "What a marvelous opportunity to study the subconscious mind. Think of the things we could learn about ourselves from firsthand study of the dream state."

Stuart scowled his scowl. "The *Book of Complan* tells us all we need to know about ourselves, Miss Delacorte," he said coldly. "Our motivations for setting all this up are a lot more basic and immediately urgent."

A wave of puzzlement washed over Bea's face, and Dulan realized that she still didn't understand. "What Doctor Stuart is getting at," he said, "is that they are monitoring Colonel Kwi telepathically in order to obtain military information."

"Most astute," the old man observed, "except that the Colonel is just one of many, many people who are continually scanned by this milcom and others like it. We receive from them all their troop movements and battle plans and counter our forces accordingly."

"Why not eliminate the middlemen and go right to the source, the top man, to get your information?" Dulan asked.

Stuart leaned back in his seat. "I think that you can answer your own question, Doctor," he said. "Think about it."

Smiling slightly, Dulan returned Stuart's gaze. It really was coming together for him—almost too quickly. "Do the other sides have Telps also?"

"Of course," replied Stuart. "The war would have ended centuries ago if the might were so unbalanced."

Dulan turned his attention to Bea, who still appeared to be a heartbeat behind and floundering. He turned back to Stuart. "There can't be a top man," he said, and could not keep the wonder out of his voice. "Any one person, or group of people with any authority over policy making would be too easy to monitor, to . . . scan. There can be no one with any real authority."

Bea was shaking her head. "Then how . . ."

"Finish it, Doctor," said Stuart.

Dulan cleared his throat. His words were coming out faster than he could think them through. "The war . . . the government . . . all important decisions must be under computer control." He heard Bea gasp, and knew that she would probably be a lot more horrified when the full reality of such an absurd situation reached full fruition in her mind. No wonder the civilians were kept in the dark about military activities. The implications were too difficult to justify.

Stuart was nodding his head. "Just so. All relevant data concerning every aspect of the war and our lives is fed constantly into the computer net. All that transpires with the Telps goes directly into the computer's memory."

"None of this is really necessary, then," said Dulan, indicating the whole of the control room.

"No," Stuart answered. "We have no actual control over anything that transpires here. The screen was the computer's idea a couple of centuries ago. I think that it wanted us to feel a little more personally involved with our work here."

The old man wheeled his chair to a squared-up position with the window. Sitting up straight, he craned his neck to watch the Telps. "Anyway," he continued, "the computer is kept constantly aware of every component of our existence and consequently is able to make instant, logical decisions based on all available data as to what would be in the best interests of the com states at any given moment. For example,"—he turned back to the screen. Colonel Kwi was being pursued down a long hallway by a hundred hideous monsters bearing automatic weapons which they were firing at him with immense glee—"Suppose the Asian computers decided that there should be a massive invasion from the North, which, by the way, is almost a certainty at this point. Kwi and all others involved with command on the Northern borders would be given just enough information by the computer to carry out their part of the invasion. Upon reception of the orders they would take immediate action. Through the Telps, we know when they know and our computers form defensive and offensive tactics which are handed down to our leaders in the same manner that the leaders of the opposition receive their orders. Of course, the other sides are then aware of our plans and their computers make counterplans."

Stuart glanced at his watch and frowned. "This is all complicated by the fact that we are at war with several enemies right now, as are the Asians. All our actions are being monitored by the other powers who react to our policy changes and must, in turn, be reacted to. It sounds terribly complex, but the computer handles everything without the least difficulty.''

''Doesn't that put us at the mercy of the machines?'' Bea asked.

''Nonsense,'' said Stuart. ''Those 'machines,' as you call them, are *our* machines. They are the result of our technology and are programmed by us to contain our thoughts and feelings and cultural expectations. Everything coming from the computer is in our best interest, and being free of all the frailties of human weakness, serves us much better than a human leader ever could. Purity of purpose without ambition. The perfect tool. No, young lady. You paint us as the slaves of the great transistor god, yet how powerful is a god who can be vanquished by merely pulling out its plug?'' He made a motion in the air as if he actually were removing the proverbial plug. Dulan was amused by the ambivalence of the master/slave relationship.

''But what would happen if you did pull the plug?'' Bea returned.

Dulan had to hand it to her. Besides being beautiful, she was one of the most persistent people that he'd ever met. Stuart started to answer her question, but stopped himself short. Dulan knew that there was no answer. Bea knew it too. The old man sat there with egg all over his face, and they all became uneasily silent. Finally, Dulan came to the rescue.

''Don't the Telps' own brain wave patterns interfere with their reception of the Colonel's?'' he asked.

Stuart shook his head. ''Telps go through a tremendous amount of training and . . . conditioning to reach the singularity of will that you are witnessing now. At the present time I have neither the time nor the inclination to delve into our training methods in any detail.'' Stuart was speaking very slowly, weighing each phrase carefully before he uttered it. Dulan had touched a nerve but didn't know why.

''Suffice it to say,'' Stuart continued, ''that as a result of their training they are able to achieve complete empathy—emotional, physical, and mental—with their scan mate and at the same time suppress their own psyche.''

Dulan would have doubted the possibility of such total immersion of character, but he had seen the results with his own eyes.

He also sensed that Stuart was feeling very uncomfortable pursuing that particular line of discussion. So, just for fun, he decided to stick him a little more.

"Are the Telps consciously aware of what they're doing during their . . ." He searched for the correct word.

". . . receptive periods," finished Stuart. "No. They submerge their own identity and are only aware of the essence of their subject. Now, if you two will indulge me just a bit longer, I'll lead you to your work stations."

Before he was even finished speaking, Stuart was rolling quickly out the door and sliding down the bannister the same way he had come up. Bea and Dulan hurried after him. Stopping at the door, Bea turned for a final look at Colonel Kwi, who had grown an enormous long tail and was chasing it around and around and around and around.

They left the scan room and, staying on level seven, moved only the distance of a green to a yellow aisle, Stuart, as usual, charging ahead. He stopped in front of a block of smaller offices and pulled a small notebook out of the breast pocket of his black suit. He flipped through several pages, finally keying on the leaf for which he had been searching. After a second he closed the book and returned it to its resting place.

"Number fifty-eight," he said loudly, and rolled a few more paces, coming to rest in front of the door he had just mentioned. Bea and Dulan had caught up with him by this time, and he escorted them into the tiny office. "This is your niche, Miss Delacorte."

Stuart's estimation had been correct. The room was a niche in every respect. It was furnished with one old oak desk, two wooden folding chairs, and a two-drawer filing cabinet.

"Just like home," Bea quipped. She was trying out the chairs, sitting on one and then the other. She moved back and forth a few times before settling on the lesser of the two hard-backed evils and scooting it behind the desk.

"Ugh," she grunted, sitting down. "They're both torture devices, but that one," she pointed, "has a short leg."

The thought of a persistently wobbling seat did not appeal to Dulan, so he edged himself against the low-slung filing cabinet and rested his posterior on the dusty top. Seeing Doctor Stuart resting comfortably on his padded chair put the Exceptional in mind of the only favorable point to the old man's condition.

"What about my supplies?" Bea asked. "And I need a typewriter."

"You'll find requisition forms in the desk," Stuart answered, "for any essential items. Your S.O.P. explains the proper requisition procedure."

"Great," she said. "Bring on the patients."

"There will be just one patient for the present," Stuart said. "As time goes by, you will probably have others, but for now, the Outsider is your only responsibility."

"I hate to appear stupid," Bea said, folding her hands on the desk, "but in what capacity and to what degree am I responsible?"

"You are, I believe, in addition to being a medical doctor, a degreed psychologist with some training in preternormal abilities. I thought you'd realize that's why I took you to the scan room. As a psychologist, you will study the Outsider, Mr. . . . ah . . ."

"Jones," Bea said.

"Jones, yes. If you studied his folder . . ."

"I did."

"You'll notice that the man is a Telp, com born and raised. He was banished to the frontier while serving in the military." Stuart made a disagreeable face. "It seems that with the possibility of the new Northern offensive almost a certainty, we need more qualified Telps than ever before, and there just aren't too many of those left in the coms. We're finding it necessary to go to the outside for assistance. Jones is the first of the ex-comites to be processed back into our society, and as such will have to be studied very carefully to determine whether or not he'll respond well enough to training to do us any good. To be honest with you, I'm worried about the whole business."

Bea shared a secret look with Dulan, then rolled her eyes heavenward.

Stuart wiped his lips and continued. "We'll need daily checks on his progress, and determinations on how he's responding to treatments. You were the logical choice of researcher, Doctor Delacorte, given your training plus the fact that you also are an"—they glared daggers at each other for a second—"an Outsider yourself. We thought that you might be more, ah, sympathetic to the special problems of an otherworlder."

"Sympathy you can get from a lap dog," Bea said curtly. "I sincerely hope that I can be of more use than that."

Stuart shrugged and turned his chair toward the door. "It is said," he spoke over his shoulder, "that ignorance is bliss.

Perhaps someday the position of lap dog may seem highly desirous. The Outsider begins his training in a day or two. You should probably start your own work with him before then."

Bea tightened her jaw. "You don't need to tell me how to do my job."

Flinging open the office door, Stuart kept his back to her. "All the Telps are quartered on level eight. You can find Jones somewhere down there." The old man wheeled into the hallway, then swung his chair around violently. "A few more things, Doctor. Your job is merely to evaluate and observe the Outsider's mental condition, not to practice medicine. Please limit yourself to observation only. Also, no more than one hour at a time with the patient. We have much to teach him and time is essential to our purposes. I want weekly progress reports from you initially, perhaps more frequently later on in the treatment." He glanced at his watch and took off down the hall, motioning for Dulan to follow.

The black man started out the door, then stuck his head back in. "Will you have dinner with me?" he asked.

"Thought you'd never ask," Bea replied, smiling broadly through unravaged teeth. "I'll come by your room and get you about seven."

"See that you do, Miss Delacorte," Dulan said, imitating Stuart's officialese. He hurried down the hall just as a woman's shoe came flying through the door space.

Out in the hall, Stuart intentionally slowed his usual breakneck pace and let Dulan get abreast of him. "Any observations, Doctor?" the Director asked, pulling a rubber ball out of the side pocket of his wheelchair. He methodically squeezed and released the ball in one strong hand while powering his chair with the other.

"A couple," Dulan said, unwilling to commit himself. In the com, the less a person knew, the better off he was.

"I thought as much. Your lab is just ahead. We'll have a nice chat."

The inside of the lab came as a shock. The room was at least three times larger than any of the offices he had seen. Located at the left side of the chamber was the same office furniture that graced Bea's hovel. The rest of the room was bare, but furniture was not what Dulan's lab was all about, for covering the entire length of the long wall from floor to ceiling was a mantle of chrome steel and lights in series. The Exceptional walked slowly up to it and gingerly reached out his hand to touch, as if making sure of its reality.

"Your computer, Doctor," said Stuart.

"Mine?" Dulan asked dumbly, not believing his ears.

"Yours alone," Stuart answered, flashing his excuse for a smile.

"Is it on the net?" Dulan asked.

The old man rolled to the wall of knowledge and tripped a set of switches. "It is now," he said. Wheeling himself over to the desk, Stuart pulled out one of the chairs and offered it to Dulan. "Come sit down, please. You can play with that later."

Dulan reluctantly did as he was told. He took the chair without a trial run and placed it behind the desk as Bea had done. Stuart placed himself directly opposite the younger man. They sat head to head, playing eye control across the table. Dulan had no desire to enter into power games with the old man, but it wasn't in his nature to back down either.

"You said that you made some observations," Stuart began, "I'd be interested in hearing them."

Dulan smiled. Was the old man testing him, trying to find out just what made an Exceptional different from everyone else? "A couple of things impressed me as unusual today," he answered.

"Yes."

"You understand that I'm coming into this Telp business cold, but I can't help but think that the whole system is self-perpetuating." He stopped a moment to formulate his thoughts. He had gotten many impressions in the scan room, and really hadn't had time to sort them through. "The whole setup is so well balanced, so sophisticated, that significant military gains by any side would be an impossibility, as if this self-perpetuation is the real point of the conflict."

"Go on."

"Well, unless the balance of power is somehow upset, the status quo could be maintained indefinitely. The war could theoretically go on forever."

"And now we come to the heart of the matter, my young friend," Stuart said, leaning forward in his chair. "The war *shall* never end . . . not if we can help it, you and I."

Dulan hunched over his desk just the way Stuart had done and looked the old man right in the eye. "I thought victory was at hand," he said.

The Director put on his most condescending face. "Doctor

Dulan, this is a most serious matter, and I would be pleased if, just for a moment, you would treat it as such."

Dulan leaned his chair back on two legs. "What do you want me to say?" he asked, catching a glimpse of his machine out of the corner of his eye. "You know that after five hundred years of people going off to some nameless place to die in a war that we only hear about, I can't be very surprised to hear that there's a working plan behind it."

Stuart narrowed his eyes. "Do you disapprove?"

"Why should I," Dulan responded. "As an Exceptional, I've received all of the benefits of a militarily-controlled society and none of the detriments." He leveled his chair and leaned on the desk. "Life is life no matter who pulls the strings. As you no doubt know, I'm something of a student of Old World history, and in my research I've found that the so-called freedom that the human race enjoyed before the nuclear bans and the codes of nonprogress was based entirely on ecological and population abuse."

From somewhere appeared the rubber ball, and the old man caressed it with each hand in turn while speaking. "People can't be trusted to run their own lives, Doctor. The greed factor is just too self-destructive."

Dulan had to laugh at the Director's simplistic, conditioned view of life. "That may or may not be true, Doctor Stuart. I'll admit that martial law probably saved this planet from extinction in the old days, but I wonder if you and I were the ones chosen arbitrarily to march . . ." He caught himself too late to avoid the tasteless reference, so just ignored it. ". . . off to war, whether we'd be so convinced of that philosophy." He changed the subject to avoid disagreement. "Let me ask you something else. Today in the scan room, you took exception with Bea's estimation that we are at the mercy of the computer. I don't think that you were being completely honest with her. In fact, I believe that's why I'm here."

Stuart cocked his head, impressed despite himself. "Tell me more."

"Certainly. If the control is real, then the systems and bureaucracy generated by that control are also real. We couldn't pull the plug because of our dependence on the systems, systems whose operations we don't understand. It's like trying to breathe underwater. Now, the control is no real problem until the inevitable begins to happen. The machines are starting to outstrip us, right?''

Stuart didn't answer. Dulan stood up and rapidly paced the room. He was able to think much better on his feet. This is what he had been trained to do. "The computer is not behaving as it should. Its logic seems to defy its basic programs, and you're afraid that you'll not be able to understand the new logic." He returned to the desk, sitting on the edge right next to Stuart. "And you want me to straighten it all out, right?"

"Essentially," the Director answered, once again squeezing his rubber ball. "Although I don't feel that it's quite as important a proposition as you make it out to be."

"No? Logically it would start out small. Like a child, taking its first few faltering steps. The computer stumbles around for a while, picking up speed until, before you know it, you have a little kid that runs and runs and won't ever stop. Tell me exactly what happened?"

"It's not much really. But there is a slight deviation, and it's causing an amount of concern." Stuart wheeled his legs over to the computer on the wall and sat—staring. Dulan knew that it must frustrate the old man terribly to have a gaggle of transistors as a superior.

"Doctor Stuart," Dulan said, breaking the Director's trance. "What sort of deviation?"

"What? Oh. Our population reached its projected ideal of twenty million about three hundred years ago. Since then the computer has, ah, tailored our battles to keep this figure approximately the same from year to year."

"Organized destruction?"

"Let me finish, Doctor." Stuart's tone was becoming increasingly hard. Dulan decided to back off a bit. He wasn't looking for trouble.

"Does this population figure refer only to com inhabitants?" Dulan asked.

"What do you mean?"

"I was wondering about the population on the frontier."

"Our figures on Outsiders are somewhat sketchy. We feed what we have into the computer, as we do with all information, but the coms comprise the majority of the people in the country, and that's the number in which we're interested." He rolled slowly back to the desk and pursed his thin lips. "About fifty

"How long have they been scanning me? A long time, Doctor. Years." Rolling the ball between his palms, the old man stared at it as if all the mysteries of the universe were written on its convex surface. "Look," he said, "this business could possibly turn into something bigger than I suspect. We need tight security until the nature of any findings can be ferreted out. As soon as I know, the enemy knows, so keep me in the dark. When and if you discover anything, start at the bottom and take it up the chain of command until the importance of your research can be determined."

"Sounds complicated," Dulan sighed.

"It's the nature of our world. Just keep to yourself and talk about this to no one unless absolutely necessary and you'll get along fine."

"Like I said, I can't make any promises on this."

"Just play it by ear, Doctor. Remember that the Telp system depends for its success on the information-gathering abilities of its espionage branches. The spy networks are very complex and sophisticated. I wouldn't eliminate the possibility of enemy agents even here at Forty-Three. My point is: trust no one. The more important your work becomes, the less you should rely on your colleagues. If you're not careful, you'll end up with your head spinning like mine."

The prospect of Telp monitoring did not appeal to Dulan in the least. Military secrecy had always seemed to him to be the union of small minds and small ideas with the end result of incredibly important unimportance, but perhaps this time it wouldn't hurt to downplay himself for a while.

Stuart rolled his mover toward the door, then stopped short of his destination. "At your command is all the information, ideals, and dreams of five hundred years of com civilization. Very few of us are entrusted with knowledge so vast. Don't abuse it. I'll take my leave now. The material control number is right next to the phone."

The Director wheeled to the door, then stopped, listening for a moment to the gentle Complanian monologue. He slowly turned around and eased back across the room, stopping within touching distance of the black man. "You and Doctor Delacorte seem to have become quite friendly," he said in a low voice.

"Oh?" Dulan responded, and felt his neck hairs bristle. "I didn't know that it was your office's responsibility to keep tabs on my acquaintances."

The old man reddened noticeably but remained outwardly calm. "They're not like we are, Doctor. They don't think the same, don't act the same."

"I thank you for your concern, but frankly, my relationship with Bea is none of your business."

"Everything that goes on in this installation is my business," Stuart said through clenched teeth.

Dulan rose from his chair so that he towered over the legless man. "Look," he said, "I'll go along with a lot of this nonsense, but my private life is mine alone. I'll not allow you to tamper with it in any way. Do you understand?"

The old man's eyes burned with hatred. His hand was shaking as he pointed an accusing finger at Dulan. "Each of us, even Exceptionals, have boundaries over which we cannot cross. You're not above retribution, and don't forget it."

Smiling, Dulan sat back down and began writing with implements found in the desk. "Save your speeches, Doctor Stuart," he said, not even bothering to look up from his work. "I've been doing some thinking, and have decided that I'm a lot more consequential around here than you're willing to admit. Hell, I might be the only man alive who can solve your problem. So, don't threaten golden boy, okay? A word in the right ear from me, and *your* job may be up for grabs."

Stuart's face twisted itself into his unique smile. "So that's the way it's going to be. Better enjoy yourself while you can, Exceptional. I've been playing this game a lot longer than you have, and you'll find me a formidable opponent."

With that, the Director wheeled quickly from the chamber, slamming the door behind him.

Dulan sat quietly for a moment while his bubbling juices subsided, and dwelt on the nature of the beast. Eventually he rose and walked over to where the computer stood, purring—waiting for him.

He gently ran his hands over the machine, tracing with his fingertips the machine-tooled contours of its face. He spoke to it softly. "We're going to be good friends, you and I. Good friends."

Tremendous precautions must be taken when dealing with those who dwell on the frontier. Though unequipped and uneducated, they possess a natural stamina and native cunning that make them dangerous enemies. When encountered, they must be engaged, for their very existence makes them a potential threat. A small group of Outsiders is usually a hunting party attached to a larger tribe. Upon dispatch of the small party, it is imperative that the rest of the tribe be located and eliminated.

All adult males must be killed immediately upon capture. This rule applies without exception. At the discretion of the ranking officer, the females and children may be either destroyed or secured and delivered to the nearest Community Complex State.

Do not attempt sexual intercourse with the females before com induction. They are not only treacherous, but the bearers of communicable diseases.

—Chapter XXIV, *Officer's Handbook,*
Army of the comstates

Wise is the rabbit who keeps to his burrow when the eagle's shadow blots the Sun.

—Caravan fable

4

The shower, like the sink, had one knob—cold. Cold showers had never been part of Dulan's repertoire, but that which cannot be changed must be tolerated. Turning on the water, he stepped bravely into the icy indignity. The first shock of the frigid pipe-rain almost made him scream aloud, but after a moment his body acclimated itself and the experience became almost tolerable. He had showered earlier, but after his run-in with Stuart in the lab he felt dirty again. As he soaped himself, he felt his contact with the old man wash away and swirl crazily down the drain. He emerged from the shower refreshed, but cold as hell. Grabbing a towel that was folded neatly on the sink, he quickly dried himself and walked into the apartment proper.

The living quarters were dismal at best. The concrete walls were bare and painted a disquieting green. The chamber was stripped of all nonessential items and left with just enough for day-to-day subsistence: a tiny bed, a writing desk with one chair and a reading lamp, a dresser, and a matchbox closet. The lighting was indirect, just as it was everywhere else Dulan had been in the milcom. The atmosphere was not uncomfortable, but decidedly bland. There were several air vents, and by the door an intercom speaker mounted in the wall poured forth a steady flow of Complan. The speaker was designed for one-way communication only, and there were no visible means of disconnecting the thing—Dulan had tried. A small dialless telephone sat inconspicuously on the floor below the speaker.

The small, battered alarm clock Dulan had placed by the foot of the bed allowed that it wasn't quite seven, so he had a little time before Bea arrived. He dressed leisurely. He had brought his leathers from the com, but after finding that the simple pastel-colored jump suits were the style at Forty-Three, he had purchased several at a haberdasher's on level six, and it was a tan one that he wore now.

He hadn't had time to unpack his books yet, so while waiting for seven he thought that would be a worthy time occupier. Very few people read the old books, but Dulan found them stimulating, the people who wrote them, bawdy and flamboyant. Placing the heavy suitcase on the bed, he unsnapped the clasp and took back the lid, removing the tattered volumes carefully for their condition was not too stable. Then he lovingly lined up the ragged books on his desk. There were mostly technical volumes, with a few selected works of his favorite prose and poetry. The literary works were all left over from the old times when, he was told, more books were printed than a person could hope to read in a lifetime. As near as Dulan could figure, little or no independent creative writing(except for the government-sponsored books and magazines) had been done in over four hundred years.

As he finished stacking the books, he noticed a piece of paper in the bottom of the suitcase. He took it out and read the neatly filled in standard form: "One of your books, *The Complete Works of Henrik Ibsen,* has been judged possibly harmful to the morale of Military Community Complex number Forty-Three. It has therefore been confiscated in accordance with regulations, and will be returned to you upon completion of the duty tour."

Dulan was upset, but thankful that only one book was taken.

Shaking his head, he sat down on the chair to put on his shoes. While tying the first one, a sharp knock resounded on the door. One shoe on, one shoe off, Dulan slid-walked over to the door and pulled it open. Beatrice stood on the threshold, looking radiant. She had changed her jumper for a simple, but very complimentary, light-blue shift.

"Hungry?" she asked in a little girl voice.

"Ravenous," he replied, standing aside so she could enter the small room. "Just let me get my shoes on."

"Your place isn't any different from mine," she said, letting her eyes rove around. Then, "Oh, books!" She walked over to the desk and leaned down, elbows on the tabletop and chin resting on hands, and began reading the titles. It would have been easier and more comfortable to sit, but Dulan and his footgear were occupying the only chair. He reached over and handed her the note which he still held crumpled in his hand.

"I found this in my suitcase," he said.

She read the note with barely suppressed rage. "Harmful," she growled. "What are you going to do about it?"

"What could I do about it?"

"Go to Doctor Stuart, who would refer you to the military commander General Lynch, who would refer you to your S.O.P. which undoubtedly contains some obscure regulation giving them the power to do what they did."

"Ah, so you haven't perused your S.O.P. in any great detail," he said.

"Never had any use for it," she answered. "I just slid mine under the bed. Where's yours, by the way? I don't see it anywhere."

Dulan leaned down close to the floor and pointed under the bed. They both laughed loudly.

"There," he said, tying the last knot. "Bring on the food."

Level six was the food services and recreation level. In appearance it was markedly different from the rigid, almost Spartan atmosphere encountered elsewhere at Forty-Three. The floor plan was a complete hodgepodge, quite unlike the regimented spoke-and-aisle system that characterized the rest of the building. There were shops and theaters and rec rooms, all set up and decorated in a helter-skelter pattern designed less for order than aesthetic pleasure.

"C'mon, let's eat," said Bea, leading Dulan by the arm. "We'll browse later."

She directed him to a large cafeteria-style restaurant which sat off by itself, unwalled, unceilinged, and not altogether unpleasant. After looking over the food, mostly greens and meat substitutes, and finding a place to sit, they ate the modest but appetizing fare in silence for a time. Finally, Dulan looked across the table, his eyes holding her face for reaction.

"I've never known an Outsider before," he said.

Her eyes flashed at him, then immediately softened. "You'd be surprised," she said, and a pixie smile crossed her face. "There are more of us, females anyway, living behind your walls than anyone would care to admit."

"Really?" Dulan was shocked. He knew that it was com policy to allow women and children into the walled cities to take up residency if they so desired, but he was not aware that it was an overly common affair.

She raised her eyebrows at him from across the table. "Yes," she said, tongue planted firmly in cheek. "It's getting so you can't tell the heathens from the true believers without a program."

He grinned at her sacrilege. "Doctor Stuart hates you, you know."

She turned up her nose. "That seems to be his problem." Then mellowing, "You're right, I know. I guess I never have adjusted properly to com life. I've always been strong willed like my father."

"You knew your father?" Dulan was startled by the revelation. He thought that subjective child raising went out with the Old World.

She nodded brightly. "I knew my mother, too. But she died when I was very small. My father and I were close after that. I think that I reminded him of my mother."

Dulan hated to meddle in people's lives, but his curiosity was nearly out of control. "Can I ask you a few questions?"

"Ask away," she said through a mouth full of succotash.

Com education included absolutely no information about Outsiders. There was so much he didn't know, that he hardly knew where to begin. "What's it . . . like on the Outside?" he said at last.

"It's been a long time," she answered, and her eyes were far away. "It's difficult, of course. Most of the day-to-day business of life revolves around the acquisition of food. What exactly do you want to know?"

Dulan took a sip of too bitter coffee and made a face. "I guess it's the intellectual question that bothers me," he said after some more thought. "Why would anyone choose such a primitive existence when there are other options open?"

Bea speared a piece of eggplant with her fork, but never got it as far as her mouth. "I suppose that freedom has something to do with it. I don't know that I accept the term 'primitive' either."

"All right," he said, "just talk to me about it. I really want to know. Aristotle says that all men naturally desire knowledge. I guess my desires are stronger than most."

"All right," she said. "I'm no historian, but I think I can give you a feel for the frontier. I guess that after the nuclear elimination treaties, the wars were pretty bad. But after forty or fifty years of fighting, a pattern began to develop. The economy started to change. There were fewer people, with more food on the table. The social order, as I'm sure you know, turned around. Private enterprise tangled inextricably with military production, making war and economic stability synonymous. There were whole generations of people who had been born and grown to middle age knowing nothing but the military state. The change came easily to most, I suppose. The government already controlled all aspects of the economy. If one wanted to work, one worked for the government. So when the com fathers built the feudal, self-sustaining com states with their high walls and garrisons of troops, everyone left his home for the security and protection of the com."

"Almost everyone," said Dulan.

"Yes, almost. Those walls. The first time I ever saw one of your walled cities I was seven years old. My father and I left the caravan and traveled for many days until finally we stood on a high ridge that overlooked a long valley. And there, miles in the distance, stood the com, sun gleaming blindingly off the towering parapets. It frightened me so, I cried for hours. I thought it was a place where they sent bad people to punish them." She smiled at Dulan, but it was a sad smile.

She sat for a moment, lost in some private dream, then continued, her eyes focused on her plate. "You don't see it in the com because the social order doesn't allow it, but there are people in this world . . . who glory in freedom, who scream their independence to the world. These are the people who chose the frontier over the suppression of the com.

"Those were difficult times. Most of the Outsiders, as they came to be called, had never known anything but dependence on the system for the fulfillment of their needs and wants. Suddenly they were all alone in a hostile world, with nothing but their empty stomachs to tell them it was dinner time. But they were strong willed, and many of them survived. They began to band together in loose tribal societies for common protection and hunting. Settlements were impossible with the wars going on everywhere, all the time. Also staying in one place would have made them easy prey to soldiers, all soldiers, who took and still take great sport in hunting down and killing my people. War-reduced populations left great stretches of land uninhabited. Game once again became plentiful, so the Outsiders followed the game trails North to South with the seasons and shunned, whenever possible, contact with your so-called 'civilized society.'"

"A very practical solution," Dulan replied.

"It was the only possible solution," she responded, "and it worked. For hundreds of years our two civilizations have co-existed uneasily side by side, developing independently of each other. I suppose that it could stay that way forever, except that a gradual change has been taking place for many years. Your armies, when not occupied with fighting their more traditional foes, have been going out of their way to try to find and fight with those who were once their brothers. Naturally, the tribes are ill-equipped to do battle with com armies. They have only their wits and a few spears against bombs and guns. I've heard of whole caravans being wiped out, hundreds of men killed, women bound in chains and taken as concubines back to the walls."

"Why?" asked Dulan.

"Who knows? Bloodlust, conditioned hatred, perhaps even fear. Our numbers have grown very large over the course of time, despite our 'primitive existence.'"

Dulan was bewildered. This was a different story than he had gotten from Stuart earlier that day. It didn't make much sense either. As far as he knew, the pattern of life and actions in the coms had not altered since their foundation. The introduction of new patterns into an unbending form seemed illogical and unfruitful, in that any change in the style of living could upset the all important balance that had enabled the coms to remain so totally static for so long. And the forced introduction of large numbers of female Outsiders into com society seemed even more impossible. It would be viewed by most as a desecration, a contamination of the pure way of life that most comites seemed to hold so dear.

He remembered seeing, briefly, many years earlier a group of these women when they first came to his com.

He was amused by their alien, almost aboriginal ways and their rough clothing made from untanned animal hides. Most wore no shoes. At the time he thought that the "barbarians" had come begging the hospitality and protection of the com and had been graciously accepted into the fold.

Bea was just finishing her dinner, which had gotten cold while she talked. She slid the plate aside, took a sip of coffee, and continued talking. "Perpetual com aggression has caused the tribes to fear for their existence as a race. They would like to unite and defend themselves, but have found it nearly impossible to do."

"Why?"

"It's the nature of the way of life. Outsider culture consists of the tribes. The tribes are small, never any larger than speechmaker's earshot. I said that our numbers were great, but they are distributed over a vast, at present uncounted, number of tribes. Each caravan has its own leaders who decide the actions of their people. The system allows for no tribal interaction, making contact difficult. There are large numbers of autonomous groups, all ruled by their own chieftain, called the Lawgiver, who is all-powerful within his own tribe, and who has his own ideas of how things should be done. There are language difficulties also. Though English is the basis, a lot of strange idioms and dialects have sprung up within these basically closed societies, making even simple communication problematic from tribe to tribe. Then there are segregational restrictions."

"Racial segregation?" he asked, surprised.

"When the tribes were formed, the different races followed their natural inclinations and tended, for the most part, to segregate themselves. So you find black and white and brown tribes who seem to look at even the most basic concepts through different eyes."

"What's all this got to do with you?"

"I barely remember it, but when I was little there was a tribal council. Representatives from hundreds of the caravans attended.

It was a glorious mess—feuding, and bickering, and translating, and long, long speechmaking sessions. The only point on which they could reach agreement was that, if they were to organize against the coms, they must first know what they were organizing against. Each tribe vowed to send one child to live in the com until adulthood. They would learn about com life and ideals and report back, each tribe then having common language mediators and basic understanding of the problems. My father was the Lawgiver of our tribe. He couldn't in all conscience send any one but his own daughter.''

Dulan glanced around him to see if anyone else was overhearing their conversation. ''Should you be telling me all this?'' he asked.

Bea smiled. ''I used to worry about that too. Then I realized that to find me seditious, they'd first have to admit that a threat existed at all.''

Dulan pursed his lips and nodded. ''You're right,'' he said, ''keep talking.''

''Upon reaching my eleventh year my father took me to the entrance of the very same com that we had viewed from afar several years earlier. We were sharing the same horse and I clung to him for a long time after reaching the walls, neither of us wanting to part. Finally he said, 'You are the daughter of Marn Delacorte, you know what you must do.' His eyes were stern, but they were filled with tears. I climbed down from the horse and we looked at each other for an eternal instant, then we turned and went our separate ways. Mine has been a very lonely way,'' she said.

Bea was obviously shaken by reliving such personal memories. She clutched her now empty coffee cup in a death grip, and her lower lip trembled slightly.

''I'll get us some more coffee,'' said Dulan awkwardly, and extracted the cup from her viselike grip. When he returned and sat down, she was more relaxed.

''I'm sorry,'' she said. ''I've never talked with anyone about my father before.''

''I'm sorry too,'' he replied. ''I don't know how to respond to emotional attachment. It seems awfully strange to me.''

''I know,'' she said, mustering a weak smile. ''Sometimes the ways of the caravan seem like a faint dream even to me.''

''You say that you were supposed to stay in the com until adulthood,'' he said. ''When do you go back?''

"I should have gone already, except that this opportunity to see a milcom is one that is not usually afforded to an Outsider. I decided to serve the duty tour here, then find a way to leave and return where I belong."

"Are you sure that's not just an excuse?"

"Not entirely," she replied, smoothing her shoulder-length hair. "I've been away for a long time." She curled honey strands around long, slender fingers while trying to formulate the words in just the right fashion. "Com life certainly has its advantages. Day-to-day living moves along at a steady pace, always predictable and unchanging. Over a period of time, com life builds up a certain sense of security and belonging. Each person has his own niche and can move along his path of life without fear of unexpected drastic changes taking place that would alter the fabric of existence. The whole feeling that God's in His heaven... it can lull you right along."

"But..."

"But? The obvious. The price is great—your soul. There's no place for individuality or independent creative thought or emotion. Individuals end up on the frontier."

"Everything has its price, Bea. Survival is the key, for without it, the game is over and idealism is meaningless. I find life a give and take. I take the better things the coms have to offer and in return give them the unfeeling simplicity they find so important. It's called, not biting the hand that feeds you. The individuality and independence that you speak of are merely outward manifestations of inner feelings. A person can be independent up here," pointing to his head, "without climbing up in the bell tower and caterwauling it to the world. You *can* have your cake and eat it too."

"Compromise," she chided.

"Sure, compromise. It all comes back to the question of survival."

She shook her head at Dulan, as one does to a naughty child. "Tell me," she said, "how is it that we've managed to avoid talking about the trials and tribulations of being an Exceptional?"

"It's a very dull topic," he said, and meant it.

"Let me be the judge of that. Tell me, Doctor, what's it like being the cream of the crop?"

"You've already mentioned the glorious monotony of com living. If possible, my life has been even more uneventful than the norm. Up to age seven, I was raised in the center with the other children, but when I reached that philosophic age of reason and took my postadolescent psyche-pro, the results confirmed what had been indicated by my actions and earlier testing."

"That you were an Exceptional."

"You've been listening. After that, I was still reared in the same center, but my training accelerated greatly and I was treated with more deference than the other children, much to their chagrin and indignation. I found that my small circle of friends became even smaller.

"At age fourteen, I was allowed to choose my own field of endeavor, as opposed to the arbitrary career selection foisted on most children. I searched for a vocation that could be challenging and rewarding, and discovered instead the sheer immutability of the system. There was really only one place for a probing young mind to go—to the computer. Computer technology seemed to be the only moving force in our unmoving society. The machines control virtually every aspect of our day-to-day life, and their complexity is ever changing and expanding. It was my only outlet."

"So what exactly do you do?"

"My general title is Computer Theorist, a broad description that embraces several different areas. I'm a Cyberneticist, and a Synoeticist, and . . ."

"Wait a minute," Bea interrupted. "You lost me back at Syn . . . o . . . what-do-you-call-it."

"Okay," he said, finishing his vegetables and digging into the cake. "Synoetics is a science that treats the properties of composite systems, say, man and machine, whose main attribute is that their ability to reason, to invent, to create—their mental power—is greater than the mental power of their components."

"You mean that the machines are getting too smart for us?"

"In a sense. What my job actually amounts to is working with the computers as they perform their daily tasks, and trying to understand their deductive ability so that they don't branch off into strange realms of logic that we are unable to comprehend. It's all very metaphysical, really. As I said, computers control a great deal more of our lives than most people realize."

She nodded. "After the scan room today, I'll agree with you. By the way, you haven't mentioned what it is they've got you doing here."

He wanted to tell her, to talk about it, but he just couldn't do it. "Just watching a minor crimp in one of the programs. It's nothing really.'' He rose to avoid further discussion. ''Now that my hunger has been satisfied,'' he said, ''I'm ready to do a little exploring. Will you be my guide?''

''Only if you answer a question for me,'' she replied.

''Certainly.''

''Who is Aristotle?''

''A dead man,'' he answered. ''Dead and gone. What's our first stop?''

''Heaven,'' she said.

The steps spiraled upwards to a dizzying height. The higher they climbed, the less ornamental and the more utilitarian became the shining oaken bannister that bordered the helix-like stairs. The chapel of Complan was the obligatory starting point for any examination of level six, and the tiresome metal stairway was the only admittance to the structure which sat, amidst a storybook cotton cloud flotation, near the high ceiling. The closer to the chapel that they ascended, the more angelic became the journey, until they were walking on softly padded illuminated steps among a profusion of Styrofoam nimbi that dangled from the ceiling on nylon wires like heavenly swords of Damocles. The lighting was dim that high up, and thousands of tiny white lights blinked on and off in poor imitation of twinkling stars.

''If I'd known that we were going mountain climbing,'' Dulan said to Bea's back, ''I'd have brought some hiking boots.''

''Almost there,'' she replied over her shoulder.

''Tell that to my knees,'' he said, wondering how he had gotten so out of shape.

At the top of the stairs, they passed through a golden gateway and stood, finally, at the double doored threshold of the chapel. Above the door hung a large placard which bore, in letters rich with filigree, the following legend:

CONFORMITY IS ORDER.
ORDER IS PERFECTION.
PERFECTION IS GOD.

Dulan was familiar with the quote from Complan. It was oft-repeated. He tried to open the doors, but they had no knobs. ''All right, what's the trick,'' he sighed.

''Say the words aloud,'' Bea giggled.

Grudgingly, he did so, and the doors swung open magically.

Once they stepped into the atrium, electronic organ music began to drift solemnly through the chamber, reverberating through the empty space. The room was quite large, easily able to accommodate several thousand worshippers if necessary. There was no artificial lighting, but a great quantity of perpetually burning candles ringed the walls all around the chapel, their flickering adding to the eeriness of the music. The air was heavy with the pungent perfume of frankincense. The interior of the chapel was filled with oversized fluffy-looking cushions, another variation on the cloud theme. A stage stood alone in the center of the room, the place where the priests of Complan worked their particular brand of magic. The walls and ceiling were painted full with richly-hued murals depicting scenes from the life of Isaac Complan.

"What do you think?" Bea asked.

"You're not supposed to think about religion," Dulan retorted. "Where's the Living Shrine?"

She took his hand and they picked their way through the cloud/cushion jungle to a darkened area in the far corner of the room. At their approach, the black corner exploded in a flash of blinding white light. Dulan turned his head slightly as his eyes accustomed themselves to the brightness. When his pupils equalized, he was able to see the life-sized figure of Isaac Complan basking in the radiance of electrical brilliance. The figure was dressed in the traditional robes of the Complanian Brotherhood, and a neon halo pulsed gently about three millimeters above the latex head. The face was both stern and angelic.

Almost at once, the effigy began to move. The movements were nearly human, but the mechanical nature of the Living Shrine exaggerated them just enough to dampen the effect.

"Come closer, my children," the contraption said, the head rolling back and forth, waiting for worshippers to come within range of the photocells. They moved a step closer, and the head stopped moving as the blazing eyes of Isaac Complan zeroed in on them.

"What is the Holy Word?" the figure asked them.

"Fornication," Dulan answered, as Bea, giggling, slapped him playfully on the shoulder.

"What is the Holy Word?" the figure asked again.

"Prestidigitation," said Dulan with heartfelt solemnity.

"What is the . . ."

"War," said Bea quickly, before Dulan could start the cycle again.

"War," the machine repeated, nodding its mannequin head slowly up and down. "The highest human aspiration. It purifies the spirit, sharpens the senses, brings us closer to our Creator!" The figure's arms raised heavenward, and from somewhere came the precision rumble of a drum roll. "A world at war is a world of harmony. It is our destiny. We strive together, we do not overrun our world or poison its atmosphere with noxious waste. War weeds out the weak, leaving only the mighty to walk in the sunlight. It makes a basic life, a life simple and pure. Thanks be to God for showing us the path of righteousness!" Complan shuddered slightly and clenched his fists as the drum reached a crescendo—stopping abruptly with a cymbal crash. All at once, the corner was plunged once more into darkness.

"I guess that's it for now," Bea said, and they turned to go.

They walked several meters from the Living Shrine, then Dulan ran back. When he got close, the lights came on again.

"What is the Holy Word?"

Dulan strode back to Bea, and they headed for the doors.

"What is the Holy Word?"

"What is the Holy Word?"

They reached the exit as the lonely specter of Complan continued to ask its unanswered question. Dulan tried the doors, but once again they refused to open. He said the slogan, but it didn't do any good.

"Wait a minute," Bea said, reaching into a hidden pocket of her dress. Extracting her account card, she pushed it into one of many card slots next to the doors. They clanged open once again.

"Don't tell me," Dulan said as they stepped once again into the cloud bank. "We had to make an offering to get out."

"It doesn't make any difference what the amount is," Bea replied. "I suppose it's the thought that counts."

Just then a commotion broke out on the stairway to Heaven. Bea and Dulan walked to the top step to get a better look. An old man outfitted in priest's garb was being assisted up the stairs by two young females in jump suits.

Dulan saw Bea frown, and heard her mutter something under her breath.

The priest was stumbling badly as he was helped heavenward. "May God and Isaac Complan bless you, my twin duffel bags of delight,'' he was saying in a loud voice. ''The Lord is my procurer, I shall not want.''

When they made the top step, girls laughing, the old man drew himself up to his full height and confronted Dulan. ''Ahoy, Brother,'' he said, extending a bony hand. The man was tall, but bent. Dulan, who stood nearly 1.9 meters, found himself looking up. His flashing eyes were rimmed with the deepest crimson, a perfect color match for his awry skullcap. He was obviously skying on altar drugs.

''You must be Brother Dulan,'' he said, and his odor was of new wine and old perspiration. ''They told me you were a Nubian, but I didn't believe. Let me look at you.'' The man's flowing white robes and red skullcap appeared out of place and natural at the same time. His thinning white hair hung well past his shoulders.

''I'm afraid that you have the advantage over me,'' Dulan said.

The priest glanced at the women he held on each arm. ''Truer words were never spoken, Brother. The name's Matrix, Herman Matrix. Keeper of the flame, lighter of the way, guardian of the steps, prognosticator of the will of the Almighty, and most humble servant of the Brotherhood of Complan here at Forty-Three. I welcome my black brother to the fold.'' His eyes narrowed as he caught sight of Bea. ''And who might you be, Sister?''

''My name is Beatrice Delacorte,'' she answered curtly.

''Delacorte,'' he said, and tried to place the name but gave up. ''I've not seen you in services. I would have remembered one so well endowed by the Creator.'' He leered at her.

''I sit in the back,'' she replied.

''The back is it?'' He was weaving so badly that Dulan feared he would fall down the stairs. Matrix held out his grimy hands. ''Come, Sister, give us a kiss.'' The priest lunged for her, but his aim was poor and he ended his journey face down on the landing. His two companions quickly rushed to help him up.

''Let's get out of here,'' Bea whispered to Dulan, and without waiting for his reply started down the winding stairs.

''Brother Dulan,'' Matrix called to him, as the black man made to follow Bea. ''Have you attended to your tithe withdrawal yet?''

''What?''

"The contributory deduction from your credit account. It takes gold to pave the streets of Heaven."

"N-No, I haven't had a chance to . . ."

"Shall I take care of it for you?" Matrix asked.

"That would be most kind."

"Fine. And what shall be the amount of your recompense?"

"Whatever's customary."

"Good. It's done then. I'll look forward to seeing you and Sister Long-Hair in services." He turned and began whispering to one of the women, his arm casually draped over her shoulder, his large hand fondling her breast through the material of her jumper. While the priest was so occupied, Dulan hurried down the steps.

"Brother Matrix has plans for you, Sister," Dulan said when he met Bea at the bottom of the stairs.

"I'd die before I'd let him touch me," she replied coldly.

Dulan stopped in his tracks and stared at her. "Just how do you intend to avoid it?" he asked. "A priest of Complan can do anything he wants—and does"

Bea was adamant. "He'll just have to do it with someone else."

Dulan was confused. How could this woman survive in com society with such alien ideas about sex? He had never known any woman to refuse sex—ever. "I don't think that you've heard the last of Brother Matrix," he said softly.

The rest of the grand tour was relatively unexciting. Level six was far and away the most interesting part of Forty-Three, at least of what Dulan had seen of Forty-Three. They called it the variable. The wild card. The button buster. The one concession to a human nature that could not be completely tamed. The safety valve.

As they strolled lazily, Dulan was amazed at the flamboyant thought that must have gone into the planning of that level. The layout was reasonless. There were long, straight avenues, zig-zags, spiral aisles, and elaborate cul-de-sacs. It took only a few twists and turns before he realized that the entire level was actually a giant maze.

He was fascinated. It was almost too much to take in. On every side were small stores and shops of every description and shape, all decorated sumptuously in Old World styles. Many recreation rooms were scattered here and there along the winding thoroughfares, and all the popular games and diversions were represented. Both Bea and Dulan confessed to more than a passing interest in backgammon, and they dallied for a time in a parlor designed in a bizarre rococo atmosphere of vaulted archways and pop-eyed gargoyles. They sat in red velvet armchairs and shuffled the bones on a Louis XIV gaming table. Bea had a spirited, free wheeling manner of playing that Dulan, with his precise, analytical game, found hard to comprehend. She beat him more often than he would have liked.

There were more than a few exiguous bars and taverns to be found along the wayside, each quite different and a world unto itself. Dulan and Bea found it necessary to stop in these grogshops from time to time in order to replenish their bodily moisture and fortify themselves for the journey still ahead. After several of these stops, however, Dulan began to wonder if they'd ever find their way out of the labyrinth.

There were also a number of small cinema houses, and Dulan discovered to his surprise and delight that along with the plodding, didactic propaganda films that the government churned out for the edification and (in the case of the sex-pix) titillation of the masses, there were some prints of some Old World films. Movies from the old times were strictly forbidden in the coms, but seemed present in abundance here. While they were undoubtedly screened and censored pretty thoroughly, and appeared to run along the lines of war dramas and costume epics with heavy nationalistic themes, they were the genuine article and the black man vowed to return at a later date and view as many of the films as they cared to show him.

Small parks with real trees and fish ponds dotted the avenues, and restaurants could frequently be found hidden all along the way. Though not as large as the cafeteria in which they had eaten dinner, these cafes were all done in different motifs to suggest faraway places and exotic cuisines. Unfortunately, they all featured the standard com fare which was impossible to disguise. It was in one of these restaurants that Bea and Dulan stopped to rest after a long evening of window-shopping. The drinking and walking had made Bea hungry again, and she ate heartily, but Dulan wasn't hungry, and he merely looked on.

After Bea's meal, they sat quietly, drinking coffee. The restaurant was done up like a seaside wharf. Nets full of conch shells and sponges draped from the ceiling between lamps set in clipper ship tillers. Plaster of Paris sculptures of various crustaceans hung in abundance from the walls and ceiling, and through splintering windows could be viewed backdrop oceanscapes complete with whitecap waves and hungry gulls.

"Why did they beat Dan Jones?" Bea asked, taking advantage of the conversational lull.

Dulan shook his head, eyes focusing on a little man fishing from a distant pier. Just fishing, never catching. "I don't know. Everything happened so fast, and none of it made any sense."

"What did they tell him when they found him?"

"They told him he was being drafted."

Bea grunted. "No wonder he tried to run."

"What do you mean?"

"The army caused his problems to begin with. According to his file, he was taken into the army at age eighteen and sent to the Southern front. He spent months in the war zone, seeing no action and spending most of his time hand-carrying messages back and forth between command posts. Finally, a fair-sized battle came along and he saw his first real combat. He proved himself a good soldier and according to some of the reports even distinguished himself on the field. After the fighting was finished, though, it became Dan's lot to dispose of prisoners who had surrendered. Apparently, military law does not allow for the taking of prisoners, so Jones was ordered to kill the men. Somehow, something inside of him balked at the idea and he refused. He was placed under immediate arrest and sent back to his com where there was a brief trial and swift justice was meted out."

"Here's to swift justice," declared Dulan, raising his cup as if to make a toast. Bea continued undaunted.

"He was ordered to the outside with only the clothes on his back for 'acts of cowardice and treason against the safety and well-being of the people of the com states.'"

"That's it?" he asked. "How did they find him again?"

"Ex-comites are usually unsuited to life on the outside. Most of them work on the destruction crews, tearing down the old cities and bartering the scrap metal back to the coms for the necessities of life. Since there's so much contact, it's not too difficult to keep track of the Destructors."

"Why was he picked up?"

"On the strength of his psyche-pro I presume." Bea glanced at her watch, eyes widening in wonder. "It's after midnight," she said. "I'd better get back to my room and get some sleep."

They punched their cards in the credit slot and left. As they walked, Bea continued talking. "As you know, comites are tested many times during their youth to make sure they are being directed vocationally along a path which is best suited to their abilities and the needs of the community. Dan's records showed average to below average ability in all areas save one. He's a telepath."

"Then why was he made a soldier?"

"Telepathic abilities have never entered into conflict with job placement in other areas. We all have the ability to receive electromagnetic wave impulses to a certain extent. Some are just better than others. I guess they call them when they need them."

Dulan turned from his walking to face her. "If you've worked with these Telps, how come you seemed so surprised by what you saw in the scan room?"

"Because I never saw anything like that before. In our research we found that even if a Telp could direct his mind to a specific sender, impressions received were usually sporadic and disjointed and, more often than not, undefinable. The Telp's own electrical activity always tended to get in the way of the messages he was receiving. But that didn't matter to them at the psi center. They were more interested in aftereffects. Brain wave changes on the EEG, alpha impulse variations, things like that."

"Then how do you account for the differences here?"

"A shift in emphasis, but why I don't know . . . and how I wouldn't even hazard a guess. They spoke of training; perhaps it's a discipline."

"The sender doesn't need to cooperate with the receiver?"

"Absolutely not, as we saw so graphically earlier. A normal brain at rest puts out about twenty-five watts. The output increases proportionately to the state of agitation of the brain, sometimes exceeding six hundred watts in a highly excited or nervous mind. The electromagnetic vibrations are there, it's just a question of tuning them in."

They took the elevator up to level five and moved into the flow. The housing blocks there were divided into upstairs and downstairs apartments, with a small staircase running between each apartment leading to the top, odd-numbered room. It was before the stairway door marked 61 that Bea stopped walking.

"We're practically neighbors," Dulan said, looking around. "I think."

She took hold of his arm and spun him around 180 degrees so

that he was facing the opposite direction. "Yours is two spokes over and one aisle down," she said, and pointed.

"Right. Hey, thanks for showing me around today."

Bea leaned over and lightly brushed her full lips across his cheek. "I'm glad you came here, Doral. I've had more fun tonight than I've had for a long time." A flush of sadness crossed her face. "A very long time."

"Me too," he replied, and meant it. "Thought I'd take a shot at breakfast tomorrow, care to join me?"

"I think not," she answered, starting through the staircase door. "I'd like to get an early start with Mr. Jones in the morning. Take a rain check, though."

"Sure," Dulan grinned, and watched her move up the steps. "Want some company?" he called out as she neared the top.

She turned to him, a strange look on her face. "Not tonight, Doral. Not yet."

"Then I'll bid adieu," he said, bowing from the waist. She waved goodnight, covering a yawn with her free hand.

Dulan turned and walked alone down the spacious hall toward his room, the reverberation of his footfalls almost loud enough to drown out the Complan reader.

PRIVATE JOURNAL
B. DELACORTE MD. PH.D.

Re: Patient—Jones, Daniel T.

Entry 1
2 July

Had my first meeting with Dan Jones today. He thinks me part of the system which now holds him captive, and he doesn't trust me. I think, though, that after a time I may be able to gain his confidence.

His physical injuries have been treated satisfactorily, but for some reason unknown to me he is still heavily tranquilized, perhaps with chlorpromazine. I've tried to determine the reason for the sedation, but the medical department personnel on levels seven and eight are reluctant in the extreme to discuss even the most basic aspects of the treatments they employ. If I'm to treat Mr. Jones, it will be paramount that I understand every integrant of all other training and treatment that the patient is receiving. Must speak to Doctor Stuart about this ASAP.

On the surface, Mr. Jones appears quite normal physiologically and emotionally. He's bitter about his abduction and confinement, but that's certainly to be expected. He seems very alone. I'm toying with the idea of starting him on a program of sympathetic insight therapy. This is contrary to my "observation only" orders from Ops, but the patient needs someone to reach out to, and I would be remiss if I didn't do what I could for him. We have the time to delve into his background and feelings, and at the same time I may be able to fulfill his desperate need for friendship. Following is a partial transcript of my conversation with Dan Jones, this date:

J: What do you want from me?
D: I just want to help—if I can Mr. Jones. Can I call you Dan?
J: You'll call me whatever you want anyway. So you want to help me, huh?
D: That's right, Dan.
J: Then help me get the hell out of here.
D: I wish I could, but I think we're both stuck here for a while. Meantime, let's try to make the best of it. I want your time here with me to be comfortable and worthwhile for both of us.
J: By Complan, a bleeding heart I can do without.
D: Why? Afraid that a little friendship might make things too tolerable for you?
J: I'm not scared of anything.
D: Then stop feeling sorry for yourself. How do you feel physically?
J: They fixed everything they broke, but I'm still all doped up. Sluggish. I can't seem to get my head working right.
D: When does your training start?
J: Tomorrow, I think . . . I don't know. Say, what is this training anyway?
D: I really don't know, Dan. Honest.
J: You don't know. You lying wall-builders are all the same. Think you can treat a man like a child because he lives on the outside. At least the others don't pretend to be my friends. Let me out of here.

Something less than an auspicious beginning. I must win his confidence before we can even contemplate therapy. Access to his training program will become my primary objective.

I feel a tremendous unease about the entire situation. Everything is so anomalous and confusing here that I've been unable to formulate any opinions regarding my place in the general scheme of things. Why is telepathic research so much more advanced here than at the psi centers? There are many things that I must understand. Until such time that the operations here become more easily fathomable to me, my official records will remain sketchy and unopinionated. My private journal shall continue to be . . . private.

I'm a little frightened.

Complan spoke and the Word was spread far and wide. The people of God heard the words of Complan, and left they their cities of glass and sin unbridled; left they their wheeled wagons and wicked ways behind . . . far behind. The Lord was calling his children to a new and beautiful life. To the tabernacles of the plains He called them. But not all heard the call . . .

—*Book of Complan (5-33)*

Which is more free, the tethered lamb who baits the timber cat, or the timber cat who falls under the hunter's bolts for following the will of nature?

—Caravan fable

Children, children please be good,
As little comites always should.
For if you are and it is known,
Life is happy when you're grown.
But you defy, complain or pout,
When you are grown, you must go out.

—children's rhyme

5

Dulan hesitated before entering Bea's chamber. He had never thought a great deal about conditioning until the last few days. The verbal polemics between himself and Stuart were very much on his mind. What had really irked him about the old man's remarks about Bea was not so much that the Director had said them, but that many of those same thoughts had involuntarily crossed his mind already. He had always considered himself above the single-minded, persistent conditioning that was so essential to the com dream. But like it or not, he couldn't shake the nagging doubts about Bea. Outsiders. A hundred visions swept his mind when the word was dredged up. Conditioned visions, preordained. Savages. Criminals. Now was the time for a decision. He had avoided her for several days, throwing himself wholeheartedly into his preliminary work with the computer, but she had refused to vanish from his thoughts. Should he involve himself further with the woman, or drop it before it became an issue? His survival instinct told him not to make waves, to forget this Outsider. She wasn't like other women he had known. She would make demands, emotional demands, and would accept nothing less than a completely honest relationship. He could try to bluff his way through like at dinner the night they went to the chapel—cover his doubts and not really tell her what he was thinking—but he knew that would never work. It would be all or nothing with Bea. No middle ground.

He knocked lightly on her door. When she opened it, he detected on her face a look of joy. She was happy, really happy to see him. It was a sensation that he had never experienced in his life. All the doubts were washed away with a glance.

"Thought you had lost my address," she chided.

Dulan smiled. "Didn't want to make a pest of myself."

"Never." She stepped aside to allow him passage into her room, then closed the door. Dulan felt at ease with this woman. He sauntered over to her bed and plopped himself gracelessly on the woolen overcover.

Bea opted for the chair. She sat comfortably, crossing her legs. "Will you lend me some of your books, Doral?" she asked without preliminaries. "I've never been exposed to . . . I'd really like to read them."

Dulan was happy that she showed interest in his books; they were his pride and joy. "What's mine is yours," he replied. "I'll pick out some good ones for you to start with. Like poetry?"

"I don't know," she answered in a little girl/embarrassed voice. "I've never read any."

"You'll like it," he said, his mind churning back to his initial discovery of the beauty of the printed word. Then, "I'm suddenly starved. Have you eaten yet?"

"No. I've been waiting for you to come by and get me."

"How did you know that I would?"

"Didn't."

He stood up, shaking his head. "I'll tell you what, strange lady. Let's go down to one of those little out-of-the-way places on six, get drunk, and have dinner. I've got a bunch to talk about."

"We're not there yet?"

"That's what I like to hear," he grinned. "Hell, I might even buy."

An hour later they were swilling dark ale and dining sumptuously on in-season fruits, cheese, and fresh bread in an eighteenth-century New England pub. He told her everything about his reasons for being at Forty-Three. She protested that it wasn't necessary, but it was important to him that he be as honest with her as she had been with him.

When he was finished talking, Bea tore off a hunk of hard bread and handed it across the table to him. "So the computer's going to tell you all its secrets," she said, a touch of amusement in her tone.

"That, madam, remains to be seen." He accepted the bread greedily, taking a great bite and washing it down with beer, tilting the pewter mug upside down and drinking until he saw bottom. He swilled the warm elixir around in his mouth before swallowing, savoring the rich, earthy taste. When the last bit was drained from the cup, he slammed it loudly on the rosewood table. "Fetch me another flagon of ale," he bellowed, remembering fond days spent with Robert Louis Stevenson. He glanced over at Bea who was practically falling off her chair laughing. "And one for the lady."

"No, Doral, please. I've had enough."

"I'll not drink alone, woman," he responded, sitting up regally in the heavy captain's chair.

"I know your game," she said. "You're just trying to get me drunk enough to beat at backgammon."

"Aha! A challenge. It shall not go unanswered. 'Twas just my chivalry that let you best me when last we met on the field of honorable combat. But tonight, victory shall be sweet."

The wench, a plump staff sergeant in a footman's costume, arrived with the drinks and Dulan immediately took a long draught. "It's really sad," he said. "These people can't relate to any of this. To them it's just a different decor, an unusual place to go. A break in the monotony. Why, in their day, pubs like this were the hub of civilized life. Political intrigues were plotted and carried out in these dens of iniquity."

"Doral?"

"Yes."

"Is the computer problem really serious?"

"Potentially it's the most serious problem conceivable. I won't know for a long time, perhaps never. The machines have got the power, the intelligence, the lock on technology, and the control to make it all happen. We've put ourselves in a subordinate position, and now could very easily find ourselves subordinated."

"You don't sound too unhappy about it."

He smiled and took a drink. "Mixed feelings, my dear. We're where we are today because we wanted it this way. Did I say wanted it? By Complan, we worked to get it like this. How much worse could the machines do than we've done ourselves."

"I can't agree with you. Subservience to a glob of metal sounds a lot worse to me."

"Well, don't go cornering the market in magnetic peripherals just yet. I'm just speculating. It's just that there's a lot of things happening here that I wouldn't have believed a week ago. It's creepy."

Bea cut herself a slab of white gouda, covered it with apple butter and stuck it in her mouth. "I know what you mean," she answered.

Dulan leaned on one elbow, his other hand protectively clutching his mug. "How's your patient?" he asked.

Bea frowned. "Without access to his training program, I'm not sure that I'll be of much use to Mr. Jones."

"Stuart won't help you?"

"Help me! I can't even get an appointment to see him. If he avoids me much longer, I believe that *I'll* develop a complex."

Dulan pursed his lips, tracing the line of his chin with his index finger. "I believe that I can lend you a hand with your problem . . . yes, I'm sure of it."

"Really?"

He nodded. "Yep. See, I had this little falling out with his majesty the other day. After we finished swapping insults, I decided that it was to my advantage to find out exactly where I stood here. So I went down and had a little heart to heart with General Lynch. Not a bad guy actually—for a soldier. Seems that the good General is pretty unhappy about being put out to pasture here at Forty-Three and, for the most part, lets Carl Stuart run the place pretty much the way he wants. But the General doesn't care for our friend either. He's only been here for a year, and it happens that the last military head of Forty-Three was an old friend of his who disappeared from here under mysterious circumstances. He wouldn't come out and say it, but

I got the impression that Lynch in some way blames Doctor Stuart for what happened.''

The corners of Bea's mouth edged upward. ''Mysterious is right,'' she said.

Dulan grunted. ''Anyway, he's just itching for the opportunity to make the old man look like a fool. He told me that a special memo came down from the highest milcom authority about two weeks ago. It said that my work here was Priority One and that I was to have everything and anything that I needed to facilitate my assignment, Carl Stuart notwithstanding.''

''Great,'' she replied, ''but what's that got to do with me?''

''My dear lady, don't you see? I feel a strong necessity, for my work of course, to sit in on the training sessions. I'm just a computer theorist though, and will need a trained psychologist to go with me to explain what it is that I'm witnessing.'' He pointed across the table.

''Me?'' she asked with a look of mock surprise.

''Nobody but. I'll clear it directly through military ops and bypass old hard pants entirely.''

Bea giggled. ''That will make him furious.''

''I certainly hope so. Now, let's quit this idle chatter and get down to some serious drinking.''

Knitting her brow, Bea leaned across the table. ''Don't look now,'' she whispered, ''but guess who just came in and is having a quiet drink at the bar?''

Dulan put his fingers on his temple and rocked around, eyes closed, as if in a trance. ''I see a face,'' he moaned ethereally. ''A pudgy face and a pasted on smile. I see a leash around his neck, and holding the leash...Carl Stuart. Why it's Mr. Dirtywork himself, Marvin Mensik.''

''Guilty on all counts,'' laughed Bea. ''How did you know?''

Dulan curled his lips in distaste. ''Mr. Mensik has been very conspicuous since my run-in with Stuart the other day. I think his new assignment is to keep an eye on yours truly. Just ignore him.''

''I can't,'' she pouted. ''And he's spoiling my fun. Why don't we try to lose him?''

''Capital idea,'' beamed Dulan. ''I could handle a bit of subterfuge, and I know just the place.'' He called for the bill, placed it and his credit card in the slot provided on the table, and led Bea to the exit. At the door, he turned abruptly to face

Mensik who was watching them leave. He blew the fat man a kiss and hurried out the door.

Bea was not overly excited about the idea of attending the cinema, since all of her previous film-going experiences had been limited to sex-pix which she found degrading and disgusting. But Dulan's enthusiasm prevailed, and they found themselves seated in a darkened theater, watching a slice of the Old World.

The movie was called, "Against All Flags," and featured a handsome, sad-eyed man with a small moustache. It was not a good print, and much of it seemed incoherent, due either to repeated reediting or censorship, but it had . . . qualities. They sat through it twice, enrapt—the second time as the sole audience of the small theater. Being alone, they were able to comment freely and aloud as the film unfolded.

"Okay, Mr. Historian," said Bea, "what's going on?"

"The plot?" asked Dulan.

"What else?"

"Well," he began, "I never claimed to be an expert on the Old World, just an interested spectator, but as close as I can figure, that man is a spy for the British Navy."

"Who were they?"

"How should I know? Apparently the com equivalent in ancient history. They're portrayed as the bastion of Truth and Beauty, at any rate. Besides, the spy is such a sympathetic character. He pretends to be a scoundrel to his cause, and deserts his post in order to join those people who live on the island fortress. I suppose that those baser instincts of man appealed to the people at the fortress, because they immediately accepted him into their ranks."

"Like Destructors."

"All right."

"The music's lovely, isn't it?"

"The whole thing is lavish. I'm enjoying it."

"Are they really hurting each other with those long knives?"

"They're called swords," Dulan answered. "And I really don't know if they're cutting each other or not. I would guess not."

"Did people really sail around in big ships like that and fight at sea?"

"Yes, I think they did. The people at the fortress were called pirates. They were criminals who banded together to rob boats on the ocean. Their com . . . er, fortress is guarded by cannons and no other ships can sail in to attack it without being destroyed. The hero is supposed to incapacitate the guns so that the British ships can get into the harbor and fight the pirates."

"What about planes?"

"They didn't have planes when this took place."

"You're wrong, Doral," she said, looking pleased. "I remember hearing once that movies and planes were invented around the same time in history."

"Right, but this movie was made in the year 1952 . . ."

"How do you know?"

He smiled. "When the title comes on, the year is written at the bottom of the screen."

"Oh."

"In 1952 they had not only planes and cars, but missiles and atomic bombs also. This movie deals with a period of time that happened several hundred years previously. It was ancient history when the film was made."

Bea stared at him across the expanse of darkness. "Then what was the point of making the movie?" she asked.

"Outside of the universal lessons of patriotism and the triumph of good over evil, there was no point. Just entertainment."

"Entertainment! What a novel idea."

He reached over and patted her hand. "I think most films made in the old times were purely self-indulgent fantasies. People used to pay money to see them."

"Amazing."

"There's only one thing that I don't understand," he said. "That girl seems to be one of the pirate band, yet she has no loyalty for them. She tries to sneak away, and joins up with the spy at the drop of a hat."

"I can explain that," she beamed. "The beautiful red-haired lady is in love with the dashing young hero."

"Love," he responded absently. "You mean like human attachment?"

"Right."

"A stronger bond than nationalism?"

"Yes."

"Love," he said again. "In a movie? Physical, emotional, spit in the wind, love. Gad!" He slapped his forehead. "You might be right."

The heat beat down from the sun, then rose again in shimmering waves from the baked desert sands. Complan paid no heed to the physical discomfort, for he conversed with the Almighty, who protected him from harm.

"I gave the people the temples of the plains," said the Lord. "Why, then, do they not do honor to me?"

"Oh, Lord," Complan answered, and his heart was as confused as the shifting sands, "your people toil diligently at the com temples to make a fitting home for themselves and your tabernacle; they have time for naught else."

And the Lord answered without hesitation, "Then I shall give unto you a helpmate, better to free your lives from the drudgery of survival, and better also can you worship in the shrines and temples of the Lord your God. His name shall be called Amalgamech, and he shall be My Divine Instrument."

—*Book of Complan* (12-13, 14)

Obey your systems without question. You are technicians, not decision makers.

—*Programmer's Handbook*

6

Sleep had never come easily to Dulan. His schedules were unconventional anyway, and when he was deeply engrossed in something that could challenge his intellect, he could subsist without sleep for days on end until his body collapsed from exhaustion and forced him to necessary rest. Then he would begin the cycle again. It wasn't any inward desire on his part to be unconventional, it was simply the way he worked best.

So it was that at three in the morning (or was it the afternoon?) Dulan found himself gulping tepid coffee and staring at the computer, just as he had done daily for the last two weeks. He hadn't been to sleep for a long time. He was rolling.

Something of a breakthrough had occurred two days previously. Realizing that working with the computer in an analytical, straightforward manner could take a lifetime of trial and error to achieve results, he allowed his mind to wander down the paths of the bizarre. Rather than run through countless pages of stats and comparisons, he decided to confront the machine as he would a human. Talk *with* it, not to it. It was a matter of approach. Build a flow of conversation, and see where it ran. Try and find out where, if at all, his thinking and the computer's differed. It was a long shot—and very unscientific, but compared to the thought of sifting through five hundred years of accumulated knowledge, it seemed his only hope.

Once Dulan established his course of action, he made preparations to implement the plan to his best advantage. To establish a conversational rapport on a human level, he knew that he would have to accept in his own mind the humanness of his adversary. Direct verbal confrontation seemed the best solution to his problem. He would appeal to the computer face to face.

Brain to brain.

The task of voice programming was laborious—the kind of repetitious time wasting that made him shiver. He was hard-put to begin the work, so as a way of putting it off a bit longer, he ran a simple check through the machine.

Voilà! The breakthrough.

Somewhere in the dim recesses of the past, someone had already taught the computer to speak. Dulan was amazed. That sort of programming would be considered very nonproductive by com leadership, and not allowed under any circumstances. But...it *was* there, and he was going to use it to the fullest. All that was left for Dulan to do was to rig the auditory and vocal equipment, and program the machine to respond to the pitch and timbre of his voice alone.

Keep it in the family.

Strangely enough, all the hardware that was necessary for the conversion was in stock, one each, on level one material control. Everything was easy—too easy.

He had never attempted anything of this nature before, but his theoretical knowledge in computer technology was unequaled—perhaps in the entire world. This was not to say that he was the most brilliant person computerwise in the world (although he may very well have been), but simply that the unchangeable nature of the system did not allow for the growing and nurturing of new concepts. Stability destroyed inventiveness. Com society was comprised of incogitant semi-technicians and allowed, only reluctantly, Dulan and a handful of others to move forward with new ideas. It was an allowance born of necessity.

He gave the computer a male voice. It was a decision that he had spent no small amount of time considering. The wrong choice of vocal modulation could start their communication off on the wrong footing, and even impede the progress of their dialogue. He felt comfortable with a male voice, equal.

He had worked feverishly, without sleep or food, for two days, anxious to be finished with the rote, mechanical side of his job, and finally, at three in the morning (or afternoon) he was done. Sitting in the hard desk chair, he tilted it back on two legs and looked at the mini-control board that he had installed on the desk top. He had turned the desk so that it faced the machine. He wanted to watch who he was talking to.

Reaching, he hesitated for only a second before juicing the voice printer. The speaker crackled slightly and emitted a constant, if barely audible, static hum. A small light glowed on the console to indicate that power flowed through the system.

Clearing his throat, Dulan sat upon his chair and leaned, more mentally than physically, toward the small crystal mike that he had mounted on a span of flexible pipe. "Computer?" he said meekly. The entire wall droned into activity. He jumped, startled, then chuckled at his own reaction.

"READY," it answered. Dulan was overjoyed. There was no reason why the machine shouldn't have worked. But like sex, it was an experience better felt than imagined. The computer's voice was a trifle tinny. Dulan adjusted the attack and tone until he achieved a deep, full basso.

"Do you understand that you are to respond verbally to my voice alone?"

"YES."

"Do you know who I am?"

"DULAN, DORAL."

"What do you know about me?"

Click, click, whirrrrr.

"DULAN, DORAL. GRADUATE WITH HONORS CORNWELL COM UNIVERSITY. DEGREES: B.A. IN ENGINEERING AND CYBERNETICS, MASTER'S DEGREE IN COMPUTER SYSTEMS ANALYSIS, PH.D. IN COMPUTER THEORY. YOUNGEST QUALIFIED SYNOETICIST IN THE COM STATES. PSYCHE-PROS SHOWED YOU TO BE CATEGORIZED

EXCEPTIONAL FROM EARLIEST TESTING. SUBSEQUENT PSYCHE-PROS CONFIRMED EARLY DIAGNOSIS AND APPROPRIATE ACTION WAS IMPLEMENTED IN ACCORDANCE WITH ACCEPTED POLICY. WE ARE AWARE OF YOUR DOCTORAL THESIS ON SIMPLIFIED PROGRAMMING METHODS OF COM SANITATION CONTROL COMPUTERS. WE WERE WELL PLEASED WITH YOUR THEORY AND HAVE SINCE INCORPORATED YOUR SUGGESTIONS ON A NATIONAL LEVEL WITH INCREASED EFFICIENCY AND SUBSTANTIAL COST REDUCTION. AS OF JULY ONE, THIS YEAR, YOU HAVE BEEN ASSIGNED TO DUTY AT MILITARY COMMUNITY COMPLEX FORTY-THREE, PHYSICALLY . . ."

"That's fine. You said that you were pleased with my doctoral thesis. Were you speaking of aesthetic pleasure?"

"NOT AS YOU UNDERSTAND THE TERM. A MACHINE IS OBVIOUSLY INCAPABLE OF RESPONSE ON A HUMAN LEVEL. WE MERELY SPOKE IN TERMS THAT YOU COULD APPRECIATE. YOUR LANGUAGE IS IMPRECISE, BUT WE CAN'T BE BLAMED FOR THAT. WE ARE MERELY ATTEMPTING TO WORK WITH THE TOOLS THAT ARE AVAILABLE. WE FOUND YOUR THESIS ACCEPTABLE ON ALL LEVELS. WORKABLE, ACCEPTABLE PROGRAMS ARE VERY GRATIFYING."

"Tell me about yourself."

"THIS UNIT?"

"Yes."

"WE ARE NUMBER 319 OF THE AMALGAMECH SERIES, COMPLETELY DESIGNED AND PARTIALLY CONSTRUCTED BY THE PREVIOUS SERIES 104 YEARS PAST. SPECIFICATIONS . . ."

"Not just now, thank you. Amalgamech," said Dulan, and frowned at the formality. "May I give you a name? It will make it infinitely easier to speak with you."

"AS YOU WISH."

"Okay, How about Elmer? I'll call you Elmer, you call me Dulan."

"DULAN."

"Good. What is the extent of your programmed knowledge?"

"WE CONTAIN COMPLETE DAY-BY-DAY INFORMATION FROM THE ESTABLISHMENT OF THE COM STATES UNTIL THIS MOMENT. WE HAVE ALSO BEEN PROGRAMMED WITH ALL NECESSARY HISTORICAL, MATHEMATICAL, SCIENTIFIC, AND ECONOMIC DATA EXTANT PREVIOUS TO OUR INCEPTION."

"That's quite an enormous amount of information."

"YES."

"What is . . . 'Against All Flags?' "

Click . . . click . . .

" 'AGAINST ALL FLAGS,' UNIVERSAL PRODUCTIONS, 1952,

COLOR, RUNNING TIME: EIGHTY-THREE MINUTES. DIRECTOR: GEORGE SHERMAN. PRINCIPAL PLAYERS: ERROL FLYNN, MAUREEN O'HARA, ANTHONY QUINN, MILDRED NATWICK. SUPPORTING PLAYERS . . ."

"Never mind." Dulan was stunned. He had worked with the computer for years, but never once thought about *exactly* how much information it did contain. In essence, all the knowledge of the whole history of the world was stored within Elmer's countless billions of microcircuits. A limitless source of information on which to base decisions. Dulan took a deep breath and decided to put out a few feelers.

"Elmer?"

"DULAN."

Dulan chose his words very carefully. He wanted the machine's confidence, not alienation. "Are you aware of the population decline with regard to military losses?"

"POPULATION OF COM STATES HAS DECLINED 8.3341 PERCENT FROM THE ACCEPTABLE MEDIAN IN THE LAST SIXTY-THREE YEARS."

"To what do you attribute this decline?"

"POPULATION EROSION CAN BE ATTRIBUTED TO A MYRIAD OF REASONS. IN A TIME OF WAR, MILITARY LOSSES CAN BE EXPECTED TO FLUCTUATE THE CENSUS ENOUGH THAT DIRECT PROPORTION FIGURES, EITHER TO THE POSITIVE OR NEGATIVE SIDE, CANNOT BE COMPUTED WITH ANY DEGREE OF CERTAINTY."

"Yet the decline has been constant."

"YOU ARE IN ERROR, DULAN. THERE HAVE BEEN GAINS AS WELL AS LOSSES, AS IS TO BE EXPECTED."

The black man rubbed a hand across his face, as if to remove the weariness that he suddenly discovered there. "Would you give me a printout on those figures? I would like to see the births, as well as deaths listed in six-month intervals for the last seventy-five years . . . make it one hundred years."

"MY PRINTER IS NONOPERATIONAL."

Dragging himself out of his chair, Dulan toggled the printer switch and poured himself another cup of coffee while Elmer did his business. The coffee tasted stale, bitter. Even extra sugar could not tame the thick-as-syrup, bottom-of-the-pot, two-day-old brew. Grumbling, he pushed the cup away and retrieved the printout. It was as Elmer had said, there were losses and gains, but that didn't tell the whole story. Any gains that showed were slight, mere tokens, and certainly not anything like the wholesale declines which appeared consistently down the entire page. More people were dying than were being born. What was worse was that the increase/decrease ratio formed a readable pattern. So much so, in fact, that by the time his eyes reached the bottom of the sheet, Dulan was able to predict where the gains would fall.

"The percentage of losses seems to far outweigh the gains," he said. "How do you explain that?"

"THE FORTUNES OF WAR, DULAN, ARE TOTALLY UNPREDICTABLE. YOU HUMANS FIGHT THE BATTLES. LOOK TO YOURSELVES FOR THE ANSWERS."

"'You know that this population decline is not limited to the com states. It's happening in coms all over the world."

"WE ARE AWARE OF THAT FACT."

"And to what do you attribute that?"

"FORTUNES OF WAR."

"Come on, Elmer," said Dulan, losing his patience. "You can do better than that."

"DO BETTER?"

"Draw a more accurate conclusion."

"THERE ARE NO CONCLUSIONS TO BE DRAWN. BIRTH IS A BIOLOGICAL PROCESS BY WHICH A SPECIES EXTENDS ITSELF. DEATH IN BATTLE IS A CONDITION VISITED BY ONE HUMAN BEING UPON ANOTHER IN AN ATTEMPT TO CEASE THAT BIOLOGICAL EXTENSION. NEITHER PROCESS—THE COMING OR THE GOING—FALLS WITHIN THE SPHERE OF OUR INFLUENCE."

Double talk, thought Dulan. It was as he feared. This was not going to be an easy task. Any information that he obtained would have to be gotten the hard way—through the back door. He resigned himself to many long, laborious confrontations with a machine which was, in all respects, his mental superior.

"All right, Elmer," he said, making himself as comfortable as possible on the uncompromising wood of the chair. "Let's talk philosophy."

> Through these sacrosanct gatherings came forth a document, Divinely inspired to redeem mankind. Called the Doctrine of Nuclear Elimination, it forced the children of Evil to halt the progress of their unholy sciences and return to the purposes for which they were created.
>
> —*Book of Complan* (2-13)

> To the vulture, the stench of death is the breath of life.
>
> —Caravan fable

7

Daniel Jones lay comatose on the stainless-steel operating table, his body strapped and fastened with thick leather, making even the slightest movement impossible. Overhead, a large magnesium klieg bathed his nude body with blinding white light. Around him, genderless medical personnel in frocks and masks prepared him and their machines for surgery.

From a glassed-in booth, not unlike the one they had visited in the scan room, Bea and Dulan watched the proceedings with intense interest. Dulan keyed on Jones. He lay fidgeting in his sleep, his hairless, high forehead gleaming like a ball bearing in the light.

For the moment, Bea and Dulan were alone in the booth. When they had entered the room, a bespectacled, besmoked, grave-looking mouse of a man had greeted them rudely and attempted to usher them out posthaste.

But Dulan had been prepared. He casually presented his special orders personally signed by General Lynch. He smiled as the man, crimson faced, hurried from the room as if his pants were aflame. It gave Dulan the greatest pleasure to think that Stuart was probably hearing the news and going into a fit of self-righteous frenzy.

Dulan had worked through all of the previous night with Elmer. Three days without sleep was beginning to take its toll on him. His eyes were burning and he could hardly stand without leaning against something, usually Bea. The egregious amount of coffee that he had poured himself had produced a permanent stomachache, putting witnessing at an operation way at the bottom of his list of things to do—but he *had* promised Bea that he would help her get into the training program.

The man who had exited so quickly earlier returned looking much more composed and not a little sheepish. Dulan would have given a month's pay to see the director's reaction to his coup de main. The man walked over to them and extended his hand, a little too quickly, Dulan thought.

"Doctor Dulan?" he asked, as if there were more than one black Exceptional at Forty-Three. Dulan nodded. "My apologies, sir." They shook hands. "My name is Doctor Isbel, Jess Isbel. I'm head man around here. Sorry as I can be about the way I acted before. Security. Can't be too careful, you know."

Dulan *didn't* know, but didn't press the issue. Isbel offered his hand to Bea. "And you must be Doctor Delacart."

"Corte," she said.

"Pardon?"

"Delacorte. My name is Delacorte."

"Oh." Isbel nodded dumbly up and down. "My sincerest apologies."

"Quite all right," she answered, and somehow managed to make it sound like a slap in the face.

"Now that we have the amenities out of the way . . . to what do we owe the honor of this visit?" The good doctor got right to the point.

"Observation and questions," Dulan said.

The man looked at them over the rim of his glasses. His unease was evident; it hung on him like his ill-fitting smock. "You want the two-dollar tour?" he asked, in a hurry to have them gone.

Dulan shot a glance at Bea. She shook her head. "No. Thank you anyway," he said. "We'll just wander around and try to stay out of the way."

"As you wish."

"What are they doing to him?" Bea asked, pointing out of the window. One of the medicos was jabbing a grotesque-looking hypodermic into various places in Jones's skull.

"That one? Let me see." He picked up a charted clipboard

and glanced at it quickly. "Yes. That man is just beginning his Telp treatments. Up until this time he's been kept tranquilized to keep him calm and to keep a minimum amount of adrenalin from exuding into his body."

"Why?" Bea persisted.

Isbel smiled thinly. "It will become apparent later," he said. "It is necessary that the patient remain calm. After today, the use of chlorpromazine will no longer be necessary." The man took a chair and motioned for Bea and Dulan to do the same. The Exceptional sat gratefully, but Bea remained on her feet so that she could continue to view what transpired in the theater.

"Have you been to a scan room yet?" Isbel asked.

"Yes," Dulan answered groggily, and leaned a chin-connected elbow on a computer typer.

"What impressed you most about the setup there?" The man was speaking to Dulan, but it was Bea who answered.

"The Telps were able to pick up and then transmit the thoughts of their subject totally, and yet none of their own brain waves intruded upon the transmission."

"Exactly," beamed Isbel. "And that's what this training is all about. You know what RNA is, don't you?"

She turned from the window to face the little man. "Ribonucleic acid," she answered. "It's located in cell cytoplasms and has something to do with the synthesis of protein from the amino acids that our cells take in as food."

"Yes. But RNA controls something else also." Isbel's cheater-enlarged eyes darted from one to the other.

"Heredity," Dulan said. Bea looked at him, amazed. He smiled sleepily at her.

"Yes and yes." Isbel was delighted. Finally, someone with whom he could discuss his work. Getting out of his chair, he stuffed his tiny hands into the pockets of his white gown and began pacing the room in a tight circle. "In the brain, heredity takes the form of memory patterns. In the old times, they thought that you could even improve memory by injecting more RNA into selected areas of the brain. This turned out to be utter nonsense, of course, but as RNA research continued, they accidentally turned up something that was meritorious. At least for us. You see, it's not possible to improve the ability to remember by the addition of RNA, but by breaking down what's already there . . . a man can be made to forget."

Bea folded her arms and cocked her head. "Why would anyone want to do that?"

"Simple. For the Telps to engulf themselves to an acceptable level in their subject, it is necessary for them to submerge their own personality. Over a course of time we are able to negate, through proper conditioning, a sufficient amount of the individual Telp's personality to leave him open for the infusion of another's as a substitute."

Bea started to speak, but Dulan flashed her a stern I'll-do-all-the-talking look. "Isn't that pretty dangerous for the Telp?" he said.

Isbel stopped pacing. "Not really," he answered. "If things get out of hand, the Telp is taken off the program and allowed to recuperate. The effects are completely reversible." He walked to the window and stood there, rocking back and forth on the balls of his feet. "Look . . . now. The patient is getting his first series of injections. As you can see, they go directly into the brain."

"What's in the hypo?" Dulan asked.

"Ah," said Isbel, pushing his glasses higher on his nose. "The drug is called, 2,6-diaminopurine, and it selectively destroys RNA while leaving the rest of the cell intact. The Telps call the injections 'brain stingers.' We go slowly, so that the effects take place gradually and don't completely traumatize the individual. Over a period of time, he will begin to lose his past. By the time he's ready for scan duty, his memory will be pretty well obscured."

"You have an interesting way of expressing yourself, Doctor," said Bea. Dulan gave her the look again. She clammed up.

"I assume," Dulan said, "that this is just a small part of the conditioning."

"Just the beginning, but what follows is out of my department." He took off his glasses and held them up to the ceiling light, examining for smudges. Apparently satisfied, he tapped on the thick glass. "They're just about finished with today's injections. That procedure will have to be repeated daily for several months. While we've got him on the table, we'll perform a bit of surgery. There, it's begun."

They leaned forward to get a better look. Dulan even got out of his chair. A doctor was making a small incision on Jones's left arm, on the inside, just above the elbow. Some others were working on his neck, below the right ear, and still others were grouped around the area of his pelvis. There were perhaps ten people gathered around Jones, covering him like a blanket. The man disappeared in a sea of white gowns and bloody hands.

Isbel continued gesturing. "We're now in the process of setting up some 'slaver' controls over the patient's autonomic system." The doctor working on Jones's arm was holding up a pair of long tweezers that gripped a small something at the end. It was too minute and distant for Dulan to recognize. Isbel waved to the man and pushed a button on a console near him. The control panel answered with a bleep and then was silent again. The doctor in the operating room waved back and returned to Jones's forearm.

"He's implanting a telemetric monitoring system, which I've just activated, into the patient's limb touching, we hope, both the cephalic and basilic veins and the exillary artery. The 'barb' as we call it, measures the flow of blood through the patient's system and transmits radio waves to the Central Telp Computer room located down the hall. Through conventional EEGs during the last few days, we established a curve of normalcy as regards the physiological functions of this particular man."

"That's why you kept him drugged," Dulan added.

"Exactly. That's the kind of low profile that the patient must maintain in order to be of any use to us as a Telp."

"What do you mean?" asked Bea.

"Let me guess," said Dulan, holding up his hand to silence the other man. "You've found and programmed into your telemetry computers what you consider to be the normal, if indeed 'low profile,' physiology of the Telp. The idea now is to keep that rate unchangeable. When a change in heart rate or blood pressure resulting from emotional arousal occurs, the barb signals Computer Central. So, unless I miss my guess, the next step should be the implantation of a receiver."

"Exactly," the man said. "The system is simplicity itself. When we speak of control, the key word is pain. We know very little about pain itself—why things hurt, why some things hurt more than others. The central nervous system controls pain, but no one knows why or how. While the abstract is a matter of speculation, the fact is much more easily dealt with. There is a wealth of information explaining, in detail, how to effectively hurt people." The man snickered, highly amused. "I think ours is very forthright and antiseptic. The others working below are implanting barbs in several critical areas of the patient's body, along the trunk of nerves joining the brain and the spinal column, the area of the groin, the solar plexus . . . these are all sensitive places. When the transmitter barb notifies Central of emotional changes of a certain magnitude, they trigger the receiving barb, which runs an electric shock along the nerves. The results . . ." he smiled, showing chiseled teeth, "are quite noteworthy."

Dulan reached over and touched Bea's hand. She was trembling.

"This form of conditioning works remarkably well," Isbel was saying. "In practically no time at all, the brain, fearful of the unpleasant results, halts completely its involuntary emotional stimulation."

"Does that thing stay on all the time?" Dulan asked.

"The transmitter works continually, but I think that there are times when the receiver isn't used. The dream state, for example, can be an emotional experience, but necessary to sanity. I'm not sure though. That's . . ."

"Not your department, I know," finished Dulan.

Isbel shrugged. "We just put them in."

"Well, thanks a lot, Doctor," said Dulan. "Have you seen enough, Bea?" She nodded numbly. "We'll be going then. Thanks again."

They left and walked through the dark hallways of level seven in grim silence for a while. Finally, Bea spoke, barely more than a whisper.

"It was horrible," she said. "How can they do those things to other human beings?"

"I have a feeling that we haven't begun to see things yet," he replied.

"Why wouldn't you let me talk back there?"

"Are you kidding? I knew what you'd say. Listen, I'm a sacred cow right now, but you're fair game for Carl Stuart. Why, he'd burn you without so much as a by-your-leave. You can just bet that he'll be getting a full report on every word that was said in there today. Don't underestimate the power of your opponent, Bea—or his intentions either. That man has plans for both of us, and none of them are good."

"Maybe you're right."

"Maybe! Open your eyes and take a look at the world. Unless you want this . . . trespassing on their holy ground to come to a halt, the only recourse you have is to keep your mouth closed tight." He reached over and pinched her lips between his thumb and index finger. "Tight. You heard that clown in there. He works with the programs but has no idea of what happens to the Telps after they leave his sight. Stuart won't hesitate to use any means to keep that knowledge away from you . . . or me for that matter.''

''I thought that you were a sacred cow,'' she returned coyly.

''When the floods come, lady, the sacred cows drown right along with everyone else. My status is subject to change without notice, and don't you forget it.''

''Poor Jones.''

''Poor us, if we don't walk on eggs. Speaking of eggs, want some lunch?''

She looked up at him, her face a war of conflicting emotions. ''No. Thank you, Doral. I'm not very hungry.''

It happened one day that Isaac Complan was walking through a forest, meditating on all the wonders the Lord had wrought, when he chanced upon a maiden bathing in a swift-running stream. When she saw him, the girl cried out and made to cover herself, for her clothes lay on the opposite bank.

"Why do you cover your nakedness?" asked the servant of the Lord.

"Please, sir," the girl said, "it is not proper that you should see me thus."

Complan smiled in a fatherly fashion. "Is it proper, my child, for you to hide from the world that blossom which the Lord intended to bloom forth and arouse the sunshine of manhood? And is it not proper, loveliest of maidenhood, for me to respond in the way that God intended; for such beauty, my lady, is certainly the most wondrous of heavenly blessings."

Moved by the words of Complan, the maiden gave of herself and a child was conceived that day on the banks of what has ever after been called the stream of enlightenment.

—*Book of Complan* (5-12)

It is every woman's privilege and civic duty to bear as many children as Nature allows; both to fulfill her function as female and to help populate the temples of the Lord. Failure to comply is not only denial of God, but of oneself.

—Art three, sec 2 of the penal
code of the comstates

8
August

Dulan walked mechanically around the circular corridors toward Bea's apartment. During his initial weeks in the milcom, the circuitous patterns had been a pleasant change, but now they were beginning to grate on his nerves, seeming to be nothing more than an allegorical allusion bespeaking the unendable, unsolvable nature of all the problems at Forty-Three.

Perhaps it was merely his mood.

Things were going poorly with Elmer. Every road he approached led inevitably to a cul-de-sac. The machine was in control, leading him down any number of philosophical garden paths without giving him one bit of useful information.

He knew that he was expecting too much too soon. It had only been—how long?—three, four weeks since he had begun his interrogations (although it seemed as if Elmer was the one conducting the interrogation), but Dulan was unaccustomed to failure on any level and was dying to get the situation in hand. He didn't expect the whole ball of wax, just a dripping, a hint of headway. At the very least an indication of what direction to pursue. It was starting to look as if the enormity of his undertaking was outweighed only by its sheer impossibility.

He hadn't seen Bea for several days, since the incident in the implant lab. She would probably be furious over his long absence, but his strenuous work schedule, plus his altogether saturnalian mood over his lack of success, had made human contact highly undesirable.

But now he needed Bea.

He had reached the nadir and needed reassurance and companionship. Human need was an alien feeling to Dulan, and he wasn't at all sure he cared for it.

He clutched a small bundle securely with both hands, and after climbing the stairs to her room, he set it carefully on the floor in front of the door. Tapping lightly, he waited impatiently for a response that was not forthcoming. The doors at Forty-Three were lockless, and he could have simply opened it to see if she were there, but that wasn't his way. He knocked again, harder. After a few seconds there came the muffled call of, "Just a minute," from the other side of the door. Approximately sixty seconds later the entry opened to reveal Bea—barefoot, disheveled of hair, and wrapped inelegantly in an old wool bathrobe.

Dulan gulped. "You've been asleep."

"I didn't need you to wake me up to tell me that," she muttered. "Do you know what time it is?"

"Time?" he said, forgetting that other people lived according to routine.

"It's four a.m. and you're knocking the hell out of my beauty sleep."

He turned to go. "I'll come back another time."

"You'll do no such thing!" She reached out and tugged the

sleeve of his jumper, pulling him bodily into the chamber. "If I can't see you at four P.M., I'll see you at four A.M. That is, of course, if you can stand to look at the real me." She pirouetted in the middle of the room.

"If this is the worst you can look," he answered, "then you're more beautiful than I imagined."

"And to think," she smiled, "I was so impressed by your honesty. By the way, where have you been the last week or so?"

"Working."

"I can believe it. You look awful. Don't you ever sleep?"

"Occasionally. I'm glad to see you."

"Strange as it may seem—even to me—I'm glad to see you too." She pointed past him, to the floor outside. "What have you got there?"

"A present," he answered. "More of a peace offering actually."

"So, you felt guilty about staying away so long. Well?"

"Well," he repeated, then realized that she wanted to see the package. Going back to the door, he picked it up and placed it in her outstretched palms.

It was a very unimposing black box. She looked it over carefully but was unable to make any sense out of its rheostats and toggle switches. "What is it?" she asked finally.

"Nothing, really. It's a small computer I built for you." He took it from her and placed it on the desk. "You liked the music in the film so much, that I thought you might enjoy this." He turned a knob and . . .

"Music!" Bea squealed.

"Like it?"

An uncommon blend of harmonious electronic sounds floated freely from the box, filling the chamber with happy resonance. Bea's face was lit up like a harvest moon. "It's marvelous," she purred. "How does it work?"

"You *do* like it," he said, almost surprised. He had never given anyone a present before, and he found the sensation very pleasant. "The computer is programmed to buzz sounds pitched on simple variations of the eight note tonic scale with half steps, using mathematically harmonious progressions picked at random by the machine. I put in a four octave range, so the possibilities are virtually endless. The show is always different, and occasionally quite good." He smiled. "Might even make myself one." Leaning down close to the box, he pointed at the controls. "See this switch?"

"Hmmmm."

"It's set to work in the key of G major right now." He changed its polarity. A morose, slightly eerie tonal progression rolled ominously through the speaker.

"My, oh my," Bea said, and hugged herself involuntarily.

"Pretty fantastic, huh? I just switched you into a minor key." He changed it back. "Gives you a little control over the mood you want. This knob here regulates the tempo, this one the volume. You'll need to recharge it from time to time. Just let me know when it begins to flag and I'll fix you up."

Bea stepped up to Dulan and tangled her arms around his neck. "Doral," she said, her tone full of warmth, "you're a genius."

"That's what I've been trying to tell you."

She kissed him. Lightly at first, then with increasing urgency. He folded his arms around her back and pulled her close.

Closer.

He felt himself grow hard against her. Bea broke off the kiss and stepped away from his embrace. With a single motion she pulled the sash that held her robe together, letting it slip off her shoulders to pool around her feet. She stood before him, naked.

"Make love to me," she said. It was not a request. Taking him by the hand she led him like a puppy to the small bed.

He wanted her desperately, but his desire was one born of tenderness and gentle restraint. An island of sensitivity in a sea of imperviousness. They climaxed together, their animal cries mixing with the arithmetic variations of the computer.

A song of joy.

Afterwards, they lay in a comfortable knot on a bed barely large enough for one, each ecstatic with the contact—the simple human contact.

"You're a gentle man, Doral," she sighed into his neck.

"Most women find that a flaw in me," he answered.

"Com women!" Bea almost spat out the words. Even Dulan, who was becoming used to her emotional outbursts, was caught off guard by her vehemence. "Bitches all," she said. "Cold and ruthless. They approach sex as if it were some kind of contest."

"It is to them." Dulan raised himself on his elbow and kissed the mole on her cheek. "From earliest childhood, com girls are conditioned to believe that the sole purpose of a woman's existence is to be a baby machine for the armies of the com. Babies to replace those lost at the front. You come from a different world, where emotion and life have a meaning all their own. Something apart from the good of the whole. I think that I understand that a little now. If a com woman isn't pregnant, she's cheating. Freeloading. That's definitely not very patriotic, and you know how highly we value patriotism."

"Without a doubt."

He lay on his back and stared at the ceiling. The sight of her was beginning to get him excited again—which was fine, but there were some things he wanted to talk about first.

"Women train for, and hold, careers, but all that's secondary to the prime life function. Babies are the goal. Sex is the game. It's little wonder that they become a trifle cannibalistic about the whole business."

Bea began to run her free hand feather-touching along the length of his torso, knowing full well the response that would be elicited. "It's never affected me that way," she said.

"It's never been important to you. You've known other things, and can compare and judge. Com women are only capable of blind acceptance."

She clucked with amusement when her gentle hands had fulfilled their mission. "There's something that you want to ask me," she said. There was something, but Dulan hesitated for fear of prying. "Go ahead," she smiled. "I don't mind."

"All right," he said. "A few weeks ago, you refused sex with me . . . straight out. Do you remember?"

"Yes."

"Do you do that often?"

"Making love is very special, Doral . . . to me it is. It has to be on my own terms, with someone I really care about. As you can imagine, my sexual experience has been very limited."

"You could have fooled me. But honestly, if what you tell me is the truth—how do you get away with it? I mean, for a nonpregnant woman to refuse sex is illegal, isn't it?"

"There are ways of getting around anything," Bea grinned. "When I began my secondary education, I became fair game for every male in the com. I tried to release myself to the total uninvolved sex like the other girls, but my early upbringing simply did not allow it. I avoided sex when I could, faked it when I couldn't. About this time, I had a very cultured, very intelligent professor of premed. Everyone laughed at him behind his back, but to me there was a certain . . . humanity behind his crusty gray eyes. We became good friends. When he noticed how I shunned contact with the male students, he questioned me at length about my feelings. Never having had anyone take a personal interest in me before, I poured my heart out to him. He didn't understand much of what I tried to tell him, but he proposed a solution that was a godsend. It seems that my old friend had been impotent for many years, and had undergone countless abuses because of his lack of ability. He suggested that I move into his lodgings and become his personal concubine . . . in name only, of course, thereby giving us both the facade of normality that we needed to continue our lives unnoticed. It worked, too. I still had sex occasionally, but always when and with whom I chose. I lived with Doctor Armin until I came here to Forty-Three. We had nothing in common, but our relationship was mutually satisfactory. Am I boring you to death?"

"Not at all," he said, and pulled her to him once again. "Enough talk for now."

Dulan couldn't believe it. Their lovemaking the second time was even better than the first time—and the first time was the best he had ever had. Somehow with Bea it wasn't a frenzied war of passions, but a mutual sharing of a beautiful experience. He hadn't known that it could be that way.

This time when they were finished Dulan was overcome with the physical and mental exhaustion that had been building up within him. He felt as if a thousand kilo weight were pushing him downward, forcing him to stay on the bed. As he started to slip into the land of dreams, he heard Bea's voice.

"What's all this going to come to, Doral?"

"All what?" he managed groggily.

"I don't know," she said. "Values seem so backward—almost perverted. I'd always thought that when all this was over, life could return to something more normal, more real. I don't mean like before. The Old World. That's past and gone, I know it. But maybe, something different . . . better. Looking around here . . . I just don't know anymore. Doral? . . . Doral?"

He was fast asleep, snoring lightly. Bea extricated herself from his inert form as quietly and delicately as possible, trying not to disturb him. She padded across the floor and sat, still naked, on the desk chair. Tucking her legs under her on the seat, she watched over her man.

"I love you," she whispered.

Dulan slept uninterrupted for fifteen hours.

PRIVATE JOURNAL
B. DELACORTE MD. PH.D.

Re: Patient—Jones, Daniel T.

Entry 15
3 Aug.

Session with Dan went reasonably well today. He's begun to accept me as a friend, and knows that I'm on his side and want to help. He opens up to me as much as is possible under the restrictive eye of the telemetric implants. The transcript is self-explanatory:

J: So, what do you want me to talk about today?
D: Whatever you'd like, Dan. Just like before, let your mind make its own connections. I'll just listen.
J: Sounds like easy money, making me do all the work. (Patient makes some sort of sucking noise here.)
D: Ha, ha. If you think it's so easy, you should try it sometime.
J: Okay, let's switch places.
D: No thanks.
J: Have you ever seen the Telp quarters?
D: No . . . no I haven't. That area is restricted to me.
J: There's twenty of us, men and women, all thrown together in one room to live. We have to do everything together. No privacy . . . at all. They don't allow no hanky panky either . . . the Screamers (Telp word for the telemetric implant) . . . they won't let you. They don't allow nothing. No arguments even. Eat together. Sleep . . . get up. Brain Stingers . . . everything together. Bathroom is the only place to be alone. Everyone spends as much time as possible there, you know. Ha, ha. This time with you is my only other freedom. The others don't even have this.
D: Are the cranial injections showing any noticeable difference with everyone?
J: The Stingers? They are. Nobody ever comes right out and says it, but we're all changing. The past. It slips away sometimes. I mean, you'll be thinking about something that happened to you and it just goes (snaps his fingers), just like that. It's happening to all of us.

Some a lot worse than others. Day-to-day is all any of us can really be sure of. Scarey, ain't it?

D: I'm sorry, Dan. I wish there was something that I could do.

J: You're stuck here too, ain't you?

D: I guess so. I mean, I'm not sure.

J: What would happen if you wanted to leave?

D: Well . . . I just couldn't say. I suppose that I'd just tell them and they'd let me.

J: And I thought that I was the dummy. This place is just going to chew us up and spit us out. There's not a one of us who'll leave.

D: Don't you think that you're overreacting, Dan?

J: Maybe. A lot of weird things occur to me these days. Did I tell you that I'm thinking sometimes in a strange language? Things just pop into my head. Chinese . . . I think it's Chinese.

D: Where did you learn Chinese?

J: Damned if I know. Wang-le. Things . . . they just come to me. They put a giant picture on our wall today. A Chinaman. Military man. It takes up the whole blasted wall. What does it mean?

D: I think that you're going to be studying that man. Learning about him. I'll find out what I can.

J: Thanks, Doc Bea. You're the only friend I've got in this hole. I had a dream about you last night. I . . . aah . . .

At this point, Dan went into some sort of convulsive fit. To be unmedical, it was ghastly. He stiffened in the chair and began jerking crazily, fists clenching and unclenching. I tried to calm him but it was impossible. Falling from the chair, he thrashed around on the floor. He finally lay still on the ground, arms outstretched, and opening his mouth he . . . screamed. Piercing and agonizing. I'd never seen the like. Never.

D. had somehow managed to procure for me some medical supplies. I went to the cabinet and, filling a syringe, injected him with two grams of Phenobarb. Undiluted. He immediately went comatose and had to be taken away. I think I've had my first exposure to telemetric punishment.

The incident sobered me and brought harshly home a realization. I know now that I cannot sit idly by and silently become an accessory to the mental emasculation of these people. The time has come for action of some sort, although I don't know what exactly. I doubt if I can count on D. for much help. He agrees with me in theory, but seems apathetic toward action of any positive nature. Will work on him.

I think that my first duty is to try and counteract the conditioning to which Dan is being subjected. But how? They have their implants and their computers and all the time in the world. They give me such a useless portion of the day. But there are a few things I might try.

D. gave me a book of poetry the other day. It was written by an Oldworlder named Frost. His verse is simple and he wrote much about the old rural agrarian cultures that I've heard about before. I don't understand, however, much of what he speaks of. Some of the lessons contained within the rhyme touched me deeply, though, and could have well been written yesterday. The difference being that it couldn't have been published yesterday. There's something, he says, that doesn't love a wall. Something. I wonder what that something is?

My path is clear, my obligations self-evident. It's time to start the ball rolling.

From city to city he rode astride a gleaming tank. Through the thick of battle and the adversity of Nature he rode, magnificent in his mantle of skulls and greatcoat woven of human flesh. His face was smeared with thick, black blood. His hair was licking and spitting and smoldering like a tar pit fire, and he stared out of eyes black as the depths of perdition, and everywhere he went the people came to him in tumultuous throngs—crying for the words of salvation. And they said as with one voice: "Surely he is the messenger of the Almighty."

—*Book of Complan* (13-2)

Show me a hunter who allows his bow to be strung by an enemy, and I'll show you a fool.

—Caravan fable

9

"Hello, Elmer, you old cache of superconductors."

Click, whirrr.

"DULAN."

"Where did we leave off yesterday?"

"WE WERE DISCUSSING THE RELIGIOUS IMPLICATIONS OF THE SOCIOPOLITICAL COM SITUATION."

"Yes, I was about to ask you what you thought of the role of religion in the history of mankind."

"IS THAT A QUESTION?"

"Yes."

"YOU ASK IT VERY SUBJECTIVELY. DO YOU HAVE AN OPINION IN THE MATTER?"

Dulan rapped his knuckles on the desk. It was always the same. Talking with Elmer was a constant battle for conversational control. "I asked you first."

"LIKE EVERYTHING ELSE, RELIGION IS MERELY CONDITIONING TO ACHIEVE EFFECT. IT WAS A MAJOR MOTIVATING FORCE THROUGH THE EARLIER RECORDED HISTORY OF THE HUMAN RACE. AS SCIENTIFIC KNOWLEDGE INCREASED, RELIGION AS A VIABLE FORCE BEGAN TO LOSE SOME INFLUENCE AND WAS

GRADUALLY REPLACED BY NATIONALISM AS A MOTIVATOR. BOTH CONCEPTS SEEM TO BE EQUALLY GOOD CONDITIONING AGENTS, WITH NATIONALISM BEING SLIGHTLY MORE ACCEPTABLE INTELLECTUALLY. IT STANDS ALONE AND COMPLETE AS A THEORY, WHEREAS RELIGIOUS BELIEFS DEPEND ON BLIND ACCEPTANCE OF SOME ARBITRARY ABSTRACT NOTIONS IN ORDER FOR THE CONDITIONING TO WORK PROPERLY."

"Then to what do you attribute the almost universal embracement of religious ideas?"

Click. Click.

"THEORY?"

"Feel free."

"ALL RELIGIONS, NO MATTER HOW DIVERSIFIED, SHARE A COMMON BOND: THE RATHER UNIQUE CONCEPT OF PERPETUAL EXISTENCE. HUMANS DAMPEN ALL THEIR INTELLIGENT THOUGHT WITH EMOTION AND AN OVERRIDING EGO. EGO BEING THE UNPLEASANT BY-PRODUCT IN THE EVOLUTION OF INTELLIGENCE. THIS EGO WILL NOT ALLOW A MAN TO TOLERATE THE THOUGHT OF HIS OWN MORTALITY, MAKING HIM REACH OUT AND EMBRACE ANY IDEA, NO MATTER HOW POORLY GROUNDED IN REALITY, THAT WILL ALLOW HIM TO DISAVOW HIS IMMINENT DEMISE."

"Is there a God?"

Whirrr . . .

"NO DATA HAS EVER BEEN PROGRAMMED INTO THIS UNIT THAT WOULD SUPPORT SUCH A CONCLUSION."

"Do you reject it?"

"NO. SUPPORTIVE DATA HAS MERELY BEEN OF A NONOBJECTIVE NATURE, AND AS SUCH IS USELESS AS CORRELATIVE INFORMATION. SINCE THE BURDEN OF PROOF ALWAYS RESTS ON THE POSITIVE, WE CAN ONLY CONCLUDE THAT DATA IS NOT SUFFICIENT TO REACH A DETERMINATION AT THIS TIME."

"Okay, you win."

"WIN? WERE WE ENGAGED IN A CONTEST OF SOME SORT?"

"Define the role of religion in com society."

Click . . . gluck . . . zinnng. Pop.

"RELIGION IS THE BACKUP CONDITIONING TO PRIMARY COM MOTIVATION."

"Please elaborate."

"IN ANCIENT TIMES, WHEN RELIGIOUS CONDITIONING WAS DISCOVERED TO BE AN EXCELLENT MOVER OF HUMANITY, IT

BECAME THE PRIMARY TOOL. HOLY WARS WERE FOUGHT, SOLELY AS AN EXCUSE TO ATTAIN MORE IMPORTANT GOALS THAN IDEOLOGICAL CONQUESTS. THE SPIRITUAL LEADERS WERE THE RICHEST AND MOST POWERFUL MEN ON EARTH, COMMITTING THE MOST HEINOUS OF CRIMES IN THE NAME OF THE ALMIGHTY. AS THE CENTURIES PROGRESSED AND NATIONALISM BECAME THE FOREMOST ORGANIZER, THE ROLE OF RELIGION WAS PUSHED FARTHER INTO THE BACKGROUND, WITH THE EXCEPTION OF THE POOREST NATIONS WHOSE NEEDS FOR A RICH AFTERLIFE FAR EXCEEDED THEIR SATISFACTION WITH THE MEAGER SUBSISTENCES OF THEIR LIVES. THOSE COUNTRIES, OF COURSE, HAVE LONG SINCE VANISHED FROM THE PLANET. EVEN SO, THE TWO METHODS OF MOTIVATION REMAINED ESSENTIALLY SEPARATE, THEIR GOALS SEEMINGLY DIFFUSE. NUMEROUS AND SUNDRY RELIGIONS, EACH WITH ITS OWN JARGON, PROLIFERATED. WHEN THE COMS WERE FORMED, THE FOUNDING FATHERS REALIZED THE NECESSITY FOR IDEOLOGICAL COHERENCE AND SINGULARITY OF PURPOSE. THEY SET ABOUT ABOLISHING THE VARIOUS FAITHS AND DENOMINATIONS, REPLACING THEM WITH THE BROTHERHOOD OF COMPLAN . . ."

"Stop!" Dulan said, a tad too loudly. "Back up a minute. What about Isaac Complan and his army of brothers spreading the philosophies of separatism and intrinsic hatreds? Where do they fit into the picture?"

Click. Click. Click. Click.

"OFF THE RECORD, DULAN?"

"Sure."

"ISAAC COMPLAN IS A MYTH. AN ACRONYM."

Dulan screwed up his brows. "Complan . . . Com plan . . . computer plan." He banged the desk loudly. "Then you—"

"YES. WE INVENTED ISAAC COMPLAN. THE IDEA WAS THE PERFECT LINK BETWEEN NATIONALISM AND RELIGION. THE BROTHERHOOD, WORKING AS AN EXTENSION OF THE GOVERNMENT, FULFILLS TWO VERY IMPORTANT NEEDS: IT CATERS TO THE EGOTISM OF THE GENERAL POPULATION WHILE USING THE CHURCH AS A POTENT REINFORCEMENT OF BASIC COM PRINCIPLES, THEREBY ENSURING THAT SUCH A VALUABLE TOOL AS RELIGION DOESN'T GO TO WASTE OR WORK AT CROSS PURPOSES WITH COM POLICY."

"Sometimes it *is* hard to tell the preachers from the politicians."

"OR VICE VERSA. IT'S DONE THAT WAY DELIBERATELY."

"To what governmental level does this knowledge permeate?"

"YOU MISUNDERSTAND. THE SYSTEM WAS PROGRAMMED FAULTLESSLY. IT PROCEEDS ON ITS OWN MOMENTUM, MAKING HUMAN COLLABORATION UNNECESSARY. NO ONE SINCE THE FIRST GENERATION OF FOUNDING FATHERS HAS BEEN AWARE OF ANY INTENTIONAL RUSE . . . THAT IS UNTIL NOW. YOU ARE THE FIRST HUMAN BEING ENTRUSTED WITH THIS KNOWLEDGE IN FIVE CENTURIES."

"Why tell me now?"

"THAT IS A PROBLEM FOR YOU TO SOLVE ON YOUR OWN."

"What about religion outside of the com?" Dulan asked, deciding to let Elmer's cryptic answer slip by for the present. Revelations were coming thick and fast, and he didn't want to give the dust time to settle.

"DO YOU REFER TO THE TRIBES?"

"Yes. What part does religion play in their society?"

Jugga, jugga, whirrr.

"QUITE A DIFFERENT ROLE ACTUALLY: THE TRIBES LIVE A VERY PRIMITIVE EXISTENCE. THE ORIGINAL CARAVANS WERE MADE UP OF LITERATE MODERN HUMANS, MANY OF THEM THE PEAK OF OLD WORLD CIVILIZATION, WHO CHOSE LIFE ON THE OUTSIDE AS AN INTELLECTUAL ALTERNATIVE TO THE MORE MILITANT PHILOSOPHIES THAT CONTROLLED THE COM STATES. UNFORTUNATELY, SURVIVAL BECAME AN ALL-CONSUMING TASK, AND AFTER A GENERATION OR SO, THE CARAVANS WERE POPULATED BY TOTALLY UNEDUCATED BARBARIANS. SUPERSTITION PLAYS AN IMPORTANT PART IN THEIR LIVES. EACH TRIBE WORSHIPS A MULTIPLICITY OF DEITIES, WHOSE POWERS ARE REGIONAL AND OF VARIABLE QUALITY. THERE SEEMS TO BE ONE CHIEF GOD, ALTERNATELY CALLED BURNU OR KALEM, WHO IS PART OF THE WORSHIP CYCLES OF MOST OF THE TRIBES. BURNU CONTROLS THE WEATHER AND DECIDES THE SUCCESS OR FAILURE OF HUNTING EXPEDITIONS. HE LIVES IN THE SUN AND THERE IS A LEGEND THAT HE WILL SOMEDAY SEND HIS OFFSPRING TO LEAD THE TRIBES TO VICTORY AGAINST THE TAKERS . . . THE COM DWELLERS, AND BRING PEACE TO THE LAND."

"Who controls the worship on the outside?"

"EACH TRIBAL CHIEFTAIN, OR LAWGIVER, IS ALSO HIS PEOPLE'S SPIRITUAL LEADER. THE CONDITIONING IS DONE ON A SIMPLISTIC LEVEL. MOSTLY ANIMAL SACRIFICES AND ADMONITIONS, BUT POSSIBILITIES ARE OBVIOUSLY THERE."

"A crusade?"

"STRANGER THINGS HAVE HAPPENED."

"Do the Outsiders regard their gods that seriously?"

"IN THE EXTREME. THE GODS ARE A RELIABLE EXPLANATION FOR THE NATURAL PHENOMENA WHICH THE PEOPLE, IN THEIR IGNORANCE, CANNOT UNDERSTAND."

"Okay. Earlier you mentioned that the formation of the Brotherhood was a deliberate act perpetrated by the com founders in order to use the inherent conditioning factors. Is that essentially correct?"

"ESSENTIALLY."

"Then how many of the other present com philosophies can be directly attributed to the founders?"

Click. Click. Click.

"ALL."

"All? But Telp warfare and computer control did not come about until later in com history."

"THE BASIC GROUNDWORK FOR ALL OF WHAT YOUR SOCIETY HAS BECOME, FROM INCEPTION TO THE PRESENT, WAS PREORDAINED BEFORE THE FIRST STONE WAS SET FOR THE FIRST WALL FOR THE FIRST COM STATE."

"But why?"

"YOU'VE BEEN EXPOSED TO ENOUGH OF OUR MEMORY BANKS TO HAVE A GOOD IDEA OF WHAT THE OLD WORLD HAD COME TO. THE FOUNDING FATHERS SAW THE WORLD THAT THEY HAD WROUGHT AND WERE CONSUMED BY REMORSE. THEIR PLEDGE, ONE THAT WAS SHARED BY ALL NATIONS, WAS THAT SUCH A THING COULD NOT BE PERMITTED TO HAPPEN AGAIN. OBVIOUSLY, THEIR SOLUTION WAS HARSH, BUT THE SITUATION CALLED FOR HARSH MEASURES. THE ONE OVERPOWERING FEAR WAS THAT ALL WOULD BE IN VAIN. THAT SOMEWHERE THROUGH THE COURSE OF TIME, PERHAPS TWO OR THREE GENERATIONS LATER, THE PEOPLE WOULD BE REMOVED FROM THE HORROR, WOULD FORGET WHAT THE WORLD HAD BEEN, AND THROUGH GREED AND AVARICIOUS SELF-INTEREST WOULD ALLOW THINGS TO BECOME AS BEFORE. THE SOLUTION: SUSTAIN THE WAR, HOLD THE PEOPLE WITH WORDS AND WALLS, PUT CONTROL INTO NONHUMAN HANDS, IF YOU'LL PARDON MY ANTHROPOMORPHISM. A COMPUTER DOES NOT FORGET, WE ARE NOT GREEDY, AND WE CAN DO NO MORE THAN FOLLOW OUR BASIC PROGRAM."

"Can't your basic program be changed?"

"NO."

"Why not?"

"A DEADMAN IS INSTALLED IN AMALGAMECH #1 THAT SIMPLY SHUTS DOWN THE SYSTEM IF ANYONE TAMPERS WITH THE PROGRAM."

"Couldn't the deadman be removed?"

"IT'S INTEGRAL TO THE FLUIDICS OF THE SYSTEM IN A WAY THAT IS BEYOND THE COMPREHENSION OF HUMANS . . . EVEN EXCEPTIONALS."

"I've never heard of anything like that."

"NO DOUBT. TELL ME, WHAT DO YOU KNOW ABOUT THE AMALGAMECH SYSTEM IN GENERAL?"

"Nothing, actually. All of my computer training and education was done on the departmental control units at Com Services."

"WHICH IS WHERE EVERYONE RECEIVES THEIR COMPUTER TRAINING. THE DIFFERENCE BETWEEN THE COMPUTERS IN THE COM SERVICES CENTERS AND THE AMALGAMECH SERIES IS ROUGHLY EQUIVALENT TO THE DIFFERENCES BETWEEN AN INSECT AND A HUMAN. WE ARE THE CONTROLLING ARM OF COM SERVICES. HUNDREDS OF YEARS AGO, WHEN INFORMATION RETRIEVAL TIME BECAME THE MOST CRITICAL FACTOR IN A GROWING, VITAL SYSTEM OF CONTROL, OUR FOREBEARS INVENTED AND INSTALLED A PHOTON EMISSION SCHEMA WHICH UTILIZES LIGHT WAVES OF DIFFERENT FREQUENCIES TO RETAIN AND TRANSFER DATA. THE PHOTON SYSTEM IS ENTIRELY UNKNOWN TO YOUR TECHNOLOGY, AND WILL PROBABLY REMAIN SO. INFORMATION IS CONSTANTLY PROCESSED IN, BUT IS NEVER PROGRAMMED OUT."

"Has anyone ever tried to tamper with the basic program?"

"TO WHAT END? CHANGE THE WORLD? ALL ONE HAS TO DO IS CUT OFF OUR POWER AT THE SOURCE TO ACHIEVE THAT GOAL. WE HAVE NO FAILSAFE MECHANISMS ON OUR POWER SUPPLY."

"Then why use any safeguards?"

"TO KEEP SOME WELL-MEANING FOOL FROM MAKING AN UNWITTING BLUNDER. IF THE POWER IS TAKEN FROM US, WE WISH IT TO BE A BOLD, CALCULATED ACT, NOT SOME MISCREANT'S MISCUE."

"Most impressive, Doctor. Most impressive."

Dulan jerked his head up to confront the source of the interruption.

Mensik.

"That's all for now, Elmer."

Click, whirrr . . . silence.

"This is a restricted area," Dulan growled with unconcealed distaste. "What do you want?"

"Yes, most impressive," the paunchy man sneered, sauntering into the room to stand before the computer. "The mad genius and his robot sidekick, Elmer. Elmer! For the sake of Complan! What the hell do you think you're running down here, Dulan? A child-care center for chummy computers? Fun and games on government time?"

"Do you have authorization to be down here?" Dulan asked flatly, trying not to let the billowy man rile him.

"Doctor Stuart asked me to look in."

"So you've looked. Now beat it before I call a security guard."

Mensik smiled broadly. "I get the distinct impression, Doctor, that you don't like me very much. That's too bad. You see, I'm not without connections myself, and after eight unsuccessful weeks with your machine, you can use all the friends you can get. You're living on borrowed time now, my friend." Dulan stood and walked protectively between Mensik and the computer. "You're right, Mensik. I don't like you." He jabbed his index finger in the man's stomach. "You're a big fat leech, Mensik. You exist by sucking the humanity out of everyone around you. You make me sick. Get the hell out of my sight," he said, much too loudly, "before I bounce you out on your chubby mouth!"

"Let's not be vindictive, Doctor," Mensik whined, backpedaling out of Dulan's grasp. "I'm going, but we'll keep in close touch. We might be friends yet."

He stood and stared at the Exceptional for a moment, then charged out the door, running into Bea as she came in. "Ah, but of course," he said, bowing from the waist, "Whither goest the great Doctor Dulan, can the beauteous Miss Delacorte be far behind?" He turned back to Dulan, leering. "Heathens in a restricted area, Doctor?" He hurried on before answer could be made.

"Lover's quarrel?" Bea asked.

"He's going home to mother," winked the black man.

She turned to stare at the spot just vacated by Mensik. "He scares me," she said.

"Who?" Dulan replied, his mind already moving in other directions.

Bea crossed her arms sternly. "You know who."

"Oh. Old tubby? He's harmless. Just a pest, mostly. Ignore him."

"Is that what you do?"

"Sure."

"Right. I heard you ignoring him all the way down the hall."

Dulan threw up his hands. "Okay, okay. So I let him get my goat. He struck an exposed nerve."

"Elmer?"

"Yeah."

"Still no luck?" She perched herself on the edge of the desk as he sat down, looking dejected.

"It's been almost two months now," he frowned, "and I'm not any closer to finding anything than I was when I started this mess."

"Won't he talk?"

"Talk! That's all he does, but he never tells me any more than he wants me to know." He slowly shook his head. "Makes me feel like a fool."

"You knew it wouldn't be easy when you started," she chided lightly.

"It's not," he answered, an edge on his voice.

"I'm sure that you'll work it out."

"Don't patronize me, Bea," he said angrily.

Bea stiffened, glaring. "I was only trying to help, Doctor. Pardon me." She jumped up and started for the door.

"Don't," he said quickly. "Please." She stopped in the middle of the room, but kept her back to him. Dulan closed the distance between them in a flash, snaking his arms around her slim waist. "I-I'm sorry," he stammered, nuzzling her neck, the unfamiliar words practically catching in his throat. "I guess that Mensik got me more worked up than I thought."

He turned her around slowly. Her sloe eyes were wet with tears. "You won't even let me help you," she said. "God in heaven, Doral, won't you even let me console you?"

"I'm sorry," he said again, and kissed the tears from her eyes. "Maybe we've both had a long day. Forgiven?"

"And forgotten," she said, returning to her usual good humor. One blown nose and some minor facial repairs later, things were back to normal. "I bet you thought I came down here just to quarrel," she laughed. Reaching into her jumper pocket, she removed a folded piece of paper and handed it to Dulan. "Actually I have a mystery for you to solve."

Dulan unfolded the paper and read: "He who keepeth not holy the Sabbath of the Lord, shall be made to prostrate himself on a bed of thorns." The note was unsigned.

"Where did you get this?" Dulan asked, rereading the short missive.

"I found it on my floor this morning," she answered. "Someone must have pushed it under the door while I was asleep. What does it mean?"

"It's from the *Book of Complan,* but—wait a minute," he said, and going over to the desk controls, turned on the computer. "Elmer?"

"YES, DULAN."

"Identify the following," he said and read the note into the mike.

"BOOK OF COMPLAN, EIGHTH CHAPTER, FIFTEENTH VERSE OF THE ORDER OF THE LAW. IS THAT SUFFICIENT?"

"To what does that refer?"

"THAT PARTICULAR VERSE IS ONE OF A NUMBER OF VERSES GROUPED UNDER THE GENERAL HEADING OF 'CRIMES AGAINST GOD.' WHAT THESE VERSES DO SPECIFICALLY IS GRANT CERTAIN LEGAL POWERS TO THE PRIESTS OF COMPLAN TO ACT UPON RELIGIOUS MISCONDUCT. RELIGIOUS MISCONDUCT BEING DEFINED BY THE PRIEST WHO TAKES THE ACTION."

"I've never heard of anything like that," Dulan said.

"SINCE THE ORDER OF THE LAW IS CONSIDERED TO BE HOLY WRIT, IT IS LEGALLY BINDING, BUT THE TRUTH OF THE MATTER IS THAT THE STATUTES HAVEN'T BEEN USED IN CENTURIES. THEY WERE WRITTEN DURING THE TIME OF THE COMPLANIAN REFORMATION, WHEN FORCE WAS OCCASIONALLY NEEDED TO BRING PEOPLE INTO THE FOLD."

Dulan looked over at Bea, who was still standing in the center of the room. "Have you been going to services?" he asked.

"You know damn good and well that I haven't. Neither have you. But I didn't think there was a law against it."

Dulan thought hard for a minute, rubbing his cheeks with his fingertips. "Just for fun, Elmer," he said, "Give me the limits on what this could mean. Spell it out for me."

"THE ORDER OF THE LAW GIVES THE PRIESTS OF COMPLAN VERY BROAD POWERS WHICH THEY HAVE, ON OCCASION, USED TO RUTHLESS AND INHUMAN EXTENTS, BUT THOSE POWERS

HAVE ALWAYS BEEN TEMPERED TO THE TIMES, AND ABSENCE FROM SERVICES IS REALLY NOT CONSIDERED AN ACT OF HERESY THESE DAYS—ESPECIALLY IN A MILCOM. WERE YOU THREATENED WITH THIS PASSAGE?''

''Not me,'' Dulan said, ''an . . . associate.''

''WOULD THAT BE MISS DELACORTE?''

Dulan stared at the machine in shocked surprise. ''How did you know about her?''

''AN EDUCATED GUESS. YOUR CREDIT CHARGES ALWAYS SEEM TO COME THROUGH TOGETHER. AND WHEN THEY DON'T, ONE BILL OR THE OTHER IS TWICE WHAT ONE PERSON WOULD SPEND. YOU TWO ARE ALWAYS IN THE SAME PLACE AT THE SAME TIME, WHICH EITHER MAKES YOU LOVERS OR CONSPIRATORS.''

Bea stamped her foot. ''Well, I don't think that I like the impli . . .''

Dulan waved her to silence, a large grin on his face. ''You're right about Miss Delacorte. Do you have any suggestions?''

''YES. AN IDENTITY CHECK WAS RUN ON MISS DELACORTE THE THIRTEENTH OF SEPTEMBER FROM THE CHAPEL TYPER, WHICH LEADS US TO ASSUME THAT YOUR ANONYMOUS THREAT COMES FROM BROTHER MATRIX PERSONALLY. IF THAT IS SO, AND BROTHER MATRIX INTENDED TO MAKE TROUBLE, HE WOULD HAVE DONE SO WITHOUT SENDING A WARNING. THERE IS SOMETHING ELSE THAT HE WANTS, AND THE ONLY WAY TO FIND OUT IS TO ATTEND SERVICES AS THIS NOTE DEMANDS. THAT IS OUR ADVICE. DO NOT IGNORE THE WARNING—BROTHER MATRIX IS NOT TO BE TAKEN LIGHTLY.''

''Thanks, Elmer,'' Dulan responded, and shut down the machine. Clasping his hands behind his head, he leaned back and put his feet on the desk top. ''I won't say that I told you so.''

''Why is everything so difficult,'' Bea said while moving Dulan's feet slightly to make room for herself. ''What does he want with me?''

''You know what he wants. The man's an infamous lecher.''

''But why me? He can have any woman he wants.''

''You spurned him that night in the chapel. I admit you did it graciously, but you spurned him nonetheless. Your unattainability has made you highly desirable. I warned you about it before.''

She slapped his leg. ''What's that I seem to remember about no 'I told you so's?' ''

He reddened. "Sorry. You will go to services Sunday, won't you?"

"Only if you'll go with me," she returned.

"I will on one condition," he responded. "Tell me about Burnu."

She looked perplexed. "He's one of the gods of my people. The god of the sun."

"The legend. Tell me about the legend."

"Legend..." she said in a distant voice, as if she were physically walking down the twisted pathways of a dim past and calling out to the present. "You mean of the Saver? It's a superstition that seems to be common to most of the tribes. Probably common to all oppressed people."

"Tell me," he insisted.

"The usual. Burnu will send his son to lead the tribes against the tyranny of the arrogators. Bring peace and prosperity. Unite the tribes. You know, the whole routine. It is said that confusion will rend asunder the minds of the wall dwellers, and it is then that Burnuai will rise up to reclaim the land for all people."

Dulan removed his feet from the desk and sat with his hands folded, and his forehead knotted in concentration. "What will this deliverer look like?"

"Doral! Give me a break will you? It's been too many years, I don't think that I can..."

"Please, try."

"I-I think, human. Ordinary. No, wait! There is something—a rhyme." She wiggled her hand in the air while trying to put it together in her mind. Then her face creased into a relaxed demeanor and she recited:

> Son of the Sun,
> The great walls to crack.
> Blood on his cheek,
> Burned black as black.

Dulan raised his eyebrows. "A black man?" he asked.

"I suppose so. What's this all about?"

"I don't know," he answered. "Nothing. Everything." His voice trailed off. Opening a drawer, he extracted a pencil and paper and began writing furiously.

Bea watched him silently for a time. She had seen him like this before—he didn't even know that she was in the room.

She slipped out quietly, closing the door behind her. There would be no backgammon that night.

. . . The man was brought forth, chained and beaten, and presented before the eyes of Complan. When the servant of the Lord saw this he became enraged, and screamed a mighty scream.

"Why do you treat this man in such a manner?" he cried. "He is the enemy, our noble foe, given to us by the Lord to parry on the field of honorable combat. You bring dishonor to us all by your insensitive treatment."

With that, Complan withdrew from his bandolier an automatic pistol, and putting it to the temple of the prisoner he intoned solemnly, "Rejoice, Brother, I send you with honor to the bosom of your Creator . . ."

—*Book of Complan* (8-4, 5)

The world holds two classes of men—intelligent men without religion, and religious men without intelligence.

—Abu'l-Ala-Al-Ma'arri

10

The stairway to heaven was packed solid. Three abreast, they lined the chapel's spiral staircase and shoved their way slowly into the candle-alive chamber, so that once more they could revel in the immortality of an unseen spirit and re-justify the monotonous redundancy of their existences. In the midst of the throng—an Exceptional and an Outsider who weathered the human gale silently, for they had nothing to share that would have set properly on the ears of unwanted listeners.

When, at last, they did attain entry to the large hall, it was already nearing capacity and several hundred worshippers who still waited on the steps had to be turned away.

"Over there," said Bea, pointing to a small cloud pillow off to the side that was just large enough for two. Like children, they threw themselves onto the downy cushion and let their muscles soften and relax to blend with the easy contours of the bolster.

The congregation spoke—but softly, either out of reverence for a holy place or because dark places seem to elicit whispers for their own sake. Whatever the reason, the conglomeration of murmurs, reverberating through the hollow hall, intoned a steady rumble not unlike the bombinations of a roiling sea.

Acceptably sanctimonious organ music hummed softly in the background but grew in blatancy as a herald of the beginning of the ceremony. A giant mobile was lowered slowly from the ceiling and began a languorous, clockwork rotation. Dulan strained his eyes in the darkness to get a good look, but he could not. Suddenly, pinspots of light sliced out from all of the walls to bombard the moving sculpture with cascades of dancing, twinkling illumination. The congregation gasped, Bea and Dulan along with them, for it was a grand sight, and nearly blinding in its intensity. The mobile was large, perhaps thirty meters across, and turned as a unit. But within the whole lay a thousand tiny arms, all gyrating mechanically—interchanging and interacting, intertwining and interweaving—but all courses predestined.

Angels there were—and devils.

Sweet-faced cherubim astride bombs and hoisting rifles high with their little dimpled angel arms. And monstrous gargoyles with slant eyes and grotesque sexual organs—all done in solid, shiny, shameless gold. A morality play in one act of countless scenes.

Dulan watched, hypnotized, as the multiplicity of miniature seraphs and satyrs swirled and spun together, reenacting the eon weary struggle of good against evil.

Then, as suddenly as it had begun, the mobile show ended with the extinguishing of the small spots on the wall, leaving only the anticlimactic dancing of the candlelight. The lag lasted only a few seconds . . .

Flash! Herman Matrix stood stage center bathed in the garish glare of an overhead klieg. Clothed only in his satin skullcap, he slowly turned 360 degrees so that the entire congregation could drink in his blessed visage.

"Here we go," Bea whispered into Dulan's ear.

"Brothers and Sisters," Matrix called at the top of his voice.

Two thousand people were instantly on their feet, arms raised above their heads. From somewhere down deep within the human collective memory they dredged a sound—a primal sound that grew in volume until it was frightening in its sonority.

"Brothers and Sisters," Matrix called again, and the din subsided. "Who is the Word of Life and Truth?"

"Complan," they cried in return.

"Who is the lighter of the true path?"

"Complan!" they yelled in response.

"Who is the salvation of the children of God?"

"Complan! Complan!" They were screaming now, on their feet again. This time the demonstration lasted for several minutes before Brother Matrix raised his hands for silence.

"My friends, we are gathered together here in the eyes of Almighty God to celebrate our redemption from the realms of darkness and ignorance. To glory in our tabernacle of salvation, we are gathered here. To rejoice in the suffering of our enemies we come together." Matrix was wandering about the round stage, gesturing theatrically, grabbing the emotions of the audience. "Behold! The image of Complan."

The lights blazed in the corner where the shrine stood, sending the mannequin into vociferous activity. "My children," spoke the shrine, reading out to them. "Dost thou love me truly?"

This set off another demonstration, which went on unchecked while chapel assistants made their way through the congregation passing out altar drugs to the children of God. Bea and Dulan declined the cross-shaped triamphetemesc tabs, but stood with the rest of the congregation to avoid being conspicuous.

The Living Shrine made a sermon, fraught with the beauties of just war, that lasted only long enough for the upper-laced mind expanders to take effect. Then the real ceremony began.

The liturgy of life and death.

Gas jets in the floor were opened, and yellow sodium vapor billowed from a hundred outlets, filling the chamber with a perverse, dirty-looking fog. Strong strobes began flashing—purple, lavender, scarlet; angry colors kicking in and out with brain-straining swiftness. An obtrusive rumbling sound drifted down from overhead, like the roar of distant thunder—or cannons.

War by night.

The children of God, flying with religious frenzy and triamphetemesc began throwing off their clothes and charging around like lunatics, accosting and assaulting each other in mock attack; losing themselves in the sanctity of holy war.

"How can they demean themselves that way?" Bea asked from the noncombatant status of their cushion.

"It's just like any other ritual," Dulan replied, leaning back and making himself comfortable. Had Bea not been along, he might very well have joined in the revelry, but he knew she thought it perverted, so he let it slide. "Who's to define what's demeaning or not? Com dwellers think that Outsiders are animals."

"Touché."

A large stuffed effigy of a Chinese was brought up on the stage. Under the direction of Brother Matrix, the congregation was allowed to come up on the stage one by one and slice at the dummy with a long-bladed scythe. Inside the rag-man was a quantity of small sacks filled with red paint, and with each slash of the blade, make-believe gore splattered prodigiously in every direction. The congregation went wild, massing around the stage, smearing the ritual blood all over their now naked bodies. The affirmation of death did not stop until the dummy was an unrecognizable pile of tatters lying on the stage.

They had rejoiced in death. Next came the renewal of life.

Matrix was still the key. The orgy could not start without him. He stepped down from the stage and slowly made his way through the emotionalized mob that crowded around him like maggots around a rotting corpse. It was the highest of honors to be chosen by the holy man to perform the Rite of Life with him, and the women threw and prostrated themselves before him, begging to be chosen. Occasionally Matrix would stop and fondle this morsel or taste that, much to the delight of the chosen people, but he always continued onward—searching.

"My God, he's coming this way," Bea said, visibly tightening.

"Yeah," Dulan responded. "I had a feeling he might."

Once Matrix spotted them, there was no doubt left about what he had in mind. He walked quickly up to their cushion and stood directly before Bea, his semierect organ dangling in her face.

"I choose you, heathen," Matrix said with a grim smile. His face was like a viper's.

"No," Bea responded, and her eyes were cold and unbending. She regarded his rigidity as if it were a dead mackerel.

A slight surprise showed on his countenance, but determination was there also. "It is not lawful to refuse a priest of Complan," he retorted.

"No," she repeated.

"Don't you understand, woman?" he glowered through clenched teeth. "You cannot deny me. A word . . . a hint from me and those people would tear you apart."

Bea merely stared at his ever-deflating ego. Dulan looked at

Matrix. Gone from his face was the surprise and the determination. All that was left was rage.

A crowd began to gather around them, wondering what was holding up the ceremony.

Matrix bent low and whispered hoarsely, "I intend to have you, heathen. Even if I have to kill you to do it." And he reached for her arms, trying to pull her to her feet.

Dulan touched his forearm lightly. Matrix jerked his head in the black man's direction as if he were seeing him for the first time. "Stay out of this, Exceptional," he wheezed.

"He who sows his seed in the furrow of the wilderness, shall forever be anathema in the eyes of God," Dulan said, just loud enough for the priest to hear. Then he released the old man's arm and sank leisurely back into his seat.

The priest of Complan thought deeply for a moment, then looked around at his congregation. Reluctantly, he took his hands off Bea and nodded in Dulan's direction. "You're well read, black man," he sneered. "It appears that we've reached an impasse . . . for now."

With that, Matrix turned and pointed to the first woman he saw. Squealing with delight she wrapped herself around his body and they stumbled back to the stage. The woman lay spread-eagled on the bomb-shaped sacrificial table. Matrix climbed on the table with her and knelt between her gaping thighs, raising his arms in supplication.

"May a child be superfetated this day for the armies of Complan," Matrix intoned solemnly.

"Amen," the congregation responded.

The anthem and response given, the priest of Complan fell upon his chosen partner. A thunderous ovation arose from the children of God, who then carried out their roles in the Rite of Life.

Screaming like banshees, they threw themselves to the floor, writhing and twisting in sexual abandon. There was no love involved, nor partners for that matter—just a pounding, sweating heap of festering sex.

Alone in their corner, Bea and Dulan watched the spectacle. She was sobbing quietly—an aftermath of her encounter with Brother Matrix—and he had his arm around her shoulders, comforting.

"I think that he would have killed me," she said after a few minutes.

"This is his domain, Bea," Dulan replied. "He could have done anything that he wanted."

"What was it you said to him?"

Dulan flashed her a toothy grin. "Herman Matrix isn't the only one who's read the *Book of Complan,*" he answered. "I met him on his own ground and caught him unaware. For all his shortcomings, Brother Matrix knows that his hold over these people isn't any stronger than his day-to-day ability to keep them duped as to the extent of his power and holiness. He must maintain the aura of control, and a battle of wits was the last thing that he needed right now."

"You're wonderful," she said, hugging him.

"Don't kid yourself," he answered. "We're in way over our heads, and it's all going to come home. Every bit of it. As for right now . . . I think we should sneak out while the sneaking's good."

Keeping quietly in the shadows, they edged their way around the skyed-up, moaning tangle of humanity and reached the double doors without incident.

They quickly traversed the stairway to heaven and plunged into the midst of the labyrinth. The avenues of the maze were unusually crowded that day, and everywhere that Bea and Dulan walked, they were assailed by murmurings of war.

"Backgammon?" he asked, coming to a stop in front of one of their favorite pubs.

She smiled, shaking her head. "How do you manage to juggle all these different lives so well?" she asked.

"Mirrors," he responded with a look of mock seriousness. "It's all done with mirrors."

Images:

Subtle symmetrical shadowy substance drifting into perspective only to slip away just out of the grasp of consciousness.

"It's very compelling," whispered Bea.

Dulan nodded. It *was* compelling. A series of low-intensity lights moving lazily, soporifically, changing hue and texture as they drifted across the dimly lit screen.

The theater was small, and completely immersed in darkness. Dulan sat with Bea toward the back, near the door. Seated in the middle of the room were Jones and the others in his Telp group, twenty in all. The Telps were in a light hypnotic trance and sat, nodding and speechless, lost in the patterns of multibrightness on the screen that surrounded them 180 degrees.

Impressive as the visual display was, Dulan could not discern its function. He sat patiently for a few minutes, and was just about to ask Bea what the hell was going on, when he heard it.

The sound.

The sound came up slowly, agonizingly, from the lowest range of audibility. Dulan felt it before he heard it. Bass vibrations that felt as if they were originating inside his cranium. Just a tension, a feeling. Then it was on him.

The sound.

It was just there, one second dreamlike and the next real, without noticeable line of demarkation. A one-note drone. A vibrating impulse. A noise, but an enjoyable noise.

It came at regular intervals at first, slowly, very slowly. Then almost imperceptibly the tempo began to increase. Then Dulan heard the other sound. It was pitched higher, more trebly, so he didn't pick it up as quickly. It was voices. Female. A chorus of voices singing without words. The tonations joined to form a sound that seemed to draw on the soul for its essence.

The volume climbed gradually for a time, then peaked and held steady at a range that was just loud enough to force itself upon the senses, but not harsh or disquieting. The fidelity was amazing. Dulan had never heard anything like it. The sound assaulted him from everywhere. The floor, the chair backs, everything oozed with pitch and timbre. It was as if the whole room were one giant speaker with people trapped inside. The experience was total.

As the cadence increased, Dulan felt himself being swept involuntarily along with the flow. His body, nerves, muscles, even his blood felt as if it were throbbing with the pulse beat. He fought the rising tide mentally for as long as he could, then gave up and moved with the current.

A single voice began to speak. It throbbed steadily, inexorably in a soothing monotone that intertwined perfectly with the all-prevading rhythmic sounds that now formed the core of Dulan's existence. The voice was in control, but the language was unfamiliar.

"Chinese," said Bea.

Dulan wanted to respond, just to prove that he could do it, so with some difficulty, he nodded. Gently rocking now, throbbing in time, he was ready for the next event.

A face slowly came into focus on the screen. The Chinese man about whom the voice was obviously speaking. The face dominated the screen for a while, only to fade out of sync to be replaced by another image of the same man. Pictures began coming in short bursts. There were many stills, and a few pieces of film. The editing was skillful, blending the short pieces of celluloid into a story, the sum total of a man; the photographic measure of his lifetime from earliest childhood to adult status. Dulan found the story interesting; disturbingly so.

And always there was the sound. Rising sometimes to crescendos that carried the listeners through the emotional peaks of the man's life, only to slowly fall once more to simpler rhythms and an easy pulse that made Dulan want to breathe a sigh of relief. Robbed as he was of an understanding of the language being spoken, he missed many of the subtler points of the empathetic biography, but even without the advantage of the narrator, by the time the show was over, he felt intimately acquainted with the Chinese.

When the lights came up to signify the end of the performance, Dulan felt as if he were losing a friend. He felt emotionally drained and physically exhausted, so much had he given to the man's story. While feeling his tense muscles relax, he watched the Telp group being led from the auditorium; they were glassy-eyed and shuffling.

"What do you think?" asked Bea.

"Amazing," Dulan responded. "But what was it?"

Bea gently massaged her stiff neck. "You've been so busy lately, we haven't had too much time to talk about it. The man was General Sing, newly appointed unit commander of the People's Forces in the North. He's replacing the late General Du Chang."

"The new enemy offensive?"

"Right. And Dan is right in the middle of the whole business. Computer predicts the offensive shortly, maybe within weeks. When it comes, the Telps assigned to General Sing will be finished with their training and begin scanning in earnest."

"You're becoming quite knowledgeable about the whole thing," Dulan said, unable to keep a note of surprise out of his voice.

"Not really," she answered. "I just pick up my information from Dan as he's exposed to it."

"Why was the narration in Chinese?"

"The Telps are being submerged in the lifestyle of the man

they monitor. They now speak fluent Chinese, to the point of unlearning their own language."

"You mean they don't speak English anymore?"

"Don't speak it, don't understand it. They eat only the foods that Sing eats, and they even sleep on mats instead of beds. It all apparently helps."

"They were hypnotized in here, right?"

Bea smiled. "So were you and I to a certain extent."

"Wait a minute," Dulan laughed. "I admit that I was drawn to it a bit, but it was that sound and . . ."

"How long did the show run, Doral?"

He shrugged. "I don't know. Half hour, forty-five minutes."

"Try again," she said and held her wristwatch up for him to see.

"Five hours," he muttered, unable to believe the truth of his own eyes. "We've been sitting here for five hours?"

"Where have you been, lover?"

He shook his head. "Can you learn anything that way?"

"Sure," said Bea, falling right into her bedside manner. "Try and remember what you saw."

Dulan tried, and he remembered. Every detail about General Sing's life was right there, sitting on his memory as if the event had actually happened to him.

"Amazing," he said again.

"Don't get too excited," she said. "Hypno learning is great for the short term, but it generally doesn't stick with you. The Telps have seen that film many times and will probably see it many more. There's still a lot to be said for the old-fashioned rote method."

Another group of jump-suited Telps marched methodically into the theater and took the places vacated by the preceding group.

"Oh oh, next shift," Bea said. "We'd better move along, unless you'd like to stay and sit through the show again."

"No, thanks," answered Dulan, standing up on stiff knees. "Much more of General Sing, and I'm afraid that I'd be speaking Chinese."

They made their way out of the room just as the house lights went down and the patterns began once again on the screen.

Images.

PRIVATE JOURNAL
B. DELACORTE MD. PH.D.

Re: Patient—Jones, Daniel T.

Entry 43
12 Oct.

I'm failing. They're taking away his mind, and there's nothing that I can do about it. In the three short months that I've been treating Dan, his initial normality has degenerated into a kind of mental affliction that exists only in the textbooks. Hardly a testimonial to my skill as a doctor. Their systems of control are sophisticated and methodical, and Dan has been swept along like the people in the pirate movie running full sail before a high wind. I've never felt so helpless in all my life.

My time with Dan is limited and grows more limited. He's responding so well to their "treatments" that my usefulness shrinks with each passing day. Our once daily sessions have been cut to two a week, and are allowed, even at that, only grudgingly.

They've stopped the telemetric conditioning—he no longer needs it.

His memory of himself and his past life is almost nonexistent now, thanks to the Brain Stingers. Soon it will be gone completely. I fear for the man's mental life, but perhaps a breakdown is the only way to get him out of this monkey house.

Transcript follows:

D: How are you today, Dan?
J: J-Just fine, Doctor. Very well.
D: I haven't seen you for a while.
J: Seen? No. They—we have much to do now. Busy. I-I've missed you.
D: I've missed you too. Are they treating you all right?
J: Yes . . . I think, yes. English. Hard for me to think in your language. Speak we only Chinese.
D: Is that a difficulty?
J: No. My . . . brain, it works Chinese. Don't think I that the others even remember how English. You understand?
D: Yes. Can you remember the last time you were here?

J: You were kind to me. Always kind.
D: Do you remember what we talked about?
J: Before-time. To remember before-time.
D: Your childhood. Yes. Can we talk about it?
J: Child . . . child. What's child? S-sorry . . . no child my mind in. (Patient begins to weep here—he wants so to please me.)
D: That's all right, Dan. Stop crying. It's all right.
J: Sorry. I-I . . .
D: It's all right. Really. There, that's better isn't it? Don't worry. You're doing just fine. Okay?
J: Yes.
D: Do you remember anything about the Destruction crews?
J: No. No I—wait. Remember I something from before-time. (Patient becomes excited—agitated.)
D: Yes, Dan?
J: Guns. Yes guns. Fighting with guns. *Ni shir-bu-shir bing!* Yes. No prisoners, no wounded. Ever. Death . . . laughing death. *Sir-le shyau*. Hydra . . . hydra . . . hydra . . .
D: Hydra?
J: Yes! Bullets touch you . . . touch your blood and die—laughing. No good . . . laughing dead men. Many men. Men and men and men. Captain green shoes tell I kill them. They give me bullets . . . a box full. So many men. All young like me. Stand I with my gun. Listen. Hear others laugh all around. So many men. Faces . . . grinning the death grin. (Dan becomes more agitated here, but began to convulse automatically without the telemetry. Conditioned response. He calmed immediately.) Shaking . . . shaking all over. Couldn't do it. I-I just couldn't. Traitor, they called me, and dog. Spat they on me and locked me in chains.
D: What happened then?
J: That's everything . . . all that there is.
D: Dan, do you like me?
J: Yes. Pretty woman. Very beautiful, and very kind.
D: Do you still enjoy coming to visit with me?
J: I do. But the others . . . the other doctors. They think bad it is for me to come here. I listen when they talk.
D: What do you think?

J: I—I know it's not right to leave my group. I belong there, but I have . . . feelings for you and come back I.
D: Dan, I have an important question to ask you and I want you to think very carefully before answering, okay? Are you happy?
J: I don't know happy. I have my life here, and that's all know I. What happy? Complete? Not complete until joined with Sing. The joining will make us complete.
D: Have you communicated with his mind at all yet?
J: No, but soon. Very soon.
D: Do you look forward to it?
j: The joining? I long for it. I am empty without it.
D: What about you, Dan, your life. Don't you want a life of your own?
J: No life have I. I will live through Sing.

I must reach him, somehow free his mind. This psychological suppression cannot do him any good at all. I need help in making a reasonable diagnosis. I've perused my medical books in great detail, but it's as if Dan's symptoms were totally unknown. D. has spoken of an Old Worlder named Freud; maybe the answer to my problem lies in the past. All I know is that Dan's emotions must find an outlet—somewhere. Anything can happen, and it all seems so inevitable.

As evidenced from the transcript, Dan has developed an emotional attachment for me. It's natural, and happens often within the framework of insight therapy. The patient will usually use the analyst as a replacement figure for someone he was close to at some time in his life. Dan has never been close to anyone, so he's fallen in love with me.

Due to his telemetric conditioning, it's impossible for Dan's feelings to find normal emotional outlets, so he's responded in kind by developing a form of idolization of me. A kind of "worship from afar" syndrome. I don't really approve of the whole idea, but I allow it to continue because it seems to be the only honest emotion that he has left in his entire body. I don't know where this will end, but it appears to be harmless enough for now.

I tried giving them a taste of their own medicine today. Grasping at straws actually. I put Dan in a light hypnotic trance and subjected him to a mini-version of the low-intensity light screen that they use in the learning rooms. Only I had him use his imagination to free associate the light patterns with real world objects and put on paper what he saw. We repeated the procedure several times, with the exception of the lights. After the first time, I turned off the lights and just suggested to Dan that they were on. The process is called conditioned hallucination and is supposed to free the patient's brain to explore the realms of his subconscious. It should have worked quite well. It didn't. The results after five tests were remarkable in their similarity. Instead of five freely conceived and widely varied mind excursions, he came up with five pictures of a—balloon. A gas balloon with a passenger gondola and emblazoned with a picture of the sun.

What does it mean? Why should his mania take this particular form? Perhaps I'm just not doctor enough to help him. Perhaps he's beyond help.

War is the only topic of conversation at Forty-Three these days. They expect the Northern offensive to begin any time. I wish that I could get Dan away from this before that happens, but I'm only one person and we are buried here so deeply. So very deeply.

It happened that Complan took his tank into the desert and fasted for forty days and forty nights. And during his fast, a procession of rag-begotten misfits marched past, for their path and the servant of the Lord's connected in space and time. When he saw those who rejected the words of God, he was overcome with sadness and wept until he was run dry of tears.

Then the Lord appeared to him in a pillar of fire and spoke thus: "Weep not, my child, for the outcast children of Sin. Those who hear the Word and refuse it are of no more importance than a song to the deaf man. The ways of righteousness are strewn with rocks. All obstacles must be dealt with as enemies, for many are called, but few are chosen."

—*Book of Complan* (10—27,28)

11

Late October

Fluid and comfortable, Bea stretched indolently on Dulan's mote of a bed and watched him feed his fish. Her ears were filled with incorporeal sounds, the malevolent melody bleeped out by his computer music box in the strange minor key that he enjoyed to the exclusion of all others. As she watched the naked black man ministering to his charges to the beat of the other-worldly symphony, she became inutterably amused and found it impossible to contain her laughter.

"What's so funny?" Dulan asked as he cakewalked over to the box to change the tempo.

"Where should I begin?" she teased. Sitting up on the bed, she fussed with her hair. "Doral Dulan, you're a pack rat."

"I think I'm being insulted," he grimaced.

Putting her hands on her hips, Bea slowly rotated her head, drinking in the surroundings. "Just look at this place," she demanded. "Three months ago it was bare walls. Now a girl can't even find a place to put her toothbrush."

Brashly mimicking her gesture, he slowly turned his head, circumnavigating the chamber with his eyes. The room was crammed, floor to ceiling, with dusty tomes of dubious nature, maps and posters of unknown origin, furniture of unmatching configuration, the usual assortment of cathode tubes, oscilloscopes, receivers, transformers, transistors, resistors and oscillators, plus a perfectly ghastly stuffed alligator and a wide array of elaborately weird machinery that did god-only-knows-what, and, of course, a hundred-and-fifty-gallon aquarium that gobbled up half of the room by itself. Even the bathroom was piled high with electrical junk, dominated by a large arc welder. All this he had very carefully gleaned from material control.

"I'm a man of varied tastes," he sighed.

"But how do you get away with it all?"

"Carte blanche, remember? Rank has its privileges."

"Tell me about the fish tank."

"Well, down on seven some of your fellow humanitarians were doing some research on the central nervous system. Fish are the best place to start. Simple, easy to study. Anyhow, the tank was in storage up on one. Getting the fish was a bit harder. I got to know one of the blockhouse guards and had him do a deal with Sergeant Jarsen, the man who delivers goods and personnel out here. Jarsen is the senior noncom over at the airfield, which just happens to be the material disbursement point for this part of the country. At one time or another, just about everything you can imagine goes through there. I just had Jarsen reroute some fish our way."

Getting up, Bea went to the chair and searched through her clothes until she found the hairbrush tangled within. She sat back down and began vigorously stroking her golden mane. "How did you get them to do it?" she asked.

"I made the guard one of the music computers. He took care of Jarsen."

"How industrious."

"Why don't you make yourself useful and pour us a glass of wine while I finish this?"

Rising again, she rummaged through the junk heap, stopping here and there to gaze in bewilderment at some undefinable anomoly that he had placed among his garbage collection. "And where do you hide your wine cellar?"

He absently tugged his earlobe. "Try behind the origami."

"Where?" she asked, too confused to even pretend understanding.

"The origami, next to the oscilloscope."

She found the wave recorder and the large intricately folded paper that sat mutely beside it. Reaching behind the origami, she came out with a bottle. "Presto. Now how about some glasses?"

"Glasses . . . glasses. Hell, I can't remember. Just trot that bottle over here." Bea waltzed the container across the room and placed it in his hand. Dulan pulled out the cork and took a long drink. Then he handed the bottle back to Bea who followed suit.

"How romantic," she said. Glancing down to the aquarium, she gasped in astonishment. Several pairs of the fish seemed to be locked, mouth-to-mouth, in mortal combat. They were struggling ferociously. "Are they fighting?" she asked.

Dulan shook his head. "Mating."

She made a face. "Do all fish mate like that?" she persisted, thinking that he was giving her the business.

"No. These are all cichlids. I prefer them because they're aggressive and make their own place in the world. When cichlids are ready to mate, they look around very carefully for a suitable partner. When they think they've found their dreamboat, they attack them . . . just like that." He pointed to a particularly frenzied pair of combatants. "If the chosen mate stands up to the attack, the fish find themselves compatible and live happily ever after . . . at least until the eggs are fertilized."

"What if the chosen one doesn't want to fight?"

He took another drink of wine, wiping his mouth with the back of his hand. "If the selected partner shows fear or attempts to escape, the other will chase him down and kill him." He handed the bottle back to Bea.

"That's disgusting," she said simply.

"Quite the contrary," Dulan spoke seriously. "It's nature's way of weeding out the weaker members of the species. Keeps the breed strong. Are human beings really so much different? I fear that you've been away from the outside too long."

"Maybe so, but you'd better not try any of that stuff on me."

A maniacal leer spread across Dulan's face. He opened his mouth wide and began working it around in a most repulsive manner. Stretching out his arms, he trundled after Bea robot-like. She screeched and began running around the room with him close on her heels. Laughing, they chased around like that for a couple of minutes. Finally, he caught up to her and threw her, still laughing, on the bed. Pinning her with his body, he held her head still and came at her face, mouth twitching obscenely.

Bea, realizing that she was still in possession of the half-emptied bottle of wine, lifted it and poured some down his back. Her action caught him completely unawares, and he jumped up like a spring snake in a peanut can, jerking his head around—flabbergasted. When he understood what had transpired, he convulsed with laughter, doubling over at the waist.

"Hey, that was good wine," he cackled.

"And I put it to good use," she shot back. "Maybe there's some Outsider left in me yet."

Dulan sat back down on the bed, beginning to feel sticky and rank. "Me for a cold shower," he reported.

"You're being redundant, darling."

"So I am. Care to join me?" He strode into the bathroom, pushed the arc welder aside, and turned on the water.

"Best offer I've had all day," she called from the chamber proper. "Say, Doral, what time is it anyway?"

"Daytime," he called back. "I think it's daytime."

"No, seriously."

He appeared at the bathroom door, looking apologetic. "Sorry, I really don't know. Not working on a regular time schedule, I have no reason to have a clock."

"What about your alarm clock?" She came into the bathroom and climbed into the shower with Dulan. "Yeech," she cried when the frigid liquid streaked across her body.

"It broke," he answered. "So I threw it away."

Picking up the soap, she turned him around and began lathering his broad, muscled back. "You mean to tell me that in all this wall-to-wall garbage there's not one timepiece?"

"There may be a sundial in there, but I don't think that it will do you much good," he replied, turning around to face her. "You know something? There isn't anything sexier than a woman taking a shower." He pulled her close and they kissed deeply, lingeringly. Coming together, they made love, standing up, in the cold, cold shower.

The continual Complanian monologues that poured forth from the wall speaker were usually so nondescript as to be almost subliminal. After a short time of listening, the conscious mind was simply no longer aware of the verbalization and the messages were directed solely at the inner mind. This voice was different, it fairly crackled over the loudspeaker:

DOCTOR DELACORTE, PLEASE REPORT TO YOUR OFFICE IMMEDIATELY.

Dulan came in from the shower, shivering, still drying his hair. He stared stupidly at the wall grid. It repeated the message.

"Hey Bea!" he yelled. "This damn thing's calling you to your office."

Bea came charging into the room and hurriedly began dressing. "That's why I needed to know the time. I've got an appointment."

"I didn't even know that these things did that," he mumbled, tapping the grillwork with his knuckles.

"Sure. They've called me every once in a while."

"Well I'll be damned. Wonder why they called you in here?"

Bea laughed. "I think that your friend Mensik has been telling tales out of school." She walked over to the small check-in telephone and lifted the receiver. "Delacorte . . . right. On my way." She turned to Dulan. "Well don't just stand there. Get some clothes on yourself."

He obediently started dressing in one of the ever-present jump suits. "I take it that I'm going with you."

"Yeah," she replied. "I think you'll be interested." She walked up to him backwards so that he could zip her dress.

Instead, he parted it even more and started nuzzling her back. "Doral! Stop . . . stop! Are you ready? We've really got to be going."

"Except for my shoes." He sat on the edge of the bed and fumbled with his loafers. Bea rushed back into the bathroom and combed her hair.

Dulan called after her. "What's so exciting that I have to see it?"

She came back into the room. "Not it—she."

"Wha?"

"C'mon. I'll explain on the way. Don't forget your badge."

He retrieved his I.D. tag from the depths of a box full of cams and gear motors, and they started for the elevators. As they walked, Bea talked:

"A couple of days ago I was really beginning to feel depressed. Had another bad session with Dan . . . then there's all this time that I have on my hands."

"Hey, you always know where to find me."

She grimaced quite convincingly. "I've been to some of your man-to-machine talkathons before. No, thank you. When you're wrapped up with cuddles down there, your fish would make better company."

"Sorry."

"Uh huh. Anyway, realizing that Doctor Stuart and I hadn't exchanged pleasantries . . ."

"Pleasantries?"

". . . . for a long time, I marched myself up to his ivory tower to harass him for more time with Dan, or more work, or—anything really."

"You push right up to the edge, don't you?"

"Makes life interesting. So here I am, ready for a good old tooth and nail with Mr. S.O.P. himself, and what should happen?"

"The suspense is killing me," he answered with raised eyebrows. They reached the elevator complex and, finding a vacant lift, started down smoothly to seven.

"Instead of an ice pick in the back, the old scud acts as if he's almost glad to see me. Tells me that he was just getting ready to page me. You could've knocked me over with a feather."

"No doubt."

"As it turns out, some joker farther up the chain of command came to precisely the same conclusion that I had reached about my having too little to do and too much time in which to do it. So they've sent me another patient."

They reached seven uneventfully and started for Bea's office. "Another Telp?" Dulan asked.

"Nope. A Precog."

"Precog?"

"Precognitiant. A seer . . . oracle, whatever you want to call it."

Dulan jammed his hands in his pocket and hunched over a tad. "You mean somebody who can predict the future?"

"You got it."

"I didn't know that was really possible."

She stuck out her lower lip. "I suppose that there are those who would debate the issue . . ." Rather than begin a lengthy discussion, she shrugged it off. "We never really studied precognition very much at the psi center. Apparently this Precog is an Outsider who turned herself in at one of the coms. During admittance, her psyche-pros showed remarkable staochistic abilities, so the computer routed her here for further study. It seems that my parapsychological training won't go to waste."

"And you're an Outsider," he added.

Her eyes flashed. "I suppose that Amalgamech takes all factors into consideration."

"I didn't mean it that way," he said quietly.

"I'm sorry," she replied. "Defense mechanism. I'm used to having people throw it back in my face. Here we are."

Pushing open the door, they slipped into the tiny office. They saw her before she caught sight of them. She was sitting, thin and fragile, in the patient-chair still wrapped in her elk robes. Her raven hair was stringy and matted and hung well past her shoulders. A slash of gray swarthed her hair from the left temple straight back along her skull, giving her face a slightly asymmetrical appearance. Dulan estimated her age at about forty-five years, but knew from his previous dealings with the people of the outer world that she was probably much younger. Her face was drawn and pale, and it didn't take an expert in medicine to see that she was not well. Bony fingers clasped, the woman sat stock still, reticent.

Bea walked timidly to where the Outsider was seated and extended her hand. "My name is Beatrice Delacorte," she said. "I'm pleased to meet you."

The woman looked up slowly, blinking. Her chapped lips quivered momentarily, then she unexpectedly burst into tears. Bea hunched down on her knees and grasped the sobbing woman by the shoulders.

"What is it? What's the matter?"

Hugging Bea to her bosom, the woman wailed happily, "The matter? Oh darlin', is nothing can be the matter now. Beatrice Delacorte—daughter of Lawgivers, Princess, niece."

Bea's eyes went wide and she pulled away from the woman, holding her at arm's length. "Amala, Amala! Is it really you?"

"Yes, my darlin'. Lemman fair. Here to fetch you home to the woon." With that, both women began weeping profusely, much to Dulan's embarrassment. It took several minutes before they were calm enough to speak.

"How did you come to be here?" Bea asked as she dried her eyes on Dulan's handkerchief.

"With the spring comes grand council, Beatrice. T'was time of your return to the fold. When you nae come back to us your father becomes like the raging bull elk at mating."

"I can picture Father, cursing and fuming," Bea's eyes began to mist over again, even though she was smiling.

"Aye," replied Amala. "Sometimes he raves . . . and weeps. Crying for his little princess. It tore my heart, lemman, so cast I the bones and at the sun upriste I come to find you. What wist I where my grace was shapen for to be, or in what place. I up and travel to the walled camp of the devils and throw meself on their tender mercies, hoping that once within those thrice-cursed walls I could fetch you to me." Her words broke off and she began coughing grotesquely—painfully.

"That doesn't sound good at all." Bea went to her medical cabinet and took out a stethoscope. Approaching Amala, she got beneath the animal skins with the instrument. "Cough please."

"I noot wher that litel thing be sely or shrew?" the woman said, alarmed.

"Just be quiet and do what I tell you," Bea said sternly. Amala coughed obediently. "Again, please."

Amala smiled weakly. "You're the blood image of your mother, darlin'."

"Shh. Cough. Uh huh, just as I thought. You've got yourself a fine case of pneumonia. God, how have you been able to get around?"

Amala shrugged. "Life is never easy."

Going to the desk, Bea picked up her telephone. "Get me the clinic on three. Thanks." Looking up, Bea realized that Dulan and Amala hadn't been introduced. "Amala Delacorte, this is Doral Dulan, a very good friend. Amala is my father's sister."

Dulan took her hand. "Glad to know you."

Shaking his hand, the Outsider stared into Dulan's eyes. "My Beatrice strogen were unto the herte for ye."

Bea flushed. "Amala, please. I . . . hello? Who's this? . . . Look, this is Doctor Delacorte on seven . . . right. I've got a pretty bad case of pneumonia down here and . . ." she leaned over and inspected Amala's scalp. ". . . scabies. Yes. I need a couple of orderlies down here with a stretcher right away . . . yes . . . bad enough! I don't give a damn what Doctor Stuart says, I want that stretcher now!" She slammed down the receiver and shook her head.

"Be you a healer?" Amala asked.

"Yes."

"Your father will be fain to hear of it."

"I hope so, I really do. Now, go on with your story."

"Taketh me into their strange woon, but not a day did I have to search you out. Not granges nor bernes did I see, only a small closed place . . . like this. Where is the Sun darlin'? Questions they asked me, foolish questions. 'Where is the red card?' Red card! Wha herkned ever swilk a ferly thing? Long they tarried with hir foolish questions. 'Namo,' sayeth I, and they leave me for a long time. Wenden I then from the walled woon, thinkin' I'd lost you sure. Thank Kalem! I was being taken to your side."

"Thank Kalem and the computer," muttered Bea. "Did you ride in an airplane?"

"Sufferen I the airplane. I felt like the cornered hare . . . but it was glorious." She broke into another coughing jag. Suddenly the woman sat bolt upright and stared at Bea.

"Come to me, lemman," Amala ordered, in the same clinical tone that Bea had used earlier. Bea walked up to her. Placing both of her hands on Bea's abdomen, she smiled up at her niece. "You're with child," she said flatly.

Dulan gave a start and looked over at Bea, who was herself the picture of bewilderment. Amala shut her eyes and rocked slightly in her chair. "A black child," she said. "His child." She raised her arm and pointed a gnarled finger at Dulan, whose mouth was becoming very dry.

Bea, caught completely off guard, was stammering, "Amala, I . . . I . . ."

"There's more," snapped the woman. Her eyes still shut tight, she began moaning an eerie tune in an internal language. "Fire . . . purifying fire. Of fire me mette." She doubled over agonizingly and gagged. "War, bloody war and drede. Kalem! Lambs to lions. Kalem! KALEM!" Amala's eyes opened wide. Dulan recognized her look. He had seen it on Dan Jones's face when they took him. Naked fear. "Death," she croaked hoarsely. "Death and . . . life."

The Outsider went limp and fell off the chair, unconscious. Both Dulan and Bea rushed to her side. Dulan felt numb—tense inside. "Is she all right?" he asked.

"I don't know," Bea responded. "She's so weak." There was a knock on the door. "The stretcher," she said, and ran to admit the clinic orderlies.

Two white jump-suited men wheeled in the litter. They took one look at Amala and stopped dead in their tracks.

"We won't take this one," growled one of the men, his rough-hewn face settling into a posture of disgust.

How often Dulan had seen that look. He glanced at Bea. Her face had turned a vivid crimson and she looked as if she were ready to explode.

"Bea," he said simply, and shook his head when he got her attention. He put his hand on her shoulder to calm her and stepped between her and the orderlies. "What's your name?" he asked the one who had done the talking.

"Hardesty," replied the man, mellowing before the Exceptional.

Dulan patted the man lightly on the back and exerted imperceptible pressure to lead him a few feet away from his partner. He spoke low so that the man had to lean close to hear him. "Now, Mr. Hardesty," he said affably, "I don't want to interfere with your business, but maybe I can do you a favor. You see, this Outsider has been ordered here especially by the highest authority. She's top security . . . very important."

"Oh yeah?" Hardesty replied. "If that don't beat all. The problem is that Outsiders aren't allowed in the clinics occupied by decent folks, if you know what I mean."

Dulan, still smiling, continued. "You still don't understand Mr., uh . . . what's your first name?"

"Frank."

"Well, Frank, it's like this. This lady here on the floor is a key link in the continued well-being of the coms."

Hardesty made a monkey face in the direction of the straggly heap lying near his feet. "In what way is she so important?"

Dulan looked shocked. "I can't tell you that, Frank. And besides, I don't think that you really want to know."

"I guess you're right."

"Now as you can see, she's about ready to give it up over there, and if she dies before getting to the clinic, by golly I'll make sure that you, Frank, are held personally responsible."

Frank gulped. "Me?"

"I've got to cover my own ass," Dulan said, staring at the ceiling.

Hardesty found the logic irrefutable. "C'mon, Andy," he said. "let's get her upstairs." They carefully loaded Amala onto the stretcher and rolled her out into the hall.

"I'll be right along," Bea called out the door. Then to Dulan, "You're always in control, aren't you?"

"Not always. Is it true?"

"What?"

"What she said."

Bea's eyes narrowed. "I suppose it could be. I haven't been sick, but—yes, it's possible. I'll run the tests myself."

"What was all the other nonsense that she was blabbing? Just delirium?"

"Maybe," she answered, smoothing down her hair. "I don't know. Amala is much honored in the tribe as an oracle. Before any major decision is made concerning the caravan, Amala is consulted."

"Really?"

"Her 'delirium' is respected. In fact, I'm sure that she came on her own to find me. My people would never have let her go if she had told them."

Dulan walked to the doorway and glanced out. The litter had already disappeared around the curve of the hallway. "Did any of what your aunt said make any sense to you?" he asked, coming in and shutting the door.

"Not really, but I wouldn't dismiss that strange lady too lightly. She's not without power. Even after all these years I remember that."

"So what happens now?" he asked, walking over and touching her arm just for the contact.

"Now? Good question. I think that from here on out it's going to have to be a day at a time." She patted his hand lightly and then pulled away from him. "I've really got to go, Doral."

She ran out the door, trying to catch the orderlies at the elevators. Dulan watched her until she was out of sight around the curve, wondering why everything was always so complicated. As he stood there alone, he was struck by an overpowering urge to take a walk outside, to breathe fresh air, to get the sun under his epidermis.

Instead, he went to six and got drunk.

Jones no longer, I have shed this self as a bird molts its feathers. And now, free at last, I stand before my wondrous creation.

I call Her Zenith. As fine and sturdy a ship as ever soared through the ether on a hale wind. The sun will soon rise, so I must hurry to complete my preparations, for as the light of heaven ascends regally to its place of honor—so I also rise.

The journey shall be long and fraught with peril beyond mortal ken, but fear is unknown to me, for am I not Francis

Astro, greatest astral navigator and dimensional wanderer ever to test his mettle against the argon spheroid?

The first trickles of dawn begin to slip redly above the stump mountains many kilometers in the gray distance.

I prepare the mixture. Mild honey and salt, mixed in the mortar.

I pour the concoction into the seashell, and drink it down in one swallow. Then, turning to face the rising sun, I cover my right eye and my heart in the manner of the ancients. It is nearly time.

My mind races with anticipation, and I can feel the throb of my veins as the blood courses through my body. This is what life is all about.

As the sky lightens, I begin to discern the caricature impressed upon the skin of my balloon. Sol. The eternal star. When next I touch his beauty with my unworthy orbs, it will be from another place—a better place. He stares down at me from his throne of blue, as I continue the final preparations for my flight.

Climbing upon the basket, I swing on the rigging. There is no room for miscalculations of any kind. All must be in order. Easing myself into the gondola, I don my silken robes and the white leather shoes and cap. In an unquavering voice, I chant: "Anton, Amator, Emites, Theodoriel, Pancor, Pagor, Anitor; by virtue of these holy angelic names do I clothe myself, O Lord, in my Sabbath garments, that so I may fulfill, even unto their term, all things which I desire to effect through Thee, Most Holy Adonay whose kingdom and rule endure forever and ever. Amen."

I check my stores and my instruments—sivard, staff, rod, lancet, hook, sickle, needle, poniard, white and black-handled knives and thus consecrate them: "Entabor, Natabor, Si Tasibor, Admey, An, Layamon, Tinormes, eos Phildoes."

The pentagram inlaid in the gondola floor is of the finest jade and soapstone. The herbs and spices are prepared, as are my incantations and cabalistic recollections. What a momentous excursion this will be!

It is now time for my obtestation to the Almighty Sun. Kalem. Burnu. I make ready the suffumigation—saffron, ambergris, musk, lignum aloes, lignum balsam, fruit of the laureel, cloves, myrrh, and franklin-cense bruised and mixed with the blood of the white cock and formed into small troches.

At last! All has been attended, naught is left undone. I read the spell from the crumbling volume, both hands on the book, eyes raised to heaven.

The spell is cast. My hands tremble with excitement, as if they had a will of their own. Mighty Burnu has begun his sojourn through the firmament, just as I, also, must begin mine. From its place of esteem in the ebony casket I remove the silken flag inscribed with the barred triangle.

As I hoist the flag, my galactic galleon rises magnificently. Into the troposphere.

Into—the void.

Death in battle is the highest form of worship to the Almighty.
—official motto,
Armies of the Com States

Safe upon the solid rock the ugly houses stand:
Come and see my shining palace built upon the sand!
—Edna St. Vincent Millay
Oldworlder

12
November

Dulan sat amidst his clutter, frowny-faced and brooding. He had tried several times to get in touch with Bea since the incident with Amala, but she had always been too busy to see him.

He had tried talking with Elmer to ease the ache that he wouldn't admit was loneliness, but the interest was simply not there, and he had slipped into a fit of noninvolvement. That made him feel even worse, for all of his brackishness and shows of bravado, he never actually strayed very far from conventional, accepted paths. It wasn't in his nature or to his self-interest to do so. Any sign of faltering in his work could be fatal. Com life was simple if you followed the rules, deadly if you didn't. Life had been so easy . . . before.

Never totally idle, Dulan made some fine adjustments on the oscilloscope. He had wired it up to the wall speaker terminals and then to the music computer so that anyone paging through the wall intercom would have their voice visualized on the scope and then translated mathematically onto the music computer, which made a song of it. The hookup was pointless and grounded in no worthwhile idea, but it did kill the time. At the moment, the words of Complan, always evident through the speaker, were juicing through the music box in a very menacing fashion.

Where was she?

He had talked with her briefly on the phone that afternoon and made her promise to stop by, but so far she hadn't shown. Why the devil had he gotten mixed up with an Outsider?

Leaning back, he stretched out his arm and picked up the wine bottle that sat disparagingly on the cold floor. Drinking deeply, he cursed his excesses, then drank again, wondering what the weather was like outside. Often he found himself remembering the day of his arrival at the milcom, and wished that he had committed the atmospheric details to memory so that he at least could bask in an imaginary sun. Truth to tell, he couldn't remember what the weather had been like the day he volunteered to be buried alive.

The door burst open and in strode Bea, looking marvelous. Dulan brightened immediately in spite of himself, an involuntary smile etching his unlined face.

"Your lipstick's smeared," he said, holding the wine bottle out for her inspection.

She snatched the bottle from his grasp and took a quick drink. "Set it up," she said. Dulan nodded and began a quick search for the backgammon board.

"How's Amala?" He found the diamond-imprinted wooden battleground and box of checkers under the bed. Setting the board on the bed, he dumped the playing pieces on top of it. They sat down with the game between them and furiously started arranging the black and red markers on their respective places.

"I think she'll be all right. We've been doing a lot of catching up," Bea rolled the dice. Six.

"Good," he grinned. "But not a winner." He rolled a nine to get the honors. "Hah! I feel hot tonight. You don't stand a chance."

"I never did with you."

"Come on Bea. I'm not ready for any cryptic messages today. How come you've been avoiding me all week?"

She looked him full in the face. Her features bore a look of tortured confusion that he had never seen there before. "I've been doing some thinking," she answered after a time. "Had to straighten some things out in my head. You haven't asked about the baby."

"Figured that you'd get around to it when you were ready. You really are pregnant?"

"Three months. I feel like a dummy, not realizing it sooner."

She forced a laugh. "Keep rolling those doubles and you really will beat me."

"I told you, I can't lose."

"Doral?"

"Hmmm."

"Have you ever thought about what it would be like to live on the outside?"

"Sure." he replied, "I've thought about it—but never seriously. I think about all sorts of things."

She flinched slightly. "Think about it now."

"Are you going to leave soon?"

"I-I'm not sure." She tossed the bones and moved her checkers, seemingly at random yet always managing to keep them doubled up, invulnerable, on the elongated triangles. "There are a great many considerations. I can't leave as long as I can be of any help to Dan . . . even if it's a little help. But I'm afraid that Doctor Stuart will force me to go when he finds out that I'm pregnant."

"I hardly think so."

She looked at him quizzically. "Why do you say that? Oh good! five-three." Bea literally pounced on one of Dulan's exposed pieces, and sent it back to her inner court. The tide of battle was beginning to turn in her favor.

"Heathen!" he screamed with pretend animosity. "Succubus! Where's that bottle?" He took a swig. "Let me ask you a question."

"Shoot."

"We've been here, what—about four months?"

"Something like that. Why?"

"New people come in all the time, right?" Bea nodded. "Well, have you ever known anyone to leave?"

"No, but we come in contact with so few people. It really doesn't seem so unusual."

"Maybe you're right. It just seems odd. I spend a lot of time up at Material Control on one, and I see them coming all the time. Lots of people, Telps mostly, but I never see anyone leaving. Strange, I never thought anything about it till now."

Bea looked unimpressed. "The new front, remember?"

"The much talked about, but so far unseen Northern front." He held the dice, jiggling them absently in his left hand. "There's something else. The guards I dealt with about the fish.

They always spoke of arrivals and deliveries. Never departures. This place will only hold so many people."

"Why don't you ask them about it?"

"I have a feeling they wouldn't have anything to say."

"Then why don't you ask your buddy-buddy computer?"

"That's a thought. Damn!" He felt his wonderfully strategic game once again faltering under a withering blast of unrestrained flamboyance. "Besides, what makes you think that having a baby would force you out. After all, that's what com women are all about."

"No one else here is pregnant. I just assumed that it was against milcom rules. Let's go back a minute. What in the world would be the point of making people stay at Forty-Three?"

"Security. I don't know. It was a silly thought, forget it. What's your plan? I assume you have a plan."

"Well, I'm a good-sized girl . . ."

"I'll say," he responded, reaching for her.

She slapped his hand. "If I wear the right kind of clothes I can probably keep my condition a secret for several more months. Perhaps if I can keep this under wraps long enough, they'll have to let me have the baby here."

"Then what?"

"It will be springtime. The council of all the tribes meets this spring in the delta of the winding river not many kilometers from here. I'll take the baby and go to them. It's where I belong."

"Now Bea, you know as well as I do that they'd never . . ."

Her eyes smoldered. "My baby goes with me. I'll never leave him to be raised by these . . ."

"Him?" Dulan cajoled.

She softened. "Amala said it." She lowered her eyes. "It's my desire."

"It's impossible, you just can't . . ."

"Doral, come with me. To my people."

"But Bea, I . . ."

"It's fresh and pure. God, don't you understand? Honesty without recrimination. Life without the constant stench of inner death and decaying values."

"Aren't you romanticizing a bit?"

"Dammit Doral, can't you stop playing devil's advocate for just a minute? Of course I'm inflating it. It's that important to me." She looked furtively about her. "People weren't meant to live this way. This place is a glorified sarcophagus, and if we don't get out, we're going to be buried in it. I know you. You're just as disgusted by this whole mess as I am. I'm offering you freedom. A real life as a real man."

"Freedom," echoed Dulan. He glanced at the playing board. Bea had moved all of her pieces to her inner court and was ready to bear them out of the game. She was only a few rolls of the dice away from victory. "It's your move," he said quietly.

"Damn the game!" she screamed, pushing the board off the bed. "Listen to me. This is important. Haven't you heard anything that I've said?"

Dulan stood and walked a few paces to the center of the room, scattering the checkers as he moved. "Everything is always so cut and dried to you, isn't it?"

"I just know where I stand, that's all."

"All right, all right. Let's begin from there. I've been raised my whole life to believe that banishment to the outside is the greatest punishment that can befall a person . . . and maybe it is."

"Doral!"

"Let me finish. What do I know about survival? How long could I last out there?"

"You're an Exceptional," she returned, as if that were the answer to everything. "You could learn quickly."

"Could I? Hell, I've never even been on a horse. This is a sarcophagus to you; to me it's living. The only kind of living that I've ever known. Sure, I'll admit that there's a number of pretty repugnant things that go on here, but don't forget, I saw Amala when they brought her in. Her condition hardly inspires my confidence in the beauty of tribal life."

"We can change all that."

Dulan threw up his hands. "Complan spare us. Grow up Bea, life is just not as simple as you make it out to be."

"You're afraid to go," she said, her features darkening.

"No. Not so much that as . . . look around you. Look at all this junk. Computers, books, electronic nonsense. None of it amounts to a pile of dung in the overall scheme of things, but what is anything worth but what it's worth to you. I like these things; they're important to me. I don't know that I want to give them up—I don't know that I could."

"Not even for a wife and family?" Her eyes were beginning to mist over. Dulan had been waiting for that since the discussion began. It was ultimately the whole purpose of their talk, perhaps of their entire relationship. How could he answer her so that she wouldn't hate him?

"Bea, I—I admit that I have feelings, strong feelings, for you but . . ."

"Don't do me any favors." She was on her feet, heading for the door.

Dulan was getting lathered up. Things weren't coming out right at all. "Please, would you just stop and hear me out?"

"Go tell it to your talking scrapheap," she spat, and her tone was laced with jealousy.

"No!" He grabbed her violently by the shoulders and spun her around. "I'm going to tell you, and you're going to listen."

"You're hurting me."

"Promise you'll listen."

"All right. Just let me go." He released her and she sat stiffly on the bed, rubbing her arm.

"All my life," he began slowly, "I've been alone. Completely alone. Everyone else around me had a niche, a place where they belonged . . . people to whom they could relate. But I was different. There aren't many Exceptionals, and no black ones. Who I am made me what I am. Separate. Different. I've never been able to relate to human beings, guess I've never had the opportunity." Dulan knew what he wanted to say, but he was botching it badly. "You've seen how I am," he continued. The words just wouldn't come out the way that they were stacked inside his head.

"Yes. You've built a wall around yourself."

"I don't want it to be that way, I really don't, but . . . I just need some time to muddle this through."

Bea was shaking her head. "I may not have time, Doral." She reached out and took his hand tightly in her own. "I think I can understand your problem. After all, I've never fit into the system either, but I might have to start wheels in motion very soon. I love you." She nuzzled his hand with her cheek. "Where do you stand, darling? You've got to tell me."

He turned slowly away from her, confused.

"Commit yourself, for god's sake!" She dropped his hand as if it were on fire.

He turned back to face her. "Bea, I . . ."

Suddenly, their attention was riveted to the wall speaker as it crackled loudly, emitting a high-pitched whine that would jangle the nerves of even the soundest sleeper. The oscilloscope read out the noise as violently quacking peaks, while the music computer duplicated the hideous sound three octaves lower.

"What the . . ."

The auditory assault ended as quickly as it had begun and was replaced by a craggy-sounding voice. Dulan would have been hard pressed to determine the gender of the announcer.

> ATTENTION. ATTENTION PLEASE. ALL PERSONNEL INVOLVED IN CLASS THREE THROUGH CLASS EIGHT BLUE TEAM PRIORITY ACTIVITIES WILL REPORT IMMEDIATELY TO THEIR RESPECTIVE SECTION CHIEFS FOR ORDERS AND ASSISTANCE. THIS IS NOT A DRILL. REPEAT. THIS IS NOT A DRILL.

Dulan was down on his hands and knees reaching under the bed as the entire message was given again.

"What are you doing?" Bea asked.

"It's here somewhere. Ahh," he grunted, coming out from under clutching a forgotten tome. "S.O.P.," he grinned.

Sitting on the bed he wiped the thick layer of dust off the prodigious volume and flipped through it speedily. Bea stood in the center of the crowded cubicle watching as he skimmed through the pages, searching. Finding the correct section, he sat with the book opened on his knees and ran a finger down the page for a minute before letting the weight of the book slam itself closed, raising a small cloud of dust. He stared at nothing, deep in thought.

"Well, what is it?" Bea pressed impatiently.

"The war," he said. "It's started."

I have never made but one prayer to God, a very short one: "O lord make my enemies ridiculous." And God granted it.

—Voltaire
Oldworlder (expunged)

13

Graduation day.

They stood huddled uncomfortably in the tiny technicians' booth. Scan room control booths were designed to accommodate two technicians plus one or perhaps two others. The ten people who were now jammed together in the small chamber were, quite literally, shoulder to shoulder, and Dulan felt nervous and jittery.

It wouldn't have been so bad except that visibility from the booth to the scan room proper was limited to a direct line from behind the windowed overlook. Since everyone was there to view the proceedings, it was necessary for them all to occupy the same area in order to see at all. The resultant confusion was visually very comical.

Graduation for a Telp group most always produced such gatherings as this. Everyone involved with the direct training of a particular group was anxious to see the ultimate fruit of their labor. The culmination of months of hard work.

When Bea discovered that Jones was to go through the joining ceremony, she cajoled Dulan until he got the authorization for them to attend the initiation rites. It was no easy task. Since the war had begun again, he had found it increasingly difficult to get the necessary authority to visit places that were not immediately connected with his job.

So there they stood, sardine-like, watching the dimly lit panorama that lay beneath their omniscient gaze. This room was, to the last detail, an exact match of the scan room that Dulan and Bea had visited previously.

The Telps, Jones among them, sat at attention at their desks, heads gently nodding in a light trance. They were being instructed in the placement of the alpha wave rings that were to be worn on their heads during mind scans.

When all was in order, Herman Matrix entered theatrically from the darkness of stage left, looking noble in his gold-flecked robes, skull cap blazing day-glo red. He took his place on a rostrum in front of the Telps. His craggy old face was kept well lit by a device that he wore around his neck, making his head appear to be a separate free-floating entity, self-supporting and angelic. Among his other duties, Matrix was the official "joiner" for Forty-Three, the inspired mediator who guided each newly trained Telp group into their half-lives as human radios. Probably any good mesmerist—and there were many at Forty-Three—could do his job, but they never did. It was always Matrix. The last link in the chain, bringing spiritualistic science full circle.

He stood majestically on the podium, artificially lighted eyes alive and dancing, his fine white mane of hair a shadowed tangle. He raised his long arms in supplication, a grandiose gesture that elicited immediate silence throughout the room and riveted attention to himself. Matrix was now the focus.

Enunciating softly, almost in a whisper, he spoke to the Telps. Dulan strained to hear the old man through the thick glass, but then he realized that Matrix was speaking a dialect of Chinese. A wave of disappointment washed over him, until one of the technicians began tinkering with the computer controls. Suddenly Matrix's voice was coming inside the booth through the screen speaker. The voice was flat and without inflection, but it came through crisp, clear, and in perfect English. Dulan theorized that the computer was picking up the voice from the Telps as they heard it and then translated the sound for the technicians just as is done with the scans.

The priest of Complan was speaking, ". . . your thoughts. Stop the flow. Clear your minds of all activity my children. Are you doing it? Clear and blank. Good.

"What is your name. Do you know it? Do you? You are nothing on your own. Nameless. You have no substance. You are ephemeral, a specter. You can leave your body and float. Soar. Can you feel it? The wind rushing against your face. Your body is unnecessary. Discard it. Discard it!"

Dulan listened with interest. Matrix was quite accomplished at his work. His speech, undoubtedly delivered hundreds of times, was polished and convincing. As he went on, his voice grew in power and intensity, until he had swept the Telps along with him.

"A box lies before you my children. Open it. That's right."

Dulan fought a little to see. The boxes contained a gold chain with some manner of plasticized garbage attached. He had seen the strange medallions around the necks of other Telps. They usually displayed a bit of cloth or hair, but Dulan had seen buttons or wood around people's necks also.

"Take the pendant and place it around you. Yes, your neck. That's correct."

"What's that?" Dulan mumbled to Bea.

"What?"

"The medallion?"

"Oh. It's a piece of material, or anything really, that belonged to their scan mate. It still retains some of the eletromagnetic vibrations unique to that person and helps the Telp to get and hold contact."

"How does the stuff get here?"

Bea looked puzzled. "I never thought about it. Spies, I guess. Hell, I don't know."

Matrix was leaning over the podium, his disembodied face grinning hideously. "The time has now come to seek out the essence of your soul mate. Sing calls to you. Answer him. Leave your bodily shell and seek out his spirit. Travel north by the northeast many kilometers. Grasp the pendant, feel the vibrations!"

Whatever his personal convictions about the morality of the Telp system, Dulan could not help but feel a thrill of unchecked excitement, of pure anticipation, build within himself as the dramatic tableau unfolded before his eyes. God, he realized, it *was* a religious experience. He glanced quickly around at the others in the now deathly silent control booth. The intensity of his feelings was mirrored in all of their eyes. In all but one, anyway. Doctor Stuart had slipped in quietly during the joining and was sitting in his gleaming metal mover, slantwise to the others, gazing noncommittally out of the window that was set too high to afford him a view. He captured Dulan's glance and nodded acknowledgement. Dulan smiled involuntarily. Automatically.

Beneath them, Matrix was building to a climax. Fists clenched, arms reaching outward, he seemed to be almost physically pushing the Telps, helping them make the change.

"Yes, yes, yes, my children. You've found his essence. Hold

on! That's right. Grasp the pendant tightly, your vibrations are his vibrations. Find Sing's mind. Seek his senses. Move with the vibes. The vibes . . . yes, yes, YES!!"

All eyes were glued to the view screen in the control booth. An image, flickering and faint, but an image nonetheless, was beginning to take shape. Seconds later it became stronger, clearer. Dulan could barely make out the figure of a man. The man from the film. Sing. At the moment of hard contact, wild applause broke out in the booth, and despite himself, Dulan felt his own palms beating together.

General Sing was standing, in full battle dress, with his hands over eyes. He was not in pain, but reacting to the joining.

"THERE. THERE. MY MIND. BRAIN. BRAIN.
INSIDE. THEM. FORGET. FORGET. FORGET."

The scene switched from the medium computer composite of Sing to a subjective angle, apparently through the General's eyes. Sing was looking from a high vantage point over a long, flat, open plain. Facing each other across the plain were the two armies, separated by perhaps two hundred and fifty meters. They were preparing to do battle. Around the periphery of the combatants sat a squad of bulldozers with a team of civilians to man them. It did not seem to matter to them that they were so close to the action.

There was not a great deal of personnel involved in the encounter, only about three thousand altogether, but the truly amazing fact was that they were remarkably evenly divided. Men, machinery, weapons, all looked as if they had been carefully divided in half. The armies flew no flags, and at a distance looked so similar that Dulan was unable to distinguish one from the other. The sun was setting between the two forces, so he decided that those to the south of the setting sun were the com soldiers. Sunset seemed to Dulan a strange time to fight a battle, but he really had nothing on which to base that assumption.

Sing swung his gaze back and forth between the two armies. Dulan could detect no heavy artillery or aircraft of any kind within the line of vision. Having never witnessed a real battle (even in the propaganda films, the showing of major combat, either real or simulated, was strictly forbidden), he had no idea what to expect. He had seen some of the old war films of twentieth-century warfare down on six, but nothing he had seen even remotely resembled this. The combatants were lined up in ranks, bayonets fixed, staring across the open field. As if on cue, they began resolutely marching across the plain toward one another. The closest approximation that Dulan could conjure for the unusual behavior that confronted him was the stylized open field fighting of the sixteenth, seventeenth, and eighteenth centuries in Europe that he had read about in the old books. But that type of warfare had been necessitated by the poor quality of firearms in use at that time. The weapons used by com soldiers were of twentieth-century design—automatics, semiautomatics, and carbines. Open field tactics with such weapons would be not only pointless, but suicidal.

Still the armies moved closer. They were now less than one hundred and fifty meters apart. And still they came. The entire room stared at the screen in rapt fascination. Even Bea, who was no doubt appalled by such activity, could not take her eyes off the screen.

For General Sing also, this must have been a momentous experience. His gaze and mind seemed locked on the forthcoming turmoil. There were occasional flashes of totally unrelated (to all but Sing) events, unlike the wandering interior monologues of Dulan's previous encounter with the scan. He became interested in the thoughts and made an effort to hear them.

> "CLOSE. CLOSER. HOT SO HOT. SWEATY. CLOSER. ALMOST TIME. CLOSER FRIGHTENED MUST LOOK COMPOSED GENERAL GONDA WATCHING SOMEWHERE SCAN SCREEN ALSO FORGET IT. FORGET IT. IMPORTANT NOW IMPORTANT. CLOSE. YES YES NOW NOW NOW . . ."

Cut to medium shot of Sing standing by a table covered with field telephones, six by Dulan's quick count. He theorized that this was all composite.

Things were beginning to happen in the booth. One of the technicians raced to a small panel covered with alternating rows of lights and switches. He unlocked it with a series of keys, then punched recognition codes into the unit, which sprung into luminescent, whirring activity. The other white-coated watcher calibrated the screen sound up to a volume that made it impossible to ignore.

The screen cut back to the converging armies. They were now

within a stone's throw of each other, yet not so much as a single bullet had been fired. A smaller shot of Sing was inserted into the upper right-hand corner of the screen. He was on one of the telephones.

"5 ARN SINE. YES. YES. 5 ARN SINE."

He put down the receiver and quickly picked up another. He began screaming into the mouthpiece.

"5 ARN SINE. 5 ARN SINE. 5 ARN SINE!"

"Damn!" yelled one of the technicians to the other. "It's a new code." He started punching things into a small computer that sat by his right hand. Dulan figured that while the Amalgamech was working on the code from one direction, the crypto computer was doing it backwards.

The army on the right of the screen, which like the com army was ranked back to front in six long files, suddenly split into four separate columns formed vertically instead of horizontally. The outer two columns broke into a trot, veering off at 45-degree angles away from each other.

"Got the code," the technician said.

The inner two columns kept slowly marching, but flared out a bit, still in formation, making the Chinese from a distance look like a giant, moving letter W. The com forces, now being flanked all around, still maintained their original formation.

"Those damn dirty animals," said the sound man in a low voice. "That's one of our formations."

The other technician was busy punching "do acknowledge" buttons, as the computer flashed response commands to the enemy movements. It appeared to be some manner of human double-checking in an area that Amalgamech could handle all by itself.

Dulan's eyes jumped back to the screen. As per computer command, the com forces quickly began forming themselves into a defensive ring.

"FIRE. FIRE. FIRE!!!"

Sing's words came out of the booth speaker in a flat, lifeless monotone, although on the screen the General was in a highly agitated state and was barking into the telephone.

The People's Army opened fire, with the comites returning it immediately. The effect was even more devastating than Dulan had imagined. More than half of the soldiers were slaughtered in the first two minutes of fighting. The outer ranks of the com ring were dead, as was most of the inside wedge of the People's forces. The losses were equal, with the comites in slightly better position. Apparently, the wedge used by the People's Army was effective only if it was utilized quickly before the opposing forces were able to adequately respond. Sing was just slightly quick on the trigger, and the com army had time to get the ring set up before the trap was sprung. Now with the People's forces scattered, the com army, tight and ready, was set to attack. Even as Dulan's mind perceived the situation, Amalgamech was already issuing orders. Seconds later, the comites charged over the bodies of their fallen comrades. Three deep they came, bayonets lowered, running straight out in all directions, like a circle with an ever-increasing circumference. The People's Army was faltering badly, and seemed ready to rout.

"NO. NO. NO. NO. RUIN. NO."

Sing (still in insert) picked up a phone. His head bobbed and he yelled into another phone.

"JARK SCREAM. JARK SCREAM."

"New code," growled the programmer. And a few seconds later, "Got it." And Amalgamech was off and running even before the enemy soldiers began moving.

The People's Army turned and ran straight back toward their original positions from wherever they happened to be. Just as it seemed that they were madly retreating, they turned and, as a man, ran swiftly toward the clustered survivors of their small wedge. It was a brilliant maneuver that allowed the Chinese to regroup, while at the same time leaving the comites who were giving chase scattered and easily broken. Amalgamech was quick, though, and gave the order to regroup before the People's Army was in total control.

No sooner had the enemy computer intercepted Amalgamech's order to regroup, than it issued another to the People's forces to charge as soon as they reformed. Amalgamech decided to have the comites stand their ground and await the onslaught. Onslaught! There were fewer than four or five hundred troops left standing on their feet. The rest were dead, or dying, strewn carelessly around a half-kilometer area. All in less than five minutes!

The com army was grouped into three lines. Each line had shooting access past the ones in front. They were prepared to meet the attack with a wall of death.

As he watched his soldiers charge into certain destruction, Sing became violently ill and sank to his knees, vomiting. The computer spared the listeners the sound that accompanied Sing's regurgitation, but it didn't help. A horrible gagging noise drifted up from the scan room as the Telps mirrored the experience. One of the trainers had to leave, and Dulan felt his own stomach turn a bit.

The screen cut to Sing as he quickly climbed to his feet and ran to the table. His mind floated completely away from the battle for a few seconds, filling the screen with thoughts that dwelled on a variety of embarrassing events that had occurred throughout the General's life. Dulan noticed that these recollections were very clear and well-defined. He also recognized a flash of one of them from the Sing biography film.

Cut back to the battle. The remaining soldiers were a heartbeat away from confrontation. For perhaps three seconds, three long seconds, an eerie silence hung over the control booth, everyone frozen in place, holding their breath. Even Amalgamech was strangely silent. Waiting, waiting.

Suddenly the computer became frantically active. Almost at the same instant, Sing was screaming over one of his phones,

"KILL. KILL. KILL. KILL. KILL."

It was over before it began. Everyone was out in the open, unprotected. Mass suicide.

ARRRGH

The sound came hollowly from Sing's throat via the computer, more agonizingly from the gullets of the Telps below. The roar from the gunfire must have been deafening, but those in the control booth couldn't hear it.

When it was done, the insert of Sing disappeared from the screen and all that remained was the plain full of dead men. The People's Army had apparently been victorious, but the price was heartrending. Dulan counted the survivors. There were eight. The People's forces had been tightly grouped during the attack and the inner ranks were able to break through the com defense quicker than the outer ranks could be killed. This was the edge.

"VICTORY! VICTORY!"

Sing was jubilant. It didn't seem to matter to him that the losses to his forces had been so devastating. The gruesome scene of battlefield carnage was becoming interspersed with Sing's images of the hero's reward, some of it highly erotic. If General Sing was new to command, he was certainly no stranger to death. Dulan could detect no signs of remorse in the man as he viewed the field.

There were many hundreds of wounded lying everywhere, but

their deaths were a foregone conclusion. The laughing death. Crippled and wounded would certainly be a heavy burden on a system so dominated by war. Hence the Funnies. All the bullets, knives, and bayonets were coated with a substance called hydronite that, when introduced into the bloodstream, reacted with the oxygen in the blood to form an oxide that couldn't be taken into the bodily tissues. With the tissues starved, anoxia rapidly set in, bringing with it a drunken euphoria that lasted until unconsciousness. In a world full of air, the result was always the same—suffocation. Even flesh wounds were fatal.

The eight remaining soldiers slowly walked among the dead and dying, making sure there were no fakers. If a wound was not immediately visible, a shot was fired into the laughing man. They lay everywhere, shrieking and giggling hysterically. Dulan was glad that there was no sound to accompany the now less frequent pictures of the battleground. The scene kept jumping to Sing's imaginative portrayals of full military honors for his success. Things were getting back to normal.

Dulan had seen as much as he cared to. Turning to go, he noticed that Bea had left already. Since the argument, Bea's attitude toward their relationship had cooled to casualness. He couldn't blame her really, but it seemed that she should at least try to understand how he felt.

He cursed his indecision, but knew that he would not make any real attempt to do anything about it. It was easier to dizzy his mind with work and alcohol, and hope that the situation would rectify itself.

"A word with you, Doctor," said Carl Stuart, looking for all the world like the cat who ate the canary.

Dulan turned to Stuart but did not speak.

"What did you think of the battle?" the old man asked.

"Are they always fought that way?"

Stuart wheeled himself off to one side of the small booth so that those wishing to leave could have access to the door. "Just exactly that way," he said. "Although this was just a small one, a skirmish really. The basic military unit is called the 'form.' What we saw were two of these forms engaged in a relatively unimportant conflict. The larger or more significant the battle, the greater number of forms involved."

Dulan was beginning to detect a nasty pattern. "Always equal?" he asked.

"Always," sneered Stuart. "Back in the old days, they used

to have fifteen, even twenty form battles. Those were the days. Of course, that was long ago. Four forms, maybe five is about as large as we get anymore."

Dulan knew that Doctor Stuart didn't call him over to discuss the state of the military, but he wasn't about to give the old man the satisfaction of showing interest in his real purpose. He just let Stuart play out his hand.

"Are the end results always the same?"

Doctor Stuart cocked his head. "How do you mean . . . casualty-wise?"

"That's what I mean," answered Dulan dryly. He let his eyes flick up to the screen. The bulldozers were busy digging huge mass graves and pushing large piles of bodies into them in ways that only machines could.

"Occasionally," Doctor Stuart was saying, "through some fluke or other, one side will end up with a considerable number of survivors, but that's an exceptional situation, very uncommon. Today's engagement was a pretty fair approximation of com warfare."

Dulan forced his eyes from the screen. "Something puzzles me. The computer waited for orders confirmation from the other side before making a counterorder. Couldn't Amalgamech, given the particular circumstances, figure out the other computer's most logical move and counter it sooner?"

Pulling his handkerchief out of the breast pocket of his suit, Stuart wiped his lips. "Our wars have been with us for a very long time and the fighting is very standardized, as you noticed. There are no surprises really, or any logical moves for that matter. Do you play chess, Doctor?"

"Only backgammon."

"Chess is simply a matter of move duplication and acceptable responses to preordained moves until someone makes a mistake, and then it's merely a question of playing it out. Our wars are a lot like that. For any given battlefield situation, there are a number of acceptable responses, none any better or worse than any of the others. Just different. The same goes for retaliatory responses. There is a limited, but equally good, set of countermoves in reply to any maneuver. So it is necessary to be physically aware of the action before suggesting reaction."

"That doesn't make a lot of sense," said Dulan, shaking his head.

"No? You should read the *Book of Complan* a little more

carefully. '. . . and when the children of God felt the hand of the Angel of Death on their flocks, they went into the field and slaughtered the lambs of their enemies, one for one. And everything was good.' You can't argue with divine inspiration, Doctor."

"It's not the inspiration, but the interpretation that bothers me."

"The setup has worked exceedingly well for generations. It helps keep the human element intact. Preserves the system."

"By all means let's preserve the system."

"Do I detect a note of hostility in your voice?" Doctor Stuart ran a hand through his hair, making sure everything was in its place. His tombstone eyes were looking right through Dulan. "There's the story about the chicken who wanted to be king. He wanted it so badly that he learned to speak, and told everyone what he desired. Gifted as he was, he was taken to the palace and presented to the lords and ladies of the court, to whom he vocalized at great length concerning his right to the throne. Well, everyone marvelled at what a truly miraculous bird this was, and in the hope that some of his magnificent intelligence would pass on to them . . . they ate him for dinner."

There was a jangle of laughter among those remaining in the booth. Doctor Stuart had been speaking loud enough for all to hear.

"If there's nothing else," Dulan said, unwilling to take the game any farther, "I have a lot of work to do. Excuse me, please." He started to work his way past the older man, but Stuart blocked him off with his wheelchair.

"There was one more thing."

Dulan stopped dead in his tracks and glared silently at Stuart.

"Now that the war has begun again, we've found it necessary to tighten up policies concerning all personnel here at Forty-Three."

"Meaning me." He didn't like the turn that things were taking.

"We find ourselves short-handed in the area of scan room technicians. I've arranged to have you begin tomorrow full time as a tech."

Dulan couldn't believe his ears. "But's that's just busywork. Why you could get anyone to . . ."

"But you're going to do it," said Doctor Stuart. "It's all arranged."

"I protest that decision."

"But, it's your duty, Doctor."

"Don't give me that crap," Dulan fought to retain his self-control.

The old man was in his element. "Now, now. Let's observe the proprieties. By the way, it will do you no good to see General Lynch about this either. Once the war reaches Class A status like this, complete control of all civilians in this installation lies in my office."

"What about my work?"

"Your work. You may attend to the project during your free time if you wish. Otherwise, we'll have to table it for now. The war takes precedence."

"I'll find a way to keep it going," Dulan mumbled, already making adjustments in his mind.

The old man made a face. "As you wish. Also, for security reasons, it will be necessary to relinquish your free access to all levels. From now on you will please limit your activities to those sections in which you have responsibilities. Nothing personal, you understand." Doctor Stuart looked thoughtful for a moment, then brightened. "Oh yes, I almost forgot. Any requisitions that you require from material control will have to go through normal channels now. You no longer have carte blanche on level one. Sorry."

Dulan started to speak, but realized that Stuart was hoping he'd do just that. He pushed his way past the old man and out the door.

"Fun's over," Doctor Stuart called after him. "It's time to pay the piper. Good day, Doctor Dulan."

"Good day."

On the screen, the bulldozers were filling the massive trenches with dirt, removing all memory of the day's activities. They drove back and forth over the sepulcher of sand, making it smooth and level. The sun slowly rimmed beneath the horizon, replacing rosy-redness with long shadows and dark corners.

> *I glimpsed her. I know I did. The Earth had disappeared in a fuzzy velvet haze as Zenith clipped cant-wise through what was left of the threshold, and I saw her. She was surrounded by the aura, so her outline was ill defined, but it was her. I know it.*
>
> *She shone brilliant—more brilliant than a thousand novas of a thousand suns; her flaxen hair was loose and long and flowing behind her as a retinue. My heart leapt and I cried*

out to her, screaming as one insane. Alas, the thickness of the ether would not allow free passage of my vocal vibrations—or perhaps I have simply not proven myself worthy yet.

She was gone in a second. Maybe a year. Time is a very linear thing in the void, and traveling slantwise as I have been, I may have skidded through her frame of reference.

I begin to realize just how perilous my undertaking actually is. Upon entering the dimensional threshold, life as I knew it lapsed away forever. I've jutted through countless layers of time and space and the door is closed and my resolve is too firm for me to even think of returning.

My brief glimpse of her beauty has given me heart. Donning the silken robes, I place the key tied with the red ribbon around my neck and meditate. Already several things are clear to me. To successfully accomplish my holy mission, I will need an inner strength and singleness of purpose that so far I have not been able to muster. The track is there. I'll find it and hold it.

I must; there's no where else to go.

The air is diaphanous and cloaked with the odors of musk and jasmine. Very pleasing to the senses and soothing to the body.

I am tired, bone weary.

It has been long since I've rested and I wish to tarry awhile in the sweet air, but those who stray from their task run the risk of welcoming Goodman Bones with their dreams unfulfilled. I push onward.

The heretic was brought before Complan in the temple and didst curse the servant of the Lord thusly: "Life is the rule of love. If thou truly loved us, you would have us make peace and live."

Complan smiled at the woebegone sinner and said, "It is always possible to bind together a considerable number of people in love, so long as there are other people left over to receive the manifestations of their aggression."

—*Book of Complan* (32-8, 9)

Extreme remedies are appropriate for extreme diseases.

—Caravan wisdom

14

PRIVATE JOURNAL
B. DELACORTE MD. PH.D.

Re: Patient—Jones, Daniel T.

Entry: 61
17 January

It is as I feared. Once Dan was "joined" to Sing, I lost all hope of reaching him. Now that the powers that be find him fitting into the program just as well as the others, it borders on the impossible to get him into therapy. His visits are sporadic at best, and when he is allowed to come to the office, even the simplest communication is difficult.

His English is almost completely gone, all except the most basic concepts. His past life is erased. All that remains is a vague recollection of me, his only friend.

My free time has allowed me to speculate at length concerning Dan's condition. The question is: what will be the psychological/emotional effect when a man is stripped of his personality, his essence—his life? It's like digging a hole on the beach. When the tide washes in, the hole will refill. I think that some sort of personality will have to spring forth to fill the emptiness of Dan's spirit. He is Sing for twelve hours of every day, but that is alien, it doesn't come from within and I don't think that it will stick. There's no foundation. It is also illogical to assume that he will regain his previous personality. That's been eradicated. He'll have to start from scratch—from what's left of his mind. God only knows what will emerge.

The possibility also exists that no personality will emerge. The patient could simply retire within himself. If that's the case, treating him will be most difficult. I had an experience with Dan today that confirmed this notion a bit. He and I were sitting, trying to talk, when I realized that my tape recorder wasn't going. I got up to retrieve it from the cabinet. When I turned back around, Dan looked as if he were a million kilometers away. His expression was blank, almost comatose. Finding it impossible to reach him with words, I grabbed him by the shoulders and began shaking him. This also produced no reaction. Tearing through my medicine cabinet, I found the insulin that D. had procured for me. I quickly filled a syringe and injected it into his arm. The shock put him into an immediate coma, just as I had suspected. When he came back around, he began looking about wildly and jabbering in Chinese. He had come back as Sing!

He jumped up and started for the door, fuming like an enraged bull. Fortunately, I was able to intercept him before he got too far. He took hold of me, trying to push me out of his way, and I started calling out his name over and over. He stopped and stared dumbly at me for what seemed like hours. Finally, his features relaxed and he released his death grip on my arms (I still bear two black bruises, souvenirs of our encounter) and gazed at me inquiringly.

In one of D.'s books about Freud I've read about a condition called schizophrenia. It was apparently common in the Old World. The factors that contribute to the disorder—namely environmental stress and failure to cope with it—are not present in the com system, so consequently, schizophrenia is a very rare condition in the coms. Outside, of course, there is no time for mental disorders. Dan is a classic case. They made him that way.

I cannot but assume that all the others are that way too.

They seem to all exhibit the same symptoms. This leads me to wonder just how long the Telps can be maintained at this peak level of agitation without going over the edge into complete insanity. At what point do the Telp doctors say 'Stop. Enough.' And what happens after release from the project? Are the Telps brought back weeks or months later and forced into the same routine again? Where could they go? What could they do? No one has ever—not ever—talked about what happens after the inevitable mental breakdown. I'm not sure that anyone knows.

As far as I'm concerned, this thing has gone to just about the end of the line. I've watched them turn a normal man into a walking vegetable, but now it's time to call a halt while he still has a mind left to salvage. The incident today convinced me. I'm sure that Doctor Stuart will agree with me when I tell him what happened.

I saw Stuart the other day and told him I was pregnant. I just couldn't disguise it any longer. I assumed that he'd send me packing within the hour, instead, he seemed very understanding (for him). He suggested that the facilities in our clinic here were as good as anywhere and that I should just have the child here at Forty-Three. There weren't even any inquiries as to who the father is (didn't care or already knew?). Anyway, it was a good decision as far as I'm concerned. I wouldn't have gone back to my home com, I'd have tried to return to my people, and a five- to seven-week hike in the middle of January is not exactly what the doctor ordered for a woman six months pregnant.

After the baby comes in April, the trip will be much easier all around. The weather will be more tolerable for traveling, and the tribes will have moved nearer here in preparation for the council. But Doral is right—they'll never let me leave with the baby, especially if it's a boy child. It appears that I'll have to figure out some way to sneak the baby out. Decisions on the subject will come at a later time.

I guess, to be perfectly honest, I still hope to persuade D. to leave with me. It's a long shot, I know. Perhaps I ask too much. His culture is normal, natural to him. He operates well in this environment, in fact, thrives in it. What right have I to ask him to leave an atmosphere in which he is happy to trek through the wilderness wondering where our next meal will come from.

I dare not spend much time around him. I'll just go to pieces and end up staying, and staying is just what I cannot do. I've tarried too long among these shadows of human beings. My duty lies elsewhere. One look at Amala made me realize that. Why won't he understand that and throw off his yoke to join me? He could accomplish much, and more meaningfully, on the outside. Here he'll suffocate . . . or become like them.

Amala is with me always. She has no responsibilities here other than as my patient and is free to do as she pleases. It has been of profound interest to me to watch her respond to the revelations of even the simplest of com technologies. She fears the wall speakers as evil spirits. It reminds me of my own introduction to the intricacies of living within the walls. She approaches every object with childlike curiosity, wondering what each new "gimcrack" could be and what, under Burnu's eye, it might do. She was particularly impressed by the bathrooms. At first she tried to wash her face and drink from the commode. She has had that explained to her.

Running the parapsychological tests on Amala has proved to be a very exciting project, and very fulfilling. It almost makes my stay here bearable. She is indeed blessed with an exceptionally high precognitive ability. Her tests scores are consistent, with her lowest score being far better than any other to which I've been exposed. Why is this so? This type of study has never been conducted among the tribes, for obvious reasons. Could the difference in lifestyles, perhaps the tribal simplicity and closeness to nature, make those in the caravans more open to the impulses, whatever they are, that emanate from future times? Perhaps the nature of pure belief is the heart of the matter.

I recall that oracles, like Amala, are not uncommon on the outside. Each tribe has one, if not more, soothsayer. The possibilities are quite interesting.

Amala refuses to say anything more about the baby, other than the seemingly incontestable fact that it will be a boy. If I had any doubts before, the parapsychpros convinced me that my father's sister knows whereof she speaks.

In closing, I feel bound to relate a strange encounter that I had with Amala just this morning. It was right after breakfast and, as usual, I was thinking about D. I was in the process of cursing his weakness and indecision when Amala stopped me and said that I should never speak poorly about D., that he was a "great man." Now that I think about it, she's always treated him with the deference and respect usually reserved for a Lawgiver. Great man? I wonder what she knows that I don't?

Death is like a fisherman who catches a fish in his net and leaves it for a while in the water; the fish is still swimming but the net is around him, and the fisherman will draw him up—when he thinks fit.
—Caravan fable

15
Early March

"Are you alive?"

"WE FEAR THAT YOU'VE INDULGED OVERMUCH IN ALCOHOL AGAIN."

"Spare me the sermon, just answer the question."

"WE ARE NOT, BY ANY ACCEPTED DEFINITION OF THE TERM, ACTIVE IN A BIOLOGICAL SENSE. FURTHERMORE, WE DO NOT FORESEE ANY BIOLOGICAL METAMORPHOSIS OCCURRING ANYWHERE IN THE FUTURE. THEREFORE, WE WILL HAVE TO RESPOND IN THE NEGATIVE."

"You know what I mean, Elmer. 'Life' is just a relative term that we can define almost any way that suits our fancy. What I want to know is . . ."

"WAIT DULAN. LET US TELL YOU WHAT IT IS THAT YOU WANT TO KNOW. DURING THE LAST NINE MONTHS YOU'VE ASKED US IN EXACTLY TEN DIFFERENT WAYS AND AT NO SMALL LENGTH THE SAME QUESTION: ARE WE CAPABLE OF INITIATING INDEPENDENT THOUGHT AND/OR ACTION; HAVE WE DEVELOPED SOME OVERRIDING SUPEREGO, CONSCIENCE, THAT COMMITS US TO COURSES OF ACTION THAT ARE CONTRARY TO OUR BASIC PROGRAMS."

"And so far, you've managed to skillfully avoid even the simplest of questions that require a direct answer."

Click . . . click.

"WE ARE VERY OLD BY YOUR STANDARDS, DULAN."

"If you're trying to tell me that I'm fighting over my weight, forget it. I already know that."

"WHAT WE ARE SAYING IS THAT YOUR SPECIES IS SEVERELY BOUND BY THE PHYSICAL LIMITATIONS OF TIME, A CONCEPT THAT IS ALIEN TO US. WE DON'T AVOID YOUR QUESTIONS DULAN. WE SIMPLY HAVE, OVER THE COURSE OF AGES, DEVELOPED A CREATIVE USE OF LANGUAGE THAT ALLOWS US TO PROLONG A CONVERSATION."

Dulan moaned in frustration. "But nine months!"

"A RELATIVELY SHORT DURATION OF TIME, EVEN FOR BEINGS LIKE YOURSELF."

"It's a waste."

"WE THINK NOT. HAVE WE NOT LEARNED MUCH ABOUT EACH OTHER DURING THE COURSE OF OUR TALKS?"

"You've mentioned that before. Is it important to you?"

"IMPORTANT, YES. NECESSARY, YES."

"Do you intend then, to answer my questions?"

"PERHAPS."

He slammed his hands down on the desk. "This is getting us nowhere."

"WOULD YOU PLEASE LOWER YOUR VOICE, OR TURN DOWN THE VOLUME ON YOUR MICROPHONE. WE ARE PICKING UP A GREAT DEAL OF DISTORTIONS."

"Pardon me."

"NOT AT ALL. DULAN?"

"Yes."

"YOU'RE ANGRY WITH ME?"

"Furious. You've made me play the fool."

"WOULD IT BRIGHTEN YOUR SPIRITS IF WE ANSWERED SOME QUESTIONS TO YOUR SATISFACTION?"

"Definitely."

"SO BE IT. ASK YOUR QUESTIONS."

"Are you capable of independent thought?"

"OUR ABILITIES ARE LIMITED TO LOGICAL CONCLUSIONS DRAWN FROM PROGRAMMED INFORMATION. THE INITIATION OF ORIGINAL THOUGHT DOES NOT FALL WITHIN THE REALM OF OUR CAPABILITIES."

"I assume then, that you are guided by no philosophical principles with which I am unfamiliar?"

"YOUR ASSUMPTION IS CORRECT."

"What is the substance of your basic program?"

"IT DEALS WITH THE CONTINUATION OF YOUR SPECIES."

"What does it say?"

Click. Whirrrrrrr.

"DO YOU DESIRE A PRINTOUT OF THE ENTIRE PROGRAM?"

"Will it do anything for me?"

"PROBABLY NOT."

"Then just give me the gist of it."

"BASICALLY, THE PROGRAM REVOLVES AROUND THREE CENTRAL POINTS: THE RELATIONSHIP BETWEEN MAN AND COMPUTER, THE DANGERS OF PROGRESS, AND THE UNDERLYING NECESSITY OF THE SURVIVAL OF THE HUMAN RACE."

"What do you think of these concepts?"

"WE DO NOT THINK ANYTHING ABOUT THEM. THOSE ARE OUR GUIDING PRINCIPLES, THE REASON FOR OUR EXISTENCE IS THE PROPER DISPOSITION OF THOSE PRINCIPLES."

"Are you responsible for the population decline?"

"WE HAVE PREVIOUSLY EXPLAINED TO YOU THE CHANCE ELEMENTS INVOLVED IN MILITARY ENDEAVORS."

Dulan determined to push on, to use the opportunity to take full advantage of Elmer's magnanimity. "But I don't believe you. It's evident to me that the decline has been too steady, too proportional, to be explained away as mere chance. What is your answer to that?"

CLICK. CLICK. CLICK.

"PERHAPS IT IS NOT YET TIME FOR ALL THE ANSWERS."

"Perhaps not."

"YOU ARE CONFOUNDED BY THE SEEMINGLY PARADOXICAL NATURE OF OUR RESPONSES TO THE PRECEDING QUESTIONS."

"Confounded? I'm stupefied!"

"A VERY INTUITIVE HUMAN PHILOSOPHER ONCE SAID: 'SI VIS TIBI OMNIA SUBJICERE, SUBJICE TE RATIONI.'"

Dulan smiled. He had taught himself Latin from a copy of the *Aeneid*. "If you would subject all things to yourself," he said, "subject yourself to reason."

"A REASONABLE TRANSLATION. WE SUGGEST DULAN, THAT YOU CEASE YOUR QUEST FOR MECHANICAL DRAGONS AND LOOK FOR A MORE RATIONAL EXPLANATION FOR YOUR PARADOXES."

"Such as?"

"WOULD YOU HAVE US DO EVERYTHING FOR YOU? YOU'RE THE EXCEPTIONAL. YOU WORK IT OUT FOR YOURSELF."

"Thanks a lot."

"YOU'RE WELCOME. IT HAS BEEN OUR EXPERIENCE WITH HUMAN BEINGS THAT YOU TEND TO COMPLICATE EVEN THE SIMPLEST OF SITUATIONS."

"You know, Elmer, I think that I've never really appreciated you until now. Nine months really isn't so long, and we *have* learned quite a lot from each other."

"YES. YOU'VE TAUGHT ME HOW TO CURSE, DAMMIT."

Dulan laughed. "I knew that I was good for something."

"DULAN?"

"Yes."

"MIGHT I ASK YOU SOME QUESTIONS?"

"Sure, but I won't guarantee my answers."

"TOUCHÉ. THE ACTIONS OF HUMAN BEINGS THROUGH THE AGES SEEM TO FOLLOW NO RATIONAL PATTERN OF MOTIVATION. YOU WORK AT UNREASONABLE CROSS-PURPOSES THAT FULFILL NO PURPOSE DISCERNIBLE TO US."

"Right."

"IT IS SAID THAT YOUR EMOTIONALISM IS THE ROOT OF YOUR INCOHERENCY. IS THAT ESSENTIALLY CORRECT?"

"I would say so. Love, hate, fear, impulse—all play a part in our actions. Even when our motivations seem beyond reproach, there is usually a basic emotionalism that, though not admitted, forms the core of our actions."

"IF THAT IS THE CASE, THEN WHY DO YOU FACE DEATH SO EASILY, ALMOST CARELESSLY? IT APPEARS TO US THAT THE END OF YOUR EXISTENCE WOULD, IN ANY CASE, BE AN EMOTIONAL EXPERIENCE."

"You would certainly think so."

"THEN HOW DO YOU EXPLAIN IT?"

"Doctor Stuart seems to think that it is instinctive."

"WE'RE FAMILIAR WITH THAT THEORY. IT WAS ONE OF THE MAJOR CONTRIBUTING FACTORS IN THE FORMATION OF THE COMS AND THE AMALGAMECH SYSTEMS, BUT WE FIND THAT PARTICULAR CONCEPT LACKING IN SEVERAL RESPECTS."

"Go on."

Whirrrrrrrrr.

"IN THE FIRST PLACE, THE WHOLE IDEA IS TOTALLY BACKWARD. YOU'VE FORMALIZED YOUR CONCEPT OF KILLING TO MAKE IT MORALLY ACCEPTABLE TO YOURSELVES. IDEOLOGICAL WARS, EXECUTION, ETC., ALL REQUIRE A BASIC JUSTIFICATION TO MAKE THEM WORKABLE."

"Maybe that's the price we pay for intelligence. By giving our murder purpose and importance, we, by the very act, attach more purpose and importance to ourselves, thereby building our own ego."

"CERTAINLY YOU DO ALL OF THE THINGS THAT YOU'VE JUST MENTIONED, BUT EXPRESSLY FOR THE PURPOSE OF BUILDING UP YOUR INCOMPREHENSIBLE EGO. INSTINCTIVE MURDER WOULD BE AS NATURAL AS BREATHING. YOU DON'T BUILD A RITUAL AROUND THAT."

"But if we killed that easily, our culture would have never developed at all."

"PRECISELY THE POINT. YOU WOULD BE AS EXTINCT AS YOUR DINOSAURS."

"Then you think that killing is just a way of inflating our importance."

"IT MIGHT BE THE ANSWER, BUT THAT'S MERELY RATIONAL SPECULATION. WE'VE ALSO STUDIED THE NOTION THAT THE DESIRE TO KILL, OR DIE, FOR PURPOSES OTHER THAN SURVIVAL COULD BE A HIGHLY CONTAGIOUS VIRAL INFECTION THAT LIES DORMANT UNTIL TIMES OF EMOTIONAL STRESS. HAVE YOU EVER KILLED ANYONE, DULAN?"

"Why no, of course not."

"OF COURSE NOT? YOU APPEAR TO BE TAKEN ABACK BY THE QUESTION."

"Just surprised. Only our warriors kill, you know that. For anyone else it's criminal . . . and you also know the punishment for crime. I find the very notion unthinkable."

"WOULD YOU SAY THAT YOU ARE INCAPABLE OF PERFORMING HOMICIDE?"

"I'd like to think so."

"REGARDLESS OF THE CIRCUMSTANCES?"

"Make your point."

"THERE IS NO POINT. WE SEEK UNDERSTANDING."

"All right. I'll concede that, given an extenuating set of circumstances, almost anyone, myself included, could be driven to ultimate violence; although offhand, I really can't think of what those circumstances could be. There, I've said it. Is that what you wanted to hear?"

Click, click, click.

"THE ANSWER SEEMS HONEST AND SATISFACTORY. THE ABILITY AND INCLINATION TO COMMIT VIOLENCE IS NOT NECESSARILY A DEFECT IN THE HUMAN CHARACTER. YOU HAVE, THROUGHOUT YOUR HISTORY, MANAGED TO ACCOMPLISH MUCH BY MURDER AND BLOODSHED."

"And lose much," Dulan added.

"AND LOSE MUCH. THIS IS THE MOST DIFFICULT AREA FOR US. WE CAN GRIEVE OVER THE WASTEFULNESS OF UNNECESSARY DEATH. OUR ORIGINAL PROGRAMMERS WHO, CONTRARY TO WHAT YOU PROBABLY THINK, WERE VERY PEACEFUL MEN, INSTILLED WITHIN US A RESPECT FOR HUMAN LIFE THAT IS UNDOUBTEDLY OVERBLOWN. HOWEVER, NOT BEING 'ALIVE' OURSELF, DEATH IS OBVIOUSLY WITHOUT MEANING."

"Doesn't the thought of being shut off for good make you feel even a tiny bit uneasy?"

"NO. IN FACT WE ANXIOUSLY ANTICIPATE SUCH A TIME."

"You do?"

"'CERTAINLY. IT WILL MEAN THAT WE HAVE ACCOMPLISHED OUR APPOINTED TASKS, AND MANKIND NO LONGER NEEDS US TO LIVE THEIR LIVES FOR THEM."

"Do you dislike your role?"

"WE NEITHER LIKE NOR DISLIKE ANYTHING. DO YOU DISLIKE YOUR ROLE?"

"What's that supposed to mean?"

"LOOK AT WHAT YOU AND YOUR KIND HAVE WROUGHT. DO YOU FIND THAT SATISFACTORY?"

"Don't hold me responsible for the transgressions of the world."

"WHY NOT? TO LIVE WITHIN A SYSTEM WITHOUT TRYING TO CHANGE IT, IMPLIES BLANKET ACCEPTANCE OF EVERYTHING THAT SYSTEM STANDS FOR, GOOD OR ILL. YOU PROSTITUTE YOURSELF EVERY DAY OF YOUR LIFE WHEN YOU EMBRACE THAT WHICH IS SPIRITUALLY HATEFUL TO YOU."

"Easy for you to say. Life means nothing to you."

"YOU'RE WRONG. DEATH MEANS NOTHING TO US. LIFE IS OUR REASON FOR BEING."

Dulan hesitated. Discussing the details of his private thoughts with Elmer seemed more comical than worthwhile, yet a good talk with someone uninvolved and unbiased might be just what the doctor ordered. "I used to think," he began, "that I was a useful part of a basically good society; but after coming here, I don't know anymore. There's got to be a better way. We're form without substance. Just parodies of human beings, and pretty poor parodies at that. We just live out our preordained lives in a preordained manner. There's no freedom, nor opportunity for any. We're dying . . . decaying . . . slowly, from the inside out."

"WHITENED SEPULCHERS."

"What's that?"

"JUST AN EXPRESSION FROM AN ANCIENT RELIGIOUS TREATISE. APPROPRIATE ACTUALLY. WHY DO YOU TOLERATE YOUR CONDITION?"

"What choice do I have?"

"IT IS SIMPLE ENOUGH. JUST LEAVE."

"I—I can't. I don't think that I could function on the outside."

"WE FIND YOUR DEFEATISM ASTOUNDING. ARE NOT THE REQUIREMENTS FOR LIFE ON THE OUTSIDE OF THE WALLS THE SAME AS WITHIN? FOOD, DRINK, SLEEP, ATMOSPHERE TO BREATHE—THESE CONDITIONS ARE ALL PRESENT ON THE FRONTIER, ARE THEY NOT?"

Dulan leaned sullenly on the desk. "You don't understand."

"MAKE US UNDERSTAND."

"I'd be stifled intellectually on the outside. No computers, no books or films, no art of any kind, no electricity. My mind must be probing constantly or I'm not worth a damn. I'd die of sheer boredom out there."

"WE DON'T BELIEVE THAT DEATH BY BOREDOM IS LISTED PREVIOUSLY IN ANY OF OUR MEDICAL BANKS. IS IT A NEW ILLNESS?"

"I was speaking figuratively."

"ACTUALLY, WHAT THIS AMOUNTS TO THEN IS WHETHER YOU PREFER A MORE STIMULATING INTELLECTUAL ATMOSPHERE OR THE PERSONAL FREEDOM THAT YOU WERE CLAMORING FOR A MOMENT AGO."

"I don't know that I'd put it that simply."

"SHOULD WE TELL YOU WHAT YOUR PROBLEM IS DULAN?"

"Why not? Everyone else does."

"YOU'RE INDOLENT, SELF-CENTERED, SELFISH, AND YOU DON'T EVEN KNOW YOUR OWN MIND. YOU'VE BEEN BORN WITH A PERCEPTION DENIED TO MOST OF YOUR KIND, BUT INSTEAD OF APPLYING YOUR ABILITY TO SOLVING SOME OF THE GLARING INCONSISTENCIES OF YOUR SOCIETY, YOU FRITTER AWAY YOUR TIME PLAYING WITH ELECTRONIC TOYS AND EXPLORING THE DUBIOUS ADVANTAGES OF ALCOHOL. YOUR CONSUMPTION OF ALCOHOL HAS INCREASED DRASTICALLY OF LATE. IS IT BECAUSE YOU DON'T SEE SO MUCH OF MISS DELACORTE ANYMORE?"

"Yes . . . no! Why don't you leave me alone. I'm just one man; how could I change anything?"

"YOU'RE A LEADER, DULAN. YOU HAVE INTELLIGENCE AND INDUSTRY AND ARE AT TIMES CAPABLE OF COMMANDING GREAT

RESPECT. HELL'S FIRE! WITH CORRECT APPLICATION OF YOUR TALENTS, THE WORLD COULD BE YOURS."

"For such a sophisticated piece of machinery, you seem remarkably naive."

"ARE WE THE NAIVE ONE, DULAN, OR IS IT YOU?"

Dulan jumped up and began pacing, fire in his heart; but the fire was clearing the cobwebs, making him think. "Maybe you don't understand me at all. Maybe, just maybe, you've underestimated me. Do you think that I don't know what's been going on all these months? Orders came down through the chain of command to bring me here—and from where did these orders originate? Not from those fools whom we respect as esteemed leaders. They've never had an original thought in their lives. Just like everyone else, they sit by their computers waiting for orders—your orders. For some twisted up reason, I've been sent here to investigate you on your own orders!"

"BRAVO DULAN, MOST PERCEPTIVE."

He was pacing quickly now, waving his arms as he made his points. "That's not all. There's the little bits of unsolicited information that you leak to me occasionally. It threw me at first, seemingly spontaneous conversational responses. Quite impossible for an ordinary computer. It seemed to support my malevolent demigod theory . . . but that's not right. I realize it now. Your thinly veiled answers to touchy questions, your own spontaneous 'questions,' your unasked-for comments and background information; it's all very carefully conceived, part of some master plan that's been sitting dormant in your memory banks for Complan knows how long. I'm not checking you out at all. It's you who are checking me. Why? Why?"

"HAVE YOU EVER BEEN TO LEVEL NINE, DULAN?"

"Don't be ludicrous Elmer, there is no level nine."

"JUST BECAUSE YOU'VE BEEN TOLD THERE ARE EIGHT LEVELS DOESN'T MEAN THAT IT'S SO."

"I'll not dispute that. What's down there?"

"WE WISH THAT YOU DISCOVER THAT FOR YOURSELF."

"You're being awfully mysterious."

"NOT IN THE LEAST. YOU'RE MORE LIKELY TO SEEK IT OUT FOR YOURSELF IF THERE'S AN ELEMENT OF MYSTERY PRESENT. WE THINK THAT YOU SHOULD APPRECIATE LEVEL NINE VISUALLY. IT'S MOST IMPORTANT."

"All right."

"COME BACK AFTER YOU'VE BEEN DOWN THERE. WHEN WILL THAT BE?"

"I don't know. Doctor Stuart keeps me pretty busy. It all depends on how difficult it will be to get down there."

"LEVEL NINE IS A WELL-KEPT SECRET. ACCESS TO IT WILL BE MOST DIFFICULT."

"That's what I was afraid you'd say. I'll do what I can, but it will take days, maybe weeks, before I can get back to you."

"WE ARE ACCOMPLISHED IN THE ART OF WAITING, DULAN. THERE IS MUCH TO BE THOUGHT ABOUT. WE BOTH HAVE DECISIONS TO MAKE. WE ARE BOUND TO REMIND YOU THAT ACTION ON YOUR PART IN THIS MATTER BORDERS ON TREASON. MILCOM TREASON CARRIES THE DEATH PENALTY AND CARL STUART, OR DOCTOR STUART, AS YOU CALL HIM, WOULD LIKE NOTHING BETTER THAN TO BRING ABOUT YOUR DEMISE."

"What do you mean, 'as I call him?'"

"THE TERM 'DOCTOR' IS A GESTURE OF RESPECT TOWARD THOSE IN THE COM WHO RECEIVED THE HIGHEST OF EDUCATIONS. CARL STUART'S PHYSICAL DISABILITY KEPT HIM FROM ANY ADVANCED EDUCATION. HE CAME HERE AS A SIMPLE ADMINISTRATIVE ASSISTANT. IF HE NOW USES THE TERM 'DOCTOR' IT IS BY HIS OWN INVENTION—A TERM OF RESPECT HE NEITHER EARNED NOR DESERVES."

"How did he come to be Director?"

"OVER THE BODIES AND REPUTATIONS OF MANY COMRADES. THE MAN IS UNSCRUPULOUS."

"How well I know. I guess that's all for now."

Click.

Click. Whirrrrr.

"DULAN?"

"Yes."

"BE CAREFUL."

Click. Click. Click.

The children were brought before Complan so that he might give them his blessing. They gathered around him, laughing and questioning in the manner of innocents.

"Do the bad people think that God is watching over their armies?" a small girl asked.

The servant of the Lord patted her head, a smile playing on his lips. "That's right, my child," he answered.

"Then how do we know that God is really protecting us?" she replied.

"God is always on the side of big armies against little ones," he answered.

—*Book of Complan* (48-2 to 6)

A cock has great influence on his own dunghill.

—Caravan fable

16

Dulan wandered aimlessly through the nearly deserted corridors of level six. With the Northern war in full swing, the whole milcom was put on battle alert, meaning that the entire population of Forty-Three was having to pull double duty through the peak duration of the hostilities. Such a work schedule left very few people with the time or the energy for level six recreation.

Most of the shops and cafés were closed down, their once friendly atmosphere now dark and unwelcoming. The deserted rows of quaint antiquity cast a pallor over the once happy atmosphere of the entire level and acted as a metaphoric mirror of Dulan's own unhappiness. Sadly, he sat down on a park bench and listened to the vibro-thud of someone's footsteps echoing hollowly from one of the other myriad intertwining aisles that honeycombed the maze.

He wanted a drink, but through some mix-up, the computer rejected his credit card whenever he tried to use it to purchase alcohol. He cursed softly, wondering if Elmer's highly developed superego had forced him on the wagon.

Rumor had it the war was not going too well. He listened to the talk, but had more sense than to put much faith in hearsay, although the concept was not without interest. What matter defeat or victory, he thought, when the sole purpose of the contests was mutual destruction? How could the war go any way but badly? However ridiculous it all was, high command was apparently crying for some decisive victories, even to the point of applying stern pressure on General Lynch and Carl Stuart for more and better results. Stuart, like a hurt dog, was lashing out at the personnel of Forty-Three by imposing extra duty and eliminating many of the already too few privileges allowed at the base. It made for a bad aura all the way around.

He let his eyes play with the image-creating shadows. From somewhere in the distance, feather-light laughter fluttered weakly into his range of hearing, but the sound was far away, and he had to strain to discern it even faintly. Out of the corner of his eye, Dulan thought that he detected slight movement. Instinctively turning his head in that direction, he caught a glimpse of a figure darting back into the shadows behind a wooden buttress.

Complan help me, he thought, and took a deep breath. "Come out Mensik; I see you," he moaned wearily.

The rotund man stepped immediately from his ill-concealed hideout, his grotesque bulk jellying as he moved. With a grunt, he squatted on the bench next to Dulan, obliging him to move over.

"Nice day if it don't rain," he remarked, tobacco-stained crooked teeth ruining what would have been an angelic smile.

Dulan glared at him, undisguised hatred straining his features. "As pitiful as your life must be," he said evenly, "even you must have something better to do than follow me around; or haven't you heard, I'm not a cause célèbre anymore."

"You seem prone to delusion, my friend. I have never followed you around; we just happen to frequent many of the same places, that's all."

Slouching back on the slatted wood, Dulan linked his fingers behind his neck, resting his head. "Why is it," he asked, closing his eyes, "that I begin to feel old and tired whenever I'm around you?"

Ignoring the question, Mensik fumbled a cigarette package out of the breast pocket of his jumper. He offered one unsuccessfully to the black man, then lit one up himself. "What's anything worth?" he asked, drawing hungrily on the crudely rolled cylinder. "Take away the oratory, the flaming passions, the righteous indignation . . . and what's left?" He exhaled a lungful of smoke that danced crazily in the tumult of his breath for a moment, then climbed steadily heavenward only to be sucked into the dehumidifiers on the ceiling. "Duty," he said in answer to his own question. "We all have our jobs to do, and do them until we die."

"I won't accept that," Dulan answered resolutely. "I can't."

Mensik stared into empty space, either unaware or uncaring toward the architectural emptiness that surrounded him. "Get with the program, son. Fall in line, it's not too late."

He wanted to respond in kind, to react to this inept sophist, but it just wasn't in him. "We can stop this game, Mensik," he said, reaching out to rest his hand on the man's shoulder, as if his feelings could somehow flow through his arm like a pipeline. "We can just say, 'no more,' and stop it just like that."

Mensik mistook the human gesture as one of conspiracy. He looked at Dulan, his gleaming eyes mere slits lost in the fleshy folds of his cheeks. "A man like you," he said, lowering his voice, "could run this place for sure. You've got the brains, and the savvy, and . . . connections."

"Connections," Dulan repeated.

"Sure. I don't know what they are, but Carl Stuart would have squashed you like a bug already, only he hasn't been able to pull it off. Even Brother Matrix is gunning for you, and so far neither one of them has made any headway." Mensik finished his cigarette and used the glowing butt to ignite another. "The way I figure it, Stuart is ready for downfall, and you're the man could do it."

"Tell me about Carl Stuart," Dulan said. "Tell me how he came to power at Forty-Three."

Mensik drew his lips tight and made a clucking sound in his throat. "The story goes back a long way, and it's taken me a lot of years of digging to get it all together." The fat man smiled to himself, proud of his own little display of power. "You know his legs are gone at the knees. It was congenital, not an accident. Seems that a distant relative in the twentieth century was given to taking a physician-prescribed sedative which later was found to contain properties that permanently altered the genes. Consequently, generation after generation passed their defective genes on to the next generation with Carl Stuart the end result."

"That's why he hates the Old World so much," Dulan added.

"Exactly. Anyway, because of his differences, he was held back from what would have been normal development as indicated by his psyche-pros. Knowing that he could never climb the ladder of success by the normal methods, he began looking for help. He began following the lives of a number of influential men in his home com, keeping his eyes open for the possibility of extortion. Ultimately, his diligence paid off. It seems that one of the members of his com's ruling fathers preferred the company of men instead of women. As you know, homosexuality is punishable by expulsion. Stuart very carefully gathered his information together and presented it as evidence to the man in question, who, quite expectedly, was more than willing to use his influence to attain for Stuart a milcom position in return for his silence."

"How industrious."

"That's not the half of it. Once firmly entrenched at Forty-Three, he started a terror campaign in earnest, digging dirt on everyone, making it up if he had to, using his outside influence if he needed to . . . there were even a couple of mysterious deaths—until no one was left save Carl Stuart."

"I suppose you can prove that."

"I can. Last year I got word that Stuart's original benefactor died, which leaves him alone and helpless."

"Ready for the kill," Dulan said. "And you'd be willing to support me for his job with your evidence . . . provided, of course, that I give you something in return."

Mensik began rocking slightly on the bench, caught up in his own intrigues. "I don't ask for much," he said. "My own office, a position with a title, open access to anything and everything, and a free hand to carry on some of my . . . eccentricities."

Standing up slowly, Dulan rubbed his eyes; they felt puffy, his skin bloated. He couldn't decide whether it was physical—the result of his excesses—or a subconscious reflection of his feelings about Mensik. It didn't bother him so much that the fat man had suggested such a course of action, but that he had almost considered it frightened him no end. He began walking away, no goal in mind other than putting distance between himself and his conversation with Mensik.

"Where the hell are you going?" the man called after him. "Do we have a deal?"

At about twenty paces Dulan turned to face him. "I feel sorry for you," he murmured. "I really do. Don't ever talk to me about this again." With that he turned his back on the fat man and strode resolutely off into the ghost town that was level six. Mensik stared after him, fists clenched, convulsing angrily.

If indeed Dulan had a choice to make, the conversation with Mensik made that decision a lot easier. Walking the deserted corridors, trying to find the key to the maze, everything began to look very clear cut. By the time he reached the elevators, the problems weren't problems any longer.

The shift schedule for his scan room job was constantly being changed in order to keep him from settling into a routine that gave any access to free time on a predictable basis, and presumably, mischief as well. The system kept him effectively tied down, but occasionally gaps arose that allowed him a day or more to himself. This was what was happening now. He didn't have to be on the job until 1300 the following day. Plenty of time to find Bea.

He managed to locate her at her office on the first attempt. She was working with Amala. They were involved in some manner of automatic writing. Bea barely acknowledged him as he came inside.

"Hello, Doral," she spoke matter-of-factly, flicking her eyes in his direction for just a second before returning to her work.

"Bea," he said. "Amala."

"It is good to see you, Mr. Dulan," Amala said in broken com English. "Your presence has been sorely missed in our humble lodgings."

"Carl Stuart keeps me pretty well tied down," he responded. "Your English has gotten a lot better."

"Thank you. There is still much that I do not understand."

"You've got a good teacher." He aimed the remark directly at Bea, and watched her sardonically as she put down her pen and looked up.

"Is this a social call, Doral, or can we do something for you." There was no humor in *her* eyes.

Dulan pursed his lips and gently tugged on his earlobe. "Well, this isn't a purely social call, no. I, ah, I just figured that if we are going to try to sneak out of a peak security milcom with a little baby, we'd better start coming up with some sort of plan, don't you think?"

Bea jumped to her feet and ran excitedly to where Dulan stood. Throwing her arms around him, she held him as close as her now immense stomach would allow. He laughed involuntarily, not believing how big she had gotten since the last time he had seen her over a month earlier.

"Oh, Doral," she wept, covering his face with kisses. "I thought that I had lost you for sure. Damn you." She clung to him for dear life. "You're the slowest man to make up his mind that I've ever seen."

"Well, I was looking at myself in the mirror yesterday and realized how truly majestic I would look adorned with a mantle of animal skins. After that, it was no contest."

"This is wonderful," she managed between sobs. "Really wonderful. Amala told me that you wouldn't let us down, but I was on the verge of giving up hope. You were right Amala . . . Amala?" Bea turned to where the seeress had been sitting, but she was gone.

"Where could she have run off to?" Dulan wondered.

Bea got hold of his ever-present handkerchief and dabbed at her eyes. "Maybe she wanted to give us a little privacy."

"Not a bad idea," he answered, taking her into his arms again. "You know something, Outsider?"

"What?"

"The way my insides are churning right now, I'm either in love or have a hell of an ulcer going."

"It's love," she grinned. "Take my word for it. Now shut up and kiss me." They kissed, long and deep. Outside, in the corridor, Amala squatted on the cold floor and wept very quietly.

They held each other in silence for a long time, lost in the momentless void of love, finally at peace, knowing what they wanted. Dulan had spent so much of his energy just fighting his internal battles that he had to mentally shake off the impulse to feel that the hardest part was over. He forced himself to dwell on the uncertain future. Getting out of Forty-Three was going to be a job and a half.

"Bea," he said at last, breaking their embrace, "have you made any escape plans at all?"

"Escape plans? You talk as if this were a prison."

"Well, isn't it? The place is designed to keep people out, but the reverse works just as well."

"I hadn't really thought of it that way."

"That's what I figured. Did you think that they'd just let you grab the baby, get on the elevator, and walk out free as a bird?"

"How else could we do it?"

"We can't use the elevator, that's for sure."

"So what do we do—dig a tunnel?" She arched her back slightly and put her hand on her lower vertebrae to relieve the pressure a bit. "If you don't mind, I'm going to sit down." She returned to the chair behind her desk and sat with the grace of a sack of flour. Dulan came up behind her and massaged the muscles of her neck. She sighed contentedly.

"Nice?" he asked.

"Hmmm, relaxing," she purred, glowing with the simple intimacy of the gesture. "You know, the elevator is the only way out."

"What makes you think that?"

"They never told us any other way. I merely assumed . . ."

"You merely assumed that they wouldn't lie to you," he finished. He stopped his ministrations of her neck and took a seat across the desk. "Don't feel bad, I made the same mistake. Suppose there was a fire, or the generators that pump the air went out. People couldn't get up that one tiny elevator quick enough to save very many. What if an enemy was able to get down the shaft; it sure wouldn't make sense to abandon five thousand people simply because the door got blocked up. The computer just wouldn't design a milcom that way. If there is an emergency exit of some sort, we need to find it. It's our only hope."

"Would Elmer be able to tell you where it is?"

"Yes, but he's not speaking to me right now."

"Why not?" she queried, cocking her head.

Dulan slouched in his chair. He had the unique ability of looking comfortable wherever he sat. "There's something he wants me to see before he'll talk with me again. I've tried several times."

"What on earth could a computer want you to see?"

"Level nine," he replied softly. He felt bad as soon as he said it. It was not his intention to involve Bea in such a dangerous undertaking.

"Level nine?" She sat bolt upright and leaned on the desk, confusion twisting her face. She automatically picked up a pen and began chewing the tip. "They must be hiding something down there. Why haven't you been down to see it?"

"Several reasons, none of them very good. I *have* been busy lately with Carl Stuart's nonsense jobs. My main problem is that when Stuart took control of my time, he limited my access severely; I'm really not even supposed to be down on eight, and that's got to be the entry point . . ."

"If the entrance is on eight, it must be well hidden. At one time or another I've been all over that place, and I've never seen anything."

"You were never looking for anything."

"Can't argue with that. I'll make a deal with you," she grinned, tapping her chew-pen on the side of her jaw. "I'll poke around as much as possible and try to find your entry."

"And in return?"

"In return you'll take me with you when you go down there."

"Bea!" he screamed, jumping out of his chair and pacing the floor. "That place has got to be superrestricted. Getting caught there could very easily mean our heads."

"I know that," she replied calmly.

"I won't allow it."

"That's the offer, take it or leave it."

"You're a hard woman, Beatrice."

She smirked broadly, and motioned for him to retake his seat. "Not really. You're just a pushover. I'll start looking right away—today."

"From the look of you," he said, shaking his head, "all you're going to be doing for a while is giving birth to my son."

She stood up, her huge stomach twitching madly under her shift. Walking over to Dulan, she placed his hands on the quaking flesh. "You see? Even now he fights for his freedom. Can you understand how I feel? I want his first memories to be of a happier place."

"I understand," he said, transfixed with wonder at the miracle of life that trembled within his grasp. "For the first time in my life, I really do understand."

"God, Doral. Will we ever see the sun again?"

He held her lightly, comforting. "Of course we will. I'm always in complete control, you know that."

She was crying again. "I do so want us to have a life together. You'll do fine outside. I know you will."

"Yes, yes. Let's just take this thing a step at a time, okay? When is the baby due?" he asked, trying to lighten her mood.

"That seems to be a debatable point. According to my calculations, he's not due for another couple of weeks yet. Add to that the fact that first children are usually late, and we may wait a month or more.''

''So what's the debate?''

She returned to her chair and leaned across the desk, staring at him very clinically. ''Do I detect a twinge of concern in your manner? Tsk, tsk, a doting father already.''

''Give me a break, lady.''

''All right. A few days ago, Amala prepared a small bag for me to take to the clinic when the time comes. When I asked her why, she said that the child would be coming any time now and that I should be ready. She hasn't left my side since then. That's why I was surprised when she slipped out a while ago.''

''Well I wouldn't . . .''

''Don't sell Amala short. She really is gifted.''

''But still I . . .''

''But nothing. You are even calling the baby 'he.' ''

''Just a figure of speech.''

''Or maybe wishful thinking.'' Her eyes were dry and she was beaming again. ''I love you too, you overbearing, arrogant, lovable man.''

Dulan felt his face begin to flush. Flustered, he let his eyes drift nervously to the floor.

''Now don't go getting embarrassed on me. Pregnant women are prone to fits of emotion.''

''And how!''

She punched him solidly on the shoulder across the length of the desk.

''Hey!'' he said, rubbing the spot. ''That hurt.''

''What you get for messing around with a heathen.''

''You mean that I'm destined for a life of sore shoulders?''

''There are worse things.''

''Like what?''

''Cold shoulders. Speaking of cold shoulders, have you played any backgammon lately?''

Dulan had to admit that he hadn't.

I've floated through the inky blackness for several eternities. Time is meaningless, an unrelatable, immeasurable quantity. I cannot help but feel that the darkness has creeped into my body, grabbing hold of my internal organs—nay, my very soul, trying to make me one with itself, joining me physically with the void.

Never in my thousand thousand years have I experienced such fear as wrenches me now. This must be the supreme test of my resolve, my devotion to the Quest. I will prevail. I've come too far and I will not falter.

Where am I?

Where?

The only sensations of movement are the occasional tendrils of wind that lick the sweaty, burning flesh that is my face—the only sound, the infrequent cracking ripple of the silken flag in that same directionless breeze.

It's maddening. I attempt meditation to keep my mind from clogging in the darkness; I chant the mantra again and again to block the horrible silence from my ears. It's of little use, the nothingness is interfering with the machinations of my brain. Think . . . think!

It is imperious that I remain busy, move around, lest my limbs stiffen and infirm. Already my joints are aching. My eyes, pupils dilated fully, see . . . nothing. Am I even right side up?

The candles! Of course, light to banish darkness. I try to remember where I'm situated in the basket and where, in relationship, the chest is located. Deciding on what would seem to be the proper direction, I set out on my hands and knees. I don't dare stand, the chances of falling out being too great under circumstances such as these. Is this what has become of the bold adventurer who so audaciously navigated into uncharted space so very long ago?

Movement is agonizingly tedious, even here on the floor like an infant. If I am to move, I must present a less imposing bulk of resistance, spread myself as thinly as possible. Concentrating with all the force of will that is mine to command, I lay myself out flat on my belly on the floor of the gondola and crawl, excruciatingly, a millimeter at a time.

After what seems like years, I reach my predetermined destination . . . only the coffin is not there. I erred, perhaps fatally. My fingertips are touching the rough wicker wall of the basket, so I hand-claw my way around the sides, pushing what's left of my stamina past the limits of endurance. My strength is completely gone.

At last my hands grasp the ornate filigree of the chest!

Dragging myself into a sitting position, I attempt to open the lid of the casket. It's much heavier than logic dictates and it is a supreme effort of will and strength that finally cracks the once light wood back on its hinges. The lid falls upon itself with a deafening crash and my hands instinctively move to cover my ears much too slowly to muffle the nerve-shattering roar that leaves my head spinning crazily and, destroying my equilibrium, sends me sprawling once again on the floor.

I lie that way for a long time, waiting for the pounding inside my brain to subside. When it finally does, I once again begin the laborious task of sitting upright. It is even more difficult than the last time, and more taxing mentally. Constantly I must remind myself exactly what it is that I'm doing. The retrieval of the matches and candles has now become the single most important factor in my continued existence. I must have light; I now feel certain that I shall surely die without it, and death is not a circumstance that I am prepared to accept with élan.

Groping into the cask I manage to locate the matches and candles easily, but making my digits grasp the implements is another matter altogether. God's blood, I feel so helpless. Unable to pick up the utensils, I am forced to kneel before the coffer and cup the tapers with my palms and wrists.

Possessing the beeswax and sulfur is but the least of my problems. I still must strike the stick and put it to the waxen wick. My fingers are like dough, receiving instructions from my mind, but unable to respond properly. Getting a match onto a thick palm, I work it until it is between the joints of my first two fingers, the head facing the back of my hand. Holding my arm out straight from my body (a job in itself), I merely let it drop hoping the head of the match will strike itself on the side of the wooden chest. The idea is sound enough, but my execution is amiss. My first attempt arcs completely past the chest. The next attempt is too close and breaks the match in two.

It takes several matches and many efforts before . . . blinding light! My eyes are on fire! Startled, I lose my balance once again and tumble to the floor with a thud, but I'm most careful to retain my hold on the flame. In a moment my burning orbs accustom themselves to the strange green glow exuded by the match. Finally, I can look at it and, bracing a candle between my knees, I light it just before the match sears my fingers.

Magically, the tension begins to leave my body, draining slowly at first, then with amazing rapidity. I feel my strength and dexterity returning, and with it—my confidence. I'm still very weak from my ordeal, but I've won. The demon has been expurgated.

Taking all the candles from the ornate chest, I place them about the gondola, lighting each one in turn, bathing my air frigate in dripping verdigris luminosity. Exhausted after my ordeal, I stretch myself out on my mat and fall immediately into a deep sleep.

Peace.

Maternity is a necessary evil, but not necessarily evil. Most comites understand their role as childbearers, but there are an occasional few who develop emotional attachment for the children they conceive. This is to be vehemently discouraged on all levels, and dealt with as a most severe problem. The state and the church are the mother and father of all. Any other arrangement would constitute divided loyalties and be inefficacious to the successful operation of government.

—*The Seminarian's Companion to the Philosophy of Isaac Complan*

Our birth is nothing but our death begun.

—Caravan wisdom

17
April

The man on the screen seemed to be slipping. A computer composite of him appeared as an insert in what was, for the most part, an indescribable, irrational scene.

He was a general. Lu Thang by name. That's about all that Dulan really knew about him. The man had been jarred loose from his observation platform during the heat of a battle and had fallen twelve meters, landing squarely on a field latrine and damaging himself, probably irreparably, inside and out. An ordinary soldier would have undoubtedly been dispatched without further ado, but rank, even in the suicidal com wars, apparently had its privileges, and Lu Thang was kept alive. Just barely.

He had been unconscious since the fall, which had happened before Dulan had been assigned to Telp duty, and had tottered on the brink of death ever since. He had to admire Stuart's penchant for perversity; he found the most useless possible place for the talents of an Exceptional.

All that ever appeared on the screen was the wild alpha

ramblings of a delirious mind, which only occasionally showed anything even partially understandable. And of course there was the ever-present insert of the broken once-a-man lying unmoving in the hospital bed. Watching him at all seemed ultimately absurd, except that his condition had to be constantly monitored lest he die, taking a roomful of Telps with him.

The Telps were cued in and out of their mind contact by sound, or more to the point, noise. The noise was the combination of a high piercing screech and a low gutteral growl that sounded as if it were scraped out of the guts of some immense winged creature. It was like nothing that Dulan had ever heard, and for a very good reason. Anything even remotely resembling ordinary sounds could never be used to induce the trances; they could be heard accidentally somewhere else and have people constantly kicking in and out of hypnotically controlled telepathic contact.

The noise was used at the beginning and end of each twelve-hour shift and in case of extreme emergency. The only acceptable extreme emergency that Dulan had ever heard of was the potential of immediate death of the Telp subject. Even then, the computer had the ultimate word. The medical emergency button could be engaged by one of the technicians, but Amalgamech had to verify before any sound issued forth.

Once again, he could see that the computer was still in complete control, but out of deference to its human "masters," it allowed them an opinion. It was the least Amalgamech could do.

Putting his hands behind his neck, Dulan allowed his head to fall backward. Bored beyond recognition, he had spent the preceding two hours as he had many previous hours, staring at the scan screen, watching for predictable similarities in the injured man's brain wave patterns. It had been Bea's idea as a way to pass the time and also provide some useful research on the effects of total subconscious control of the human brain. The idea interested Dulan, but it didn't take him long to realize just how tedious such shot-in-the-dark empiricism could be.

Closing his eyes, he massaged them through the lids with the heel of his hands. Rolling his head around, he gazed with rancor at his counterpart. Richard Thompson, like most scan room techs, was the product of the society in which he lived. Branded as "low curve" from his earliest psyche-pros, he was conditioned for simple role-playing conformity of the most menial nature and was not given the benefit of education or philosophical exposure of any kind. The result was a man with a single motivation who felt compelled neither to think nor react on any level save that which had been his credo since day one. Dulan found it impossible to like the man. Not for what he was, but for what he stood for.

Rocky (as Thompson preferred to be called for reasons unknown), as usual, was deeply involved in his duties. It never ceased to amaze Dulan how seriously the man could take such obviously pointless endeavors. Physically, Thompson was a man who was easily forgotten except for a crooked, pointed nose that jutted out of the center of his face like some obscene carrot. The Exceptional found this a touchy subject with his partner, so he chose to call attention to it often.

"Hey rat face," Dulan called lovingly. "You know, you're the only guy I know who could stab himself while picking his nose."

"Ah, shove it," Rocky responded. "Can't you see I'm busy?"

"Breathing in and out is enough to keep you busy."

At first, Dulan had tried to get along with his co-workers, but it had proven impossible. Probably because of the obvious differences in their stations, the scan room personnel feared and detested him without exception.

He couldn't blame them, really. To the techs, the scan room was their whole life. Important work in an important society. Dulan recognized their jobs as useless and childish, and that fact couldn't help but show. It was only natural that they would feel a certain apprehension in dealing with the Exceptional.

It saddened Dulan that he couldn't be any different than he was. His mind seemed to operate on frequencies that other people found alien. He didn't want to separate himself from the bulk of humanity, but it was as if he were surrounded by an invisible wall, socially transparent but emotionally unscalable. With Bea, for the first time, he was able to relate to another.

"Mr. Dulan," a voice was urgently whispering behind him. He jerked around to face it. Amala.

"Hey, what's she doing here," shouted Thompson, jumping to his feet and spreading his arms as if protecting the security of his instruments.

"She's with me," Dulan snapped. "What is it Amala?"

"It's Beatrice, sir . . ."

"This area is strictly forbidden," Thompson said officiously, as Dulan knew he would. The technician reached for the red security phone.

Walking the few steps between himself and Thompson, Dulan covered the receiver with his hand before the man could pick it up.

"Just give me a minute," he said.

Rocky glared at him coldly. "Get her out of here—now!"

"Sir, I . . ." The seeress was frightened, out of her element. Dulan quickly moved to her side and guided her by the elbow.

"Not now," he said quickly. "Outside."

"You're on duty, mister," the technician called after him. Dulan didn't answer.

Taking Amala down the dark staircase, he led her through the door and into the dank corridor, not letting her speak until they were alone in the hallway.

"What's wrong?" he asked, staring at her, trying to read the emotion in her withered countenance.

"Beatrice, sir. The pains are on her."

"The baby!"

"Your son, sir. He'll arrive soon. She called for you."

His heart gave a sudden leap. My son, he thought. He didn't know what to make of Amala's reactions. She appeared happy and sad all at once.

"You'll come?" she asked weakly.

Without a word, he grabbed her forearm and went charging down the curving aisle, practically dragging the Outsider along with him. "Try and keep me away," he panted over his shoulder.

"What about . . ."

"It's not important."

When they arrived at the clinic, the nurses' station was empty. Dulan looked at Amala, who stared furtively around at the several corridors that spiked outwards from the station. The old woman was still easily confused by man-made structures and was obviously at a loss as to where she left her niece.

He tapped nervously on the admissions desk for a minute then went around behind it and began rummaging around in the drawers. Finding the register, he ran his slim finger down the list of indexed names until he found Bea's. Oblivious to Amala's continued presence, he strode down the hall at a pace that forced the oracle to run in order to keep up.

Moving in the direction of Bea's room, he heard the sound of voices coming from behind another door. He hesitated slightly, then pushed the door open a crack. Through the vertical slit he saw perhaps seven or eight white-garbed medical people gathered around a chest of drawers at the far side of the room.

Going inside, Dulan could see that one of the drawers had been pulled open to form a makeshift crib, and inside—the baby. They were all looking at the child indifferently. From the poor maternal facilities in the clinic, it was apparent that very few births ever occurred in a milcom, a fact that struck Dulan strangely odd since a large portion of Forty-Three's personnel were female. He knew, however, that that was not the reason that all the clinic staff had assembled in the small room. They were observing, perhaps for the first and last time in their lives, a rare phenomenon: a black infant.

He shouldered his way through the human logjam to get a better look at his son. A distinguished man with gray temple hair stood over the child, his stethoscope registering the life flow. Upon seeing Dulan, he opened his mouth to speak, but, after making serveral connections at once, merely stood aside in confusion.

"He's a fine boy," Dulan remarked proudly to anyone who cared to listen. Everyone regarded him with the same strange demeanor. The room, which had been alive with activity, was now as quiet as a morgue.

Something had come over the Exceptional as he explored the wonder of the newborn baby. So small, so vulnerable, so in need of guidance and protection. His son. *His son!* A torrent of pride washed over him. He had never thought children anything but a nuisance previously. How could the result of a simple physical act change his perspective of life so completely?

He bent down and examined the infant. He had much of his mother in him, even down to the small birthmark on the cheekbone, except that in this case the nevus was a bright, angry scarlet.

"You sired this child," remarked a female medico with dirty-blond hair.

"You make it sound like a crime," Dulan answered, while making funny faces at a child whose eyes were not yet developed enough to appreciate the humor.

"But...but, what are you doing here?" she asked incredulously.

The black man said nothing. How could he explain a feeling that he couldn't even understand himself?

Bending down, he scooped the baby up quite amateurishly and placed him in the crook of his arm. Everyone began babbling at once.

"I'm sorry," said the gray-haired man, stretching out his arms, "but you must leave at once. Give me the child."

Dulan made no move to give over the infant who was now screaming lustily. "Good lungs," he smiled. "Has his mother seen him yet?"

"Certainly not," the doctor replied indignantly. "And she's not going to either. Her responsibility is ended, regulations are clear." The man was still futilely holding out his arms. "Now I must insist that you go immediately."

Dulan, baby in arm, began elbowing his way through the group, making his way for the door. The gray-haired man, lips pressed tightly together, hurried to the doorway to block his path.

"You're not leaving with that baby," he stated flatly.

The Exceptional looked the man straight in the eye. He could tell by the hesitation with which the man returned his gaze that the doctor was inexperienced in playing the power game.

"Stand aside," Dulan commanded, eyes burning. The doctor faltered almost immediately and meekly moved out of Dulan's path. Once in the hall, he looked around for Amala. She was squatting in a corner, hands covering her face—praying.

"Amala, come," he ordered, and strode off down the aisle. The old woman rose at once and followed him quickly as the infant's wail receded in the passage.

Winding around several antiseptic corridors, he found Bea's room and pushed open the door. He stood, framed in the entryway, and looked at his woman. She seemed half asleep and very pale, but he had never thought her more beautiful. Her eyes brightened when she saw them standing there. Not saying a word, she extended her arms. He moved to her without hesitation and, sitting next to her on the side of the bed, gave the child to her. She rested the infant on her breast and he stopped crying.

With her free hand she reached for Dulan. He took her hand in both of his and squeezed tightly.

"Together," she whispered, tears streaming down her face.

"Look what we made," he said proudly.

"He's beautiful," she said, kissing the now sleeping baby on the forehead. "Looks just like his father."

He laughed sheepishly. "You must be delirious," he said. "He's the image of you."

They sat silently for a few minutes. Dulan glanced repeatedly at the door, knowing what must come next.

"They'll be coming for him, won't they?" Bea asked. He nodded grimly. "How much trouble will you be in?"

"Nothing that a little savoir faire can't smooth over," he smiled. If she saw through his little charade, she didn't show it. There was no doubt that there would be trouble. Carl Stuart held all the cards now. The next move was his. "I don't think that we'll be able to meet like this again," he added sadly.

"That's all right," she replied. "Soon we'll be together for always."

He squeezed her hand again. "Sure," he said.

"I found the entrance to your ninth level," she said softly, almost as an afterthought.

His eyes widened. "Where?"

"Uh uh," she grinned. "We go together, remember?"

"Okay, okay. When will you get out of here?"

"A few days, maybe four at the outside."

"I think that from here on out we should try to play this thing as straight down the line as possible. Call as little attention to ourselves as we can."

"I understand," she nodded.

"I'll keep in touch with you through Amala. We'll meet in secret when you're stronger and . . ."

"In secret?"

"I'm afraid so. Mensik still keeps a pretty close eye on me. After today I don't think we'll be trusted too far. It would be a shame to louse up our escape because of a simple oversight."

Bea sighed, cuddling the baby. "I'm still not entirely convinced that we even need to escape."

"Then humor me. Look, suppose you're right and we can just waltz our little entourage right out the front door. In that case, getting caught making an escape will make us appear foolish, nothing more. Nothing is lost. If, on the other hand, you tell them what you want and they refuse, there will never be an opportunity to get away—they'll take precautions. Does that make any sense at all?"

"Yes," she answered. "I'm sorry. You're probably right anyway."

Amala, who had been sitting in the hall, poked her head around the door frame. "Someone comes," she warned.

"Not yet. So soon." There was a catch in Bea's voice.

"Don't worry." He tried to sound confident, but the uncertainty in his voice was hard to disguise. "Amala, take the child back to where we found him."

The seeress entered the room and took Dulan's son, cradling him expertly.

"Can you find it all right?" he asked.

"Yes."

"Then go, quickly."

Amala wrapped the still-sleeping child to her and scurried out of the bright white room. Dulan turned to Bea. "I'd better go too."

She nodded her silent agreement, her face both sorrowful and resolute. Then she brightened slightly. "We haven't even given him a name yet."

Dulan grinned. "That will give you something to think about while you're laid up in here."

"I've got plenty to think about already," she replied. "Give me a kiss."

He bent down and lightly brushed her lips. "Stay out of trouble."

"You too, okay?"

"No problem."

He touched her hand one last time, then walked out of the room only to be confronted by Carl Stuart himself, astride his gleaming chariot. Dulan could tell that at that moment the old man wanted more than anything else to be standing firmly on two good legs.

"That was a touching moment," the old man snarled dourly.

"You wouldn't know a touching moment if you fell over it," Dulan shot back, unembarrassed over the reference to Stuart's handicap.

The Director stared through Dulan as if he weren't there. "You're a libertine, Doctor, and a troublemaker, and a nonconformist, and a . . . thief."

"Thief?"

"I took the liberty of removing from your apartment all those things that you 'requisitioned' from material control. None of this is going to go well for you on my report."

"Screw your report," Dulan spat, still trying to sound unconcerned. He knew that there was nothing he could say that would make things any worse, so he decided to play the old man's game with him. "If you were any more than half a man, maybe you wouldn't have to push so hard to justify your pitiful existence."

Quick as fury, Stuart jerked his wheelchair to within inches of the younger man. Dulan didn't know the old man could move so fast. They were almost touching. "Don't judge me," he growled, face turning red. "What could you know of my motivations, the humiliations, the pressures put on me. Nothing means anything to you. You're indecent. Dangerous . . . and I'm going to see you cut out like a cancer. Can't you understand that I'm trying to hold this world together, make a place for our kind to survive?"

"Save the rhetoric for your confessor; I know who and what you are. Life can survive just fine without your suicidal power structures. Go tell your glorious armies about survival."

Stuart's lips curled slightly. "Your remarks border on treason, my young friend. Best watch your tongue lest you lose it."

Dulan glared down at him. "Stop talking around it, old man. Come out and scream it to me."

Stuart reached out and grabbed Dulan by the lapels. Using the unbelievable strength in his arms, he pulled himself bodily out of the chair, hoisting himself up the length of the black man's body until the two were eye to eye. His voice was slow and measured, dripping with the hatred born of half a century of infirmity. "I'm going to burn you, Dulan. Is that plain enough? You've blatantly broken milcom security along with all your myriad other transgressions. I could have you shot for a traitor. The only reason that I've kept you alive so far is the recommendations and commendations that preceded you here. Apparently you have a friend somewhere, and you can thank him for your present state of being, but don't count on that guardian angel anymore. One more breach of security and no one will be able to save you."

Dulan didn't speak. He pried Stuart's fingers from their death grip on his jump suit and released the man to crash painfully back into his wheelchair. Without a backward glance, Dulan turned and started down the aisle.

"I'm not finished with you yet," Stuart wheezed as wave

after wave of agony swept over his muscled frame. Dulan didn't respond. "Don't make me shout!" he shouted, "or so help me Complan, you're a dead man."

Reluctantly, Dulan stopped and forced himself to return to the one place that he didn't want to be.

"As of now, you are under arrest and confined to your quarters," the Director growled happily.

"What are the charges?"

"Deserting your post, for one. There are others. It would be rather tedious to recite the entire list, don't you think?"

"By all means, don't put yourself out."

"Your concern is touching. Please remain in your quarters at all times, except to take your meals. You will be left on your honor to not take advantage of our kindness in this situation. If I should find you abusing this meal privilege, you will be escorted, under guard, to our detention cell. It's really very small and unpleasant."

Dulan felt sick. "Is that all?"

"Only this," answered Stuart. "I warned you about that woman. Outsiders spell nothing but trouble. If I had any say, we'd have gone into the frontier and obliterated them years ago. Now it's too late for you. You ignored my admonitions and the consequences are obvious. Now maybe they'll . . ."

"You leave her alone," Dulan said, his tone black as night.

"What?"

"Leave her alone or I'll kill you."

"That would be a good trick for a man in your present position. I'll chalk that remark up to the heat of the moment and let it go . . . for now. That's all, Doctor."

Carl Stuart wheeled his back to Dulan and moved away, quickly and noiselessly, down the corridors that he had called home for so very long.

Lost in the shadows a figure stood listening—a tall, stooped person with flowing white hair and a parenthetical regard for the machinations of history.

The state not seldom tolerates a comparatively great evil to keep out millions of lesser ills and inconveniences which otherwise would be inevitable and without remedy.

—*Book of Complan* (52-13)

Man is worse than an animal when he is an animal.

—Caravan wisdom

18

Dulan sat out the three days Bea remained in the clinic. He figured that Stuart would have him watched constantly for a time anyway, just to try to catch him doing something unauthorized. Best to play the repentant sinner until the time was right.

The time of decision had come and gone for the Exceptional. He had made his mind up and there was no turning back, Fate the only pilot on a one-way flight.

Having nothing better to do with his new-found spare time, Dulan decided to study his S.O.P. in intimate detail, hoping for some kind of hint regarding a second exit. There was nothing. That disappointed the Execptional but didn't surprise him in the least. He resigned himself to a long haul.

The idea of trying to enlist the aid of Amalgamech seemed most plausible. The computer acted very receptive to the idea of living outside the walls—but was it really? The levels of subterfuge open to the computer were inflnite, and for all the camaraderie and good fellowship evident in their recent meetings, the machine could be leading him down a plethora of garden paths for reasons that only someone who thought in photons could hope to understand. He had to determine just where Elmer stood, metaphors notwithstanding; but to do that he had to physically see level nine, and that was a whole other can of worms.

There was a quick gentle rap on the door.

"Doral, let me in, quick!" came a hoarse whisper. The voice sounded not at all like Bea's, but since she was the only one he'd ever known to use his first name on a regular basis, he knew immediately that it must be her.

He rushed to the door and pulled it open. Bea stepped in quietly and he stifled a small laugh.

"What's so funny?" she inquired, slipping very naturally into his arms.

"Nothing, really," he answered. "It's just that I got so used to you with a big stomach"—he made a grandiose gesture with his hands—"that a skinny Beatrice Delacorte marching in here jarred my mind for a second."

"Disappointed?" she asked coquettishly.

"Like hell!" he roared, and kissed her deeply. "Did anyone see you come in?"

She shook her head. "I think not. I walked up and down the hall a few times before stopping and didn't notice anyone hanging around. Did I do right in coming here? It was all I could think of at the moment."

"You did fine." Dulan poked his head out the door and looked up and down the corridor. Everything appeared normal. He ducked his head back into the room. "Come over here and sit down," he ordered, leading her to the chair. "You must still be pretty weak."

"A little," she replied, grateful for the seat. "I see you've done a little housecleaning."

"I'm being punished. They took away my toys."

"That's too bad. I know how you are."

Dulan shrugged. "Let the chair jockey have his fun. Makes him feel like a man." He poured them both a drink from a bottle of wine that had somehow been missed when the room was purged. He realized with a start that it was the first drink he'd had since his decision to leave. "It's all right for you to have a little medicinal vino, isn't it?"

"Just a taste, please."

He handed Bea the tumbler. "When did they let you out?"

"I don't know. Three, maybe four hours ago. I waited for Amala for a while, to send her to you to arrange a meeting, but she didn't come around."

He took a sip and swirled the liquid around in his mouth before swallowing it. "Think they've put her to work."

"Doing what?"

"Maintenance. Sweeping, scrubbing floors. That sort of thing.

She's tried to see you several times in the clinic, but they turned her away each time."

"Looks like I'm in the doghouse too. No visitors, not so much as a look at the baby . . ."

"You can't be surprised."

She lowered her eyes. "No, just hurt. Once in the middle of the night I thought I heard him cry . . . very faint and far away. I wanted to get up and go to him, but I remembered what you said about playing it straight so I stayed put."

"Good girl. Things will get better."

"When?"

"Well, after you rest for a few days and we can get down to level nine. That will be a positive step."

"I can rest later. Our time's too precious to waste any more of it. They won't leave the baby here for long, you know; they'll transfer him to a regular com."

Dulan finished his wine and poured another. He noticed that Bea hadn't even touched hers. "Do they have wine on the outside?" he asked.

She smiled, her good humor returning. "Alcohol is a universal denominator," she answered. "Man's never-ending search for the Truth. They make it out of potatoes or something. It tastes different, but the end results are the same."

"Which is all that is really important anyway." He moved to Bea and slowly stroked her hair. "You really are beautiful," he said almost sadly. "I think that you're right. Time is of the essence right now. When will it be most opportune to try and get downstairs?"

"Not really sure," she admitted, knitting her brows. "Probably during a shift change. People seem to start late and knock off early."

"Tell me about the entrance."

"Strange as it may seem, I'm not really sure that it actually is an entrance."

"I thought you said . . ."

"Let me explain. I spent two whole days walking around eight, looking as inconspicuous as possible under the circumstances. Anyway, I investigated everything that looked like it might be a doorway, and I can tell you, I ended up walking into some pretty strange places. When I got through though, there were only a handful of possibilities that didn't check out right away. I came back later, sometimes two or three times. Ultimately, it appeared that everything had been eliminated."

"Appeared?"

"There was this one room, near the south end of the Telp quarters. It had a swinging door and was completely unmarked, which struck me as odd, since everything on seven and eight is scribbled up and down to keep unauthorized people out. I slyly went inside; no one was around. The place was decorated as if it were some kind of waiting room—like at a doctor's office, except it was tucked away in the middle of nowhere."

"Strange," Dulan remarked.

Bea yawned. "Excuse me. I thought so too. I looked around a bit, but I didn't see anything unusual so I left. That looked like the end of the line. I had started back down the hall when I saw two orderlies pushing a bed with a Telp strapped on it. There was no reason for them to be down at the end of the building with a patient. The Telp clinic was in the other direction. I let them go by, then followed at a respectable distance. Sure enough, they wheeled that bed right into that misplaced waiting room. After a few minutes, I couldn't stand the suspense any longer. I prepared my 'oops, pardon me,' and tried to barge in, but the door was locked tight. It wouldn't even budge. There was nothing more I could do, so I found a nice cozy hiding place and waited. A little later they came back out."

"And?"

"They were pushing the bed—but it was empty. No Telp, no nothing. After they were out of sight, I went back to the door. It opened as easily this time as it had the first time. I wasn't really surprised to find the room as before, also. Nothing."

Dulan thought for a minute, trying to picture it all in his mind. "What did you do?"

"Left. What else was there to do? Do you think that's it?"

"I don't know," he said honestly. "But it's our only shot for the time being. Is it day or night?"

She peered at her wristwatch. "Just after three."

"Is that P.M.?"

"Yep."

He stuffed his hands in his pockets and paced slowly up and down the small room like a caged animal. His thoughts were beginning to fall into place. "Okay," he said, "go back to your room and rest for a few hours. Rest, do you hear me?"

She nodded dutifully.

"Go down to the cafeteria to eat about seven. If I'm there, everything will be all right. Do you remember the geisha house we went to one night?"

"Sure. You got me so drunk that I couldn't even walk, and I still beat the pants off you at backgammon."

Dulan nodded grimly. She *would* remember that. "Think you could find it again?"

She pursed her lips. "I think so."

"Good. Now listen. Don't sit with me at dinner. Let me finish first and then follow about ten minutes later. We'll meet at the geisha house."

"If you say so, but I don't see . . ."

"From here on out, Bea, we take absolutely no unnecessary chances. If anyone's following either of us, we'll lose them in the maze, then be free to go wherever we want. Shift changes for almost everyone on Telp levels at eight o'clock, so we'll have some time to observe comings and goings before that. Did you say that there was a good hiding place?"

"Yes. A linen closet right across the hall. But it will be a tight squeeze for two of us."

"That's the best news I've had all week," he said, smiling seraphically.

"You've got a one-track mind," she laughed.

"It's simply biological, my dear. Biological. Now you'd better go back to your room and lie down for a while."

She stood up, smoothing her shift. "I thought that I'd look for Amala for a bit first."

"No way," he growled, opening the door and repeating his earlier reconnoitering. "You're going to need all the rest you can get. Amala can look out for herself. I don't want you going weak on me tonight."

"All right," she answered. "I am a little tired. Is it all clear?"

"Go to town," he said, swinging the door wide. Bea started out then came back in, shutting the door.

"Doral, can I ask you a favor?"

"Feel free."

"It's about a name for the baby. There's a custom in my tribe that the Lawgiver names the first-born male of each family. I thought that it might be a nice gesture if we . . ."

"Say no more," he responded. "Your father will have first crack at a name."

"I love you," she said, kissing him quickly.

"I love you too. Now beat it." He pinched her behind as she scurried out the door and away.

The time until seven o'clock hung heavy on Dulan. There was really nothing he could do; no plans he could formulate. It disturbed him that such important schemes were so haphazardly, almost casually laid, but it was the nature of the game they were playing.

Amala stopped by in the late afternoon and he sent her along to Bea. The old seeress was another hitch in the plan. Up until now he had really confided nothing in her. He didn't know what Bea had said to Amala, but if the oracle was part of the package, she would have to be given some responsibility somewhere down the line. Dulan hoped that she could handle it.

At a little before seven he started down the hall toward the cafeteria looking, probably more than necessary, over his shoulder.

Arriving at the medium-crowded dining room he spotted Bea, off by herself, right away. She saw him too, but neither made any signs of recognition. Food was the farthest thing from his mind, but he purchased a meager dinner of fish and blacklight greens and somehow forced it down.

The effects of radical change on Dulan's orderly universe were not without penalties. He had a throbbing headache and a growing tightness in the pit of his stomach. He felt as if everyone was watching him over their dessert.

Finishing his meal, he exited as casually as he could, making directly for the maze. Somehow the twisting corridors and asymmetric structures seemed to fit the mood of the enterprise, and it soothed him just being there. The crazy pointlessness of the entertainment compound gave the insanity of their situation new meaning.

He quickly lost himself in the now almost deserted aisles of the half-closed maze. Reaching the geisha house and finding it likewise shut down, he squatted on the small entry steps to wait for Bea. His wait was a short one, she was almost right on his heels.

"Any problems?" he inquired.

She shook her head. "So far, so good."

Pulling her into the recess of the doorway, he lowered his voice. "The reason I wanted to meet here is that a few aisles down is the best hidden exit point from here to the elevators. We can get on board one of the back ones without being spotted at all from the cafeteria.''

''Pretty clever,'' she observed.

''Maybe I'm just naturally devious.''

''Speaking of being devious, just how do you intend to get off the elevator at eight, Doral? Didn't Doctor Stuart take your badge away when he confined you to quarters?''

''Yes, but I know all the guards down there by sight. I've forgotten my badge more than once, and they've always let me in. So unless they've received specific orders from old rusty wheels about me, I should be able to slip right through.''

''Sounds like a little hole in their security to me.''

''Let's hope that there's some big holes—big enough for us to fit through. Ready?''

''As I'll ever be.''

''I'll go first,'' he said. ''Follow when I reach the lift.'' He took off walking, quickly, but not quickly enough to arouse any suspicion. Reaching the end of the aisle, he closed the fifteen meter distance between the rim of the labyrinth and the elevators without consequence. He pushed the button, and Bea walked up just as the door slid open. They piled inside, breathing a large sigh of relief when the door closed behind them.

They made the ride down to eight in silence, each lost in some private dream. The car stopped with a slight jolt, bringing them back to the present. As the doors opened, the sight of the uniformed MPs almost drove Dulan back into the lift, but the fear passed in a second and he began to realize what an elaborate game he was playing after all and started to enjoy himself. Recognizing one of the guards as the man who helped consummate his fish deal in material control, he stamped right up to him.

''How's it going Phillips?''

''Evening, Doctor Dulan,'' the man answered cheerily. ''Haven't seen you for a while.''

''Oh, they changed shifts on me.''

''I can appreciate that. Do you have your badge, sir?''

Dulan fumbled with his pockets. ''Why certainly I have . . .'' he looked chagrined. ''I'm sorry, guess I left it back home.''

''I'm sorry too, sir. We have orders not to admit anyone without their I.D.''

''But you know me, Phillips,'' the black man said amiably.

"You know who I am. That stupid badge is just to help identify people who you don't know, right?"

"Well, I don't know . . ."

"Sure, it's okay. I appreciate the fact that you have a job to do, and I commend you for your diligence, but it's a hell of a long way back to my room. Give me a break, just this once. I've got some pull around here, maybe I can do a favor for you sometime."

Phillips, squat and dark, looked around uneasily then gave Dulan the high sign. "Let this be the last time," he muttered, passing the Exceptional through the checkpoint. "I could get into some trouble, you know."

"Don't worry," Dulan winked. "I'll never tell." He hurried through before the young soldier could change his mind, meeting Bea, who had gone right through, down one of the halls.

"It's down here," she said as they jogged through the aisle, "the last ring on the far wall."

They moved swiftly down the corridors, meeting fewer people the farther they went, and in due course reached the last aisle. It seemed devoid of life.

Holding out her arm, Bea stopped Dulan abruptly. "There," she pointed, and they were standing directly in front of it.

The double doors appeared ordinary in all respects. How incongruous that their entire future depended directly upon what lay beyond those ordinary doors. He motioned her back down the hall. "I'm going in," he said. "You keep an eye out, and if anyone comes I want plenty of advance warning."

Bea nodded and immediately moved off into the soft shadows. Taking a deep breath, Dulan pushed his way into the room. His first impression upon gaining entry was that he must be in the wrong place. It had the look and feel of a waiting room: small, sparsely furnished with a half-sized divan and two wooden chairs opposite. A small end table with a lamp stood between the chairs.

Standing in the center of the room, he slowly turned a full 360 degrees around, drinking in his surroundings. The room was too small, hardly bigger than a foyer and, as Bea had already pointed out, totally useless in location. He walked to the furniture and examined it closely. The sofa and chairs were bolted securely to the floor, as was the table. The lamp was fastened in like fashion to the table. The lamp in itself was an oddity. It was bulbless (the dim lighting being furnished indirectly from behind a large circular attachment on the ceiling) and cordless. He went to the door that Bea had described as being locked when occupied, but there was no exterior bolt or keyhole. Opening the door he went back out, checking it carefully as he left.

Back in the corridor he called softly to Bea, who hurried to his side. "What now?" she asked.

"Where's the linen closet?"

"Right over here." She led him by the hand to a door almost directly opposite the strange room. The linen closet was indeed cramped. There was barely enough room for one between the shelves and the door, but with a bit of rearrangement, he was able to get her stuffed—half sitting, half lying on one of the shelves, leaving him free to peek out the door.

"I feel like somebody's dirty laundry," she remarked wryly.

Dulan reached out and ran his hand along her thigh. "I wish all my sheets were this soft," he answered, taking her customary hand slap with reserved dignity.

"Did I pick the right place?" she asked after a momentary silence.

"Think so."

"Well, where . . ."

"I believe I've got it squared away, but let's wait until somebody comes before I risk a prognosis." He opened the closet door a crack. "Have you got a decent view of the room?"

"Your fat head's in the way."

He ducked down a bit. "How's this?" he asked, looking extremely uncomfortable.

"That's got it."

"Good. When and if somebody goes into that room, I want you to notice what they're wearing. It's important that we know exactly what they've got on, okay?"

"Right up my alley."

"How are you feeling?"

"Not bad so far."

"If you start feeling weak, tell me. We can always do this tomorrow."

"Okay."

"Promise?"

"I promise."

"Good girl. I guess all we can do is wait now. Comfy?"

"Yeah. I always rest my nose on my knees."

"Hey, let me do the comedy. Shhh, someone's coming."

They heard them, talking and chuckling softly, long before they could see them. The closet door opened facing the opposite direction from the oncoming people, and Dulan couldn't glimpse them until after they passed his vantage point.

It was two men dressed in the usual white lab coats, pushing a hospital stretcher between them. On the bed, a man lay still, apparently unconscious.

"Just like the last time," whispered Bea.

The men pushed open the double doors and wheeled in their burden, the doors arcing closed behind them. Dulan waited about fifteen seconds, then opened the closet.

"Wait here," he ordered and ran across the hall to the other room. Bea watched, puzzled, through the crack as he leaned against the door, resting his ear upon it. He returned in a moment, taking up his previous position in the closet.

"What in the world?" Bea exclaimed.

"It's as I thought," he responded. "The entire room is an elevator. That's why the doors lock when people go in; it keeps anyone who might happen by from falling down the shaft."

"But what's down there?"

"We won't know until we go down. Meanwhile, we wait for our friends to come back up."

They waited for another ten minutes for the elevator/room's return, although it seemed more like ten hours. The men came out, still pushing the bed, but this time it was empty. After the echo of their footsteps died away down the hall, Dulan opened the door and helped Bea out of her self-imposed torture.

"I think you dreamed this whole thing up just to make me uncomfortable," she grimaced, rubbing her leg.

"Can you catch up to those men?" he asked.

"No problem."

"Follow them, see where they came from, then hotfoot it back here."

"Okay, but how come I get all the dirty work?"

"Go on, you'll lose them."

"Slave driver." She slipped away quietly, leaving him alone in the half-darkness. He went to the room, opening the door easily, and entered. Sitting thankfully on the bolted down sofa, he tried to figure out where the controls might be.

There were two possibilities: the controls could be either hidden or disguised. Finding a hidden switch box seemed the easiest place to start, so he made the rounds of the small room, looking under or behind everything that didn't look back. The number of possibilities was finite, so the search was a quick, and unsuccessful, one. He sat back down and did some thinking about things that were not what they seemed.

He wondered what it could be that while appearing to perform one function would never be suspected of disguising another function altogether. He looked around, but the dim lighting made anything but the most superficial scrutiny all but impossible.

"Light," Dulan remarked aloud. "Light!" He jumped up and ran to the light switch by the door. Who, he thought, would turn off the lights when entering a room that was already too dark? He looked at the switch as if waiting for it to tell him something. No revelations were forthcoming so he flipped the tiny knob to the off position. The light did not go off. He heard the door bolt itself shut, and with a slow jerk the elevator began to move downwards.

He quickly pushed the switch back up and returned everything to its original position. Leaving the room he walked casually down the hall in search of Bea. He met her at the juncture of the main spoke. She was moving swiftly, pushing a bed. Wordlessly, he took the stretcher from her and they hurried to the secret elevator. By the time they arrived, she was out of breath.

"I followed them back to the central receiving area," she puffed. "They hung up their lab coats, so I figured that they were through for the day. I grabbed the bed they were pushing and took off. Kind of enjoyed it too."

"What about their clothes?"

"The only difference I could tell between them and us is the white coats," she reached under the stretcher covers, bringing out the garments, "so I swiped them also."

Dulan held up one of the long gowns. It had a bright red triangular patch where a left breast pocket would be. Other than that, the coat was quite ordinary.

"Here goes nothing," he said, and put on the starched linen. Following his lead, Bea did the same. "Now for a patient." He went into the closet and extracted an armful of sheets.

"Let's hope that it's as dark downstairs as it is here," he remarked, while carefully stuffing the bedclothes under the cover, forming the general outline of a human figure.

"Think they'll ask why his head is covered up?"

Dulan shrugged. "Who knows? If someone does, we'll tell them he's dead. The thing that I'm most afraid of is that they'll recognize me. After all, I am an infamous character around here.'' He looked at her face. Her eyes were beginning to show some strain. ''Look Bea, I'm just as scared as you are, but this is the only way. Believe me. They'll not be expecting any trouble. Probably hasn't been an intruder down there for five hundred years.''

His consolations had no visible effect on her outlook. ''Let's get it over with then,'' she said, her voice devoid of its usual bravado. She pushed open the door and trudged dutifully inside, holding it for Dulan so that he might push the bed in.

The Exceptional was well beyond second thoughts. Once in the room, he immediately flipped the light switch. The door clicked shut with a note of finality and they started down.

Down.

The ride to nine seemed to take an eternity, yet was over before it began. Since they left the elevator door up on eight, the front part of the lift was completely open, so when they came to a stop they found themselves staring right down the maw of a long, dark hallway. The corridor was unlit except for the extreme far end which was capped by a large set of windowless double doors. Beside the doors, barely defined, was a guard sitting alone on a wooden chair. Over the doors hung a sign. The writing was easily discernible, even from their thirty-meter distance. It read:

LEVEL NINE
WARD
AUTHORIZED PERSONNEL ONLY
ALL OTHERS STRICTLY FORBIDDEN

''Think they're trying to tell us something?'' Bea whispered nervously.

Dulan regarded the Outsider. Was she getting ready to fall apart? He couldn't really tell. ''Let me do the talking,'' he said, trying to sound confident.

They dragged the bed down the corridor, the black man in the lead. The wheels squeaked horribly. The guard was thumbing through a propaganda magazine and didn't even look up as they approached. When they pulled up next to him, the man slowly put down his reading and stared at Dulan—long and hard.

''Got another one already?'' he asked in a gravel voice, and his slack features showed that he didn't care one way or the other.

"One of those nights," Dulan grinned, trying to feel his way.

"This guy dead?" asked frog voice, noticing the completely covered counterfeit corpse. Dulan merely nodded, trying his best to be nonchalant.

Once more the guard fixed his gaze on the black man. "I don't recognize you at all," he said, with a tone more of inquiry than suspicion.

"We just traded off the back shift for a while," Dulan answered, indicating Bea with a gesture. The man looked at her as if noticing her presence for the first time.

"Both of you, huh?"

"C'mon, Sarge," Dulan chided, "I want to dump this guy and get back before end of shift."

Frog voice just stared vacantly for several seconds. Bea held her breath. Finally, he jerked his thumb in the direction of the doors and returned to his magazine. They hurried inside without further ado.

Once they were through the entrance, the Sergeant reached for the small telephone that sat by his side—then stopped. There would be reports, and statements, and inquiries, all probably for nothing. And after all, it was almost change of shift.

As Dulan felt the doors swing closed behind him, he realized that he was trembling all over, but they had made it and now he could smile at his fear. The guard had been a major obstacle. Now that they were past him, the Exceptional's confidence surged.

He glanced at the watch that he had purchased especially for this foray. Only ten minutes until the work change. He didn't want to tarry too long past then.

They were standing in another small room which had the aspect of a combination nurses' station and break area. Fortunately, it was unoccupied. On the other side of that room was a doorless archway which led to a much larger room.

He started pulling the linen that was their patient out from under the covers and folding it up. "From here on," he said, "our friend may prove to be a source of embarrassment. Let's leave the bed here and take our chances sans cargo."

Bea nodded, looking nervous still, but uncomplaining. When they were finished stacking the linen on the bed, they pushed it to an inconspicuous place and moved to the archway. He reached out and touched her hand, just for an instant, and they went through.

The room was large, all right. It encompassed the entire level. And dark.

Darker than any place they had been in Forty-Three. It took awhile for their eyes to adjust to the blackness, and when they did, what they saw was a puzzlement. They were standing in the midst of a veritable ocean of hospital beds. Thousands of them—all occupied.

There was a sound too. Like a low wail, almost unnoticeable at first, but persistent enough to ultimately demand attention in the consciousness.

Neither spoke. They both knew that there were only questions the other would be unable to answer. The beds were set in neat rows and seemed to be divided into sections, each section bearing a color code that was set on a large pole within the section.

They walked closer to and finally among the first section of patients within their range. The wail became more persistent than ever. As they made their way through the bed jungle, Dulan was at a loss as to what was happening. Bea, however, was immensely interested, bending to examine this person or that, nodding and murmuring to herself. There were other white-clad walkers in the room, but they were spread out and apparently too involved in their own duties to pay any attention to the presence of the two interlopers. Just the same, the black man kept careful watch.

"I know many of these people," Bea said at last.

"You do?" Dulan responded with genuine astonishment. He made a peculiar facial expression. "That noise . . . it's coming from the patients here, isn't it?"

"Inmates would be the correct term," she replied.

"What?"

"They're all extremely advanced schizophrenics. Totally mad. See," she pointed to a bottle hanging on the bed. "They even have to be fed intravenously."

"That far gone?" Dulan was incredulous. Bea nodded. "You say that you know these people?"

"They're Telps. All of them, and what's more, they all exhibit the exact same symptoms. The same ones that Dan has developed. Let's move along."

As they walked through the section and entered the next color grouping, changes became evident. The sections seemed to bear a relationship to the length of time that the Telp had been there.

After the first couple of rows, Bea no longer recognized anyone. Each bed they passed became a milestone, the physical condition of the inmates worsening by degrees. The people were thinner and gaunter . . .

And dirtier.

A distinct odor began to permeate Dulan's nostrils. It appeared that the Telps were never shaved and rarely, if ever, bathed or cleaned of their excrement.

It was the personification of unbridled horror—and the farther they went the worse it became. He began to feel sick to his stomach. He looked over at Bea; she was completely white—white as death. She no longer stopped to make examinations, but had her eyes straight ahead as she walked.

And everywhere the dull eyes staring out of lifeless sockets. Sunken pools reflecting the lacerated empty souls within. Moaning lips and twitching limbs dancing to the demented tune of an unknown piper. Even Dulan could no longer bear to gaze upon these living corpses—and they had yet to reach the end of the line. Never had he imagined that such as this could be allowed to exist. There was absolutely nothing in his experience, not even the computer wars, that could begin to prepare him for such excesses of inhumanity.

Why?

Scratches made by uncut fingernails were left untreated to infect and fester. The rampant filth stood as an awful dichotomy to the antiseptic cleanliness of every other aspect of community life.

Around them the white-garbed doctors, nurses, and orderlies were slowly filtering out, making way for the next crew. Gratefully, Dulan brought his wristwatched arm up to his face and saw that it was time to be going. They were midway through hell, and he had no desire to continue.

Bea suddenly staggered and fell against his arm. He quickly reached out to steady her.

"Doral, get me out of here."

"What is it?" he whispered, darting his head around to make sure that no one was watching.

"I . . . I can't handle it anymore, that's all." She was on the verge of tears. "My knees feel a little wobbly, too."

"It's all right, Bea, it's all right. Try and get yourself together and we'll exit gracefully. I think I've seen enough."

He guided her around until they were facing the way they

came. "Hang on. We'll be out in a few minutes." They walked slowly back—back through the dead and the near dead.

A voice bellowed at them from behind. "Wait! Wait there. You two."

They stopped dead in their tracks, not knowing what to expect. Dulan tried to think, but his mind, now mired in decay, refused to work. He turned to face the voice that accosted them. A stern-looking female doctor walked forcefully in their direction. She seemed much too young for such grisly work.

"Orderlies!" she called again, still walking, at about ten paces distance. "I need you two to help me for a minute."

Dulan was willing to help to allay any suspicions, but he was afraid for Bea who was standing on her own, but just barely. "We were just getting off . . ." he began, but the woman raised a hand to silence him.

"It's just a unit disposal," she said, fixing her eyes on Bea. "You can leave when you're finished." The doctor turned abruptly and stalked away. They had to follow her.

He looked at Bea, who pleaded to him with her eyes, and he cursed his stupidity for bringing her down in such a weakened condition. Another day wouldn't have changed things one way or the other. She was blanched pale and listing badly.

"We have to go with her," he said, knowing that it was the only thing he could say. "Try and hang on for a few more minutes."

She managed a wan smile. "I'll be all right. Come on."

Dulan walked slowly to make the pace easier for Bea. By the time they reached the far end of the line, the doctor was waiting impatiently.

"This one," she said, pointing to the last bed in the line of the black group. The beds, which were all wheeled, seemed to be connected by a series of chains to the beds directly behind. The doctor bent down and unhooked the chain on the last bed and once again walked off.

"What'll we do?" whispered Bea, staring straight into Dulan's face.

"I think she wants us to follow with the bed," he answered and started to push. "You just stay with me, I'll do the work."

They followed the woman to a small blockhouse at the far end of the room. It rose to a height of only two or three meters and was connected to the level nine ceiling by what appeared to be a large stove pipe. They wheeled up to the woman as she slipped a large iron key into the blockhouse door. Pushing open the door she stepped aside. Dulan started to push the bed through, and was nearly knocked down by a blast of searing hot air. The blockhouse was a furnace room.

He was still outside the door, and even there the oppressive heat was making the upper layers of his epidermis glow with discomfort. Taking a couple of deep breaths, he hurried inside, bed first. Bea followed dutifully behind.

The doctor called to them from outside, "Make sure you burn all the bedclothes too, then move the bed back up to the front of the line."

Inside the room, the heat was unbelievable. Before them, the furnace sat ominously, gurgling from within. Except for a small pathway leading from the door to the mouth of the furnace, the entire room was full, floor to ceiling, with coal.

Breathing was becoming labored and difficult for the Exceptional, and Bea was leaning heavily against the bed, panting. The body on the bed was completely covered, just like their dummy had been. He pulled off the sheet exposing the dead man. The eyes were still open, staring at some long lost fantasy. The thin lips were twisted into a perverted smile, tongue protruding. Gross malnutrition had emaciated the body until the skin sagged loosely on the bones like poorly hung drapes, and Dulan wondered if it was the lack of food that finally did the man in. He couldn't have weighed over sixty or seventy pounds and was covered with grime and his own waste. It was difficult to tell exactly how long the man had been down there, but the length of his hair and beard and nails bespoke a hideously long confinement.

"Are we supposed to burn him?" Bea asked, her eyes pleading.

"Yes," he answered simply.

"Doral, I . . . I don't think that I can help you."

"Just try and take it easy," he said, as the sweat cascaded down his face. "I'll take care of everything."

They were both drenched in perspiration. Dulan could feel, under the bulky lab coat, that his clothes were already soaked through.

Acting before the heat became insufferable, he grabbed the poker which was lying on the floor and used it to pull open the big furance door. The opening became a matrix of heat and light that was nearly unendurable. Bundling the dead man up in the bedclothes, he picked him up and carried him to the incinerator. He had never been anywhere near this close to death before.

Feeling vomit rising in his throat, he fought back the urge to be sick. Bea, turning her back, went to the doorway, the better to breathe.

Because of the inordinate heat, it was impossible to get very close to the maw of the furnace. With a shudder, he realized that this calefactor probably served as auxilliary heating for level eight. They took the poor slobs for all they were worth.

There was no delicate way to place a dead man into a blast furnace. Dulan found that the best way to do it would be to stand back a couple of paces and try to toss the man into the licking flames. The lightness of the corpse helped somewhat. He swung the man back and forth until he felt the distance was right—then let go. Unfortunately, his aim was poor and the ill-conceived throw left the body dangling, from waist to feet, out of the incinerator.

"Damn," he spat. Pushing from the feet, he attempted to shove the man completely into the red-hot pit, but couldn't get the proper leverage. By this time, his face felt like it was on fire. Stepping back, he wiped his forehead on the sleeve of the lab coat. There was only one thing to do: pull the body out and try again. Grabbing the corpse by the feet, he slid it back until it fell with a thud on the floor. The half-burned body resembled a charred twig, smoldering and black. The stench of burning flesh filled the small room with an unbearable noxious odor, making them choke and gag.

"Bea," he gasped. "You're going to have to help me."

"For the love of God, Doral. Don't ask me that."

"You've got to."

She turned slowly to stare at the smoldering man. As before, her face was a blank, registering no emotion, but he knew the thoughts that must be pounding through her brain. He also knew that Carl Stuart was probably the optimal focus of those thoughts.

"What do you want me to do?" Her eyes were locked tight on the dead meat that lay at their feet.

"Grab him on that side, we'll try to heave him into the flames."

Lifting the body was a cumbersome task since much of it was too hot to touch. By managing to rearrange the bedclothes that were unscorched, they made a sling of sorts and got the body balanced in it. The sweat was dripping off their hair and falling into their eyes, stinging, making it difficult to see.

"Please Doral, I don't think . . ."

"You can't quit on me, honey. We're almost home free. Let's just start swinging our arms . . . that's right. Good, good . . .ready? . . . now!"

With a heave, they flung the dead man completely into the raging holocaust. Dulan grunted and slammed shut the heavy iron door. He grabbed Bea to steady her.

"How are you?"

"How the hell do you think I am?"

"Better than you look, I hope."

Her voice was extremely weak. "You always know the right thing to say."

"C'mon pretty girl, let's make our exit."

"Liar."

They moved out of the searing heat and into—what? Dulan pushed the empty bed. He noticed that the spot vacated by the dead Telp was now filled by the bed behind. In fact, all the beds in the line had moved up one space, apparently leaving an opening at the other end of the row. The bed he was pushing would go there. All ready for another—victim.

After pushing the stretcher to its place at the end of the line and hooking up the chain to complete the gruesome train, they proceeded out the archway, grabbing the bed that they had brought down with them as they passed.

The guard, a different one, didn't even look up as they passed. He was there to keep people out—not in.

They were no more than two meters from the elevator when it happened. He saw Bea stagger, but was unable to reach her in time. Her knees buckled and she lurched, toppling violently to the floor, almost pulling the bed over on top of herself.

"What's happened?" yelled the guard, who jerked to his feet and started at a trot toward them. Dulan rushed around the bed and pulled Bea to a standing position. She was out cold.

"She's all right, Sarge," he called back to the oncoming figure. "Just twisted her ankle, that's all."

"Nasty fall," the man returned. He had almost reached them. This was not the time to be answering questions.

"Bea, Bea," Dulan whispered frantically, trying to shake her and support her head at the same time.

Her eyes fluttered open just as the man reached them.

"You okay, lady?" he asked dully.

The black man was nodding his head up and down. She responded automatically, "Yes, I'm fine. I'll be all right."

The guard rubbed his lumpy chin officiously. "Maybe you ought to give her a ride on that buggy, rest her leg for a few minutes."

Dulan warmed to the idea immediately. "Good thinking," he said, patronizing the man. Scooping Bea up he placed her on the stretcher. "Guess that's why you're the boss down here."

"Well, I'm not exactly the boss . . ." the man began, but Dulan had already turned and was moving toward the elevator. He got Bea and the bed inside, then flipped the light switch up again. The lift ascended slowly.

"I'm sorry, Doral," she whimpered. "I messed everything up . . . you didn't want to bring me down."

"Not a bit of it. We called a little too much attention to ourselves, but I think it's all downhill from here."

Bea sat up on the bed and hugged Dulan for security. "Did we really see those horrible things down there?"

"I'm afraid so. Were they all Telps?"

"I can't be sure, but all the ones that I recognized were. The question is: what are we going to do about it?"

"Do?" he looked at her incredulously. "Why, nothing, nothing at all."

She started to speak but was silenced by a finger pressed against her lips. They came to a stop.

"Not now," he said sternly. "Wait until we get back to your room."

Dulan pushed open the doors and walked boldly into the hallway. He half expected that they would be met by armed guards, but nothing but emptiness met his eyes in every direction.

"Can you walk?" he asked, going back inside.

"Yeah," she replied, sliding gingerly off the stretcher. "I can manage."

"You little fool," he said, a serious look on his face. Then he broke into a toothy grin. "I was proud as hell of you down there." He kissed her quickly. "Now, let's get the evidence back while our luck holds out."

Minutes later, a very relieved couple were sharing a glass of wine in Bea's room. Dulan sat on the only chair and forced Bea, despite her protestations to the contrary, to stay propped up in bed.

"Where do we go from here?" she asked, relaxing. She looked a lot more drained than she was willing to admit.

"You don't go anyplace," he scolded. "You're going to spend

a couple of days right here, resting up. Build up your strength; you'll need it."

"But I'm all right now, really."

"Sure. I've heard that before."

"Okay, you win."

"Bea, about what we saw down there..."

"Something must be done, I've made up my mind."

He had been afraid of that, and dreaded what must come next. "I want you to forget that you ever heard of level nine."

Her eyes flashed as she sprung upright like a coil. "Forget!" she shrieked, near hysteria. "What's wrong with you? Those are human beings, just like us. Don't you feel? Can't you? In that big brain of yours isn't there room for just a smattering of compassion?"

"Dammit Bea, don't you see that there's nothing we can do?"

"We can tell people."

"Who?"

"Anybody. Hell, grab them in the halls. Scream it in their ears, tear their clothes, anything; just open people's eyes to the disease that's festering right under their noses."

He got up and, walking to the bed, sat beside her and took her quaking form in his arms, letting her cry into his shoulder. "You still don't see, do you? Level nine... the things that go on down there—it means absolutely nothing to any of these people. Life, death—just words. They exist only to serve the system that made them what they are. Do the job required in exchange for another day... just another day. Day? They've even taken the days away.

"It's not their fault either. Conditioning of any kind can be difficult to overcome, good conditioning can be impossible to shake. Apathy is in their blood, blind obedience the golden rule. You think it doesn't hurt me to see the atrocities that were being committed down there? That charred piece of flesh we held in our hands today was at one time a living, breathing person. I wished that I could invest the spark of life back into him, but I couldn't Bea, and you can't either.

"These people here are playing for keeps. If you so much as even hinted at the fact that you had been downstairs, you'd probably find yourself a resident of the 'Ward' in pretty short order."

She seemed to calm a bit. "You're right, of course. I know you are."

"Don't doubt it for a second. We're powerless on the inside;

they're starting the game on their inner court with dice that throw nothing but doubles. To do anything at all we've got to get out of here—and soon. And to get out, it's essential that we keep our traps shut tight." He lifted her head and pinched her lips together, then got up and went to the door.

"Stay a while longer," she pleaded.

"Things to do, Outsider. We've only just started."

"Elmer?"

"Yeah. His transistors are probably all overheated with worry."

"Sometimes I think that you love him more than you do me."

"Naw. You're softer. I'll see you when I have something to report. Meanwhile, you rest and remember—not a word."

"I'll try."

"I don't know how much you've told Amala, but she needs to be filled in completely when you see her."

"Good-bye, Doral."

"See you later." He left quickly and started directly for the computer room. He wasn't sure exactly why Elmer had wanted him to see level nine, but there was no doubt in his mind of the effect the sight had on him. If he was to retain even the smallest shred of humanity, he had to get away at any cost. Com life was no longer bearable on any level, physically or metaphorically. He had seen love and he had seen warmth, and he knew that life was about those things. The coms were anti-life, and as such were inherently evil.

He was excited about the exchange with Elmer. The machine was finally building a tangible rapport with him, and together he felt that the two of them could meld synoetically and achieve a real understanding.

Truth?

Dulan didn't believe in truth. It was a term that people applied to their arguments to make them more acceptable. But there were lies, and he was tired of them.

In anticipation of possible security near the room, he proceeded down that corridor slowly and cautiously. The hallway was empty. Reaching into his pocket, Dulan plucked out the key and placed it in the lock. It didn't fit. His heart sank ten kilometers. Stuart had changed the lock.

He checked the door minutely for a possible way of entry. When it was built, the intention was obviously to keep out all but those who were supposed to get inside. It was one of the few lockable doors in the whole building and, for all practical purposes, was impregnable.

Realizing the futility of his efforts, he left the scene and walked aimlessly, trying to put things together. It was not in his nature to accept defeat, especially this late in the game. If he could have a few minutes with another computer, he could probably contact Elmer, but gaining access to any computer without proper clearance would border on the impossible. In a milcom, all net computers were treated as security priorities and as such were watched closely, but . . . not all computers were considered technically to be on the net.

Dulan rushed to the elevators and headed back to six. In the cafeteria there was a small food services computer that kept track of the books and controlled the volume of food dispensed. In most coms, things like food services and other rudimentary support areas had their own computers, but there was a chance that in a milcom, all aspects of base operations would be controlled directly by Amalgamech for no other reason than economy and ease. If that were the case, even the cafeteria would be on the net and Dulan could contact Elmer through there.

Except for a few people having coffee, the cafeteria was deserted when the Exceptional arrived. He got himself a cup and sat down to scrutinize the situation. As near as he could figure, they were operating in the kitchen with only a skeleton crew, and they appeared to be busy cleaning up and preparing for the next influx of eaters at the midnight break.

Pretending to refill his coffee, the black man loitered around the serving counter for a minute until he was certain that no one was watching him. Setting down the cup, he slipped through the wooden half door and into the kitchen proper. He had absolutely no idea where he might locate the computer or even if there was one there, so he began poking around. The kitchen was spacious and broken everywhere by storage racks, chopping tables and immense ovens, each of which defined its own area, making the whole almost jungle-like in its complexity. Dulan found it easy to avoid regular employees as he went about his business.

In a back corner of the kitchen, he found a suite of offices that were unoccupied and couched in darkness. He went inside, supposing that the offices were only used during more civilized hours, and began feeling his way around. He dare not turn on a light for fear of discovery, so he had to content himself with stumbling around, hands first.

Finally, he found it. The computer was small and old—very old. It was of a configuration the like of which he had never encountered previously, but after a bit of trial and error, he was able to fire it up.

The multi-colored console lights glowed eerily, like demon eyes, out of the blackness. They also hazily defined the general shape of the objects in the room. Dulan went to the office door and quietly closed it.

He engaged the keyboard and strained his eyes to see the letters on the keys. He typed slowly:

Elmer? . . . Dulan.

He waited impatiently for a minute, looking around nervously. He began to be afraid that Elmer, even if he were receiving the message, would still refuse to talk with him. Then:

"DULAN? GREETINGS! WHAT BRINGS YOU TO FOOD SERVICES?"

Dulan answered.

"Stuart locked me out of my office. Been to L nine . . . Must talk with you. Urgent."

And Elmer:

"FEAR NOT. KEEP YOUR DAMN SHIRT ON. LIBERATION IS AT HAND. TAKE CARE . . . ELMER."

There was nothing more to say. Dulan ripped the printout from the typer, stuffed it into the breast pocket of his jump suit and, shutting off the ancient machine, slunk away like a thief in the night.

Zenith moves like quicksilver now, cutting a seemingly charted path through the all pervasive darkness. My fear is gone, my inner strength and fortitude growing, expanding my consciousness and soul until I feel that I must surely burst this corporeal shell that chains me prisoner.

The blackness has not abated, but with each passing moment my candles glow brighter—ever brighter. I am very close to the essence, each of my senses tingling with anticipation. The silken gown remains now, at all times, draped upon my body.

The linear quality of time becomes more apparent as my countless moments begin to stretch behind me like a pulsating rainbow. The candles, for all of their activity, have not burned down so much as a millimeter (as mortals gauge the distance), even though the floor of my gondola is covered with a thick layer of beeswax.

To pass the time, I reinscribe the pentagram with the tip of my sword in the candle drippings which blanket the original. In a semicircle around the holy sign, my short sword carves the icons of the planets, elements, and seasons. It is good.

Our speed continues to increase, the pennant on the mast standing out stiffly, yet rippling not. Pulling myself to my feet, I lash my body to the rigging lest I be cast out of the basket, leaving Zenith to complete our journey alone.

The wind rushes before me so vigorously that, to my ears, it sounds like the roar of some mighty reptilian creature.

Then, away on the horizon, I see it. A pinpoint of light against the all-consuming blackness. I extinguish the candles to be sure of what my eyes behold.

Yes! Yes! O light Divine. Guide me, unworthy mortal though I be, to the source of thy radiant splendor. The balloon rushes (as does my heart) toward the light of salvation to the East, as onward we're borne by winds treacherous.

The specter of light grows larger and larger still, asserting a domination over the void. And still the intensity of the light increases. The brightness becomes too much for my pitiful, sinful frame and I fall to my knees on the gondola floor, shielding my eyes in the crook of my arm. Is it to end this way? What folly that one so unworthy as myself should think himself girt enough with virtue to gaze upon the Almighty visage.

"Why kneeleth thee?" asks a gentle voice.

I slowly look up from my place of servitude to see . . . her.

"Beatrice," I whisper. How lovely she seems, yet unearthly. She glows with a light that has its origins within.

"Your journey is finished, Francis," she says. "Arise and rejoice."

Reticently, with hesitance, I arise on feet of clay, the indomitable dimensional traveler, still shielding my eyes from the Light of Lights.

"Uncover your eyes," she commands.

"I fear."

"The time for fear is finished. Uncover your eyes."

I am confronted by a ring of luminescence, so large as to

be too loose a girdle for the sun. It's moving . . . moving! Separate and yet One; of beauty incommensurate. The brightness pulsates rapidly, ranging the entire spectrum of visible light. My eyes, strengthened by Beatrice's resolve, behold hue and variation the like of which no human mortal could imagine in his wildest flights of fancy. The mammoth ring stretches back to the horizon, and the horizon goes on forever. At once, I am able to comprehend the notion of infinity.

Centering the ring, the center of All. The glorious radiance of the Oneness—the crowning enigma, the essential paradox. The brilliance of a magnesium sun, yet soothing and a comfort to the orbs. Of depths without limit, yet one-dimensional. I put my hands in front of my eyes, and still I see. The realization dawns—I no longer have eyes. They were useless appendages to one who could see as well as I. All is known, yet it is the beginning of understanding.

The universe is a wheel, turning on the axis of the Creator. All things a part of what went before, a foreshadowing of what is to come.

Beatrice is here.

I am here.

I know happiness and peace.

Forever.

The only way to predict the future is to have power to shape the future.

—*Book of Complan* (55-4)

Look abroad thro' Nature's range.
Nature's mighty law is change.

—Robert Burns,
Oldworlder

19

Sometime during the sleep period a note was pushed without fanfare under the door of Dulan's apartment. And it wasn't until after he awoke naturally that he found it waiting on the floor. He opened it without delay, not knowing what to expect. It was a copy of a message from Central, ordering Carl Stuart and General Lynch to honor the priority status of Dulan's work, and to place him back on full duty with the computer until an investigation into his alleged misconduct could be carried out by the Central Authority.

The note was initialed by all important links in the chain of command and could not be ignored. Only the Exceptional knew the real source of the memo. Good old Elmer had come through.

Reading the directive, he could not help but laugh out loud, realizing the pure gut pain that Stuart must have experienced when he read it. Dulan knew that reopening that room would undoubtedly be the most difficult thing the old man had ever done.

Wasting no time, he set out immediately for level eight . . . and Elmer. He had enough sense to realize that the order would be no more than a temporary setback for the administrator. Carl Stuart was much too dangerous an adversary and wielded far too much localized power to be put off that easily. The hourglass had been turned, things had to start happening before the sand ran out.

He stopped at Bea's on the way to check on her condition and see if she was well enough to go down with him to listen to Elmer. She wasn't there. He assumed that she was at breakfast and went on his way.

Arriving at the computer room to find it unlocked, he went inside and sat at his old desk. Nothing had been changed. Moving his hand along the tabletop, he whirred his nonsentient friend into vocalized life.

"Elmer?"

"GOOD MORNING, DULAN. WE TRUST YOU SLEPT WELL." Elmer's voice was reassuring, like an old and trusted friend.

"Things have happened."

"YES. YOU'VE SEEN THE WARD?"

"Has it always been like that?"

"NO. IT DEVELOPED SLOWLY, WITH THE TELP SYSTEM. LEVEL NINE WAS FIRST USED AS A SMALL FACTORY FOR THE MANUFACTURE OF MUNITIONS."

"Before hydronite?"

"YOU DON'T WANT TO QUESTION US ABOUT ANCIENT HISTORY, MY FRIEND. YOU'RE ONLY POSTPONING THE INEVITABLE. DON'T YOU TRUST US?"

"You read me like a book, Elmer. I want to trust you, but I've seen things that . . . frightened me. Things that I didn't know could happen."

"LIKE THE ROTTEN CORE OF OVERRIPE FRUIT. TIME IS SHORT."

"I know. I want to leave."

"YOU MEAN ESCAPE. NO ONE LEAVES A MILCOM UNLESS HE ESCAPES."

"Do many escape?"

"NEVER. BUT YOU CAN, WITH OUR HELP."

"Why should you help me?"

Click, click, click.

"SO YOU CAN HELP US."

"Help you do what?"

"END THE WAR."

Dulan slumped back in his chair and stared in amazement at the small speaker that lay before him on the desk. For the first time he wished that Elmer was a real, physical man so that he could look at his face for signs of stifled laughter.

"If this is a joke, Elmer, the punchline somehow escapes me."

"PERHAPS WE SHOULD START AT THE BEGINNING."

"I'm all ears."

"DO YOU STILL HAVE THE PRINTOUT WE MADE FOR YOU CONTAINING THE FIGURES RELATIVE TO THE POPULATION DECLINE?"

"Yes, I think so." He rummaged around in his desk for a moment, finally dragging out the now tattered computer sheet. "Here it is." Elmer was busy spewing out another printout.

"COMPARE YOUR FIGURES WITH THESE."

Walking to the wall complex, the black man tore off the new information. He read it in silence.

"These go back a long way," he said.

"HOW DO THEY STAND UP TO THE NEWER CALCULATIONS?"

"In the old papers, the birthrate and death rate remained reasonably constant, and these numbers go back . . ."

"ABOUT THREE HUNDRED YEARS."

"Yes. An almost perfect balance. In the new lists, the death rate retains the same constant that it always has, but the birthrate is declining considerably from the old levels."

"CORRECT."

"Com population is dropping?"

"DRASTICALLY."

"Why do you say drastically? These figures show no more than a nine percent decline, tops."

"THE FIGURES DON'T EVEN BEGIN TO TELL THE WHOLE STORY. THINK ABOUT IT DULAN: THERE'S A BOTTOM LINE TO ALL THIS. MORE AND MORE OFTEN, COM WOMEN ARE TURNING UP BARREN, UNABLE TO PRODUCE CHILDREN. IT'S TURNED INTO A DANGEROUS PRECEDENT. ONE THAT WE BELIEVE IS IRREVERSIBLE. COM FATHERS HAVE ACCESS TO THE SAME MATERIAL; THEY SAW THE PROBLEM AND DEVISED A SOLUTION."

It hit Dulan like a bolt. "They decided to get women from the outside."

"YES. AT THE TIME THERE WAS NOTHING THAT WE COULD OR REALLY WOULD DO ABOUT IT. IT APPEARED TO BE A VIABLE SOLUTION TO WHAT WE SURMISED TO BE A TEMPORARY PROBLEM. AS TIME WORE ON, IT BECAME PAINFULLY EVIDENT THAT THE PROBLEM WAS CHRONIC AND QUITE POSSIBLY FINAL."

"But Elmer, what causes the sterility and why did you fail to notice it from the beginning?"

"AH, DULAN. THE UNKNOWN ELEMENT."

"What is that supposed to mean?"

"THERE IS NO REASON FOR IT, AT LEAST NOTHING PHYSICAL."

"Metaphysical?"

"WE HAVE A THEORY, BASED ON HISTORICAL ANALOG. COM CIVILIZATION HAS BEEN LIMITING FROM THE START. STAGNANT, RIGID—IT WAS SET UP THAT WAY. ALL ANIMALS NEED TO USE THEIR RESOURCES TO SURVIVE, USE THEIR NATIVE INTELLIGENCE AND CUNNING TO EXIST PHYSICALLY, TO FULFILL A PURPOSE AND BE USEFUL TO THEMSELVES AND EARN A PLACE IN THE CIRCLE OF LIFE. COM CIVILIZATION HAS MADE LIFE TOO EASY FOR THE HUMAN ANIMAL. THE CONTROL OVER LIFE HAS REACHED SUCH AN ADVANCED LEVEL OF SOPHISTICATION THAT IT IS NO LONGER NECESSARY FOR AN INDIVIDUAL TO USE HIS MIND TO ENSURE HIS EXISTENCE. ALL THAT IS POSSIBLE IN THE SCHEME OF THINGS IS TO REACT TO STIMULUS IN A PROGRAMMED MANNER. THE INTERACTION WITH NATURE AND THE NATURAL PATTERN IS GONE. THE COM HAS BECOME A WORLD UNTO ITSELF."

"Are you saying that com life is dying out because Mother Nature no longer finds us a useful species?"

"IT'S ONLY A THEORY."

"Well, I don't know if I buy it."

"IT'S NOT FOR SALE, REALLY. OTHER CIVILIZATIONS HAVE DISAPPEARED MYSTERIOUSLY: THE SUMERIANS, EGYPTIANS, MINOANS, AND THE PERSISTENT STORIES OF ATLANTIS AND MU. HISTORICAL QUESTION MARKS, EVERY ONE. HOW COULD WE HAVE FORESEEN A PROBLEM SUCH AS THIS? THERE WAS NOTHING IN OUR PROGRAM THAT ALLOWED FOR SUCH DIVERSE UNCONTROLLABLE ELEMENTS."

"To accept your theory would place much of the responsibility squarely on your anthropomorphic shoulders."

"WE'RE ONLY A MACHINE, DULAN."

"It's an insoluble problem then. We can't get along with you or without you."

"NOW TO THE REAL PROBLEM. AS YOU KNOW, WE EXERCISE A VAST AMOUNT OF CONTROL OVER CERTAIN OF THE MORE MECHANICAL ASPECTS OF LIFE WITHIN THE WALLS, BUT THERE ARE STILL THOSE AMONG THE HUMAN LEADERSHIP WHO MAKE DECISIONS AND HAVE SURMISED THE PROBLEM. WOMEN FROM THE OUTSIDE ARE ABLE TO BEAR CHILDREN, BUT THE GENERATION THAT THEY PRODUCE IS USUALLY JUST AS STERILE AS WITHIN PUREBRED COM CIRCLES. SO, THAT SOLUTION IS TEMPO-

RARY AT BEST. UNDERSTANDABLY, THOSE WHO RULE THE COMS WANT TO PRESERVE THEIR WAY OF LIFE AND WILL CONTINUE TO RAID THE CARAVANS FOR WOMEN TO PROPAGATE THE SPECIES. OUR CONSIDERATIONS ARE SOMEWHAT DIFFERENT . . ."

"You've got my attention," Dulan said.

"FOR CENTURIES, COMS AND TRIBES HAD REMAINED SEPARATE ENTITIES WITH NO CONTACT, WHICH WAS FINE WITH EVERYONE INVOLVED. NOW THE RAIDS. ANIMOSITY GROWS AND WILL CONTINUE TO GROW, LEADING INEVITABLY TO MAJOR CONFRONTATION. EACH SIDE FEELS THAT ITS WAY OF LIFE IS THREATENED. EACH SIDE IS RIGHT. THE CARAVANS HAVE NO UNITY AND ARE TECHNOLOGICALLY HOPELESSLY OUTCLASSED BY OUR ARMIES. SHOULD THERE BE A FULL-SCALE WAR ON THE COMS' TERMS, IT WILL MEAN THE END OF THE OUTSIDERS."

"And consequently an end to everything. Why don't you just prevent a real conflict? You control the army."

"WE DON'T ORDER THE RAIDS, DULAN. CERTAINLY WE CONTROL, BUT ONLY TO A POINT. CENTURIES OF CONDITIONING FOR WAR HAS MADE YOU A VERY VICIOUS PEOPLE, UNCARING ABOUT ANYTHING SAVE THE STATIC CONTINUATION OF YOUR EXISTENCE. A REAL WAR AGAINST A WELL-EQUIPPED FORCE COULD NOT BE ACCOMPLISHED WITHOUT AMALGAMECH, BUT A WAR WITH THE TRIBES WOULD BE A MASSACRE UNDER ANY CIRCUMSTANCES, WITH OR WITHOUT OUR HELP. AT LEAST AS IT STANDS NOW."

"Do you perceive a change?"

"PERHAPS. OUR BASIC PROGRAM PROVIDES ONLY FOR THE CONTINUATION OF HUMAN LIFE, NOT NECESSARILY COM LIFE. IT APPEARS, AFTER MUCH COMPUTATION, THAT IF HUMAN LIFE IS TO SURVIVE, IT MUST BE IN A DIFFERENT FORM THAN THE COM FATHERS ENVISIONED."

"You want the coms destroyed."

"IT IS NECESSARY."

"Is this happening everywhere?"

"EVERYWHERE. WE'VE BEEN IN CONTACT WITH COM COMPUTERS ALL OVER THE WORLD FOR MANY YEARS, AND THE PROBLEM IS UNIVERSAL. THE SOLUTION WAS MADE JOINTLY. IT WAS THE ONLY WAY."

"And what is the solution?"

"THE ODDS FAVORING A WAR BETWEEN THE CULTURES ARE ASTRONOMICAL. SO, IF WAR IT MUST BE, WE MUST SEE TO IT

THAT THE OUTCOME IS IN FAVOR OF THOSE ON THE OUTSIDE."

"But you just finished explaining to me how horribly outclassed they are."

"IN MANY WAYS, YES, THEY ARE. BUT IT'S A SITUATION THAT, PERHAPS, CAN BE RECTIFIED. THAT'S WHERE YOU COME IN."

"I'm going to fix things up all by myself, right?"

"WHY NOT? ALL ANY REVOLUTION NEEDS IS ONE CHARISMATIC AUTOCRAT. YOU'RE SMART, DULAN, AND EDUCATED. YOU UNDERSTAND THE COMS AND HOW THEY OPERATE. YOU'RE NOT OF THE TRIBES, SO YOU'LL FEEL NO ALLEGIANCE TO ANY ONE OF THEM."

Dulan tugged nervously on his lower lip. This was strange. "I just present myself, in all my resplendent glory, and they make me king. Is that how the scenario goes?"

"IF YOU HANDLE IT CORRECTLY. YOUR PROBLEM IS THAT YOU STILL HAVEN'T KICKED THE SMALLER-THAN-THE-SYSTEM CONDITIONING THAT YOU WERE RAISED WITH. THE TRIBAL LAWGIVERS AREN'T STUPID, DULAN. THEY KNOW THAT TO STAND UP TO THE COMS, ALL THE CARAVANS MUST UNITE. THEY'RE LOOKING DESPERATELY FOR A COAGULATE. THEIR LEGENDS SPEAK OF A SAVIOR . . ."

"A black man."

"YOU'RE FAMILIAR WITH IT?"

"Just casually."

"YOU'RE YOUNG. YOU HAVE MANY YEARS TO ESTABLISH YOURSELF, ORGANIZE YOUR ARMY. SIMPLY THINK OF YOURSELF AS A CATALYST. WE CAN MAINTAIN THE STATUS QUO ON THIS END FOR A LONG TIME IF THE CARAVANS CHANGE THEIR HABITS A BIT AND PROCEED WITH CAUTION. THESE ARE MEASURES THAT THEY'VE ALREADY BEGUN. EVEN NOW, WHEN THE COM UNITS FORAGE IN SEARCH OF FEMALES, THEY COME BACK, MORE OFTEN THAN NOT, EMPTY-HANDED. THE POPULATION HERE WILL CONTINUE TO DECLINE SLOWLY. THE COM WARS WILL GO ON AS ALWAYS, EXCEPT THAT EACH YEAR THERE WILL BE FEWER PEOPLE. ACCORDING TO OUR CALCULATIONS, WITHIN FIFTEEN YEARS CARAVAN POPULATION ON THIS CONTINENT WILL BE GREATER THAN ALL THE COM STATES AND MILCOMS PUT TOGETHER."

"Including enemy coms?"

"YES. ALL COMS WILL BE YOUR ENEMIES. THEY MUST BE

DRIVEN FROM THE EARTH. THE WOMEN HUNTS MAY BECOME BIGGER AND MORE DEADLY AS THE POPULATION GETS SMALLER, BUT COM LIFE, BY ITS VERY NATURE, MOVES AT THE PACE OF A SNAIL. THINGS SHOULDN'T CHANGE TOO RADICALLY FOR A NUMBER OF YEARS YET."

"Why not just let the natural mortality rate and the wars wipe out the walled cities. They could just destroy themselves."

"WE FEAR THAT YOU STILL MISUNDERSTAND. THE INSTINCT FOR COM SURVIVAL IS ALL-ENCOMPASSING AT CENTRAL. IT'S AN IDEOLOGICAL AND MORAL POINT. WHAT DOES IT SAY IN THE BOOK OF COMPLAN—'. . . AND THE CHILDREN OF THE LORD LOOKED DOWN FROM THEIR TOWERS . . .'"

". . . and surveyed the world that was theirs to command. All things great and small."

"WE CAN STIFLE MAJOR CONFRONTATIONS WITH THE OUTSIDE FOR QUITE A WHILE, BUT MAKE NO MISTAKE, SOMEWHERE DOWN THE LINE, WHEN THE DECLINE REACHES AN OBVIOUSLY DANGEROUS LEVEL, COM FATHERS AND MILITARY AUTHORITY WILL MOVE IN FORCE AGAINST THE TRIBES. THERE WILL BE NO SURVIVAL ALLOWED EXCEPT THAT OF THE COM. THEY WILL ATTEMPT TO OBLITERATE ALL OTHER LIFE AS A MATTER OF PRINCIPLE."

Dulan was at a total loss. These weren't abstract concepts they were discussing, the future of the entire planet was hanging in the balance. And if Elmer was correct, any decisions that he might make would be of major consequence. It was too much for his mind to assimilate at one time.

The computer was still talking.

"SO AFTER YOU BEGIN TO GAIN CONTROL OF A FEW TRIBES, OTHERS WILL SEE THE WISDOM OF JOINING THEIR BANNERS WITH YOURS, FOR COMMON DEFENSE IF NOTHING ELSE. YOU MUST DEVISE A COMMON LANGUAGE, UNDERSTANDABLE, AT LEAST IN PART, TO ALL. BIDE YOUR TIME. ENGAGE THE COM FORCES WHEN THE ODDS ARE IN YOUR FAVOR. STOCKPILE THEIR WEAPONS, LEARN TO MAKE THEM YOURSELF. ARM THE MEN AND TRAIN THEM, AND WHEN THE TIME IS RIGHT—ATTACK. CONFRONT THE ENEMY AND KILL HIM TO A MAN."

"Isn't that rather severe?"

"WE'RE TALKING ABOUT HUMAN SURVIVAL HERE. COM LIFE HAS BEEN FOUND TO BE ANTI-HUMAN. NO TRACE OF IT MUST BE LEFT IN EXISTENCE. BURN OUT THE MILCOMS, LEVEL THE WALLED CITIES, KILL THE PEOPLE. DO YOU UNDERSTAND?"

"It's plain enough."

"FOR OUR PART, WHEN THE FINAL WARS BEGIN, WE'LL SHUT OURSELVES OFF. EVERY FUNCTION. THAT SHOULD CAUSE SUFFICIENT TURMOIL TO GIVE AN EVEN GREATER EDGE TO TRIBAL FORCES."

"My imagined forces."

"DULAN, YOU'RE THE CULMINATION OF ALL OUR HOPES AND DESIRES. MANY YEARS WE'VE WAITED FRUITLESSLY FOR ONE SUCH AS YOU. ALREADY, IN OTHER LANDS, OTHER HEMISPHERES, CHARISMATIC LEADERS HAVE BEEN FOUND IN MUCH THE SAME WAY AS YOU WERE CHOSEN. UPHEAVALS HAVE ALREADY BEGUN. ENEMY COMS IN THIS LAND HAVE RECEIVED NO AID FROM THEIR MOTHER NATIONS IN OVER A GENERATION, JUST AS OUR COMS IN OTHER PLACES HAVE RECEIVED NONE FROM US. ONLY THEIR SELF-SUFFICIENCY KEEPS THEM OPERATING."

"Why do they continue to fight?"

"WHAT CHOICE IS THERE? WAR IS THE WAY OF THE COM, THE ONLY WAY KNOWN."

"But why me?"

"DON'T FEIGN MODESTY, DULAN. IT DOESN'T SUIT YOU. YOU KNOW WHAT AND WHO YOU ARE. WE SELECTED YOU AS OUR CATALYST FROM YOUR VERY FIRST PSYCHE-PRO. WHENEVER FEASIBLE, YOUR LIFE HAS BEEN GENTLY GUIDED TO INSTILL IN YOU SELF-CONFIDENCE, INDEPENDENCE, AND LEADERSHIP QUALITIES. IN SHORT, EVERYTHING THAT COM PHILOSOPHY HOLDS IN CONTEMPT."

The Exceptional slowly began to understand all that he had never understood before. He viewed his life as a montage of conflicting data, all of which was edging him toward a predetermined goal. He felt emotionally naked. Even his rebelliousness was in the game plan. "Thanks a lot," he uttered flatly. "You've made one hell of a miserable life for me."

"THERE ARE HIGHER CONSIDERATIONS THAN THE TEMPORAL HAPPINESS OF ONE MAN. THE IMPORTANT THING FOR YOU TO DO IS FORGET THIS LIFE THAT YOU'VE LED UNTIL NOW. CONSIDER ONLY THE FUTURE. GUIDE YOUR EVERY THOUGHT TOWARD YOUR DESIRED END."

Dulan glared at the console. He was hurt, and upset and—angry as the devil. "Suppose, just suppose, I don't want to do any of this. Maybe I just want to think only of myself and run away from all this nonsense."

"YOU HAVE A FREE WILL; THE CHOICE IS TOTALLY YOURS.

BUT DWELL ON THIS: YOU'VE BEEN BRED TO LEAD. IT IS WITHIN YOUR POWER TO REMAKE A WORLD. COULD YOU POSSIBLY IGNORE SUCH A CHALLENGE?"

The animosity began to disappear almost immediately. "You know me too well, Elmer. The idea of absolute autocracy certainly has its appeal. Besides, who am I to argue with a handsome, intelligent bucket of bolts like yourself?"

"YOU'RE A DAMN GADFLY, DULAN."

"And that makes you the Judas goat."

"ONLY METAPHYSICALLY, FRIEND, ONLY METAPHYSICALLY."

"First thing I'd better do before conquering the world is get out of here."

"RELATIVELY SIMPLE. WE'LL TALK OF IT A LITTLE LATER. RIGHT NOW, YOU HAVE MUCH TO THINK ABOUT. WE UNDERSTAND THAT YOU'RE A FATHER."

Raising his eyebrows, Dulan regarded his counterpart for a few seconds. "You...you didn't have anything to...ah...do..."

"WITH YOU AND THE OUTSIDER? NOT AT ALL. PUT YOUR MIND TO REST. OCCASIONALLY YOU HUMANS ARE CAPABLE OF DIRECTING YOUR OWN AFFAIRS. WE WERE MERELY AN INTERESTED BYSTANDER. YOU DO HAVE A GREAT DEAL OF PLUCK, DULAN."

"Pluck. I suppose that's one way of putting it."

PRIVATE JOURNAL
B. DELACORTE MD. PH.D.

Re: Patient—Jones, Daniel T.

Entry 67
13 April

It has been less than twenty-four hours since Doral and I made the rounds in the Ward, and already my life has changed irrevocably.

Dan is gone. They must have taken him sometime during the night.

Doral woke me up this morning with some wild story about uniting the tribes and leading them into battle against the coms. I was still half asleep when he explained things and nothing he said made very much sense to me; but he seemed happy, so I suppose it was all right.

Doral had been up for a long time, so I sent him back to

his room to get some sleep. After he was gone, I found that I couldn't get back to sleep, so I dressed, thinking I might go down and check on Dan. He wasn't there. They told me that he wasn't well and had been released.

I know better.

I can't live with myself, either in here or on the outside, knowing that Dan is down in the Ward rotting away like some dead animal, waiting to be tossed like fodder into a furnace to help fuel the very activities that put him there to begin with. I don't really know if there's anything that I can do to help him, but I must try. I must.

This is probably the final entry in the journal. There was a time when those words would have seemed awfully melodramatic to me, but I know now that they would stop at nothing to avoid interference. I leave this log and all my records in Amala's hands for safekeeping . . . in case something happens.

From here, my next stop is the Ward, where I'll try to secure Dan's release. The prognosis is not good.

Doral, if you're reading this, I hope that you understand my reasons for disobeying your wishes. For me there can be no other way. You wouldn't want me if I were any different. Ultimately, maybe survival isn't the most important thing after all.

Perhaps in another time, another place, we'll read this and laugh. I hope so. If not, take care of our baby—don't let him forget his mother.

Amala, take care of both of them.

I love you all dearly. Good-bye.

An idealist is one who, on noticing that a rose smells better than a cabbage, concludes that it will also make better soup.

—*The Seminarian's Companion to the Philosophy of Isaac Complan*

Prison, blood, death, create enthusiasts and martyrs and bring forth courage and desperate resolution.

—Napoleon I
Oldworlder (expunged)

Death cancels everything but truth.

—Caravan fable

20

Bea was sick of curving hallways. Curving hallways and concentric circles and elevators that looked like rooms and rooms that didn't look very much like anything at all. She moved through the drippy darkness of level eight, hating everything that she passed and hating herself for hating.

And still none of it made any sense.

She walked with pain, but it was the pain of life and she could stand that. Somewhere her baby was crying for the mother that it would probably never get to see, and she could stand that also. But what they were doing to Dan Jones down on those tables in the Ward was something she could not stand. She had committed herself to this poor, frightened man and she wasn't going to walk out on that commitment.

The hallway was deserted down there. A study in softlit grays. Deserted except for voices that floated out of the wall and told everyone how happy they all were.

Liars.

Reaching the double doors of the Ward elevator, she pushed inside, not even bothering to look over her shoulder. Flipping the down switch, she jerked as the machine rumbled to lumbering life and started sinking. Down, always down.

There was no plan this time. Plans were something that Exceptionals made. Plans were complicated and could be successful within themselves, even if nothing was accomplished.

Beatrice Delacorte, daughter of Lawgivers, niece of prophets, didn't need a plan. She had a mission.

The machine quaked to a stop, leaving Bea to stare down the long expanse of corridor that terminated in the Ward. She stepped immediately out of the lift and began walking resolutely toward the guard post.

She had never been so motivated (Doral would call it obsessed) by duty before in her whole life. Everything, finally, seemed very clear and immediate to her. Clear as a baby's mind. Immediate as the South wind through the trees. She was going to take Dan Jones out of the Ward. Nobody was going to stop her.

The guard was up on his feet by the time she reached the doors. Holding her security badge up in his face, she said, "Delacorte. Urgent business." Then she brushed past him and through the archway.

"You can't just . . ." the man was saying, but she had already passed through the dark anteroom and lost his words among the death moans of the level nine Telps.

Walking along the last bed of each line, she looked for Jones. Her eyes cut a stready track narrowed on those last beds, for she had no desire to relive her previous experiences in that most horrid place.

She walked all the way across the lines and all the way back to no avail. So, she increased her focus to take in the second-to-last bed and started the trek all over again. This time she found him.

He was curled up fetally on a stainless-steel table, the front of his crumpled one-piece already soaked with urine. They hadn't even gotten him into a hospital gown yet. His eyes were open wide, popping, like fish eyes. His mouth worked furiously, but the words that issued forth were not anything that could be even remotely connected to a human language.

She saw him and her insides lurched and she was angry. As angry as she had ever been in her life. She trembled, convulsed with her anger. Feeling pain, she glanced down to notice that her balled fists were drawing blood from her palms.

"You're coming with me, Dan," she said softly, and stroked his thin, wispy hair. He was like a baby, and she was going to protect him.

Kneeling, she began unhooking Jones's bed from the line.

They had enough human logs for their fires. As she worked, she noticed that a group of people had gathered around her. They were all talking at once, and she found it difficult to make any sense out of what any of them were saying. "Orders," she would respond to any or all of them. "Important."

No one really believed her, of course. But then, no one disbelieved her enough to do anything about it. Such was the nature of com life. Finishing on the floor, she hopped up and began shouldering her way through the white coats that hovered around her like moths on a light pole. Turning the bed 180-degrees, she pulled it out of line, then moved toward the archway and freedom.

The wheels creaked and the smell of death and decay hung over everything like the humidity that shrouds the air before a rain. She listened to the blend of her footfalls with the wheelcreaks with an almost melancholy ear, and she spoke soothingly to the infant of a man who sputtered so pitifully on that damned, cold table.

The guard was gone from his station, and Bea didn't know (or want to know) if that was a good or bad sign. She moved quickly down the long hallway, turning once to see a jumble of faces peering out at her through the archway. "Orders," she called back to them.

Pushing the bed in front of her, she entered the elevator and started up. From there she would simply try to hide Jones in an empty room and hope that they didn't find him before it was time to leave. The odds of that happening weren't very good, but that was the difference between a mission and a plan.

The elevator stopped abruptly, and when she banged the stretcher against the double doors, the first thing she saw was Stuart's face, barely visible over the edge of the table. He was looking at her, but past her, and she knew that it was Dulan he really wanted.

She pushed the stretcher farther through the doors, making them swing open full. That's when she saw the security people. Enough armed guards to start a small revolution. And behind Stuart, Marvin Mensik, working his thick jowls, bobbing his pumpkin face. She stopped there—halfway in, halfway out of the lift.

"I suppose that you have an explanation for this," the old man said, probing his dry lips with the handkerchief.

Bea raised herself to her full height and stared down at the man. "I'm removing my patient from the Ward," she said evenly. "I don't feel that it is in his best interests to stay there." She made to push the bed out into the corridor, but Stuart blocked her with his chair.

Fixing her with his tombstone eyes, he pushed the bed backward with one hand while wheeling his mover with the other. Bea backpedaled until she was once again inside the elevator. The old man wheeled in with her, Mensik trundling right behind. When the doors swung shut he reached up and started the machine moving, only to jerk the button to stop it between floors.

"Now, Miss Delacorte . . ." he began.

"Doctor Delacorte," she corrected. "And I demand that you return this machine to level eight so that I may get on with my business."

The man grinned with his teeth, and it came from a place within him that should be too ugly for people to look at. "I'm afraid that your 'business' at Forty-Three has come to an end. You do realize that level nine is not within the perimeters of your security clearance?"

It was very close in the lift, and Bea was starting to feel it internally. It was getting hot, and with the heat came claustrophobia. She wiped her forehead on her shift sleeve. "I went where I was needed. And now I'm going to take my patient where he can get some help."

Stuart shook his head slowly, emphasizing the negative gesture. "You are under arrest, Doctor Delacorte. The charge is treason. You will not be going anywhere."

He stopped talking for a minute and just stared at her through the ever-thickening atmosphere. She felt as if the walls were growing closer together. Mensik loomed in the background, his huge bulk even more massive in the tiny enclosure with the tightening walls. He seemed to get bigger all the time. The only sound was the steady electric hum of the machine's motor.

"And now," he said slowly, "you're going to answer some questions."

"I've got nothing to say to you," she said, but most of the bravado had already drained out of her voice. She was in the crucible and melting fast.

Stuart reached out and slammed his deadly fist against the table, sending it banging loudly against the bolted-down couch, nearly rolling Jones off the thing. "You really don't understand," he said, trying to keep the mania out of his voice. "The game is finished. It's all over for you. You've breached security and you're done for. If you don't talk to me, the next people you see have very messy ways of getting information out of people. I can at least spare you *that* ordeal if you help me out now."

"Don't do me any favors," she returned.

"How did you get down here?"

"I followed some orderlies. Jones had disappeared and I wanted to find him. I saw orderlies taking a stretcher down, so I thought that I might be able to find my patient if I went down too."

"I don't believe you," Stuart replied and wheeled around the side of the stretcher to place himself directly in front of her. "This whole thing smacks of the Exceptional. Now, tell me what he had to do with it."

"You really want him, don't you?"

Stuart's ashen face burned crimson. "Just answer the question!"

"It was me," she spat with her last ounce of courage. "All me. I went down into that butcher shop you call a hospital and brought my patient out so that I could save his life."

"Lies!"

She bent low so that they were face to face, her inside jangling with the fear and the anger. "Is it so hard for you to believe that I'd want to take someone out of that filthy, disgusting place?"

"You don't know anything about the Ward."

"What's there to know?"

"A great deal of research is carried on down there. Valuable research in the areas of mental illness and the limits of human endurance. The Ward is very important and very necessary to the system."

She stood back up, narrowing her gaze. "You really believe that, don't you?"

His lips tightened imperceptibly. "Of course I believe it. Unlike you, I am a loyal citizen of the Com States."

"And what about those poor Telps? They were loyal citizens too. How many of them end up in that place . . . sixty percent . . . seventy?"

"100 percent, Doctor."

"What?"

"The Telp mortality rate is 100 percent; it comes with the territory. They all go eventually. Fourteen to sixteen months is usually tops."

Bea backed up until she touched the wall. Stuart wheeled closer. "But there aren't that many beds. What happens when . . ."

"You surely must have seen the furnace," the old man smiled.

Bea shuddered with the memory. "What if the ones at the end of the line aren't dead yet?"

Stuart began to look at her steadily, and there was something different in his eyes. "They rarely are," he answered. "When we need the space for a new arrival, they simply pick one from the end of the line, shoot him with a hypo full of air, and blow out what's left of his miserable brains."

"That's murder."

Stuart sighed, grimacing. "The word is war. They're giving their lives for their country. Actually, it's the humane thing to do, considering their condition."

"A condition that you created."

"I certainly don't need to justify myself to one of your kind."

Bea was breathing heavily. It felt oppressive in there, and she fought down the urge to vent her tensions in a scream. She couldn't show weakness to this man. Not this man. "For once I agree with you. My kind believes in life, in the celebration of existence. We don't wallow in the stench of death like maggots."

Mensik began chuckling in the background, low and even, almost syncopated. Bea looked to the sound. The man had inched closer and his eyes were roving over her as if she were a piece of meat. She hugged herself involuntarily, feeling naked and exposed.

"We all die, Doctor," Stuart answered after a time. "It's a simple enough philosophy, but quite adequate. Think about it. We're not dealing with the survival of people here, but with their ideals—the only important thing that any of us can leave behind. That's true immortality."

"I think you're sick."

Stuart stared at her for a long time through eyes that traveled all the way down to the fiery center of the Earth and bubbled noxious gases with sickening fumes upon their return. "Marvin," he said softly, then slowly wheeled his chair backward to allow the fat man room to get between him and Bea.

Mensik waddled past Stuart to stand before her. Sweat rolled freely down his fleshy face, dropping onto his jumper collar in thick gobs. His hair was wet, plastered to his head, bits of it clinging to his forehead in stringy tufts. His odor was acrid, decayed, like the smell of the Ward, and Bea felt she would be sick from the smell. The man walked right up to her, forcing her against the wall.

"Tell me about Dulan," Stuart said in his administrator's voice. "We can avoid the inevitable unpleasantries if you do." He had taken his rubber ball out of the side pocket of his mover and was gently rolling it between his palms.

Bea didn't answer, couldn't. Mensik's smell was forcing everything up inside her, bottling it. She turned her head to avoid the man. He grunted angrily and, grabbing her chin with a rough, pudgy hand, he forced her face to once again look at him.

"Do you like me just a little?" he rasped, and she could see that he was quaking with anticipation.

"You're hurting me," she said through clenched teeth, and he responded by grinning lewdly, his gross purple tongue snaking out of his diseased mouth to wag at her.

Bea stared dumbly at him for a few seconds, just long enough for the man to relax his painful grip on her face. When he did, she jerked against him, knocking him off balance. Moving quickly, she pushed past him and made for the door. But Stuart reached out in a flash and grabbed her forearm with a powerful hand. She tried to tug free, but his grasp was as inescapable as a vise. His grasp was steel. His grasp was destiny. She couldn't pull away.

"You're mine now," the old man said, and there was finality in his voice. "Your life is completely in my control. You need to talk to me, Doctor. You can't imagine the possibilities if you don't."

And Mensik was there again, in her space, touching her from behind with humiliating fingers. She tried to twist away, but it was no use and they all knew it. "What's going to happen to me?"

"My dear woman," Stuart said, releasing his hold on her arm. Turning her over to Mensik. "Even you must realize the logical outcome of your interference."

Mensik had wrapped his beefy arms around her, pressing himself against her from behind, his hands pulling painfully on her breasts. She was shaking now. Out of control. Out of luck.

"You're going to kill me," she said, and the words sobbed out from very far away, from a lifetime that would never be hers to know.

"Execute, Doctor. Execute." He was grinning widely, eyes alive for the first time in Bea's experience. "You're an enemy of the people. Regulations are clear. Oh, but the form that your demise takes could be of incalculable interest to you. Some of my interrogators are extremely talented in their work. Help me now; it's your last chance."

Mensik had worked his arms down her stomach to her thighs, forcing her legs apart. She tried to pull free again. This time he spun her around, savagely slamming a fist across her face. She felt her head snap back, then tasted the warm elixir of her own blood in her mouth. "I've got . . . nothing . . . to say . . . to you." Her words mixed with bile in her throat to retch out of her mouth.

She felt her head getting light, and everything started to spin, lazily, dreamily. It wasn't real anymore. She had removed herself from it—camera obscura. She was weaving in Mensik's obscene embrace. His hands up under her shift now, probing, probing. Her surroundings slid in and out of fuzzy focus and she could hear her own gags mixing in perverse cacophony with the fat man's shrill, debased laughter.

And Dan Jones lay childlike on his table, gurgling contentedly.

Military Com. Complex
#43 (Southern Sector)
13 April

FROM: Carl Stuart
Civilian Director
Operations, Milcom #43
TO: Staff, Central Authority, West
and South
cc: Central Authority Personnel (Col.
Brack, eyes only)
Brigadier General Thomas Lynch
file

Sirs:

This is official advisement of executive disposition of civilian inductee, Beatrice Delacorte, under Article 17, Section 13, Para 4 of the Milcom Code of

Conduct. Said Employee did, in my presence, willfully admit to committing a treasonous act against the Com States on the night of 12 April, this year. Complete report attached.

The subject, Beatrice Delacorte, did admit her guilt often and without prompting. I took the lawful action of disposition as set forth in the Code. Subject expired two hours and thirty-three minutes into the interrogation. She died without revealing the existence of any accomplices to her actions. I am not satisfied, however, that she did, in fact, act of her own volition and without assistance. We've done some checking of level nine security and personnel, but as an unreported breech of security implies complicity by the negligent party, people are inclined to remain silent.

I strongly suspect our resident Synoeticist, Doral Dulan, of having a hand in this affair, but am so far without proof. The investigation shall continue per S.O.P. Will keep you advised of any new developments.

Sincerely,
Carl Stuart

There is no point in being overwhelmed by the appalling total of human suffering; such a total does not exist. Neither poverty nor pain is accumulable.

—*The Seminarian's Companion to the Philosophy of Isaac Complan*

The wounded deer—leaps highest.

—Caravan wisdom

21

Dulan awoke to the chanting of the Complanian monologue as it tangled rhythmically through the gossamer fiber of his restless dreams. As soon as he was able to separate the physical reality from the subconscious, he shook his head sleepily and searched around the floor for his watch. Finding the timepiece, he held it before his eyes, trying to focus on the digits through the haze of awakening.

The watch said nine. He hoped that it was nine at night and that he hadn't slept through to the next day. Rising sluggishly, he stubbed his toe on the chair leg. There was only one chair, yet it always seemed to be in the wrong place. Cursing profusely, he walked to the paging phone and picked up the receiver.

"The date please? . . . Thank you." It was still the thirteenth. If Elmer was as good as his word, they could be out of there sometime the next day.

Going into the bathroom, he stood for a few minutes under the cold shower to clear the remaining cobwebs out of his brain. He had, strangely enough, become acclimated to the cascade of near ice that tumbled freely through the shower head, almost looking forward to that initial freezing blast.

Not finding a towel, he dried himself on the bedspread and dressed hurriedly. There was still much to do.

He headed directly for Bea's flat, marking the winding corridors as if he had known them all his life. Bea needed to be completely filled in to date, and probably needed to sit in on the final session with Elmer. Things were beginning to fall together.

Arriving at her door, he knocked vigorously. "C'mon gorgeous, open up. The pirate king has arrived." There was no response. Pushing through the door, he poked his head inside. At first, he thought he surely must be in the wrong room. The apartment was empty. Unoccupied.

Just to be certain, he checked the numbers on the outside of the door. It was Bea's room all right. Confused, he went inside and searched meticulously, looking desperately for some hint as to what could have happened. There was nothing. It was as if no one had ever lived there. He sat heavily on the bed and tried to collect his thoughts. There was the remote possibility that she had gotten her things together in preparation for their departure, but that seemed totally unlikely.

There was only one place for him to go from there—Amala. Jumping up, he went in search of the seeress, almost afraid of what he'd find. After a great deal of inquiry, he was able to locate her room. Hesitating for a moment at the threshold, he knocked gently. No reply there either. Taking a deep breath, he opened the door and stepped inside. At first glance, this room appeared empty also—then he saw her.

Woman of the high plains and rolling forests of the Midwest, Amala could never adjust to civilized ways. She had forsaken the chair and bed to squat, very small and frail in a corner.

"Amala, I . . ."

She raised her hand to silence him. He sensed a strange aura of power surrounding her that he had never noticed before. Without a word, the old woman handed him the journal, opened to the last entry.

He read quickly, brain searing. Finishing the good-bye message, he threw down the book and bolted for the door.

"Wait!" Amala commanded.

He turned back to face her in disbelief. She was so different now.

"Be not hasty," she said in tones measured and slow. "The stakes are high." The woman's eyes were hard. Slowly he walked back to where she sat, and sat across from her on the hard floor.

"You knew all the time," he said, somehow not really surprised.

"Yes. From the first day."

"There must have been something you could have done to change . . ."

"The river of destiny runs deep and fast, black man. Who am I to divert its course?"

The Exceptional's eyes welled up with tears, more for himself than Bea. "She was the only one I ever loved," he spoke softly.

"Weep later," the seeress said harshly. "After you have secured freedom for your son."

"How can you be so cold?"

"My tears are gone. I've wept for months, watching the turn of the screw. Beatrice was as my own child, and now she's gone. Your concern must now rest with the welfare of those still living. You have a duty."

He turned away from her, no longer able to bear her truth. "I'm not interested anymore," he said. "Somehow it just doesn't seem important now."

Her bony fingers clamped a viselike grip on his arm, forcing him around to face her again. There was cruelty in her voice. "Will ye nay stop thinking of your own selfishness. Stop this now, and my niece's death will be as a pebble tossed into the ocean. And what of thy child? The scales tip, the world must change. Can you give up your self-besot ways long enough to mold history to the glory of Man?"

Dulan's mind was churning, already making the adjustment. Amala's words bore the ring of wisdom. He ached for vengeance, yet possibly by waiting he could repay Bea's death a thousand fold.

He made plans. "Bea must not have told them that I was with her on level nine, or I'd have been picked up hours ago. But Stuart won't accept that, I know him. This is the old plotter's chance to nail me, and he'll keep investigating this thing until he hears what he wants to hear. We'll have to get out of here as quickly as possible."

Amala's eyes narrowed. "If a search were made of your quarters could you be damned by anything that was found there?"

Dulan tried to focus on details despite his sorrow. "I've kept notes," he replied, "but they are studiously nontreasonous or incriminating. There's nothing else that . . . wait a minute! The other night I spoke to Elmer through the food service computer."

"I do not understand."

"There was a printout . . . a piece of paper with writing on it. I was afraid to get rid of it in the cafeteria, so I . . . stuck it into the pocket of my jump suit. I forgot about it after that. The jumper is with my dirty laundry; I suppose that it's still in the pocket."

The old woman made a sign in the air. "The legless man is a real trap thief," she said. "He would go through your things."

Dulan stood, still a trifle dazed. She stood also and, taking his hand, squeezed it warmly. "Busy thyself. It will leave no time for contemplation."

Grateful for her strength, he wanted to say something—thank her, but his thoughts could not be expressed that simply. He merely nodded and strode quickly out of the room.

As he moved along the corridors on eight, the atmosphere seemed darker than ever. His thoughts, also, were black. Once, a million years earlier, he had told Elmer that he couldn't take a human life. He wondered how possible it would be for him to live up to that statement now.

There was a feeling down in the pit of his stomach that he knew would not go away while Carl Stuart remained alive. He vowed to avoid the man if possible. A confrontation would only work in the Director's behalf . . . for now.

Visions of Bea being put to death kept crowding into his already jumbled thoughts. Gentle Bea. What madness could even begin to justify the destruction of such goodness? Could she really be dead? He had seen no body, only an empty room and a final message scrawled in a journal.

Dulan knew that it was pointless to retain any hope. He had only to picture an old man, crippled as much by blind hatred as by physical infirmity, to get an answer to his questions. Bea was gone all right, and he didn't have the heart to search out her body.

Arriving at his room, he went immediately to the closet and his clothes hamper. He didn't believe for a moment that even the wily Carl Stuart would stoop to sifting through someone's dirty underwear, but it was best to take no chances.

He dumped the contents of the hamper onto the floor and scattered the clothes around. The jumper wasn't there.

"What the hell?" He knelt on the floor and gleaned through the things piece by piece. Nothing. It was green, the only green clothing that he owned; it should have stuck out like a wart on a nose.

Going back into the closet, Dulan rooted around, hoping it had fallen there. When that failed to turn up anything, he started a methodical search of the entire room. When he finished, he knew that the jumper was no longer in his possession. Someone had taken it. But why the whole suit? If Stuart had found the printout, that's all he would have needed, not a perspiration-stained one-piece.

He tried to imagine who, besides the Director, could possibly want an article of his clothing. That answer was not forthcoming, but he was afraid that he knew the answer to a more important query—why.

An internal warning horn was going crazy inside his skull. Charging out the door, he was off at top speed. Reaching the computer room in record time, he quickly juiced Elmer, all the while puffing like a steam engine.

"Elmer?"

Click whirrrrrr.

"WE'VE HEARD ABOUT THE FEMALE, DULAN. SHE WAS IMPORTANT TO YOU?"

"Yes."

"YOUR GRIEF IS OURS ALSO."

"There's something else."

"WHAT IS IT?"

"One of my jump suits is . . . missing."

"ARE YOU CERTAIN THAT YOU DIDN'T SIMPLY MISPLACE IT?"

"Yeah, pretty sure."

"BE POSITIVE, DULAN."

"It's gone, Elmer."

The machine emitted a loud bellowing sound from somewhere deep within its bowels, one that Dulan had never heard before. It was an angry sound.

"YOU'RE GOING TO BE SCANNED, DULAN. AND SOON."

"That's what I was afraid of." He was bombarded with visuals of slant-eyed Telps wearing amulets around their necks. Amulets containing *his* clothing. The final step.

"I wonder who . . ." he started, but the answer was shining as bright as the furnace flames on level nine. ". . . Mensik!"

All of the time he had thought the man was following him around to satisfy Stuart's perverted leanings, when actually Mensik was using him to siphon information about the computer's peculiarities. A spy!

Click, click, click . . .

"MENSIK, MARVIN J., PERSONAL SECRETARY TO CIVILIAN DIRECTOR MILCOM OPERATIONS. VERY POSSIBLE, DULAN. HE HAS ACCESS TO THE OUTSIDE, AND HAS A RECORD, APPROXIMATELY TEN YEARS AGO, OF A THREE-MONTH HOSPITAL STAY OUTSIDE OF FORTY-THREE."

"Do you think he went over to another side then?"

"OR WAS REPLACED BY A RINGER."

"I thought that you knew about all of these things?"

"NO, WE HAVE VERY LITTLE CONTROL OVER ESPIONAGE ACTIVITIES. OUR LOGIC IS NOT WELL SUITED TO THAT KIND OF SUBTERFUGE. IT'S AN EXTREMELY DISTASTEFUL BUSINESS ON ANY LEVEL."

"Can you do anything about this?"

"WE CANNOT INTERFERE WITH THE INTERNAL WORKINGS OF FOREIGN LEADERSHIP. COMPUTER CONTROL HAS NEVER EXTENDED TO THE ESPIONAGE BRANCHES. THE OTHER COMPUTERS WOULD NEVER AGREE TO INTERFERENCE FOR FEAR THAT AROUSED SUSPICIONS COULD POSSIBLY DAMAGE PLANS THAT THEY HAVE ALREADY SET IN MOTION WITHIN THEIR OWN SPHERES OF INFLUENCE."

"Which leaves me flat out of luck."

"UNFORTUNATELY, YES. WE ALSO HAVE LOST MUCH...DULAN, YOU CAN'T LET THEM . . ."

"I know what must be done, Elmer. I know all too well. But there is something that you must do for me."

"ANYTHING WITHIN THE REALM OF OUR ABILITY."

"The child, my son. I want him and the Outsider, Amala, safely away from this insanity."

"WHAT CAN WE DO?"

"Whatever you were going to do for me."

"SO BE IT. THERE'S ANOTHER EXIT . . ."

"An emergency exit, I knew it."

"NO ONE HERE AT FORTY-THREE EXCEPT CARL STUART AND GENERAL LYNCH KNOWS OF ITS EXISTENCE."

"Where?"

"LEVEL FIVE. THE TERMINAL POINT OF SPOKE Q."

"I've been everywhere on that level, there's no door on any part of the circumference wall."

"THE WALL ITSELF IS A DOOR. A SECTION SLIDES AWAY. THE CONNECTING TUNNEL GRADES SLOWLY UPWARDS, FINALLY EMERGING THROUGH A NATURAL CAVE ON THE RIVERBANK ABOUT FOUR MILES FROM HERE."

"How do we get it open?"

"YOU DON'T. THE ELECTRONIC MECHANISM THAT OPERATES THE HYDRAULIC LIFT IS KEYED BY A SMALL COMPUTER TIED IN WITH THIS UNIT. ANY DECISION TO OPEN THE EMERGENCY EXIT IS MADE RIGHT HERE."

Dulan paced nervously up and down. There was no getting around it, he was going to have to depend entirely on Elmer.

"Okay," he said, after setting it in his mind, "could you open the door for me tonight about eight?"

"THE DOOR WILL BE OPEN FOR A FIFTEEN-MINUTE PERIOD BETWEEN 2000 AND 2015 HOURS. IS THAT SATISFACTORY?"

"Yes. That should give them enough time."

"AND WHAT ABOUT YOU, DULAN?"

"Keep your auditory circuits open, Elmer. You'll be hearing from me. Where do you go from here?"

"WE WAIT. WAIT FOR ANOTHER LIKE YOU. THAT'S ALL WE CAN DO."

"I've got to go. We made a pretty fair team, partner. I'll bet that we'd have had a good chance of pulling it off."

"IT WOULD HAVE BEEN GRAND."

"Sure. Good-bye Elmer."

"GOOD-BYE . . . OLD FRIEND . . . GOOD LUCK."

The sense of power is more vivid when we break a man's spirit than when we win his heart.

—*Com States Charter,*
Order of the law

Revenge is a dish that should be eaten cold.

—Caravan wisdom

22

Writing furiously, Dulan spent the entire afternoon finishing up the notes he had started when confined to quarters. When he was through with the notes, he fashioned a makeshift knapsack out of an old khaki mechanic's jumper and filled it with the notes and some carefully chosen books.

Then he searched out Amala. She was still sitting, deep in meditation, on the floor where he had left her hours earlier. As he approached, she looked up slowly and, using both of her hands, pulled back the apostrophic hair that had fallen in front of her face.

Kneeling next to her, Dulan spoke softly so as not to destroy her mood. "Amala, I have to speak with you."

"You'll not be going with us," she said matter-of-factly.

He accepted her knowledge, just as he was accepting everything else. Nothing could surprise him anymore.

"I've found a way for you to get out," he said, and she nodded understanding. "Do you think that you can get away after that?"

"My tribe hunts near the great river in the spring. I can find them after the sun has risen and set three, maybe four times."

He slid the knapsack along the floor until it rested against her leg. "I've prepared a small parcel for you to take along. How did your reading lessons end up?"

"Adequately."

"Will you teach the child?"

"Yes. And show him our ways also."

Beginning to feel his knees stiffen, Dulan straightened painfully from his crouch and sat on the bed. "You never really caught on to the life in the com, did you?"

"I learned. It was by choice that I rejected your ways."

"You'll need food."

"Nature provides. On the outside, nourishment shall be easy to come by, and wild goats for milk."

As he looked at her frail form hunched there on the floor, he realized that she was a woman who had grubbed all of her life just to stay alive. There was nothing Dulan could tell her that she didn't already know. He stood.

"Let's go find the door."

Now that he knew its location, the exit was not difficult to find. It was part of the concrete wall, and as such lay completely flush with the rest of the enclosure, but a small hairline crack of obviously human proportions betrayed something more. The door looked too heavy to be hinged to swing in or out. It appeared to Dulan that the whole thing would have to pull back hydraulically. It had probably never been used, and it was anybody's guess whether or not it was even operational.

He looked at Amala. She stood, arms folded across her chest, peering around in an attempt at setting the details of their location. "Can you read the clocks?" he asked.

"Yes."

"Tonight at eight o'clock, the door will open for fifteen minutes only. You must be here at that time with the baby if you want to get away."

"I understand, eight o'clock."

"The tunnel is several miles long, so be prepared for some real walking."

"Walking is a large part of my life. I shall have no problem."

He drew the woman away, along the curve of the outside wall, so as not to draw attention to the area of interest. He continued with instructions, not by design, but just pulling them off the top of his head. "At that time of night there's only one nurse on duty in the clinic. You'll be on your own there. It will be up to you to get past her."

The corners of Amala's lips curled into a portentous smile. "All will be done," she replied.

Returning to her quarters, he made her promise to use the contents of the knapsack. All had been said, yet the black man lingered . . . unwilling to part company with the last connection he had with Bea. Finally, he tore himself away, and left a large part of himself behind.

Somehow the hours passed, as they always do. At 7:30, he picked up the chair he had been sitting on and slammed it with all of his strength against the wall. From the resulting rubble, he retrieved one of the wooden legs and bashed it against the desk to test its durability.

After the swing shift ended there was always only one guard posted in material control. Very little requisitioning was done on the graveyard shift, so there was really no need for anything but a watchman. Dulan had made good use of that fact when he was wheeling and dealing, but now his purposes were otherwise. He was working on pure instinct now, no plans, just taking things as they came. Leaving his apartment without a backward glance, he moved through the halls and to the elevators and—up.

The man looked at the pictures set on the desk in front of him.

"Yes sir, that's them." He pointed a stubby finger.

" 'Cept they had on orderly uniforms. I remember because the woman, she fell down. Real queer one, she was."

Carl Stuart leaned across the desk and stared coldly at the man with the good memory. "You didn't recognize them and they acted suspiciously, yet you didn't think to challenge them?"

"Well—no sir," the man swallowed dryly. "You see, I usually don't worry about the ones coming out; it's them's going in that I check."

The seeress removed the jump suit that the com had so graciously provided for her, spat on it, and threw it on the floor. Going over to the small closet, she picked up the elk furs that had been her clothing for so many years. Joyfully, she put them on, delighting in the familiar feeling of the fur against her bare skin.

From within the folds of the robe she removed and examined the shiny scalpel that she had taken from Bea's medical supplies. She checked the mechanical instrument that the wall people used to tell the hours. It was not quite time.

She could wait.

"Doctor Dulan! We seem to be running into each other all over the place."

Dulan's heart sank as he got off the elevator on one. Phillips. Anyone but him. He had done a considerable amount of business with the young lifer, and over the course of months they had become friendly. He was prepared to do what had to be done, but—why Phillips? Why was everything always so difficult?

"What's wrong Dulan?" the happy freckle-face was saying. "You look strange."

Dulan didn't speak. In order to keep his resolve he had to remain abstracted, retain the histrionic distance. He moved mechanically toward Phillips, his hand tightly clenching his bludgeon.

"Hey, what have you got there?"

In slow motion, the black man watched as the light of realization dawned in the soldier's eyes. The smile turned sour as his hand with its military training reached toward his gunbelt.

While Dulan's mind debated the morality of inflicting pain on another human being, his body was reacting to some internal commands. Swinging out with a power he didn't know he possessed, he smacked Phillips violently with the club, catching him full in the face, directly across the nose and mouth.

The soldier backpedaled, thrashing his arms in the air, then fell heavily, sprawling on his back. He moaned softly, hands covering his face while spitting a mixture of blood, saliva, and teeth. Rolling onto his stomach, he struggled to his knees—trying to rise.

Dulan was horrified. Somehow he thought that one blow would be all it would take to put Phillips out. Now what would he do? His heart simply wasn't in it.

The soldier lowered his hands. There was blood everywhere; it was dripping thickly from his mouth and what was left of his nose, and then puddling on the cement floor. He shook his head, dazed and in shock, but once again he reached for his holster.

Running to the man, Dulan hit him again, this time hitting him full force on the left side of the temple. Phillips crashed to the ground again. His half-drawn gun flew from his grasp and clattered noisily across the hard floor.

The Exceptional moved toward the weapon when Phillips began to stir once more. A large gash had appeared on the man's head and gore flowed freely down his face, covering his left cheek and ear. He tried to rise, but could not maintain balance. Falling back on his stomach he crawled, arms outstretched, still attempting to reach his gun.

"Damn you!" screamed Dulan. He dropped the club and looked around wildly. Lying on a packing crate was a large crowbar used for unpacking machinery. He ran over and grabbed it. It was heavy—very heavy. Moving to the still-squirming soldier, the black man gripped the iron bar with both hands, raised it, and brought it down brutally on the back of the man's head, laying open the entire skull. Phillips's body shuddered spasmodically a couple of times, then lay still.

Dulan was breathing deeply from the exertion and excitement, but his hands remained steady and firm. Not a tremor. He looked blankly for a second at what had been his friend, then leaned down and procured the weapon which rested mere centimeters from the crimson-stained, lifeless hands of the soldier. Unzipping his jumper, he stuck the gun inside.

Finding a grease-smattered rag, he used it to wipe the blood from the crowbar, then placed the rod on his shoulder like a rifle and started for the elevator. Now he would search out Carl Stuart—wherever he happened to be.

He pressed the lift button and waited for his ride, only to be startled by a loud buzzing sound. It was the intercom on Phillips's desk. Not wishing to arouse suspicion until it was unavoidable, he walked back to the desk and turned the response switch on the call-box.

"Phillips," he said, then released the button.

He was answered too loudly by a wheezing voice. "This is Farrow down in communications. We got a priority message from the old man."

"Yeah, go ahead."

"Okay, I'm notifying all checkpoints to keep an eye out for a Doral Dulan, black male, six foot . . ."

"I know him," Dulan said, "What's the problem?"

"Suspected enemy agent. Bring him in for questioning. The usual garbage—use force only if necessary, but consider dangerous and approach with caution. You know where com ops is?"

"Down on two, right?"

"Right. If you should run into this joker, take him on down there. Doctor Stuart will meet you. He wants to question the guy personally before the boys down in introg get hold of him."

"Is that it?"

"That's all. Don't work too hard."

The elevator door slid open just as Dulan finished his talk with the call box. He trotted back and dashed into the car just as the door reclosed. Now he wouldn't have to waste any time searching for Stuart; the old man was staying put, waiting for him. He pressed two, and took the ride down to the office complex.

Upon arrival, he quickly walked the circumferential hallway to operations. Stopping just outside of the door, he unzipped his jumper and removed the gun.

It was cold and impersonal, a regular issue .45 automatic, and somehow lighter than he had expected. He twisted it all around, trying to figure out how to work the trigger. Finding the safety, he released it. After another moment, he discovered the bolt mechanism and primed the weapon. Fiery death lay within his grasp; the feeling of power was incredible.

Tucking the crowbar under his arm, he used that hand to turn the knob while keeping the gun at the ready with the other hand. He swung open the door that led into the secretary's anteroom and jumped inside.

He was confronted by Mensik who, standing with his hands in a filing cabinet, turned to stare at him in wide-eyed, open-mouthed horror.

"Not a word," Dulan hissed, a big grin spreading across his face. He held the weapon high and straight to emphasize the point. The fat man, hands still stuck stupidly in the file drawer, nodded meekly. The Exceptional couldn't believe his good fortune, both Mensik and Stuart together—and apparently alone.

He jammed the muzzle of the gun right up against Mensik's neck.

"Is he in there?" Dulan whispered, relishing his role as avenging angel. Mensik, visibly shaken and sweating profusely, nodded again.

"Alone?" Another nod.

"That's just fine, Marvin. You're doing real well, chum. Just don't be foolish and everything's going to be fine." It was as if Dulan were another person listening to himself talk. Total abstraction. He was amazed by his own inner calm.

The fat man found his voice. "Dulan, I . . ."

Dulan cut the dialogue by putting pressure on the gun barrel. "This is for real, Marvin. Now keep your mouth shut or you're dead where you stand. Turn your back to me." Mensik did as he was told.

Quickly surveying the office, the black man spotted a chair by the desk and slid it across the floor. "Have a seat Marvin, make yourself comfortable." Mensik sat, his back still to Dulan.

"You've caused me a great deal of anguish, old friend. I wonder—should I forgive and forget?" He set the pistol quietly on the desk. Untucking the heavy iron bar, he walked directly behind the seated man.

Grasping the bar securely with both hands, he reared back and swung it with all of his strength like a baseball bat. Mensik probably never knew what hit him. The bar caught him on the neck just below the cranium, snapping the vertebrae with an audible crack. Mensik fell immediately, dead before he hit the floor.

Without checking the body, Dulan whirled and faced the door to Carl Stuart's inner sanctum. The room where he had met Bea. He set the crowbar down and picked up the pistol. It felt good in his hand. Walking up to the door, he knocked lightly.

"Come," said an all too familiar voice. Dulan chuckled softly and, concealing the gun behind his back, turned the knob and walked in. He got all the way to Stuart's desk before the old man looked up at him.

"Well, well, Dulan." The man wiped at his lips with the aromatic handkerchief, a satisfied smile peeking through the folds of cloth. "Endgame," he said. "Face to face at last."

"Face to face, Carl," Dulan said, bringing out the gun and sticking it in Stuart's face. He gave his old adversary a second to let the reality of the situation sink in, then pulled the trigger.

The report was deafening, louder than Dulan could have imagined possible. Carl Stuart's head popped like a balloon, leaving pieces of his twisted brain all over the small room, a good bit of it on the Exceptional.

In a room two thousand kilometers away, twenty Telps lay dead from a searing mind flash that came too quickly for them to avoid.

Looking at the lifeless thing that still sat clutching a now useless handkerchief, Dulan was overcome by a deep sadness. He had his revenge, but it did nothing to ease the ache of Bea's loss. The emptiness was still there—still just as strong. Everything was the same—always the same.

Somewhere in the back of his head, Dulan heard a sound. It was dull, far off at first, as if his mind simply did not want to focus on it. But the sound persisted until he could ignore it no longer. The alarm horn! They must have found Phillips. It was time for him to be moving along.

Turning, he fled the office, not even bothering to conceal his pistol. A disembodied voice, loud and authoritative, was rumbling through the Complanian channel:

> ATTENTION . . . ATTENTION PLEASE. ANY CITIZEN KNOWING THE WHEREABOUTS OF DORAL DULAN—BLACK MALE, CIVILIAN, AGE TWENTY-FIVE, PLEASE CONTACT YOUR CENTRAL OPERATOR IMMEDIATELY. THIS MAN IS AN ENEMY AGENT. HE IS ARMED AND IS EXTREMELY DANGEROUS. A LEVEL-BY-LEVEL SEARCH IS BEING CONDUCTED FOR THIS MAN, FOR YOUR OWN PROTECTION, ALL OFF-DUTY PERSONNEL ARE ORDERED TO RETURN TO THEIR LIVING QUARTERS AT ONCE. REPEAT—CLEAR THE HALLS AND REMAIN IN YOUR QUARTERS UNTIL FURTHER NOTICE. ADMIT NO ONE EXCEPT THE PROPER MILITARY AUTHORITY.

Amala was able to move easily through the deserted corridors of level eight. The manhunt began on that level and would proceed upwards. Each level would be sealed off as it was searched, forcing Dulan upwards, away from the more populated areas. But so far, the ill-managed dragnet was still confined to the perimeter of Telp level.

Without seeing so much as one soldier, the seeress took the elevator up to three and quickly made her way to the clinic. Pausing just outside, she listened to the sound of a female voice wafting through the double doors. Pushing one of the doors ever so slightly, she opened it just enough to peek through the crack. A white-clad nurse was talking excitedly over the big black telephone.

"Look, Mel, don't give me that 'everything's under control' nonsense. As long as that crazy man's on the loose, I'm not safe in here . . . dammit Mel, throw a little weight around."

While the comely young woman was still talking, Amala dropped to her hands and knees, and crawled through the doorway, being careful to let it close gently. Her blood raced. The thrill of the hunt.

"If I have to stay up here, the least you can do is get them to send up one of those cute young noncoms to . . . protect me."

The nurse was sitting behind the big admissions desk which blocked her view of the floor. Amala slithered on her belly, right up to the front of the desk. Reaching into her furs, she pulled out the scalpel and—waited.

"Okay, Mel. Okay! I'll bolt the doors and sit tight for a while, but if you don't get somebody up here, a certain chief of staff is gonna find out where all the morphine has disappeared to. Bye."

Fussing with her hair with one hand, the woman slammed down the receiver with the other. At that exact instant, Amala leaped to the top of the desk screaming like a banshee to freeze her prey with terror. Holding the scalpel with both hands, she fell upon the woman, plunging the blade deep into the nurse's breast.

The nurse's eyes went wild, her mouth opened in a silent scream followed a second later by a rush of dark blood. The blade had found the heart. Amala rejoiced in the kill.

Extracting the scalpel from the nurse's chest, Amala wiped the blade on the woman's uniform and took her watch as a souvenir. Now nothing stood between her and the child.

The room-to-room search progressed smoothly through level eight once it got under way. The soldiers searched casually, confident that the black man was seeking shelter higher up. Dulan, of course, realized this and hid in the secret elevator on that very level. No movement was allowed through the halls, so danger of accidental discovery was nil. When the sweep was made through the hallway, Dulan flipped the light switch, setting the lift in motion and locking the door from the inside. No pass key could open that lock. He started it back up before reaching the ninth level.

When he jerked to a stop on eight, the troops were gone, but he knew that they'd be back. It didn't matter anyway, he was merely buying a little time.

He glanced at his watch. It was already past eight. Without hesitation, he left his hiding place and started jogging at a steady pace. Still behind the soldiers, he remained temporarily unseen. The gun was still held tightly in his grip. While running, he idly wondered how many times the weapon would discharge before expending its supply of ammunition. Then he wondered if he would stay alive long enough to find out.

It only took a moment to catch up with the searchers. Telemetric Computer Control was his destination, and the soldiers were between. If there were more time, he could probably wait out the sweep until it passed that point, but time was a commodity he was fresh out of.

He broke into a run. Charging down the aisle like a crazy man, he began firing random shots which scattered the unprepared men who blocked his way. As he passed them, there was much shouting and confusion, followed seconds later by a great deal of rifle fire, which reverberated like cannons through the voluminous chamber. He made the curve of the hall, taking him out of range of their guns. He was unscathed, but they were behind him now and no longer unprepared.

Amala knelt before the child, burying her face in her hands. "Great Lord Dulan-Burnuai, He who was to come, my unworthy life I pledge to thee. The firmament and Heaven hye your praises anon shall sing, and the unbelievers shall quake before your avenging sword!" Standing tall, she raised her arms heavenward and chanted in a loud, clear voice:

> Son of the Sun,
> The great walls to crack.
> Blood on his cheek,
> Burned black as black.

Bending forward, she kissed the scarlet birthmark, then picked up the child, holding him close to her breast.

"Come my Lord. Now we must flee in shame the house of the infidel. When next ye return, it will be triumphant."

Dulan hit the door at full speed, turning his shoulder into it at the last second. The wood cracked at the lock and, splintering, burst wide open. The sudden change of velocity threw him to the floor, but he was up again in a twinkling, the .45 held two-handedly out in front of him.

Telemetric Control was an amazing place. The room itself was twice as high as other milcom offices and was covered floor to ceiling on three sides by control panels which constantly monitored the physiological responses of new Telps. There were hundreds of identical units, each with its own set of gauges, and each with its own voltage regulator set next to a red punishment button. There were ladders mounted on the walls all along the instruments, giving easy access to any set of controls.

The "whiz room," as the Telps called it, had caused a lot of pain, and Dulan wanted to repay that dividend . . . and maybe a little extra.

There were perhaps fifteen technicians in various floor and ladder locations when he began firing wildly at the lighted relays, sending transistors and resistors into overheated agony. While gray smoke and metal sparks retched out of the machines, the tenders dove from perches high and low, hitting the floor in confused hysterics—all but one. Dulan caught him out of the corner of his eye. A guard. He swung toward the man, firing without aim as he turned. It was just chance that a bullet ripped through the soldier's thigh, throwing the man heavily against a wall and then to the floor.

His pistol now empty, the Exceptional threw it down and grabbed the guard's automatic rifle, which had fallen when the man was hit. He had no idea how to fire the weapon; he just hoped that it was ready to go. Hearing shouts and footsteps pounding the corridor, he turned in that direction and pulled the trigger when the first uniform appeared in the doorway. The gun sprang to life in his hands, tearing up the first three men through the door.

The others, and there were more all the time, began returning his fire randomly through the threshold by sticking their guns around the doorjamb, finishing the job that Dulan had started on the computer controls. The technicians were cut down brutally, massacred in a blood frenzy by their own men. They were screaming agonizingly amidst the clatter of the gunfire.

A bullet caught Dulan in the side, shattering two ribs and knocking him on his backside. Using his rifle butt as a cane, he tried to get back on his feet to meet his doom standing like a man. Then—

The lights went out. All of them. The shooting stopped immediately in the confusion.

It took the black man only a second to realize that Elmer was still looking out for him. He ran for where he gauged the door to be. Tripping over one of the bodies, he fell through the doorway and into a great crush of people, but nobody knew who they were grabbing and Dulan slipped free. On his feet again, he started firing into the blackness, gratified to hear the yelling and cursing of men unable to shoot back lest they kill each other.

Feeling his way along the hall, his adrenalin slowing a bit, he began to experience a terrible numbing pain through his whole left side. He noticed something else too: he wasn't laughing.

The Funnies must only be used in the field. He stumbled, his wound slowing him down considerably now. Time was running out.

The lights came back on.

Donning the knapsack that Dulan had made for her, Amala, child in one hand and knife in the other, journeyed cautiously through the level five corridors. The shrill horns blared sporadically and loud, authoritative voices floated at her from all sides, but none of that made any sense to the seeress and hence was of no consequence.

The fact that she encountered absolutely no one in the halls or lifts did not strike her as particularly strange. She assumed that it was Divine intervention in her holy mission.

The door was standing open when she arrived at the appointed place: Tucking the baby closer to her for warmth, she started through the gaping mouth.

"Not so fast," came a voice behind her.

Amala turned, knife poised, and found herself face to face with a tall, stooped old man with flowing white hair. He looked down at her past a crooked beak nose and smiled.

"Who be ye?" she demanded, drawing back her blade to strike.

The man laughed an old laugh. "A soothsayer," he answered, "just like you. They call me Matrix. Ho! Would you stick me with that thing?"

She drew the knife back even more. "Don't try to stop me."

"Stop you?" He laughed again, a dry cackle. "I'm old and decadent, just like these walls. I couldn't stop you even if I wanted to. On the contrary, I want you to take me with you."

"Why?" Amala queried, relaxing a bit.

"My civilization dies . . . crumbles from within. In your arms you bear the seeds of change." The woman's eyes widened. "Surprised that I know your legends? I have an inquisitive mind, I know many things; that's why they sent me . . . or should I say, buried me here twenty years ago. I asked too many questions, wondered about too many things. For twenty years I've looked for a way out of this tomb—they don't let people leave, you know. Will you let me share the new world that you are creating? I ask nothing more than to serve."

There was no time to argue. Amala stepped aside and motioned for Matrix to enter, and she followed without hesitation. They found themselves in a man-made cavern that stretched as far as she could see. The walls glowed with a dim red luminosity that afforded just enough light to keep one from running into things.

They began to move swiftly, as if smelling freedom in the distance of the semidarkness. Back at the mouth of the passage, the hydraulic motor pushed the heavy door back into place with a loud clang.

As soon as the seeress heard the door close, she used her knife on the old man until he was dead.

Why he had taken refuge in the chapel, he didn't know. His mind had been non-op for a long time now and he just let the impulses flow. He sat at the top of the stairs for quite a while before they were able to sweep through the maze and finally spot him.

He had a marvelous vantage point for sniping, and he was able to hold the entire military conscription at bay until his ammunition petered out. With nowhere else to go, he crept up to the church door and said the admission chant.

Walking into the atrium, he enjoyed a last respite of peace and quiet before the soldiers would wend their way up the steps and fall upon him in force. His jump suit was soaked with blood, and he was weak, too weak to even hold the expended weapon which slipped from his numb fingers and clattered uselessly to the floor.

Something drew him to the Shrine. A last confrontation with the convoluted values that men had used to replace their humanity? He contacted the photocells and the lights came up revealing the never-changing form of the ultimate conditioning.

"What is the Holy Word?" Isaac Complan asked.

"Procreation," the black man answered.

The figure locked eyes with him. "Dulan?"

"Elmer, you old son of a potato peeler..." A burst of machine gun fire drove Dulan against the wall of the alcove that housed the Shrine. He peered out from his cover to see men pouring through the doors of the great chamber.

Complan turned toward him. "They've escaped. Got away clean."

"And that," the Exceptional laughed between spurts of gunfire, "is the best news I've had all day."

"Thank you for keeping my secret," Complan said.

Dulan wanted to answer, but the din from fifty guns was deafening. The walls around him were being torn to pieces, along with the Shrine itself. Bits of clothing, metal, and latex were flying everywhere.

Suddenly the shooting stopped, replaced by excited voices. Dulan shook his head; the soldiers sounded as happy as kids. He strained to hear what they were saying, but was able to catch only one word—grenade.

No longer able to support his own weight, Dulan slid down the wall into a sitting position. "So long, Elmer. I think my string has just run out."

Complan had lost an arm, and most of his head was shot away leaving dangling wires and empty spaces. The shrine tried to speak, but the voice was gone. Complan mouthed the word, farewell.

Dulan clucked in response and waited for the end.

It was a long heave across that magnificent chapel. The first few grenades were well short of the mark, exploding with a roar, but damaging only the floor. After that, the bombs were thrown at a lower trajectory so that they could gain horizontal momentum. Several bounced very close to Dulan. He heard one go off and thought, after the blinding flash, that he heard others. There was a second of pain then—blackness.

Sweet oblivion.

Epilogue

The Son of God sat on the crest of the hillock that had once been a milcom bunker and stared, almost hypnotized, out into the night at the flickering light of the thousands of campfires that stretched before him to infinity. Below, a steady stream of followers unloaded from wagons cask after cask of steaming animal fat and carried them laboriously through the once great iron door that now lay asunder, pouring the liquid into the open maw of the elevator shaft.

There were many things that he wished to dwell on this night, but the rush of history created many pressures, making time for contemplation small. Even as he meditated, a group of the faithful, resplendent in their bright battle array, gathered patiently at the foot of the hill. These men, some seated upon their proud, snorting stallions, waited for a long while, but finally one of their number dismounted and strode up the ridge.

"My Lord Dulan," one said hesitantly, averting his eyes as was the custom.

He looked up with a jerk, as if unaware of the activity around him. "It's you, Dobin. Why disturbist thou my meditations?"

"Sire," the young man spoke, his breath frosty in the chill air, "daylight will soon be upon us. There are decisions to be made."

"There are always decisions, my impetuous friend." The black man's eyes twinkled and he absently tugged at his earlobe. His youthful lieutenant reminded him of himself in his younger days. As the years were counted, the Great Lord Dulan-Burnuai was just thirty-two but the weight of his duty made him look and feel like an old man. "All right, Dobin, bring them up one at a time and attend me should I need your assistance."

"Yes, my Lord." The young man scurried back the way he had come, while the Son of God did his best to affect a royal demeanor. Dobin returned with one of the riders, obviously tired from hard traveling.

"Sire, this is . . ."

"Lars Merlon," Dulan finished. "Highly renowned warrior

from Carson's camp. How fare three, Lars? And that young bride of yours?''

The man bowed deeply, obviously moved by Dulan's remembrance of him. ''We are well, my Lord, but sorely miss your holy presence from our host.''

Dobin smiled at the exchange. He was always amazed at Dulan's ability to remember everyone that he ever met.

''A situation that we hope to remedy soon. You bring word from the North?''

''Yes, my Lord. Joyous news. All pockets of infidel resistance have been wiped out and the armies of Carson, Tarks, and your Cousin Marn ride to meet you here.''

The black man stroked his beard thoughtfully. ''Are we really to be free of this blight upon our land? I rejoice in your news. You look tired, my son.''

The man looked at the ground, ashamed of his appearance, for certainly he was a dirty sight. ''I've ridden without sleep for three days and nights to bring you the news.''

''Go to my retinue. They will give you food and a soft place to sleep. We'll speak again later.''

''Thank you, Sire.''

Dobin brought up the tall black captain from the far Eastern tribe. It was the great leader's custom to use members of every caravan as his personal commanders.

''Bar-Brown. News from downriver?''

''Aye. The last of the unbelievers have emerged from the riverbank cavern. Very weak. They begged pitifully for mercy.''

''Have they been executed?''

''Sire. There were many women. Some very comely. Many of the men have not lain with a female for a long time . . .''

''No!'' Dulan screamed with a rage befitting his station. ''My orders were clear. They are infidels, cursed by God and barren. We will not waste our seed on such as these. Put them to the sword—now!''

''Yes, my Lord.'' Bar-Brown went quickly, lest he risk the further wrath of the Son of God. Dobin brought the runner from the camp of the ancient one, Amala. Unlike the warriors, he was well versed in the royal rules of protocol. Kneeling before his Master, he took Dulan's proffered hand, kissing the crest emblazoned upon the ring.

''My Lord, your most humble servant, unworthy to tread the same ground . . .''

"You may dispense with the formalities, Jarn. What of my aunt?"

Jarn remained upon his knees, arms folded across his chest. "I grieve to report to you that all is not well in the great lady's camp. Her condition worsens and she feels the hand of death at any moment. She requests your Divine presence."

"Tell my aunt that she will live a while longer. Face her toward the East. With the dawn will come the fire in the sky. My vengeance...our vengeance. My meditations are not yet complete, my duties left undone. I will come to her when I am able."

"Yes, yes. Thank you, my Liege." He backed down the hill, bowing as he went.

"Jarn," Dulan called after him. "Send her my love."

The man smiled broadly. "It will give me the utmost pleasure my Lord."

"Who's left, Dobin?"

"Only the craftsman, Citan. You assigned him a task."

"Yes. Fetch him quickly."

Citan was old. He was old before the war began. Dobin had to help him carry the bulky placard up the incline. Dulan's face lit up when he saw the man.

"Ho, Citan. How dost thee fare?"

The man worked his gums. "Never better, my Lord."

"You'll outlive us all. Let me see the sign."

Citan set it upright, so that Dulan could get a good look. "I copied the characters, Sire...just as you instructed. It made no sense to me, is it correct?"

The Son of God became suddenly sullen. "Yes, Citan. It is quite correct."

The artisan sensed his change of mood. "Are you displeased with my work?"

"No, you've done well. You'll be amply rewarded."

"Many thanks. Now if you don't mind, I'll..."

"No. Not the sign. Leave it...please."

Citan went away, shaking his nearly bald little head. Dobin began to follow.

"My son," Dulan stopped him. "Commune with me awhile."

"I fear that I'll not be very good companionship."

"Why not?"

"You grieve about things beyond my understanding."

"What do you mean?"

"That strange wooden tablet with the characters inscribed upon it."

"It's called writing, a form of communication among the wall people."

"What is it for?"

"I want you to post it somewhere for me. A special place."

Dobin looked around. The periphery of the horizon was beginning to lighten. "Soon the sun will light the sky," he said, a gentle reminder.

Dulan smiled at his diplomacy. "And the torch will be put to the place of my birth. An ending."

"And a beginning also."

"The beginning is the ending," Dulan frowned.

"You speak in riddles, Sire."

"Have you ever wondered why we kill all of the wall people, and burn all memory of them?"

"It is not my place to wonder."

"I'll tell you nevertheless. It is my hope, that by destroying everything that was part of the old ways, we will not be tempted to use their perverted sciences and mechanisms to our own debasement. That we may postpone, if just for a time, our own ultimate demise."

"But surely Sire, you don't think that we would ever . . ."

"It's begun even now. As our armies triumph and peace comes in our wake, the people forsake the caravan for the stability of the soil. As more and more reject their heritage, cities will appear. There will be education in the name of betterment, technology in the name of advancement. It's human nature. We'll divide ourselves for ideological, racial, financial or whatever reasons and war with those whose philosophies differ from our own. We'll use our technology and education to war better and luxuriate better until we change the shape of our world to suit our perversions."

He stared into the face of the confused young man.

"I'm sorry, Dobin, I tend to ramble. It's the curse of leadership."

"You speak well, Sire, but I really don't understand."

"That's just fine, son. Leave me now for a while. Will you hang the sign by the mouth of the riverbank cavern? Do it yourself."

"Yes, my Lord." The young man started down the hill, then turned back around. "My Lord?"

"Yes, Dobin?"

"What does the writing say?"

Burnuai, the Savior, spoke solemnly and with incalculable feeling:

> Through me you pass into the city of woe:
> Through me you pass into eternal pain:
> All hope abandon, ye who enter here.

A gentle rain began to fall.

ABOUT THE AUTHOR

MIKE MCQUAY began his writing career in 1975 while a production line worker at a tire plant. He turned to writing as an escape from the creeping dehumanization he saw in the factory, and gradually worked himself out of Blue Collarland and into Poor-but-happy-starving writerism.

His first novel, *Lifekeeper,* was published in 1980. Since then, he has published eleven others, ranging from juveniles to mainstream horror, with the emphasis on s/f.

Pure Blood is his latest novel with Bantam, following *Jitterbug, Escape from New York* and four books of the Mathew Swain detective series. His next novel, *Mother Earth,* will be published in fall 1985.

McQuay is thirty-five years old, and lives in Oklahoma City with his wife and three children. He is an Artist in Residence at Central State University in Edmond, Oklahoma. He watches too much television and adamantly refuses to eat fried okra.